I0822481

THE SONG OF THYSSIA

S.J. STILES

EDITED BY:
S. ESPENSCHEID
M.M. SLOAN

Copyright © 2024 by S. J. Stiles

All rights reserved.

No part of this book may be reproduced in any form or by any electronic or mechanical means, including information storage and retrieval systems, without written permission from the author, except for the use of brief quotations in a book review.

The Song of Thyssia is a work of fiction. Names, places, characters, and incidents either are the product of the author's imagination or are used fictitiously. Any resemblance to actual persons, living or dead, events, or locales is entirely coincidental

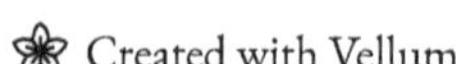

To Mel:
Thank you for listening.
Those who listen change the world.

Content Warnings

Dear Reader,

I included this list to serve as a "heads up" for any potential topics that might be upsetting to yourself or someone else. I do not consider my style of writing to be particularly brutal outside of the fantasy genre conventions but below are some of the topics that you might want to know about ahead of time:

Death (On and off page)

Death of a parent

Depictions of abuse including biological and non-biological family members.

Abduction

Beheading/amputation (On and off page)

Reference to torture (off page)

Malicious wounding

Necromancy/Alchemy

General violence associated with swords and sharp objects.

Animal injury (off and on page)

Poisoning

Possession

Depictions of an ableist character
Mild language

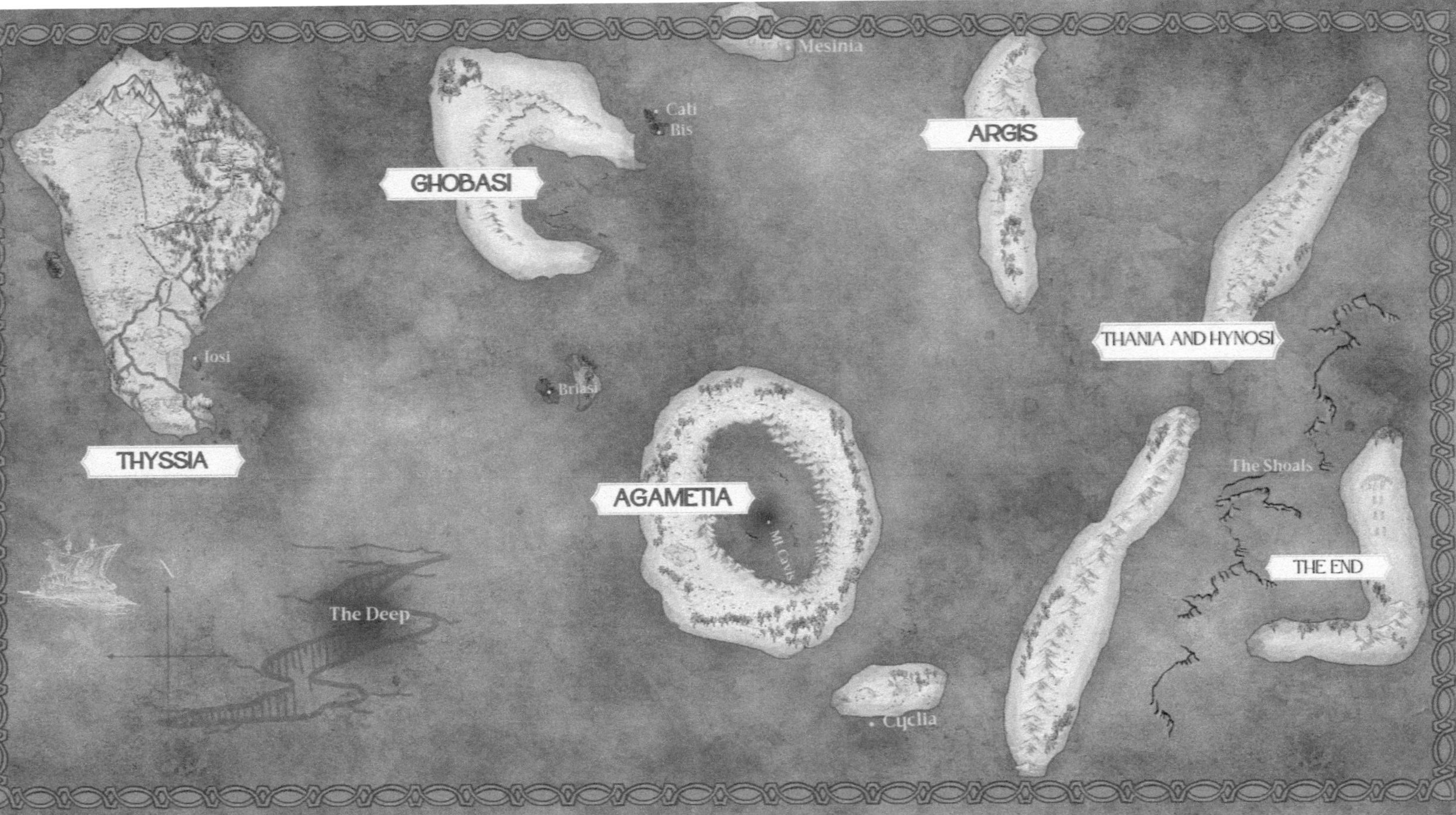
Mesinia
GHOBASI
Cati
Bis
ARGIS
THYSSIA
Iosi
Briasi
THANIA AND HYNOSI
AGAMETIA
Mt Cavis
The Shoals
THE END
The Deep
Cyclia

Thele's Keep

The Great Tree of Autumn

The Hall of Judgement

House Spessia

IOSI

THYSSIA

HEIRS OF THE GHOBASI EMPIRE

TIRANUS
Deceased

TYRAXUS — SEFTI
Deceased Deceased

LYSSIA - - DECIUS — TREJEN BASAN
Deceased Deceased

ROMULUS
674 AE

JESNIA — CASTIA — PORSIA
675 AE 673 AE 673 AE

MOUNTAIN BORN HEIRS

AHTALAH — DARREN — REGULUS
Deceased Deceased

KATHA - - FREYDEN
Deceased

AERIN — BJORN — GAILAH
675 AE 676 AE 679 AE

HEIRS OF HOUSE SPESSIA

ALLAGRIA

ALTIMAIS
Deceased

TORIN — ALEXI
672 AE 677 AE

AE: AGAMITIAN EXPANSION

Prologue

Autumn of 701 AE

If my deeds could measure my life, free of regret, then let that be a song to the people of Thyssia.

-Cias
High Priest of the Autumn Kings
Decius (675) Trejen (700) Romulus

The Thyssian Archipelago rose from the deep as six treacherous islands. They were islands that were forged from stone and sand, with kings and conquerors alike. Long ago, the gods gave each kingdom a relic to protect. In return, their peoples would remain safe from the servants of the Void. Years bled into centuries as their respect rotted into complacency. Thyssia, the Mother island, sheltered three kingdoms on its soil as it reached across the sea. In the east, Trejen's forests neatly encircled the verdant meadows while new trees crept closer each spring. Cerulean river lands carved through the island under the watchful eyes of house Spessia and everyone drank from its meandering depths. All of this was overshadowed by a solitary broken mountain. Their people's separation from the gods fractured its stony face into a chasm, a wound that released any magic the mountain held within its stone. Their relic was ruined by abomination in the wake of Haydrian's touch. Haydrian was an alchemist who relished in the hope of immortality. As the kingdoms of Thyssia disregarded their duty to the nine, so waned their fear of the Void.

Chapter One

Spring of 700 AE
Katha

Fire engulfed Freyden's body as Katha, Queen of the Broken Mountain, watched the flames dissolve his pyre. Her consort and king lay lifeless while his sun-colored hair vanished in a blaze of red. She stood in stoic despair as the entire mountain gathered to mourn their king.

Until today, Katha only wore green, but as she stood before the pyre, black mourning silk flapped behind her in a banner of grief. Her silver-streaked chestnut hair tucked beneath a veil of night and a crown of gold. The sea roared in the distance and the wind stoked the flames into a dance; she saw her memories of him between the crackle of pitch and flares of orange.

Caked in mud, he fought for her hand among the champions and knights until he alone remained. Freyden stood victorious with broken bones, missing pieces of his armor, and blood trickling from his shattered nose. The smell of sweat and soil lingered in her memory as she had crossed the tourney field. She remembered his blue Nadr eyes that stole the air from her lungs like the breath of winter.

Katha's hands shook as she stood before him, the hilt of Freyden's blade firmly gripped in her poised hands. She returned it to him as she declared him the next King Consort of the Broken Mountain. His closed lip smile sent warmth through her skin as he kissed her hand.

"I know little of fate, but I know it joined our lives for a reason. Ever since I carried a sword in your service, I knew what that reason was. If I may call you Katha, then you may call me Freyden."

Pain shot across the queen's chest and she gripped Aerin, her first-born, by his sleeve for strength. He stood beside her as did Bjorn and Gailah, their three children grown and her only proof of Freyden's love.

His presence served as a bastion of peace between the realms and that peace cracked with every passing day as his absence burrowed deep in her heart. It formed a cavern so great that while her entire heart longed for him, Katha lost part of herself to the fire as well.

The heat from the pyre burned wildly in a torrent, and its warmth from where she stood was too great. She stepped back and Katha's eyes fell upon Freyden's mother. After years of disagreements, the two matriarchs were united by sorrow.

She stood watch until her joints became stone as every courtier shared their tears. After the hundredth "Your Majesty", she stopped listening with distant eyes. Her memories invaded and took her far from the fire.

The pillar of smoke rose towards the east, billowing over the budding spring trees of the forest. They had claimed Freyden there, her companion and conscience made flesh taken by bands of rebels slaughtering as they went. Growing bolder each time, now her husband of twenty-five years waited with the gods. She hated the forest. Everything ruinous belonged to the trees.

In her memories, Trejen flashed before her, surrounded by the golden leaves of their eternal tree.

Trejen was young, his face shorn and his sienna skin gleamed under the afternoon sun. A crown of yellow oak leaves curling around raven hair, Decius' laurel, with tears brimming in his eyes. He perched on his brother's war horse on the crest of the meadow looking down at her. He would not come down to the tourney field. Her mind remembered it well, torturing her with the memory of those old days. Her foolish hope still lingered in her chest as she desperately pleaded for Trejen to fight for her, but that love died with King Decius and Queen Lyssia on the day Trejen claimed the crown of his people.

No longer her betrothed, but King of the Great Forest. Katha arranged the tourney for Trejen alone, to fight for her hand and the love they once shared, but Trejen fled with his golden cloak waving in a coward's retreat. Freyden claimed the crown of the mountain and her heart with it.

As the sky mirrored the colors of the fire, the pyre collapsed into embers and ash. Only her guards remained beside her between the snowy hills of the mountains and the thawing meadows below. Glowing embers stared back at Katha as their king disappeared further into the rising smoke.

She stared too long into the fire and saw Haydrian's eyes ignite with strange desire. Before she knew she could love another, she begged Haydrian to make things right, to bring Trejen back to her. When the gods could not help her, she sought the help of the Void.

Her fingers dug into the palms of her hands. Its hellscape flashed before her eyes, a place without light. She walked the breadth of the sentient wasteland every night as it tormented her. A reminder of the separation she formed between the living and the gods.

Katha felt the breaking of the mountain rattle through her as stone cried out to the gods.

Their kingdom was alone. She knew her enemies would come for her, their children, and all semblance of the things she held dear. They would come for the Queen of the Broken Mountain, the Queen who owed a debt to the Void.

Chapter Two

Spring of 700 AE
Trejen

"Please don't look at me like that, Cias." Trejen sighed through clenched teeth as his priest and healer attended to his wounded side.

His skin sang and his eyes watered against the sting of the odorous tinctures.

"I'm not some wounded stag with an arrow in its belly."

The high walls of his chambers echoed the timbre of his voice. They were alone.

The elder priest sighed and shook his head. His soft, hunched frame shuffled about.

"Apologies, your Grace, but empathy is a part of my profession." Cias breathed as his crooked and winter worn fingers discarded the bandages from the king's side.

Trejen winced again and fixed his eyes on the mosaic on the floor where its tessera spelled out the history of their people. The lustrous ceramic tiles formed an oak leaf border that surrounded a depiction of a battle at sea. This battle was fought before Trejen's time, a battle fought long ago when Spessia ruled all the isles. In the corners, various monsters unfurled like flowers across mosaic waters. Beyond the leaves and monsters, a map of the archipelago rested in the center of the floor. The largest portion of the floor was claimed by their island, Thyssia, followed by the five smaller islands, all of them known as the Footsteps of the gods.

"So, there is nothing to be done for it?" King Trejen whispered, then closed his eyes as his head met the back of his chair.

"Despite your pain, I am pleased that your body tells me rot does not claim your wound."

Cias' encouragement did not ease the coiling dread in his gut. Trejen felt another tug at his side and opened his eyes. This time, a cold grey gaze stared back at him.

His grandfather Tiranus loomed over the room in a carved movement of marble, a vestige with fury carved into the lifeless lines on his face. The statue's glorious prestige mocked him as a reminder of the Ghobasian empire they had lost to the sea. Painted on the statue's stone, shades of gold decorated his armor, including the crown of oak leaves upon his brow, the crown that now rested upon his desk. It pained him to wear it. Tiranus was the greatest of emperors with lesser sons and even lesser grandsons. Only remnants of his empire lived within the trees, after King Darren cleaved the empire in two, the jewel of the autumn king became the final outpost of Emperor Tiranus. Trejen flinched as Cias probed along his side and the king shook his grandfather's memory from his mind. A legacy of bitter days was all that became of the Emperor's greatness.

Cias peeled back the matted, blood-soaked oak leaves from the blackened gash in Trejen's side.

"Our sacred tree has given all. The golden oak's brightness fades as autumn passes. Our healing art loses its power as its light fades away."

Trejen tightened his grip on the armchair. The knife wound bore deep into the king's abdomen.

"How long?" The words burned on his tongue. The barren room stared back at him, a square room meant for men with greater purpose and a throne that did not belong to him, a throne he kept warm for his nephew, his brother's son and heir.

"I am no seer, but the poison festering in your veins is not a merciful one. A poison conjured and alchemical. It will be slow, but you may survive the solstice." The softness on the old man's face shifted, revealing that he would bury yet another king in Cias' time or service. "Months, maybe a year, two if it is the cruelest variety, but you must rest, my King. Excitability will only draw the poison closer to your heart."

Trejen held his breath as the priest ground another golden oak leaf into the mortar.

"Speak of this to no one. Romulus will need to be readied before I fall to this."

"Anything but discretion would be treason, but you must tell him soon, my King." Cias bowed, then turned his attention to his salves and poultices.

He was the caretaker of their sacred tree and a voice to the gods, a position with little power but a greater capacity for good. He was a patient man, soft in spirit and kind of heart, from the shores of Misenia. A man who held the secrets of the world within the iron chest of his heart.

"As your physic and, dare I say…friend, send Romulus to the gathering. Do not press your body beyond its capacity."

Cias was right. The gathering would overextend him greatly, but everything within Trejen's body knew he needed to be present. The priest finished dressing his wound and began collecting his tools.

"As your king, you know I must go. If this is to be my end, then let me secure allies for my nephew." Trejen breathed through his teeth, pushing upwards from the chair.

Cias clasped his hands before his ochre tunic and bowed his head. "You have always been selfless, my king. I do not advise you to go, but I only speak for the gods. I am not one of them."

Silence drifted across the marble room of Trejen's study. The marble walls entwined with intricate oaken carvings amplified the quiet of the room.

"You have my thanks, but ask the gods if they will spare me enough time to find a queen for my nephew."

The priest froze and nodded, but only after a pause that confused the king.

Retrieving his medicinals, Cias bowed and left the room.

Trejen brooded behind the clutter of duty piling upon his desk.

Wind flowed in through the window behind him, drafting in the earthy scent of spring. Golden shimmering leaves swayed in the breeze's rhythm. Limbs extended towards the palace and spiraled towards the sky. The tree glowed against the spritely, budding leaves of the forest. The lone trunk stood tall in the center of the courtyard. An ancient oak frozen in eternal autumn, a relic to the God of Healing. The veins of the noble tree glimmered in ethereal streaks of gold, resplendent and proud in the afternoon sun. Each leaf was connected to the source of its power and it was said that the fallen vessels were filled with the spirits of those who had passed. The priest had forbidden anyone to pluck a leaf before its time. Yet, even Trejen doubted the extent of its power. If it were a force so great, why did his body fail more every day? The gods had blessed each kingdom with a relic to protect, but when the mountain split, the other two were never the same. Their tree was dying.

Beyond the guarded walls of the square shaped keep, the twisting Ilsnadad river swept through the forest to the lower Spessian river lands. It glittered and snaked through the sun-filled leaves. The river's revered current carried the fallen to their place among the gods. Trejen could see the watery path those before him had traveled. It was a journey that ended with the forever rest beneath its rippling surface, a long journey for all except those who wore the crown. When the king's boat came to the sea, the priests would remove the body and keep it safe underground. His brother, his father, and he too would soon rest encased in the crypts beneath the keep. It was far too dangerous a thing to leave the body of a king to the mercy of the sea.

Aerin

Far eastward, beyond the halls of the forest of the free folk, seated high in the pass of the Broken Mountain, a castle thawed under the rising spring season. Thele's walls were thick and grey like the mountain itself, a fortress invisible in the cold dark of winter. The ice-crusted stronghold dripped in the day's brightness. Little rivers from the dying winter snow ran down towards the valley and away from the jagged peaks, a keep his ancestor's had named for the God of Strength.

Darting above the prince, a hawk with rust-colored markings glided upon the morning winds.

Aerin rode forward through the mountain passes with ease. The Knights of the Chasm, a legion of men appointed by his uncle Regulus, at his side departed for their fortress. They guarded the ruinous gorge that housed their armies. What had once brought shame to their house was now the seat of their strength.

The chill of the mountain air embraced him, a welcome greeting to the eldest prince of the mountain. He approached the pointed granite gates of his family's keep with a heavy posture in his saddle. Piles of snow slid from the turreted rooftops in loud, crashing heaps of slush.

Prince Aerin's riding boots sloshed into the icy mush as he dropped from his saddle, leaving a sloppy trail of footprints in the snow. He smiled as he brushed away the watery crystals that accumulated on his shoulder, a smile that felt foreign and awkward, muscles he had not used in many months. He could still see his horse's breath plumed in the morning air as he walked through the outer courtyard and greeted the squires who raced to meet him.

"Shall I announce your arrival, your Highness?" A voice rang out from the steps of the great hall. The words dripped with sarcasm. Aerin turned and his younger brother slammed into him.

"Bjorn!" Aerin wheezed against Bjorn's bear-like embrace. "It's good to see you,"

He never got used to the idea of having to look up to meet his younger brother's gaze. Bjorn was pure Nadr, mountain born. Their only similarities were their mother's chestnut hair but flecked with hints of auburn in the sunlight. Where Aerin was lithe and lean, Bjorn stood built from stone. Every aspect of him was broad from his biceps to his belly. He was stronger and more fearsome than Aerin could ever be. But none of that mattered. Bjorn was his only brother and he would never let harm befall their family. He carried the weight of their burdens like everything else–with quiet, selfless strength.

"No bears this season, but more raiders are gathering on the edges of the forest."

Bjorn's cheery demeanor stilled. "They're venturing higher into the hillside, brother. We need you home more than ever, especially if..."

Soft footsteps crunched through the snow of the courtyard.

"He's not home for more than a moment and you're already calling for the banner men!" Gailah's quiet but pointed voice called out to them as she carefully dodged the piles of melting snow in silken slippers. "You've had his ear long enough. I'm here to take him to mother before Cress and Balix find you. They'll tear you to bits."

Gailah teased and rolled her eyes at Aerin's as she took his arm.

Gailah was the youngest, but she held the reins over the royal family. She was unafraid of butting heads with her brothers, but wise enough not to cross their mother. She bore the coloring of winter in her icy blue eyes, ones that matched the sky beyond the tallest peaks. As Gailah pulled him towards the keep, her white wisps of curling silver hair danced in the air and tumbled down along her spine. She was so unlike her brother's with their warm, ruddy skin. Her rounded cheeks and soft upturned nose carried the kindness of their father but his ferocity still glimmered in the corners of her eyes.

"Thank the nine you're home." she whispered as she pulled her arm tighter in the crook of his elbow.

"Bjorn's worried. He pretends he is fine, but it is worse than he knows." Aerin whispered to his sister as their footsteps echoed up the grey polished rock steps of the palace. Two bears hewn from stone guarded the doors of the Great Hall. Emeralds rested in their eye sockets as golden sunlight danced in their facets. Gailah and Aerin passed beneath their carved paws and between the towering doors. The stronghold bore tall windows of Agametian glass, carved into the face of the

Great Hall. Long dead kings watched as the siblings departed the courtyard.

"How is she?" He asked. Aerin's fingers twitched as he fought the tussles of his hair.

Gailah narrowed her eyes.

"Stubborn as ever, but she'll be glad to see you, too." His sister smiled as the guards opened the doors in a synchronized clanging of locks and iron.

Their keep would belong to him someday, but now, after losing their father, that promise now loomed with threatening jaws.

As they entered the Great Hall, Aerin's skin tingled from the warmth of the fire. Gailah loosened her cloak and led her brother through the dark and arching corridors. Tapestries and furs lined the walls that trapped the heat within the mountain walls that surrounded them.

"If she mentions it, tell her I have no intention of marrying Lord Rorick. I know he will make an offer at the gathering." Gailah whispered.

His sister spoke of the youngest lord of the mountain and the bane of Gailah's childhood, but he had not come to the gathering in many years.

Katha and Gailah hardly spoke to each other in the months since their father's death, and it bothered Aerin terribly. His mother buried her grief in duty and diplomacy, a duty that she now pressed upon his sister.

"I will marry a princess from Ghobasi that I have never met." Aerin sighed as he massaged annoyance from between his brows. "You and Bjorn will marry whomever suits our people best.... Pay no mind to Lord Rorick. Mother would not waste your marriage to someone who already is in our debt, but Sister, I know it is an odd thing being moved around like pawns on a board."

He hid the disdain in his voice with sarcasm and Aerin flexed his fingers as he stood before the gilded doors of his Mother's chamber.

Chapter Three

Trejen

As evening fell, the King of the Great Forest dined with what remained of his family. His charge and crown prince, Romulus, slouched beside him. He was a brooding storm cloud of raven wavy hair and warm sienna skin.

Trejen's commander, Lord Barrock, occupied the other end of the table. A broad man and fierce protector of their people. He wiped the gristle from his once red, now silver beard with his sleeve as his gauntlet clacked against the table. His people were from the oldest of blood lines that belonged to Thyssia.

Meanwhile, Eric, his cousin and naval overseer, sat awkwardly in between.

"But she must marry someone... why shouldn't it be Romulus?" Eric's words slithered across the dining table.

Trejen's face hardened as Romulus seethed with his two tine fork tightly in his grip.

"If you're so fond of her, Uncle, then I will gladly let you marry the mountain princess!" Prince Romulus slammed his hands on the wood and rose from his seat with the oak table creaking from the force.

With reddened cheeks, Romulus exited the dining hall in a swift, furious movement. His steps resounded like a charging bull. Then the doors slammed against the polished walls, shaking the decorative weaponry and rectangular shields that hung on the marble.

"Let him go..." Trejen waved.

"What is he on about?" Eric's eyebrows arched with questions as he watched his nephew storm from the room. All the while, Eric raised his hands, feigning innocence as he reached for his glass.

Lord Barrock glanced between his king and the naval officer beside him as a worried expression splayed across his face.

"The prince is in a hard age and season. Even among the animals of the forest, young stags will attack for no apparent reason," Lord Barrock said as he separated the shoulder bones of a roast chicken. "As a father, I've been in your place before."

He looked at Trejen, and the king felt a pang in his chest. He clutched the knife at his place setting, hiding the pain in his eyes. He could never be the father his nephew needed him to be. Trejen chose Romulus long ago, protecting his birthright and throne, but that would never replace the gaping hole left by Decius and Lyssia's death. It was a cruelty that had separated him from the only home he had ever known.

He exhaled deeply as the pain subsided. His knuckles no longer flared white as he released his knife.

"He doesn't have the stomach for politics." The king sighed with frustration as he studied the wine in his cup.

"As if you ever did? They practically branded that crown on your forehead." Eric smirked then stabbed at his food.

"No decent man has a stomach for politics." Trejen quipped and watched his cousin roll his eyes.

"Are there decent men?" Eric asked.

Lord Barrock's gaze bounced from one end of the table to the other, a spectator. Lord Barrock's brows hid his usually jolly expression beneath a mask of confusion.

Eric smoothed an unnoticeable ruffle of gathered fabric along his shoulder clasp as he drummed his fingers on the table.

"The spring gathering will happen with or without you. It would be a slight to the judges and the rest of the kingdoms if we did not make an offer for the princess' hand." Eric's eyes wandered from the high carved ceilings of the dining hall.

The walls of the dining hall bore a carved oak tree. Magnificent branches of hammered gold took the shape of their sacred tree. Delicate oak leaves hung above them, reflecting candlelight.

"Lord Barrock? Would you do your kingdom the great service of attending the spring gathering on my behalf?" King Trejen goaded as he looked at his old friend's bewildered face.

"I would follow your Highness into the fiercest battles with nothing but my bare hands, but I think..."

Eric's chair cut Lord Barrock off as it screeched against the stony floor.

"Queen Katha will present Gailah to the gathering just as she did her sons. If Romulus is absent, then you forfeit a valuable alliance and all the lowlands that she stands to inherit!"

King Trejen paused as he met his cousin's gaze. The mention of Katha's name sent his mind a crippling blow. Trejen avoided the gathering with every fiber of his being. To him, it was nothing more than a taunting parade, an assembly of the life fate had denied him. He would not torture himself year after year to sit in his beloved's presence, but only as an observer to the grandeur of her reign.

Eric sneered as he spoke.

"You shame your brother's mem..."

The reference to Trejen's dead brother filled the room with a quiet chill.

"Treason hangs on the end of that sentence and you'd be wise to remember it." Lord Barrock's face was as firm as his broadsword and his glare was just as sharp. "You've spoiled my appetite with all this bickering."

"We will attend the spring gathering, but you will not be in my company." Trejen's words were steady and flat as his glare silenced his cousin. "I will make an offer for Gailah's hand in marriage to Romulus, but I have no hope of expecting Romulus to comply."

"Ah." Eric bit his tongue. "Please give King Freyden's widow my condolences. I hear he loved her very much." He bowed as he stood from the table. "My men will summer with me as we sail for the shores of Ghobasi."

Lord Barrock aggressively murmured into his beard.

The only sound after the doors closed was the flickering of candlelight. Lord Barrock's goblet clanked awkwardly against the wooden table.

"Your family is worse than mine." He said after a large gulp of wine. "That man makes me never want to taste bread again."

"Barrock, your family is quite pleasant. What a cruel comparison." King Trejen smiled, burying the twinge of pain that flashed across his face at the mention of the late king consort.

Freyden was a kind man and far nobler than most in both the Mountain Court and the Autumn Kingdom. His prowess with a broadsword was fit for legend. It was cruel that a raider's arrow took the swordsmen down. Queen Katha, his Katha, had chosen Freyden for a reason. That only made guilt rise high in his chest. Freyden's blood covered faced flashed across his mind. He clutched his knife again. Trejen chased the dead king from his thoughts.

"At the gathering, I have a favor to ask of you." Lord Barrock shifted in his seat as he changed the topic to lighter conversation. "I would like to make an introduction for my daughter. The second princeling from the Mountain Kingdom? Bjorn? I believe he's called. I'd like the chance for them to know each other a bit. Though it is embarrassing to ask you such a thing when..."

Trejen smiled and shook his head. He breathed through the stabbing at his side.

"Your daughter may travel with our company. Maybe someone will get some enjoyment out of the whole affair." Trejen laughed weakly as he swirled the wine in his goblet.

"Thank you. She will be very pleased to hear it. He's an honorable lad, and she deserves a husband with a good heart." Lord Barrock's demeanor had eased considerably. As the two of them dined, Trejen merely sat with his oldest of friends.

. . .

KATHA

The Queen of the Mountain was dressed in deep emerald velvet, a fabric so dark green that shadow seemed to erase trace any of the hue. Her billowing sleeves nearly reached the hem of her gown as she sat facing the intricate Agametian windows of her chamber. Her long, dark braid dangled gently over the back of her chair. The emerald crown of the mountain sat perfectly still as her head tilted downward. Karak, a great brown bear, slept with his massive head in her velvet lap. Her loyal companion carried a small piece of Freyden with her wherever they went. In her hand, an ivory comb encrusted with emeralds gently scratched at the fur on his brow. His face wrinkled in delight as she combed through his fur. Freyden had gifted them to her as wedding presents long ago.

An orphan bear cub and a heartbroken bride were now an inseparable pair. Many thought that Karak was a magic bear, that he was secretly a shapeshifter, or that the queen could speak the secret language of beasts and animals, but none of this was true. Like all orphans, what he had needed was a home. Katha smiled as her bear's rounded ears twitched with every stroke.

"Mother..." Prince Aerin's voice was soft as the wooden door creaked against the crackling fireplace ambiance.

Katha's fitful heart swelled.

"My son, it is so good to have you home. Is Gailah with you?" Katha's expression only shielded some of her concern as her half smile faded quickly. She looked around her son's shoulder through the entryway.

"She led me here, but she knew you wanted to speak to me alone. What has happened?" Prince Aerin spoke as if the walls had ears. Karak stirred at the sound of his second favorite family member.

"I'm here, old boy." He said, and he ruffled the fur between the beast's shoulders.

"Oh Aerin, it's worse than you could imagine." Her tightly set jaw twitched and rested her fingers between her brow. She set the comb on her side table. "The raiding parties are growing bolder and they are venturing farther than the shade of the forest. There have been threats from the Spessian courts. Meaningless threats, but the real threat at hand is the raiding parties that haunt our every step. We must not distract ourselves with the words of arrogant princes."

"They threatened you?"

"No. Gailah."

"What?"

"They threatened war and countless horrible things if we did not wed her to their prince!"

Aerin's fists balled at his sides.

"What was your response?"

"Nothing. Unless it comes from Allagria, her grandson's words have no teeth."

Aerin's countenance fell, and she saw her son chew on his cheek before he spoke.

"I have no word of the disappearing men. I searched every village from here to the sea. Men go missing every day! We must alert the judges! If the Autumn Court will not permit our armies on their land, then we must force the judge's hand. They are whispering of alchemists—"

Aerin struck a raw and tender point in her heart.

"The alchemists are gone. They are no more and I will extinguish any that dare show their face on our island." Katha's words were fierce. She spoke to her son, but the queen needed to believe her words as well. She wrapped her arms around her torso.

"Then we don't go to the gathering." The prince's face hardened and his gaze fixed on the snowy peaks in the distance. "With father gone, they will excuse our absence as mourning. Send Regulus, but if we are in danger, then we shall not go down."

Her fingers traced the stiff velvet along her arms. The Spessian prince's words still echoed in her mind. Katha straightened in her chair and she felt Karak stir. She thought of Trejen and their memories crept across her skin.

"We must go down. We will draw them out. A unified house, stronger than ever. Gailah needs us to be wise. Her presentation is all that matters." Katha knew they could not hide in the mountains forever. She held her hand out to her eldest son and gripped it tightly. "We may not have your father to protect us, but we have each other. We are not alone. Alert our allies in Ghobasi, it has been far too long since we called on them and if war is coming, then we must be ready."

Chapter Four

Alexi

White marble pillars shone in the afternoon sunlight as the ancient columns above the terrace bore the weight of the magnificent Spessian palace. Alexi stood on its raised watchtower as quadriremes glided through the harbor. White-washed stone houses dotted the slopes of the Riverlands. Vibrant spring hues erupted in climbing floral vines across the seaside villages. His brother had come home victorious with his fleet sailing swiftly behind him. The small isle of Iosi glimmered on the distant horizon. Alexi unclenched his jaw and rolled his shoulders back as he braced himself for Torin's arrival.

The round alabaster courtyard beneath him housed fragrant trees that swayed with the coastal breeze. Their pink flowers fell in delicate clusters on the paving stones while plebeians muttered about. Green hills absorbed the fading evening sun that reflected from the high white-washed cliffs. Spring arrived earliest in the riverlands.

A small fountain babbled in the center and despite the surrounding sounds, to Alexi, the world was quiet. A roaring battleground consumed his thoughts. His finger teased the broken skin around his thumbnail as anger waged within him. In the distance, Alexi watched Torin descend from his warship like an onyx peacock. The muscles along his spine tensed as he adjusted his weight along the balcony's railing. His hazel eyes fixed on the fountain as his fist tightened. His grandmother's words dug themselves deeper in his mind. The blood forged promises made in the secrecy of night gnawed at any loyalty he held for his brother. Their matriarch had spelled out his orders and sealed Torin's fate.

A songbird's sharp cry split the evening silence. A plume of feathers tumbled from a flowering tree in the courtyard. Spiraling in its wake, a sparrow hawk darted with its limp prize. The hawk was no stranger in their court. Torin was the keeper of the hounds and of the hunt. His sparrow hawks often plucked their food from the orchard and today was no different, but it was different to the songbird.

Alexi's silver hair moved in the breeze, and he despised his resemblance to his brother. He mirrored him in every sense, save for the features that made Torin great.

Torin's broad shoulders carried a royal blue Spessian cloak that drifted behind him. His elder brother climbed the great steps before the palace, a general in his own right. His irksome sea-blown hair feathered on the breeze and amid the roar of the crowd, a legion marched behind Torin, venerating their would-be king.

Alexi tightened his hand around the sword at his side, though untested in battle. He would strike Torin down, but not today. Alexi was the more patient of the two. He would wait for the gathering, let his brother show his traitor's hand before he shed his family's blood. Torin's legion disappeared within the gates of the barracks as flowers fell from the rooftops in celebration of their safe return.

Alexi hoped Torin enjoyed his waning glory.

The statue of their grandmother in her prime stood before the palace gates. Alexi felt the statue's piercing gaze, and he relaxed his grip.

TORIN

The sun had just disappeared beneath the cloak of twilight while moon hung low over the Carridean in white striated veins of light across the harbor. Wrinkles ribbed the pads of Torin's fingers as he returned from the thermal pools beneath the palace. In the water's warmth, his thoughts unraveled with the tension in his body as the steam turned to droplets on his skin. He moved impatiently around his chamber and searched for food to silence the gnawing pain in his stomach.

It did not matter if the battle began at sea or if the land absorbed the blood of his enemies, Torin was exceedingly proficient at killing. That was what they had trained him to do–what they expected of him. Torin was the Crown Prince of the Riverlands, the son of conquers and named blessed from birth in the line of Spessian succession.

No amount of glory left him satisfied, but in the quiet of the night, Torin stared into the darkness and he paced the breadth of his room. The entire palace was silent save for the pounding in his chest and the stars burning above the sea. As he stared through the windows and looked over the smallest isles, he thought of a girl. A girl he did not know who was in grave danger. The silhouette of his prized companion arced through the sky and Torin's pulse raced as desperate hope filled his heart.

All of his messages to the Queen of the Mountain had returned with silence. He prayed this time would be different. He crossed to his desk and unfurled a small piece of parchment, and drew a quill in his hand. It shook in his grip and the tip of his quill cracked as it met the parchment, Torin cracked with it. He slammed his palm against the desk. The prince could no longer stay quartered in his chambers.

He threw open the doors of his room and slipped into the midnight air. As Torin followed the open interior balcony, the square shaped hole in the ceiling bathed the lower compluvium in moonlight. Its pale glow shone across the courtyard mosaic and a gigantic sea serpent devoured itself amid the sparkling tiles. Nine spines protruded from its back. Shadow covered two of its spines, but the darkness divided a third from the light that revealed the rest of the mosaic's story. Strings of constellations surrounded the serpent and the nine divine of the Archipelago looked on as it swallowed its tail.

Long shadows from the carvings on the balcony weaved through Torin's steps as he urged forward into the night. Nine columns holding up everything under his feet as he moved through the warm spring air, and every crevice had eyes that watched him. Impatience guided his footsteps as he moved towards the falconry tower. His shoulders tensed from days of battle at sea that even the baths could not unwind.

What truly bothered the prince was not his aching body, but the silence from the mountain that only sank his mind into a frenzied rhythm. The world around him fractured with each day that passed as their enemies drew closer. The pillars of who Torin believed himself to be quaked under the blight that plagued their people. A blight that wore the crown of the riverlands, a blight that called him her grandson. He obeyed her every command, without hesitation, but not this. The depravity of her orders snapped any tether of loyalty he had to his queen. Spessia would belong to him someday. No true king would bow down in the face of evil.

Torin stood in the tower of his family's keep. A place of refuge for the prince. Magnificent birds of various species flew and wandered about, but only those that hunted by night. The others hunkered down in small feathery clusters with happy chirps.

A red-breasted hawk with grey and tan feathers drifted about on the breeze. She circled the tower as broad turns marked her descent. The hawk sliced through the moonlight and she announced her arrival with a mighty rush of feathers as she ducked through the tower window. Kelligh was Torin's prized hawk. She was the oldest hawk in his keeping and the mother of the rest of them.

Tonight was different. Her priority was not with him, but to the chirping chorus just beyond the window. Three fledglings filled her nest near the tower window–too young to fly, but old enough to know that their next meal had arrived. She had returned with a songbird in her clutches.

Torin's late mother gave Kelligh to Torin when he was hardly more than a child. A woman he remembered in glimmering memories and what he could recall, his mind tried to bury. Torin stroked the top of the bird's feathers and she chirped gently. He searched the cuff at Kelligh's ankle, yet there was no parchment curled through the metal clasp. Torin's hands trembled, and he swallowed against the defeat that boiled beneath his ribs. He choked back the urge to yell as he bit down on his teeth. Torin held his head in his hands as the coiling pang of his entrapment twisted like a knife.

Torin would betray his family for a stranger. Nausea coursed through him as he sat back and watched his hawk move through the room.

Kelligh bobbed about delicately on the edge of her nest as she nudged and groomed her fledglings. They were round, soft, and stout little things. Their eyes were too large for their tiny heads as they tilted about looking for their mother.

Torin extended an open, ungloved hand to the noble bird. His wrist, forearm, and hand all bore small scars from the years of practice and handling the predators he held so dear. Kelligh shuffled her way along the nest and with a taloned claw as she climbed her way onto her master's wrist. From her happy squawks, he could tell she was pleased with her catch as her small hawks feasted upon it.

Torin's eyes watched through the tower window as clouds gathered in the distance beneath the starry horizon and shadowed ships dappled the harbor far below. Beyond them, cutting through clouds, the Broken Mountain loomed far in the distance. Its shadowed peak rose high above the great forest that separated Spessia from the mountain clans. Its shattered face absorbed moonlight into its chasm fortress.

Torin released Kelligh from his wrist and despair accompanied his every footstep that receded towards the royal apartments. The gathering presented a window to protect his people from his grandmother's fate. The people of Spessia did not deserve to pay for the sins of their queen. If he challenged her amid the kingdoms, and the judges as well, perhaps he would escape the hands of death that followed him. If he did not move, Torin was as good as dead. Gailah was as good as dead. If she fell, then their kingdoms would cease to exist, and Torin along with it.

Gailah

Like a bemused house cat, Gailah tucked her feet beneath her as she curled into the warmth of the sun-filled library window. Each pane, a work of art, was a gift from the Agametian glass makers to the kings long before her. Those windows were a memorial to the loveliest island, one that erupted into a basin of lava and death. Smoke was the first sign of

Agamitia's despair before the angry core of their island buried every Agametian in ash and condemned their artistry to the Deep. Only three palaces boasted such finery, and the craft of glass work mystified them all.

If her life were different, and the void had not grown jealous of the Agametian's craft, Gailah would have cherished the opportunity to learn the magic of their skill. But in this life, Gailah had taken her father's place as the orator and storyteller. Each night, she read aloud to anyone who would listen. It felt cruel to leave her father's volumes alone in the library's darkness. The great forest shone in the distant sunlight, blue sky hung over the river lands beyond the trees.

Eastwards, the farthest isles were only specks on the horizon if she squinted. The people called them the Footsteps of the gods, as if each small piece of soil surfaced from where they trod long ago. Their entire world rested in the heel touches of the nine.

The claw shaped isle of Ghobasi boasted sharp coastal cliffs that made for treacherous crossings, but its red clay soil contrasted the turquoise Carridean passage.

This was one of the many advantages of their place on the mountain. The view of the island chain never ceased to take her breath away. She imagined what it might be like on those distant islands, but Gailah could only dream. She had never left Thyssian soil.

A pillow supported her as she jotted in her leather-bound journal. Tatters of papers fell around the edges of the book and into the pools of her skirts.Her other hand fiddled with the silver bear etched torque around her neck.

"Ranking your suitors, I suppose?" Bjorn's boisterous voice echoed through the library.

She sighed, slamming her book closed.

Bjorn stood in the doorway with a sly grin.

"No, just writing your eulogy, brother." She said with a wink as she jumped down from her windowsill.

Bjorn playfully clutched his chest, pretending to be in pain.

"Your dagger's wound, dear sister." Bjorn dipped through the doorway. "But really, what keeps you in the window all day? Surely not planning your nuptials already?"

Gailah rolled her eyes and tucked the journal beneath the cushion in the window.

"Enough."

Bjorn's eyes saddened a bit, and Gailah sighed. She paused and held her journal in her hands.

"Promise you won't tell?" Gailah narrowed her gaze at her elder brother. Her fingers wrapped tighter around her elbows as she enveloped herself in a hug.

"On my honor, as a Knight of the Broken Mountain." He softly placed a hand over his heart with a comically arched brow. "It will be as if you never told me."

She removed the book from the window sill cushions and held it tightly between her fingers.

Gailah plopped down on the velvet chaise that sat in the middle of the royal library and let the loose pages fall open across her lap. He steadied his elbows on the seat behind her. Bjorn's eyes widened, and he clicked his tongue in surprise.

"Where did you get all this?" Bjorn's voice filled with alarm.

His large hands swiped the book from her lap.

"You promised you wouldn't tell!" Her voice dropped to a threat filled whisper. Her face bore a look that all siblings know and heed well. He placed the book back in his sister's hands.

"I won't. I'll break a bone before I break a promise, sister." the warrior said with a playful smirk. "Even if alchemy is forbidden in our kingdom.... as well as every other kingdom.... and punishable by exile, dear sister. You'll have bigger problems than suitors knocking at your door. Please be careful Gailah. I hope you study for curiosity's sake and not for practice. Wiser people have died for this..."

All the playfulness retreated from his face. Her brother's sad eyes flicked quickly over his sister before he turned towards the fireplace.

Its crackling embers filled the library as the two siblings steeped in their shared secret. She quietly closed the cover, tucked the pages away and made the journal disappear under the flowing fabric of her skirts.

"Have you considered any more proposals? I assure you they are not all bad," he said, forcing a change in the conversation.

"You haven't met all of them." Gailah said with a pessimistic laughter. She brushed away a stray lock of wavy silver hair. "You do not know what it is like. What if he's cruel? What if he's dreadfully dull or if it's custom to kiss his feet every night? Or if he bites the tines of his fork when he eats?" She shivered at the thought.

Gailah liked the idea of marriage, but the principle of an arrangement depleted all joy from the concept.

Bjorn sat beside his sister, his hands clasped between his knees.

"Or... now give me a chance to speak. What if he can make you laugh or he wants you to read marvelous stories aloud before a glowing hearth with the sweetest wine? What if his cloak keeps you warm when the winter's chill cuts through even the thickest castle walls?" He turned to face his sister. "You will not be a prisoner to some prince or king... Well, that is only true if he doesn't exile you for..." Bjorn looked to the alchemy journal she tucked away. "Do not close yourself away because of it. Besides, I'd never let you marry a monster."

"What would you do, brother?" She scrunched her nose and tucked her grey blue gown beneath her slippers and repositioned herself on the chaise. It was carved from soft wood and her fingers brushed the small bears widdled into the arms. "If you were me and I were you?"

"Find the richest second-born son on this bloody continent and enjoy every penny and minute of responsibility free life. But unfortunately, I'm your brother, so you'll have to settle for the second richest second-born son." He said with a self-satisfied and ridiculous grin.

"Be serious." Gailah's said with a shakier voice than she would like.

Bjorn swallowed and nodded his head.

"Apologies, but if I were the most sought after maiden in the kingdom? Well, I'd marry anyone or no one at all." He said with a definite nod, but his eyes stopped at the portrait of his father standing beside his mother's throne. Gailah followed her brother's gaze, which rested on the sunny warmth of her father's face.

"Fate decided for them and I'd hope the gods, fate, or whomever is in charge of those decisions grants such a pairing for me as well." Bjorn said, and she saw the twinge of pain that flashed across his face.

Even now, Gailah still heard her father's footsteps in the castle.

Chapter Five

Bjorn

Above him, the yellow morning sun drenched the forest canopy, dark emerald hues bled into warm, flourishing leaves as light shone through the trees. He welcomed the glowing sun after his journey through the darkness at dawn. Bjorn galloped through the forest without permission or royal escort. He crossed the border of the Autumn Kingdom without a shadow of hesitation.

To Bjorn, this was not a place of verdant life but a crypt, with limbs buttressing its arching vaults. He found no refuge beneath its shade. He had traced horsemen's tracks through the watery mud of the road for hours now. From the depths of his dreams, the trees visited him every night, as invisible attackers assaulted his sleep. Each time they visited, the dream's ending remained the same. He could not save his father. Bjorn's pulse thundered with every rustle through the forest. His mind shut out the surrounding sounds as he hammered forward, silencing the panic that rose beneath his skin. The flashes of greenery blended together as he rushed towards the site of their attack.

Without warning, smoke slipped into his senses delicately and caught him unaware. Bjorn slowed his horse's pace, the scent befuddled him.

Bjorn dismounted from his horse with a dissatisfied grunt. The tracks he followed dissolved with the mud of a washed out embankment.

The only traces of the raiding parties were invisible in the thick clay soil.

He smelled the distant smoke once again, and his stomach churned at its emptiness. His senses heightened at the thought of who might be bold enough to light a fire within the trees. There was no known village in this part of the forest.

Only someone wanting to be found would cook something so inviting that it made the air tastier than it had the right to be. As the prince moved, the scent danced around him, leaving a lingering and enchanting presence in the air. He reached for the rations in his pack, but the cold crumble of dried venison between his fingers only worsened his curiosity. He weighed the cost of the detour against the urgency in his mind, but as Bjorn returned the venison to his pack and mounted his horse, he let his curiosity get the better of him.

It was not long before the scent of smoke revealed itself in a white smoke column rising between the white birch-woods. Their bright leaves glittered in twisting chains of jewels amid the trail of smoke and sunshine.

Bjorn led his horse on foot as he swerved between the trunks smaller than his frame and saplings scratched his shoulders in a delicate wall of undergrowth.

While dust danced through rays of splitting sunlight just beyond the trees, a lush glade captivated the prince. A crackling fire churned beneath a boiling pot. Behind it there was a circular moss covered cottage constructed from limestone. Its shoddy chimney produced inviting puffs of smoke that collected into small clouds above the forest. Freshly caught rabbits and forest foul hung along the cottage, ready to be skinned. A twisting brook sang over rapids beside the encampment, a wholly idyllic and charming place. Bjorn's heart warmed, and he took a step forward.

"Mountain born are not welcome here." A sharp voice snarled as a knife dug bluntly into his low back. Bjorn's heart stopped, and he raised his hands slowly. The reins fell to his feet. Bjorn could not see who spoke and turned into the dull press of the blade.

"I mean you no harm." His words were steady, but his pulse beat wildly in his neck. He saw a flash of red, no, auburn.

"And what if I do?" The stranger's voice was female. He blinked rapidly as he tried to recall any hint of her approach. No crunch of leaves or broken twigs. His only warning was her blade at his back.

"Then I am your prisoner by all rights of men. I am trespassing and I beg your apologies. I have no interest in disturbing your peace." Bjorn exhaled deeply.

The woman scoffed from behind him.

"You disturbed my peace by riding your poor horse, your ridiculously large horse, to its near death through my woods! My snares will be empty for at least a week because of the peace you disturbed." she spat.

The pressure of her blade lessened, but then he felt a tug at his waist. Bjorn threw himself around as she quickly sliced through his sword belt. It clattered to the ground beside him as his breath quickened, and he swallowed with a widened stare.

The voice belonged to a copper-headed female who stood no higher than the prince's sternum. For his size, this was the average height of a woman.

Her narrowed gaze camouflaged with the bright greenery behind her. Small pieces of fern and little twigs littered her mangled braid.

Bjorn could not distinguish freckles from spattered mud. He had seen deer with more meat on them, but she had the temperament of a cornered bear. Bjorn had violated her sacred forest sanctum and found a place never meant to be discovered. Her face was a mix of fear and confusion.

"Your woods?" He raised a thick eyebrow at her declaration. "They belong to King Trejen, do they not?"

"No one travels this far unless they mean to go unseen and you have no escorts." She glared down the length of her raised blade.

"But I see everyone. Turn around!" she commanded.

"Are you alone?"

"Are you alone?" she retorted and kept her hunting knife between them. "Why would I answer that question? Telling a strange man if I'm alone in my home." The woman sneered.

Bjorn raised his hands and stepped away from his sword.

"Yes, I am completely and utterly alone, well, besides him." He nodded to the horse that grazed a few paces away. Inside, his heart tightened at the truth in his words.

She looked at the horse, then back at the prince .

"Good. If you're lying, I'll kill you."

"I mean you no harm. I will be on my way, but I would like to ask you something." His hands lowered slowly. "Since you see everyone?"

"Why would I tell you anything?" She sneered.

"I can pay?"

Her face softened, and her blade found its sheath on her agile figure. "What makes you think I need your mountain coin? Our people will barter or pay with Triani, but I cannot use your silver."

He snorted and looked around the clearing. She followed his gaze and crossed her arms. Her copper braid flounced around her as a loyal serpent.

"Three questions for as much gold or amber as you're carrying. I can trade those anywhere."

Bjorn smiled tightly and moved for his saddle. Never taking his eyes off the stealthy forest dweller.

"How about three questions, a portion of whatever is making my mouth water for 50 pieces of gold and amber?"

"50 pieces of gold and amber, a meal..." She rolled his words around in consideration. "...and whatever bandages you are carrying." She responded as she pulled back her sleeve. Blood seeped through a piece of cloth that looked days old.

His eyes widened, and he felt something flutter across his chest. He was no healer, but he knew the signs of infection. His eyes softened.

"You may have the bandages as penance for the peace I disturbed. Do you have a healer nearby?"

He drew the cost of his food from his saddlebags with the bandages in hand. A healing salve slipped between his fingers as well.

"I do not need your pity, prince." Her words sharpened on his title, and his pulse spiked.

Before he could respond, she disappeared inside her cottage door. A small, rounded door that proved to be an obstacle for the prince as his head scraped the doorframe.

She crouched in front of a small fireplace supported by small grey stones.

Painted white flowers with violet centers encircled the wall around the hearth. Small trinkets lined the mantle, ranging from shiny bits of broken jewelry to dull, crystal shards. Her beige tunic was knit from sheep's wool and her boots seemed tied together with bits of old leather. The price of his visit could buy her everything in her possession ten times over. She moved from the fire towards her work table. She watched him as he surveyed every aspect of the room. The ceilings almost touched the crown of his head and as he studied the room, his eyes danced over the rounded edges of the painted flower petals. He ducked his head lower to follow their pattern along the mantel, but he stopped as the forest dweller cleared her throat.

"Paradisia," she said while she arranged a few large bowls in-front of her. "Rare, almost mythical things. They are said to only grow near the relics of the gods. Some even say that they only thrive on the soil of sacrifice."

"And what are they good for?"

She chewed the corner of her lip. "That will cost you."

He paused, forgetting the words on his tongue as he locked eyes with her. He could not place what seemed so familiar about the woman, like he had known her for a lifetime. She waited for his response, looking at the Prince as if he'd suffered a blow to the head. Bjorn steadied himself, then moved towards her.

"Where in this forest did you find cinnamon? That only grows in Ghobasi soil" The prince chuckled as he sat himself at the table on a stool carved from the stump of an oak tree.

She placed two glazed plates on the table with pewter mugs that sloshed with water.

"It's not cinnamon. It is a bark that tastes similar, and it only grows on this side of the forest." She said as she placed a small slice of warm bread on his plate.

Bjorn unraveled the delicious golden strands of braided bread. The center parted with intoxicating steam from the cloud soft layers.

"This is delicious." He said with a mouth full of bread and a constellation of crumbs on his trimmed beard. Hunger amplified the taste of everything, but the bread's sweetness was unparalleled. He felt a wave of shame wash over him and he studied the wood grain of the table. "Again... my apologies for disturbing your solitude, but in the... the abruptness of our meeting, I did not introduce myself. I am—"

"You're Bjorn, son of Queen Katha and King Freyden. Second son of the Broken Mountain.... I know who you are," she said with a simple shrug while her knife sliced up the roast rabbit for them to eat.

"How?"

"I see everyone and everything that happens in this forest. Absolutely. *Everything.*"

His thoughts raced as hoped coiled in his chest. If she was as observant as she claimed, then she could be the key to the monsters behind these trees.

"Senna."

"What?"

"You were going to ask what my name was? At least that is the proper thing to do, but I am not a prince." She said with a smug grin. Her hands moved in memorized grace as she prepared their food.

Senna.

Her name struck him like a forgotten memory and it unsettled him. She finished preparing the hearty serving and Senna sat opposite the Prince as he enjoyed the roasted vegetables and rabbit in-front of him. He did not let a single morsel escape between gulps of water. She sat silently while he finished the meal.

"You've eaten. Now ask your questions." Her hands wrapped around her curved mug and turned her gaze out the small cottage window. He nodded as he marked the closed nature of her expression. He could not place her age. She was young, but she felt as old as the forest itself.

He reached into a small purse at his side. The cool Spessian steel touched his skin, and his stomach recoiled. Cruel memories flashed across his mind as the heaviness of the arrow clanked on the table.

"Have you seen this before?"

She reached for the crossbow bolt that killed his father. Her brows arched. Her fingers turned the metal bit in circles before her eyes.

"Of course I have," There was sadness in her sigh ".. these infernal onyx bolts have marred every tree along the forest edge. The raiding parties carry them by the dozen, if not more. They tear through these trees, with no regard, as if the forest belongs to them. They stole a shipment of Spessian steel, and our forest has never been the same."

Bjorn's life had never been the same.

She returned the arrow to its place on the table and resumed her retreated posture.

Bjorn clenched his teeth and took a deep breath. Quelling the storm that had brewed under his skin for weeks now. A thousand words perched, ready to scramble from his lips. His hands shook as he reached for the bolt.

"Where were they headed? If you know their comings and goings, you must tell me." He tucked the bolt back into his overcoat.

"North, East, West, and even somewhere South, but less now after Prince Romulus found that poor priestess torn to pieces. I heard her crying through the forest, but..." she shuddered. "The entire forest could hear it, but I could not find her."

Bjorn skin crawled. He had heard whispers of what Senna described, but what she recounted sent a chill down his spine. Senna rose and collected their plates from the table.

"So they are everywhere and nowhere all at once? Wonderful."

She chopped a small collection of root vegetables and plunked them into an iron pot as she turned to the seated prince.

"Are you truly alone here?" Without intending to, he used his last question on something that troubled him from the moment they met.

"This is my uncle's cottage. He fled when... your mother decided his work was no longer acceptable."

"An alchemist." The strange objects tucked away in the corners of the room all made sense. As well as the crystals on the fireplace. Bjorn now noticed small runes etched into the table and the surrounding furniture.

"Where has he gone?"

"Out of questions." She said, without a shred of amusement.

Still seated, he placed the bandages he owed her on the table. "Thank you for your kindness."

He stood, and his head nearly hit the ceiling. In two paces, he was beside her.

Bjorn spoke, but his words failed him.

He ducked beneath the small door frame.

His black horse now lay on its side and rested peacefully in the glade while its tail swished happily in the golden the sunlight. Bjorn laughed quietly then nudged the beast up from the grass.

Senna stood in the door with her tassel of a braid hung over her shoulder.

"I will head east but this evening I will return this way.. Will you be here then?" Bjorn asked as he hoisted himself onto the back of his horse.

Senna sighed and studied the frayed end of her braid.

"Possibly... but bring more gold."

BJORN THUNDERED through the meandering forest, but a bit more mindful this time of the sound of his horse's footsteps. If Senna heard him coming, the raiders would as well. Warm sunlight flicked through the swaying leaves of the treetops, casting a soft shadowy light across the ground. Not far ahead of him, a glinting piece of metal caught his eye. Framing the road, grey, craggy stones grew from the earth. Pressing forward, a white stone archway appeared through the trees. Its face illuminated by the streaks of sunlight that poured down around its rune covered surface.

In a few more days, the spring solstice sunlight would align perfectly with the columns.

Bjorn crossed beneath the threshold of the archway. The heaping shape of a burial mound came into view. Grass and moss overtook its soil and even small white blooms littered over its heap. This grave was old but older still were the graves further behind it, marked by small stone circles. Any markings were long washed away. The glinting metal waved its reflecting light, and the prince spotted the small pendant tied to the trunk of an oak tree. The prince knew the meaning of the tree, the sacred emblem of their kingdom's relic. Its healing powers were renowned above all other methods.

Bjorn reached for the small triangle of steel. He felt a jolt as his skin touched the pendant. His fingers traced the raised runes along the edge. At its center, in the common tongue, etched words proclaimed:

BEGIN AT THE END

The wind teased at the back of his collar.

He rolled the amulet in his hand, and on its back there was a second set of symbols. Symbols he had seen in Senna's cottage, as well as in Gailah's journal. The hair at the back of his neck stood straight as his thumb rolled over the crude alchemy symbols. Under the pads of his fingers, the engraved symbols began to singe his skin. Bjorn quickly scanned his surroundings for raiders.

Nothing moved beyond the stones.

He loosed the leather ties from the tree; he pocketed the metal totem and scanned his surroundings. There were no signs of the raiding parties, no camps, no casualties, just things forgotten or things that didn't want to be found.

He walked through the surrounding area and found no trace of Spessian steel. Bjorn turned to face his horse and behind his beast's shoulder, a stone slab covered in brush caught his attention. The grass surrounding it was new, which was surprising for the forest. It bore the same phrase as the metal totem, but the symbols across it were entirely different.

"*The alchemist's name perhaps,*" he thought as he saddled his horse. His hand dipped into his pocket to feel the risen words on the token once more, and it tingled against his skin.

Bjorn was on dangerous ground. His mother spearheaded the alchemist's eradication, but clearly, their supporters had not heeded the judge's command. His presence, as a Prince of the Broken Mountain, would not be welcome here. He dug his heels in further to follow the western road.

The late afternoon sun dropped lower in the sky and filled him with worry. He would not stay the night trapped among the trees. He kicked his horse into a gallop in hopes he would make it back to Senna's cottage before twilight.

. . .

SENNA SAT STRINGING a longbow as he entered the glade with the sun ready to plunge below the tree line. The light from her cottage fire illuminated the doorway in a heartwarming orange glow he could feel beneath his ribs. Senna did not look up from her work as he dismounted. There was a soft copper glimmer in her hair from the sunset behind her. He chuckled when it seemed she had gained more twigs in her braid than when he had left.

"I found something odd in the forest and I need your help to read it." He said as he extended his hand with the metal totem dangling from his palm.

Senna's face blanched as it swayed from the leather strands.

"WHERE DID YOU GET THAT?" Her eyes widened and her bow fell from her hands as she flew from her seated position.

"A cemetery, a few hours east of here." he said, tilting his head in curiosity at her reaction to the small, seemingly inconspicuous object. "All buried there were alchemists."

He hated saying the word.

"Cemetery? There is no cemetery on that side of the forest..." Her brows furrowed, she snatched the totem from his hand and turned it over in her palm.

He stifled back the reply, *So you don't see everything then?*

"You should not have taken this..." Her voice wavered, and the sound startled the prince.

"Why? What is it?"

"It's a key. Well, in the right hands, anyway. It belonged to my uncle." Her tone lowered as she examined the symbols.

"I found it tied to a tree near a stone archway."

"Archway? Oh, the solstice...." she said as she brought her palm to her forehead. "That cemetery is special, sacred even to those who practice alchemy. The cemetery can only be entered when sunlight of the same season from which they carved the archway shines upon it. Any other time, it is lost to the trees."

"Why would they hide a cemetery?"

Bjorn moved closer to study the totem alongside her. She smelled of warm smoke and freshly hewn wood, a subtle but comforting thing.

"Grave robbers. They would prize a clutch of alchemist burial sites. The bones of an alchemist are some of the most valuable ingredients used in their practice. A lifetime of magic settles deep in their marrow. You're lucky you're still alive."

"Why is that?" He said, crossing his arms across his chest.

"Because they protect what is theirs, they line most burial sites with poison or a trap."

"I did not touch the burial mounds, just the metal."

"Again, lucky."

"Where is your uncle?"

Bjorn felt her go rigid beside him.

"No, no personal questions. I've told you everything I know." She mumbled and lowered her gaze.

"How much will those answers cost me?" Bjorn said, as he began digging in his saddlebag for gold.

"No gold, just this." She said as the totem disappeared into her hunting jacket.

They stood in the glade, silent as the peace that belonged to her returned to its place. Song birds sang in swooping dances of blue and yellow. The stream babbled louder than before. Bjorn focused on her gaze. Senna's eyes were a shade of uncommon green, flecks of yellow dotting her irises, a shade that reminded him of the lowland meadows before the mountain.

"How is your arm?" Bjorn asked, and he felt somewhat foolish.

She paused, rolling up the lower part of her sleeve. "Better with the bandages. I found the salve you left behind. Thank you for that."

There was no bite to her words, no sarcasm, or a roll of her eyes.

"Do you need more?" He took a step closer after he pulled the rest from his bag.

"No. No, I'm fine. It will heal with time." She said with a closed lip smile, taking a step backwards, putting distance between the two of them and it buffeted inwardly as well.

Senna bent to retrieve her bow from the forest floor.

Bjorn stood still, his hands filled with bandages stacked high within his fists. Senna racked her bow behind her shoulder.

"I prefer to hunt at night. I'll be leaving shortly, so don't wait around too long." she said, sliding her quiver over her spine.

Their mutual silence returned. The forest grew louder again, and he realized she did in fact, have freckles across her nose. He smiled as they reminded him of embers rising from a campfire.

"If I were to find myself on this side of the forest again, would you be here?"

Senna sighed.

"You have so many questions, Prince." She pulled the hood over her head, covering her hair and her striking freckles. Bjorn spoke, but before he could get out a word, Senna disappeared behind the cottage.

Chapter Six

Trejen

Trejen smoothed the corners of his cloak as he sat at his oaken desk. Letters, inquiries, and demands piled up on each corner of the wooden surface. Each stack seemed to climb higher than the four square courtyard guarding their keep.

The deep aching wound at his side nagged at his thoughts with every pulse and passing thought. Its throbbing pain served as a reminder: Trejen spent his dwindling moments in vain. The poison coursing through his veins moved in torturous ebbs. Trejen clung to his strength in his bones. Reaching to the nearest stack of demands, he drew forth a small charter that required his attention. His fingers shook as his fate sunk its teeth deeper. Even in his last moments, he found the resolve to bear the weight of his golden shackles of responsibility for a little while more. The evening sun mirrored the glow from the golden tree and drenched his chambers in ethereal light. As the wind shifted through the leaves, its beams rippled through the open windows of the room, glistening across the opalescent tiles. He let the glow of the room linger across his skin as he filled his lungs with the solace that followed the golden glimmers. His fingers fumbled with the wax seal of the Ghobasi crown. Basan's seal pressed into the page, but something was different. Too much amethyst wax pooled around the edges.

The hinges of his chamber screamed as a young page bursted through the doors.

"My apologies, your Highness, er.. um.., your Majesty." He breathed at a rapid pace with his hands on his knees. "Royal banner men from the mountain are here and the rest of them will be in the fourth courtyard in moments, if they are not already there."

As soon as the boy uttered the word "mountain," the quill fell from Trejen's fingers, then the charter fell away to the desk. The broken mountain stood out among the tesserae on the floor. Its proud face mocked him with its gaping chasm mouth. The home he could never return to stared back at him. The best years of his life belonged to its snowy peaks. In the months that followed his coronation, Trejen reminded himself daily that he was no longer going home, for that was what the mountain became to him. His grandfather had sold him to King Darren as a token of peace to end decades of war, but instead Trejen had found his home there. The crackling fireplaces, laughter, quiet evenings in the library, and all of it made his chest ache–an ache far deeper than the wound at his side. All of those memories faded away the moment Decius surrendered his spirit to the gods.

Trejen's breath quickened. He was unprepared for a personal audience with Katha. He could spend a lifetime steeling himself to be in her presence, but it would not be enough. Guilt reached through him.

Trejen felt his nails dig into the wood.

Had they come for him?

Would this be the end of his legacy?

He smoothed the silver edges of his dark stubble. The king fought the urge to arm himself. His sword rested only an arm's reach away. Katha carried her family's sword and bore it with honor, as was the way of the mountain.

Had she come here to fight him?

His crown rested atop a dust covered tome. He reached for the oak leaf laurel and placed it on his brow. A soft eclipse remained in the dust. Its twisting metal scraped against the palm of his hand.

Why would she come now?

His palms sweat. The doors of his study parted, and Trejen followed his guards down to the fourth inner-most courtyard.

Beneath the soft golden light of the great oak tree, emerald banners swayed as Knights of the Chasm entered the gate. A formidable battalion stilled their weary beasts as the gates closed behind them. Parting the troop like a wave, a cloaked figure rode forward. A male cloaked figure. Something inside Trejen eased, as he knew now that Katha had not come. The horse's hooves loudly drew every eye to the cloaked rider. A single gloved hand gripped the reins.

Trejen's heart fell further at the sight of the lone glove. This visit would be far from pleasant.

To Trejen, Regulus was an unpredictable hurricane of a man. One moment sensible but compassionate, then a viper baring its fangs in the same breath. Regulus was not evil because he lacked his sword hand, Regulus was untrustworthy because he protected himself above all else. The day Katha called for Regulus' head burned through Trejen's mind as her uncle approached him on horseback. She spared Regulus' life, but even as the blade fell, he did not cry out as she took his hand instead.

The Autumn King swallowed as he stepped forward to greet the councilman of the mountain.

"What brings you to my forest, Lord Regulus? You did not petition any escorts to accompany you?"

Regulus removed his hood and feigned a tight smile. He produced his other arm, the evidence of his treason. Theatrically, he used it to bow at the waist from his steed. The darkness of his features contrasted with the sharp icy eyes beneath his thick ebony brows. He glanced at the green cloaked warriors that surrounded him.

"Your escorts proved useless in our last visit to the forest, your Highness, I have brought my own." Regulus spoke in an aggressive staccato. "I am here on behalf of my dear niece, and would ask you lend me your ear? I have ridden a long way to speak with you." His words were terse despite their hollow enthusiasm. His teeth seemed almost sharp despite their crookedness as his red chapped cheeks framed his mouth. The icy mountain air spared no man.

"Your men may refresh themselves in my hall and have their horses watered in my stables. I know that journey challenges even the most experienced rider." Trejen welcomed them, but his eyes carefully monitored the battalion in front of him.

They were knights that would have been his, knights that belonged to the mountain king.

Regulus' dismount was graceful for a man of his age.

"You honor us. Let us carry on our business elsewhere. The business of Kings and Lords is above the likes of them." Regulus said, as his eyes narrowed at the stables hands that scurried to the horses.

Trejen breathed through his teeth, but softened a little as Lord Barrock entered the courtyard. He was fresh from the training grounds. Trejen smiled at his friend and commander of the armies of Autumn. Lord Barrock's eyes widened. The commander cursed in a tongue foreign to their guests.

"Lord Barrock, would you join us upstairs? Lord Regulus has just arrived with pressing matters from the Mountain." Trejen spoke with a nervous lilt to his voice.

"You'll not make me a politician yet, but I will join you, nonetheless." Lord Barrock sighed as he tossed his sword to his squire. He gave a stern and unfriendly nod to Lord Regulus. There was no love or admiration in this kingdom for the craven lord.

THE THREE MEN gathered in the quiet of Trejen's study while the councilman from the Mountain paced the room. Trejen's joint ached with the stiffness of time and the sun no longer poured in through the pane-less windows. Only cold shadows shifted around the room as a dim glow reflected across the white marble floor.

"You may find my purpose unsettling to you, your Majesty" Lord Regulus dramatically paused as he stared down the king of the forest. Trejen sat heavily on the high-backed throne in his study. Lord Barrock stood beside him.

Regulus examined every groove of Trejen's face. The councilmen, ready to pounce at any thoughtless or hurried response, but that was never Trejen's way.

From the moment Regulus arrived, their battle had begun.

"We send our deepest sympathies to your noble house. Losing the King Consort is a heavy burden." Trejen said with stoic empathy.

Regulus exhaled through his nose. The older man turned towards the statue of Tiranus. Regulus hated the emperor more than any living man, but the dead held a greater claim.

"I find it rather curious that your grandfather conquered so much, yet in two generations, all of his conquest is gone. Does Altanah's blood still stain the sands of Sefti's fighting pits?"

Regulus' eyes gleamed with the pain of old wounds.

He spoke of his sister, the eldest princess of the Mountain and the war that shattered an empire.

Lord Barrock's hand dropped to his side. His fingers grazed his sword in defense of his king.

Trejen's pulse fluttered in his neck.

Tiranus had killed his own son, Tyraxus, Trejen's father during the spectacle of Altanah's death, and all for the love he bore the princess who refused an emperor.

"If you would like Cias to recount the history of our people, I can have him brought to you. Surely your news is more pressing than the actions of the dead."

Trejen was just a boy then, the day his father jumped the barrier of the fighting pits and died for a woman who was not his wife.

"An interesting choice of words, your Highness." Regulus returned his gaze to the king. His chin dipped lower to his chest and his tired eyes scanned Trejen's study.

"Tiranus would be proud of you, but I believe he created the conventions of war after his conquest, did he not, your Highness?" He paused as he watched the face of the king and his lord commander. Regulus weaved his words with the careful intention of a spider.

"Enough with it! Speak your piece or be done with it all." Lord Barrock barked out as he tensed his grip around his sword.

A smile crept from the corners of Lord Regulus' lips. The councilman's hand dipped into his pocket. He paused just for a moment before he strode towards Lord Barrock with his hand extended.

"My knights are very thorough and they serve their queen proudly. My men found this on the body of a man raiding our lands. The same band of raiders that felled the late king." Regulus produced a bloodied golden broach. The broach was in the shape of a golden oak leaf. A sigil of the Autumn King, Trejen's broach.

"There must be a mistake..." Trejen's gaze hardened as he took in every piece of the bloodied broach. His fingers tightened around the arms of his chair.

"Do you deny it?" Regulus' voice graveled.

Sweat beaded at the nap of Trejen's neck. The weight of his throne pushed against his back.

"I will question every man until we can prove otherwise, but if it occurred, then it has occurred without my knowledge. Should we find any of my knights in league with raiding bands, their life will be forfeit." Trejen spoke sternly as he felt a heaviness in his chest. His eyes never left his blood-soaked pin in Lord Barrock's hand.

"I was there that day, your Highness. When the shadows of the forest became flesh and my king fell. I saw many things that day. Would not Queen Katha have an interest in hearing this development? My queen would be irrevocably distressed to know it may implicate you in Freyden's death. You are familiar with her sense of vengeance, are you not?" Regulus again searched for a reaction on the king's face. "Please send a word if your search produces any traitors."

"You have my word." Trejen's own weary voice frightened him. He felt the blood drain from his face. There would be no traitors found in his kingdom unless he faced the traitor beneath his skin. "Give us time and until then your discretion is invaluable"

"Know my secrecy comes at a price. My Queen is eager for her daughter to wed. Her gaze rests on your nephew. Produce the man responsible for our king's death and I'll keep silent on my opposition to an alliance with your people."

"My foremost concern is for my nephew, and I do not speak in riddles." Trejen spat as if he could see the thoughts spinning behind the Mountain Lord's eyes.

"Your nephew is unmarried, is he not?"

Trejen despised the curiosity in Regulus' voice.

"Indeed, he has no wife but a paramour that he will not be parted with.." Trejen's eyes narrowed.

"See that they part and make an offer of marriage when Katha presents her daughter at the gathering, and see they bring the traitor as well. You have a fortnight to find him. If you cannot do this, then my knights will uproot every tree in this forest until we find him."

"Tell me, in what kingdom does a Lord give orders to a King?" Lord Barrock's sword now rested between the king and councilmen.

Trejen raised a hand, blocking his general's path.

Regulus smiled as he walked backwards. His emerald cloak swaying against the tile.

"Heed my warning." He sneered, "I look forward to seeing you and your people at the gathering. A delightful affair, to be sure."

Chapter Seven

Katha

THE QUEEN STOOD watch from the highest windows of the mountain keep. Spring fires burned in clusters across the sloping hills below. Their flames danced in the night, like the candles that lined the magnificent temples deep underground. All of them abandoned to the dark, save for devout priests that tended the flames beneath the mountain. However, along the hillside, devotion showed itself in the farmers that kept the bonfires lit till dawn. Tending the warmth that defended the spring blooms along with their hope for food by summer's end.

Katha was silent as tinges of the crystal death seeped across the windowpane. It was a frost that stole the youth from everything in its clutches. It was the killing kind of frost that announced the beginning and the end of the seasons as it arrived in swaths of blue and white. That same kind of frost dwelt within her fingertips and burrowed to her bones.

Katha saw her regrets in the geometric patterns of ice clinging to the darkness of the morning when her walks would finally end. Each rigid, frozen pattern that paralyzed everything in its wake. Each one was a choice that led her family closer to the nightmares that plagued her.

Katha's hand slid down the railing of the grand staircase as it coiled upwards behind her. In her hand, she carried a single candlestick, and the other carried the long white train of her dressing gown. Her chestnut hair fell past her shoulders in plaits as she descended. She heard the soft pat of her beloved bear. Karak was only a few paces behind her. She found her silence as she walked the halls each night. He followed her until he too needed rest. The sound of his footsteps grounded her with every cool stride through the night. Her robes moved in step with her pace.

The entire stronghold slept save for a few watchmen. They were familiar with her restlessness as they stood unbothered, but at attention beside the torch light. Most nights, her journey left her to sleep on some cushioned chair, tucked away anywhere but the emptiness of her bed.

She found it unbearable without her husband. There was no warmth or comfort to lie beside. On the coldest nights, when the north wind rattled the Agametian glass, the queen slept before the fire with her head propped up by her great bear. The crackling wood shutting out the whispering voices outside her window and in her mind.

Whispers of the promise born in the dark, a promise of a heartbroken girl.

The long empty hallways mirrored the pathways in her mind, where she wandered through her memories of long ago. The tapestries and paintings hung free of judgment as they lifelessly watched her roaming figure. No one questioned her, nor did any listless soul dare interrupt her pacing.

As hallways transformed into corridors and chambers, her memories guided her to the deepest part of the keep. The grand ballroom stood abandoned and blanketed in shadow. Its dance floor had sat empty the entire winter, oil and water mixed more freely than grieving and dancing. Iron chandeliers were apparitions that hung down the center of the high ceiling in lightless circles.

The soles of her slippers moved as gracefully as firmly set teeth. They scraped against the tiled floor as she entered the room, no courtiers to bow to her and no musicians to silence at her approach. She moved through the darkened room with indifference. As if to stir the past to life, she glided through the dust at her feet. Powdery motes clung to the melancholy corners of her heart. The happiness that had plinked off goblets in waves of laughter echoed only in her imagination.

The only glow within the ballroom now flickered at the end of her candlestick. A fraction of light compared to the constant roar of revelry she had almost forgotten. All of their treasured memories were now inside a lifeless hall whose arching columns housed a skeletal corpse of a room.

She longed to see Gailah dance again, to see her smiling face glide carelessly across the room.

She crossed the floor to where their thrones sat empty, covered by white draping. She wrapped her dressing gown even tighter around her waist as she held herself in her arms. Hours ago, Karak had left her side and gone to sleep before the hearth. As she lowered her candlestick to the foot of the dais, she climbed the stairs to her seat. She had memorized this climb from girlhood, a queen too young for her crown. She sank into the covered throne and closed her eyes as she guided her braids around her shoulders. Beneath her eyelids, the soft swell of music filled the room in slow crescendos. Next, the gentle rush of fabric as couples swirled in each other's embrace.

Has it really been twenty-five years?

She had promised Freyden a lifetime. Twenty-five years was a cruel trade, as she now grew old alone with their children.

Her heart warmed at the memory of his hand at her waist. How they glided around the room at their wedding feast. She smiled and eased into the chair. She almost laughed at how nervous he had been. The light reflected off the gilded accents of her gown and across his straw-colored hair. As they spun and twirled, she remembered how he had whispered in her ear.

"*They say dancing is like sword fighting and they're all liars. Tis far more dangerous.*"

She smiled as she kept her eyes closed. Forcing the warmth of his embrace to stay a little longer, before reality stole him from her.

After many nights of dancing alone together, she had taught him every step a king should know. They practiced until the stars came out and some nights even longer. She could feel the stubble of his beard against her cheek as they floated around the dance floor. How he had swept his hair back beneath his crown. She had fallen in love with him in many places and many ways, but their love first showed itself here.

A king and queen swaying and gliding until their feet blistered. Slowly, and with every step, he caused the high walls around her broken heart to crumble. In return for her dancing lessons, her king consort had taught her to handle a blade. They had settled many of their marital arguments that way. If Freyden earnestly lost to his wife and queen, she often questioned why they had fought to begin with. Now she wished they had never fought at all.

"Pardon, your Majesty."

Katha froze and Freyden dissolved into vapor. Opening her eyes, she found herself halfway across the room. Her arms stretched wide, her hands posed as if the ghost of her husband held his arm about her waist.

The voice who called out belonged to Theor, the war chieftain of the Mountain. A man ten years the Queen's senior and the only person who had known Freyden longer than she.

"There is nothing to pardon. I should sleep, but my thoughts keep me from it." She had long since lowered her hands and folded them together at her waist as she addressed the chieftain.

He nodded as if he understood. His black hair had shifted to silver with the patience of autumn leaves. Moonlight poured in through the skylight and illuminated his armor against the darkness that surrounded the ballroom. Alchemist fire had claimed half of his jaw and left white ridges of skin where his bristly beard refused to grow.

"You have nothing to regret, your Majesty." He bowed and turned for the door of the ballroom.

The queen felt her words rush from her lips.

"If I had abdicated." She started and her hands shook. The words that had tormented her for weeks spilled out. "Then...Then they would have never come for him. Freyden should be here, and it is my fault. I chose him. I did not fire the arrow, but I put a crown on his head an—"

Theor did not flinch, nor did he look at his queen like she was mad, but with an unfamiliar softness.

"If I may speak plainly, your Majesty," Theor interrupted her, "If you had abdicated, you would have denied him the joy of his lifetime." His eyes were kind despite his war hardened facade. "He only ever wanted to be at your side. Freyden was the finest knight in my company. He trained harder than the rest because he knew he was protecting you. Let him rest in that honor, my Queen. He would've taken a thousand arrows if it had meant you were safe from harm."

Their eyes met for a moment and her cheeks colored in embarrassment, but his words were a kindness that quenched the fire of grief in her chest.

And with that, he bowed at the waist, his sword ready in its sheath. He disappeared into the corridor as his clicking armor faded into the shadowy depths of the keep.

Katha turned towards the night washed colors of the room. The brilliance of the room dulled by the shadows standing watch of her night walks.

She heard the voice of her father, Deren, the alchemist's king, the bane of emperors. *"Woe to the sons of Tiranus, woe to those who carry the blade of treason. Woe to the slayer of kings. If the Mountain falls, let it claim the trees as well."*

Fever had claimed his mind before he died, but his last words remained etched in her spirit.

Her breathing hitched in her chest, and her pulse thundered through her neck.

The queen saw something move through the moonbeams that filled the room.

There.

On the far side of the ballroom, a figure stood before the windows. A golden laurel on his brow. Katha gasped as a cold dew settled across her skin. The air in her lungs chilled at the sight of his face.

Decius.

Trejen's brother looked at her with hallowed, yellowed eyes. His neck was boneless and swayed like a broken tree limb. His tattered golden cloak dragging behind him.

Katha slammed her eyes shut and buried her face in her hands, trying to shake his memory from her mind.

He is dead. He is dead. He is dead.

The queen's heart beat convulsed against her sternum. She closed her eyes tighter.

He did not breathe; he did not beckon. Decius only stared.

"*No.*" Katha muttered between gritted teeth. She rang her hands and pried her eyes open.

There were only shadows beneath the blanket of the night. She quickened her pace and the sound of her fearful footsteps filled the room. The hinges of the doors creaked, but then at last she heard him cry.

Decius' voice groaned in her ears.

"*Lyssia? Lyssia?*"

She slammed the door to the ballroom, silencing the dead king's mournful words that echoed through her mind.

Gailah

Orla, the mistress and head cook of the Mountain keep, bustled around the caravan, making note of all their provisions.

She tucked away a satchel of morsels in Gailah's things. The princess had found less pleasure in food and drink since her father's burial, but Orla fussed endlessly over those who had not eaten enough. As she secured Gailah's saddle for the third time, she ran a hand up her horse's neck.

"Aye, head up, your Highness. I'll not watch you pitch from your saddle."

Orla knew Gailah could ride well, but her words warmed the princess more than any cloak.

In a slithering mass of green, their caravan descended the slopes of the mountain. Snow clusters melted along the rocky trails. Their horses' hooves mixed with snow and soil into a thick path of mud. The spring equinox called all the houses to the center of the island. Moving with the changing of seasons, it was a chance for their people to begin again. Marriages arranged at the spring gathering were tied in unison at the end of summer when the houses gathered before the chill of autumn came to the island.

Gailah tightened her sage-colored cloak around her shoulders. Her hair tumbled loosely as she swayed in the saddle's rhythm. Bjorn rode at her side and Aerin slightly farther ahead of them. Gailah teased at the leather reins in her grip.

Her mother had gone ahead without a word, she had climbed upon her four horned saddle, silent and stoic, and without a single embrace.

Gailah's impending presentation at the gathering loomed like a buzzard. The eyes of the island picking apart her flesh, scheming at what they could take from her. She relished in the early spring air as the morning sunlight painted the rocks. Her mother paid for trunks of gowns for her presentation. Gailah loved them all, but she had no need for piles of gowns. She needed her mother–the mother that held her, advised her, and showed her what it meant to be queen.

Her chest tightened in the crisp, swirling breeze. The version of her mother she needed most was now burned and buried with her father.

She kept her eyes focused on the road, drowning out the tune her brother whistled beside her. The Chasm watched them with its ruinous mouth of rock and blackness, a ruined alchemist's vault that their people turned into a fortress. The stronghold rested deep inside its cavern and only showed itself with a few spine-like watchtowers.

Gailah's stomach recoiled as they passed under its gaze. Her great uncle, Regulus, rode out in a stream of Calvary. They fashioned their cloaks in the deepest shade of green.

The lands of their people still bore the scars of the alchemists' exile and uprising. The meadows grew back in wild, flourishing fields, but the soil and stones did not forget. Their grandfather had created the order of alchemists to take back Thyssia from Tiranus, but he never intended for them to stay. Deren never intended for the alchemists to sink their fangs into the veins of power that belonged to the island.

The Knights of the Chasm flanked the caravan, and despite her unease at the fortress, their protection was paramount. Their mother rode leagues ahead of them, protected and separate. The wild bands of raiders had only exposed and humiliated their family, but if they attacked again, her family traveled separately.

"Gailah?" Bjorn's voice broke through her thoughts.

The princess blinked back at the sunlight and drew her eyes away from the Chasm and its knights.

"You looked like a boat lost at sea, sister." Bjorn could not hide the concern in his voice.

"I feel it." She looked down at the horns of her saddle. She chewed the inside of her cheeks. "I wake up every day and I feel like I cannot breathe."

Bjorn moved his horse closer. Her brother's eyes narrowed and the softness there made Gailah's eyes water. Bjorn had her father's eyes.

He rode silently beside her and she knew he struggled to find the right words. She had no need of words; she needed her family and Bjorn knew that, too.

Bjorn dipped his head to the side.

"Gailah... you would not believe.." Suddenly his voice lowered. "*Aerin loves gossip like a mother hen.*"

As soon as Bjorn had dropped his tone, Aerin's head whipped around. He slowed the pace of his horse and slid his mare between his siblings' horses. Aerin looked at the two of them with curiosity. A clever smile appeared on Bjorn's face.

"Gailah.. Are you pre—"

Aerin's words died. He shouted and squirmed in his saddle just as his eyes turned wild. Kicking his horse into a canter. Aerin's shoulders haunched and his face became a furious shade of red.

From the back of Aerin's cloak, a pile of watery ice and snow dripped down his neck.

Bjorn's laugh bellowed, and its cadence rumbled in Gailah's chest, a warm sound that washed away her melancholy spirit that clung to her ribs. Bjorn's fingertips were a chilled shade of pink as slush dripped from his hand.

Bjorn's eyes creased and closed. His laugh was almost breathless. Gailah did not warn him as Aerin gathered his attack from a snow covered boulder.

In a warrior's movement, Aerin buried his brother's unassuming face in a heap of slush. Gailah winced, but she felt her own laughter bubble up. It felt almost foreign and refreshing all at once. She filled her lungs with air and her laughter was louder and brighter than before.

Bjorn cleared his slush covered face and smiled at his sister. His perpetually rosy cheeks mirrored Aerin's, but as they laughed together, Aerin hid a vindicated smile.

A few paces ahead, Theor ordered them to keep moving. There was no annoyance on his face, as if the surly war chieftain needed to see his king's family themselves once again.

Chapter Eight

Trejen

Golden cloaked bannermen gathered in the courtyard for their departure while Trejen sat ready in his saddle as a few golden leaves tumbled through the air. Acolytes swept them into their robes and swiftly fled to the temple at the base of the majestic tree. All the acolytes save for one.

Romulus moved through the gates ahead of them, keeping a distance from the rest with a blue cloaked acolyte riding ahead with the crown prince. The king sighed as he saw dark strands of hair billowing around his nephew as they departed for the gates. Despite her hooded silhouette, he knew it to be Oxana, the prince's paramour. If Romulus had any say in it, then she was always in his presence. Trejen knew how dangerous that feeling could be.

The gathering was a short distance from the forest. The hall of judgment stood in the center of the continent. Its high stony walls where the borders of the three kingdoms converged. Small clusters of villages surrounded the palace, their efforts supported the judges and their needs. When Tiranus's empire fell, Deren installed the judges to preside over the matters of the island.

The young budding leaves grew bolder in every shade of bright green, but the sky seemed far away now that the canopy had thickened. The shade it cast made the sacred oak tree glimmer like a candle in a cave. Their sacred tree watched them as their column moved slowly beyond the reaches of the keep. The forest itself came alive, like a moving, breathing being. Its limbs swayed in unison underneath the wind.

As a child, the king had remembered the oak's brilliant light shining across the isles. Now its light seemed to dim with the setting of every evening sun and he felt himself growing dim along with it.

Trejen failed to straighten in his saddle but he supported him with the horns in front of him.

The king could see his nephew's dark curls bouncing as he rode at the front of the retinue. Cias' words echoed in his mind. The priest remained at the castle with those who could not ride. He gave Trejen poultices and tonics for the pain, but it was only a brief respite.

The pain never left him, even in his sleep he felt it. Even at a walking pace, the lumbering movement of his horse sent burning waves through his body.

He stilled his breath as he gritted his teeth.

He dreaded seeing her again. Not for the sake of seeing her, but because he longed to see her and that feeling wedged itself deeper with each passing day. He no longer believed himself to be the man she could love.

He lost that right.

Trejen traded that place in her heart and in its absence, the poison devoured what remained of him.

As the world around them passed by, he could feel the tall spires of the hall of judgment drawing closer.

He could remember the scent of her hair. They had hardly spoken more than a few sentences since their engagement ended, only formal greetings and well wishes that felt like shards of glass.

Painful and vivid memories flashed before him

"We will leave tonight!"

Katha's words echoed through his mind. She had come to him, rain soaked, wearing his golden cloak while tears stained her cheeks.

"You and me, and nobody else. No crowns. No glory. Just us."

"He needs me."

Trejen was so young then, and Romulus was only just a babe.

He never forgot the look in Katha's eyes. When their end became a moment forever etched in the memory of her heart. When the mask she bore to the world became the one and only part of her, he would get to see.

"I needed you too."

His hands tightened at the reins as his side reminded him she would never need him again.

The retinue weaved between the trees with their golden cloaks aflame in the afternoon sun. In the distance, a spring storm rolled in beyond the reflective banks of the river lands. The breeze that tossed the oak leaves above shifted, as if the clouds were ready to unleash themselves across the continent.

The sun shone brighter as it contrasted the sky in beams before the storm's arrival. The ground needed water, and the trees would be glad for the cleansing downpour.

He sighed and tightened his grip on the reins. Trejen hoped they would make it to the gathering before the clouds burst open.

He could still see his nephew's hair through the trees. They had not spoken since Regulus' visit.

A futile search for the nonexistent traitor occurred with no trace of the king's assailants, but Trejen withheld any productive methods of questioning.

The king retched at the thought of torturing his men for a crime they did not commit.

There was a bitterness inside him that threatened his sense of compassion like a vengeful apparition, hunting the softness in his spirit with a scythe. It was a bitterness that yearned for the life he would not get to see, the life that he had lost, and the man he had become, a man he did not recognize.

All he held onto was the hope that his secrets would die with him, for he could not bear the thought of her hatred. He could not die knowing she was ashamed of him. He needed to know that his sacrifice for Romulus would have been worth it and that Decius could rest knowing his son sat on the Autumn throne.

Trejen hoped seeing Gailah in person would change Romulus' heart towards their potential betrothal.

The softest pink petals of spring twirled in the air as they neared the last hollow of the great forest. Dark limbs arched above the road and their shadows crossed the worn paving stones in webs as the light streamed through the canopy.

Trejen's thoughts rocked between the fear of Katha's eyes as she saw what had become of him and the fear of what could never be. He knew the forest was alive but as he sauntered beneath the ancient trees, he swore he could hear them breathing.

Wind tousled his hair beneath his golden laurel, but zinging past his head, an onyx dart shot through the air.

Thud.

Thud.

A second sliced beside him, a near miss to his horse's neck. Trejen's feeble heart convulsed with pain and the dim light of the forest transformed into a blur of flesh and steel.

"WE'RE UNDER ATTACK!" Lord Barrock called from the front. "PROTECT THE KING!"

Dark, hooded figures surrounded them, crashing from above and all along the forest road.

Romulus leapt from his saddle as he tossed the acolyte, Oxana, the reins. With a swift smack, the horse cried out as it fled for its life. His nephew charged for the men that roared through the small trees lining the road.

A rune painted man fell from the tree above and Trejen's heart stopped as the knight directly before him toppled beneath the force of his weight. Blood pooled between the stones at his horses feet and as the raider pulled the knife from his knight's neck, Trejen's horse reared chaotically on his hind legs.

Trejen drew his short sword, and he galloped towards Romulus. His side no longer mattered, nothing else mattered.

Eerie whistling arrows fluttered through the trees while their men fell to the forest floor. The hollow thud of lifeless flesh rippled through his ears.

He saw only Romulus. His sword was heavy in his hand as he thundered forward.

The world fell around him and the king tumbled from his saddle. Trejen's heart seized in his chest as rune painted arms slammed into him and threw Trejen to the ground.

The forest shook as his head collided with the ground but the man who pinned him was now just a body. All life fled his attacker's face as Trejen realized his sword held the man upright through his chest. The graceless fall from horseback had plunged it deep within him.

Lord Barrock dropped beside the king. His rectangular shield was high above them as arrows continued to fall. Their furious momentum pounding the soil, tree trunk, and golden knights without discretion.

The Commander shoved the corpse off of his king as Trejen removed his sword. Spit pooled in his cheeks from fear and exhaustion. Cias was right, he was not strong enough for this journey.

"His blood, not mine," Trejen spat quickly as he rose to his feet. His mind wobbled from the fall and his side screamed from the impact. Swirls of green and blue danced across his vision as he stood.

Thud.

Thud.

As Lord Barrock held his shield higher, a steel tipped arrow plunged into the shell of his shield.

It wasn't any steel–black Spessian steel.

Lord Barrock snarled and he drove his sword into anyone who dared near them.

As his frantic pulse kept its speed, Trejen stood and blocked a bloodied axe from ending his commander's life.

Trejen threw his weight into his sword. The raider stumbled backwards in a clumsy display. Some moved with lethal grace while others fumbled in a sleeplike state but a stray arrow found its mark deep in a raider's head.

He fell and died at Trejen's feet, it was an arrow meant for him.

It had come from just beyond the forest road. A crossbowman frantically placed an onyx bolt into his weapon, then aimed it at the king's chest. Before Trejen could lower his shield, a flash of silver steel burned in his periphery.

Romulus wrestled with the crossbowmen to the ground. The prince grappled with the bow as he stabbed the raider's bolt into his neck.

His nephew rose, blood spatter painted his face, and the forest became silent in a way that only warriors know. A momentary silence before the sound of dying men filled Trejen's ears.

Trejen ran to his nephew's side as every joint and muscle in his body cried out.

There were many injured, but few knights were truly among the fallen.

Trejen wrapped his arms around his nephew, but the prince did not return his embrace. Romulus's body was rigid with cold and visceral shock.Trejen studied his nephew's undaunted face. His skin burned as he seethed with the fire and fury of battle.

Just beyond where they stood, a gold cloaked knight inspected the body of a fallen raider, one whose soul still lingered in his body.

"This one's still breathing!" The knight called out.

They gathered around the dying man as Lord Barrock held a dagger to his throat.

"Who are you?" Lord Barrock barked.

The wounded raider only smiled. His eyes were a delirious, milky blue. Lord Barrock drew back the man's hood to reveal his face smattered with blue painted runes.

Runes that darkened to shadow. The peoples of old Thyssia had painted their bodies in this way, long before Tiranus slayed the last King of Autumn. They were a people who scarcely wandered the island.

The man's blood-smeared face became frantic and wild as he scanned the trees above them. Leaves crunched beneath his body as he twisted and contorted against the soil.

"Who are you?" Lord Barrock demanded again, this time his dagger broke skin while rubies of blood spilled out along the blade.

"Many." The raider said through blood filled teeth. He smiled again, but his wounds overcame him. His body arched oddly, like his soul fought to leave his flesh. Then suddenly, his body went limp, but the madness in the raider's expression remained the same. His eyes only held a lifeless grinning stare into the canopy.

Trejen's skin crawled as the sound of his voice echoed in his ears.

Many.

Lord Barrock sheathed his dagger as he stood. He grabbed Trejen by his arm as he spoke under his breath.

"These men are of the same party that killed King Freyden." His voice was hardly audible. "Will this body suffice the Lord of the Chasm?"

Trejen's skin prickled. Lord Barrock was right in almost every regard, save for one. He would not make his friend his conspirator as well.

"Bring the man with us," Trejen ordered.

Proof is what Regulus demanded, then this would be his proof. Trejen felt the urge to retch again.

The plinking sound of rain pattered against their armor. Heavy raindrops fell from the sky. The king looked upwards as the clouds burst open.

Each droplet felt heavy against his tired skin. Thunder rolled like the voices of the gods. Streams of rainwater coursed down his armor as the blood washed onto the soil below. All at once, rain covered the island.

Chapter Nine

Gailah

Walls that climbed high enough to touch the clouds surrounded them as their family gathered in the outer chambers in the Hall of Justice. Gailah's breath hitched in her chest and her pulse fluttered like the tattered wings of a butterfly as the large doors parted before them.

She stepped forward into the inner throne room, where the judges and sovereigns assembled. While flanked by her brothers on either side, Gailah trailed behind her mother as the procession entered the Great Hall.

Her sage green gown cascaded in loose layers, then tightened at her high waist as pale golden embroidery adorned the fabric that swirled around her arms in open sleeves.

The Queen of the Broken Mountain entered as she had done at many gatherings before. Her mother donned a gracious smile, noble and resplendent with the crown of their people high on her brow.

Karak lumbered beside their mother, unbothered by those gathered on the sides. As they curved around the marble reflecting pool in the center of the floor, Gailah drew her shoulders back and lifted her chin towards the assembly.

She would not hunker beneath the weight of the islands' prying eyes. To stop her hands from shaking, she toyed with the Nadr ring on her little finger. Sigils from every house bobbed and swished among the banner man lining the wall. Soft drums lulled the rhythm of the lutes into a steady melody as the song of the mountain played.

"None of them are above you Gailah, *all men kneel before the gods.*" Bjorn whispered beside her.

He uttered a phrase that she had heard a thousand times–a Nadr phrase that belonged to the first Thyssians, words etched into the hilt of their father's sword.

The muscles in her face relaxed slightly and she counted the swells of her breath. She focused on the light that surrounded the room.

Large Agametian glass windows bathed in the morning sunlight. She moved forward behind her mother's emerald train as her own gown rustled against the marble floor.

She scanned the room of faces. Their eyes were hungry, roving needles pricking across her skin. She waded into their bog of whispers with every step towards her mother's throne.

Something was wrong. Their house was always the last to arrive–an honor given to the oldest and noblest of houses.

Ahead of them, Trejen's throne sat empty.

The decorative gold leaves curled around the empty silver seat like tightly clenched fingers. In its metalwork, they etched the patterned wood of their great oak tree. A throne made of pure silver with velvet cushions fashioned a seat inside its trunk.

The crowd uttered the king's name in a hushed chorus.

Her heart sank through her stomach.

The outcome of this gathering would change which throne she stood beside.

If their absence meant they had no interest in a marriage proposal, then her only other option rested beside the Spessian throne. Queen Allagria, the matriarch of the Spessian Riverlands, occupied her throne with a menacing stare as Gailah tried swallow the fear rising in her throat.

Their matriarch hunched into her throne with a painfully arched spine. Gailah felt the queen's eyes more piercing than sunlight. Allagria of house Spessia seemed older than time itself. Though her body failed her, she was not to be underestimated. It was rare for Thyssian royalty to live to an advanced age, a venerable and suspicious feat.

Gailah kept her eyes locked with the queen. She would not let her body show her fear. She brought back her shoulders and let the light glimmer across the golden fibers weaved into faint green sleeves of her gown.

What Gailah failed to see was a Spessian prince step forward.

Her brothers had already ascended to their seats on the dais. Even Karak pawed his way up the steps before he curled himself at the Queen's feet.

First, she heard his footsteps, then the sway of his presence beside her on the stairs, and at last as she faced him, cold gray eyes stared back at her. The prince's attire was so foreign to her.

All of it was meant for the warmth of the river lands and the current of the sea, especially the black leather band of straps that hung from his waist and fell just above his knees. The bite of mountain air would claim every bit of his muscular legs if he dared set foot in her homeland. Silver sea snakes decorated his breastplate as the sigil of his house seemed to devour each other from the clasp at his shoulder.

She lifted her gaze from his onyx breast plate and sapphire cloak.The whispers of the room dissipated in a curious rush. Torin's gray eyes creased as he smiled politely.

His silver hair fell around his neck and the width of his jaw while he had gathered the rest of his hair behind his head. Gailah felt Bjorn's and Aerin's irritation in their angered stares.

"I am Prince Torin of house Spessia. May I offer you my hand, your Highness?"

Gailah's eyes widened, and her heart panicked at the double meaning of his words.

He extended his sword-calloused hand, and she inhaled sharply. Her skin prickled under her mother's horrified gaze. The figurative and literal insinuation grappled in her mind like lions and her cheeks flushed. The prince studied her face, and it only worsened the tumbling pulse in her chest.

"You may." She spoke with pretended ease.

As the courtiers watched in anticipatory silence, Gailah placed her fingers in his patient hand. She quieted the thoughts that reported back the warmth and sureness of his grip.

Every smile and passing word from her lips was a piece in the game that would determine her fate forever. The hand he offered was likely as calculated as the polite nod she gave him.

His smile was tight and controlled. She pressed her hand downward into the strength of his grip as she lifted the hem of her skirts. They ascended the steps together, and she looked upward to her seat.

Ignoring the wide-eyed gaze of her family members, she wanted to look anywhere but the prince standing beside her. She felt his grip tighten ever so slightly before his hand fell away to his side.

Gailah found his eyes again. She meant to thank him, to say something with propriety and acceptability, but every word fled from her mind and all she could muster was a curt nod.

He smiled, but this time a smile that showed a hint of fear. The light in his eyes dimmed. He bowed at the waist, but as he did, Gailah realized the younger Spessian prince was watching them.

Everyone was watching them.

A scowl grew across his younger brother, Prince Alexi's face, a tight lip scowl framed by cheek bones as high and sharp as the cliffs. Alexi's stare sent a shiver down her spine, but Gailah did not remove her gaze as Prince Torin returned to his place beside Queen Allagria.

Their deep blue cloaks absorbed the surrounding warmth of the room, only buffeted by the prince's deep black armor, a resource more valuable than jewels, stronger than stone.

Spessian steel mines ran deep beneath the coastal shelf of the river lands. As the princes stood at their grandmother's side, their readiness for battle heightened her senses as she settled into her cushioned seat.

The spring gathering was a celebration, but it often became a political brawl and bloodshed was almost inevitable.

The mountain throne was far less ornate. Hard lines followed the edges of the chair, dark shades of gray and charcoal alternating in its pattern.

Her mother's skirts enveloped it as she seated herself in her queenly chair. The room filled with an awkward pause as Trejen's empty throne shifted the gaze of the whispering room.

Gailah exhaled deeply again as the room no longer watched her movements.

Groups of scouts gathered in the courtyards, readying themselves to find the Autumn King. Through the windows, Gailah saw storm clouds dissipate in the distance.

A loud clamor rang out, and the large wooden doors swung open. A soft breeze rushed past her gown as it curled around the legs of her seat.

Gailah arched in her seat as the King of the Great Forest finally entered the hall with his men.

The rain had not spared the people of autumn. It drenched the golden cloaked knights; it smattered their armor with mud. The king's ghost-like face made Gailah dig her nails into the wood of her arm rests. Gailah had never met the Autumn King. Her attention shifted to her mother.

A muscle flexed along Katha's jaw as he approached. Gailah watched as his gaze fixed on her mother's face. Queen Katha rose in acknowledgement of the Autumn King. Gailah felt something odd coil in her chest as the King looked up at her mother.

The raw and sharp bite of grief found her heart as she longed for her father to be here. Trejen no longer looked at her mother, but his eyes drifted to where she sat. The king studied Gailah, and she noticed the deep rings around his eyes which looked more severe under his creased brow.

There was blood across his armor, too. The oak tree hammered into his breastplate ran red with blood. Beneath his golden laurel, his black, silver streaked hair slicked away from the downpour.

She straightened her spine and refused to meet his gaze. He passed by them and climbed the dais to his throne without a word or explanation for their delay or appearance–just a cold fog of confusion that blanketed the room.

Scanning the crowd for Romulus, Gailah's pulse quickened upon spotting his raven curls. Among the gathering, the crown prince navigated with an equal measure of composure, and glimpses of his warm sienna skin revealed themselves through the throng.

Romulus' hair was a roguish frenzy, but it framed his graceful, high cheekbones. She knew the prince by name only, but she found herself captivated by the way he moved through the room. Everything about the prince heightened her curiosity.

That cold fog of confusion thickened as she blinked back in surprise.

The young prince had his fingers interlocked with a scarred priestess. She stood beside yet behind the young prince, almost invisible behind his golden cloak.

She wore a Misenian acolytes gown, the color of a blue mountain songbird. She wore her hood over her ebony curls as a soft, almost invisible essence radiated from her presence.

An essence that spoke of the healing arts of their great oak tree, her scars glimmered as if they melded her whole again with their magic. Her body bore evidence of the torture she endured. Deep crags covered her body like the cracks in a broken mirror. Even Oxana's left eye bore a remnant of her anguish.

Gailah's mind stumbled at the sight of their hands intertwined. The tales of her torture and rescue had reached every corner of the island. What the gossips of Thyssia had failed to share was that Romulus was in love with her.

Only a fool would deny what she could see plain as sunlight. Romulus looked at Gailah with indifference–no, something deeper.

Disdain fluttered in his eyes and set her teeth on edge.

Gailah met the priestess's eyes, and everything stopped. Her heart, her breathing, and even the sounds of the room. A golden glimmer sparked along the acolyte's scars the moment their eyes met.

Rabidly, the woman threw herself forward. Almost animalistic, as the priestess surged the dais.

Gailah scrambled backwards, her seat shrieking against the stone floor. Romulus lunged for the priestess, but she was too quick. The room erupted as steel rang out from every direction, ready to kill the priestess who charged the mountain throne. Her mother's furious voice deafened her ears.

"How dare you!"

Gailah's body failed her. Frozen as the woman pointed panicked fingers towards her.

"He's alive, he's coming!"

Her voice was pure blistering anguish. A piercing sound that cut into Gailah's mind.

The gold filled cracks across her eye flashed a cold light. Her muscles jerked along her neck as if some unseen force twisted against her bones.

Romulus cupped her face, whispering inaudible, grounding words to the priestess. She fought against him, clawing at his bare skin.

"He's alive!" Oxana cried out in a voice so loud the windows seemed to shake.

Each time she spoke, her muscles twitched wildly, almost feral.

"Restrain her!" Trejen's voice cut through the woman's cries.

Everything slowed around Gailah as she saw the pain on Romulus' face.

He kissed her brow and held Oxana tightly in his arms, barking back at anyone who moved to touch the acolyte.

A frost-like chill settled across Gailah's skin. Oxana's face became eerily still. Her cold blue eyes were on Gailah but softer, foreign, and distant now.

The priestess spoke again, "Roots, rocks, rivers, all of them crumbling, fumbling, dead." Oxana said in a happy, breathless voice, but spoke only to the air.

She wrapped an arm around the prince's neck and lazily twirled Romulus' hair around her finger.

The height of Gailah's fear came crashing down, and nausea prickled in her throat at the sound of Oxana's words.

Her pulse hammered against her chest and she pressed her frigid hand against her breastbone, clutching the soft fabric of her gown. Sweat tingled down her back and she closed her eyes to find her breath.

Blue sparks flashed under her closed eyelids as the chaos quieted around her.

"Get her out of here!" Katha's words sliced through the room. Gailah's eyes stayed closed as the room decrescendo in a flurry of fabric and sheathed steel.

"How dare you parade her around in such a shameful way? Have you no honor, King Trejen?" Queen Allagria's aged voice shocked Gailah's eyes open.

Romulus was already at the entrance of the Great Hall, fire in every step as he carried the priestess from the gathering.

Oxana's voice still lingered in Gailah's mind.

As the assembled courts settled like flustered chicken feathers, the room seemed to sway and her vision became unsteady.

Gailah swallowed, trying to shut out every fear-filled word and lifted her eyes to the crowd.

Her heart raced as she watched Trejen's knights surround him where he sat without his nephew.

With her mother's anger emanating from her throne, she steadied herself and her mother kept her eyes fixed on the back of Karak's gigantic head.

Gailah tried to earn her mother's gaze, but she felt nothing from the throne beside her.

Bjorn and Aerin had moved closer to her during the outburst but in Gailah's periphery, Torin sheathed his sword. He had only been a few paces from the mountain throne.

Chapter Ten

Trejen

Romulus disappeared from the room and tenderly protected the woman he loved. In another world, Trejen would've been proud of him, but not this world. The room eroded his pride into contempt. The boy he raised to be king could only think like a lovesick knight. He did not weigh the cost of his actions; he only moved with his heart.

The dwindling hope he held for their people washed away with the muddy spring soil.

Trejen moved slowly as he stifled a hobble, though not just in body but in his heart and mind as well. Trejen felt her eyes. His pulse soared and shook within his chest. Her presence pulled him to her with a great force that ached beneath his sternum. It brushed away the dust that lingered on the corners and crevices of his soul. He had committed to memory the sage and honeyed color of her eyes yet now, as he found Katha's gaze, he studied every fleck anew.

The green of her velvet gown reflected the sunlight around her lace covered shoulders. Life had ravaged him, but not her. The graying edges of her hair only framed the eyes that once held him so dearly.

He bit down on his teeth. Her eyes softened, and she nodded with the piety of a priestess. The pity on her face flayed any pride he had left, Katha turned her gaze from him as the flit of her stare tore open the old wounds in his heart.

As she looked over at her beloved bear, Trejen could feel Freyden's ghost standing just behind her throne.

Chills ran across his hands and neck, his eyes found somewhere else to rest. The ghost tormented him alone, but it extinguished the gentle fire in his heart. He had lost her once long ago, now twice, and still he would lose her for an eternity.

Trejen seated himself upon the oaken throne and hid the pain raging through him.

To his relief, Lord Barrock was the first to address the assembled regents. He puffed out his barrel-like chest as roosters often do with his red beard draped across his armor.

He stood before his king as he faced the crowds.

"I need not explain to you why we come soaked in both blood and water!" His voice echoed, "Raiders move unchecked and unfettered across our island! They scourge our great forest and will come for all we hold dear.' Lord Barrock faced the mountain queen. His commander gestured to the large doors. "As you know better than anyone else, your Majesty. View the *monster* who took part in King Freyden's death."

Monster.

A twisted voice spat in Trejen's mind. He could not look at her. Katha's silence tortured him. He felt sick as they presented her with the bait of his deceit.

A sound buffeted through the courts and as Trejen's knights dragged the corpse of the rune-covered man, they dropped him before the thrones. The warrior's body thudded against the marble, and Trejen found Regulus' eyes in the crowd.

"Your courage and honesty becomes you, Lord Barrock," Aerin said as he stepped forward and studied the corpse. "Let us display the man as a warning to all those who would kill a king."

The bile in Trejen's throat burned as he swallowed.

"Let us not waste breath until we can end their terror among the trees." Lord Barrock addressed the room. "Every kingdom must take part so that we may rid our island of them."

They dragged the corpse from the room. A streak of red trailed across the floor.

Lord Barrock's earnest heart wounded Trejen worst of all. He would follow Trejen to The End itself, but Lord Barrock did not know who or what he was abetting.

Queen Allagria scoffed.

"Our rivers will not run with blood simply because the forest cannot fend for itself. We have lost shipments of our steel to their raiders already. We will defend what is ours, but none of yours." The ragged voice of Queen Allagria called out to the commander.

Trejen held his breath as Katha moved to speak. Every rustle of her velvet gown captivated him.

"Your river lands turn to streams, do they not?" Katha countered, rising from her throne. "and those streams carve creeks along the forest floor..." The tone of her voice was empty of all emotion. Her icy tone sounded so foreign to him when fire used to drip from her tongue.

"Those creeks spring from the deepest caverns in our beloved mountain." Katha cleared her throat and her face soured towards the Spessian Queen. "Your rivers are nothing without the mountains and the trees."

The matriarch's eyes narrowed, and she rested the weight of her hands on her staff beside her throne.

Her onyx throne dripped in sapphires. Each one graduated in size and rippled in jeweled meandering rivers down the surface of house Spessia's seat.

"I will not shed the blood of my countrymen for your inability to control your populace. Your grandfather would agree with me.."

Trejen breathed sharply through his teeth as his body wanted to rise from his throne. Everything within him protested with pain, but as he struggled, the large doors at the end of the room opened and the judges entered the Great Hall.

In the center of the room, three simple wooden stools sat empty. The three ornate thrones surrounded the simple seats.

Cassia, Osiris, and Sherat.

The judges entered as a company dressed in simple beige robes held together by strands of leather. A single scroll of parchment hung from their belts as a reminder of their vow to justice and fidelity. The eldest of the judges served on behalf of house Spessia.

Each of them elected on behalf of the people's best interest. Their lives were simple. They did not live in castles and the people met their needs.

The judges acted as intercessors between man, king, and the gods. A judge could have no family, no desire for power or position.

They did not bow at the waist, nor did they bow their heads.

Their position was above the propriety of courtiers.

The judges found their seats at the center of the room. They would give each house an opportunity to present their grievances, quarrels, and negotiations. However, the gathering began when the judges spoke on behalf of the people.

Cassia, the mountain's judge, addressed the gathering. She was a woman with graying blonde hair that stood taller than the rest of the judges. Trejen knew Cassia from girlhood, but she was a woman now, and she was the image of discernment.

"Our winter has left many scars across our Thyssia. None greater than the loss of our king, but I do not stand before you to grieve." Cassia clutched a scroll in her fingers. "I stand before you to demand action and answers on behalf of those who cannot speak for themselves." She unfurled the parchment. A list of blurred ink tumbled down before her. "Fifty seven families sleep restlessly as their husbands and sons have vanished from the villages and countryside. There are more, the unseen, those who do not have families to grieve them. Our scribes have recorded every disappearance, but each day, a new name appears on this list."

Trejen sat forward in his chair.

"Your people are disappearing. Do not waste your words. Honor them by bringing them home or any others from being taken by this nightmare."

Cassia retracted to her seat as Osiris rose to continue their proclamation.

Osiris was a man older than Trejen but the newest elected to the judges' council. He served the people of Trejen's kingdom and was fair and slow to speak.

"Until we find these men, each kingdom must provide shelter and provisions for those affected by their disappearance. As well as, one legion of calvary to scour the island."

Whispers fluttered through the room. Osiris gave Sherat a moment to speak, but the eldest judge stared blankly across the room. The Spessian judge was a disgrace to his position, yet no one from his kingdom protested his incompetence.

Cassia leaned forward in her seat and, as the Spessian judge dissociated into a haze, she took his silence for herself.

"For the consideration of those gathered here and for the blessing of the gods," Cassia smoothed the front panel over her robe. "On behalf of my people, and for the benefit of our kingdom's gathered here today. Queen Katha presents her only daughter for the consideration of a marriage alliance. On her wedding day, Gailah will stand to inherit all the land promised by her father's people and the domain of all its wealth. We will only consider an offer worthy of our people."

As the judge spoke, they instructed Gailah to rise. Commotion thrummed in the room like a great hive of bees. No one would dare make an offer before the entire gathering. Rejection on this scale would be a fate cruel enough to deter an army. They only made these dealings in private. If something could not settle between regents, they would leave the judges to decide.

Trejen needed to speak with Katha on behalf of his nephew before the Spessian Queen had the chance.

Chapter Eleven

Aerin

Moonlight poured in through the windows of the hall. The thrum of merriment from the ballroom rippled through the stone hallways that surrounded him.

The promise of overflowing goblets and beautiful women seemed to help the courtiers forget the encroaching death that waited behind every rock and tree. Maybe their false smiles were all the same and they too could not consign to oblivion the feeling of paralyzing dread.

Behind the privacy of closed doors, his mother, along with the other regents, talked long into the evening of what to make of the priestess's outburst, marital negotiations and how to find the disappearing men.

As he followed them, the guards shut the doors in his face. Aerin tracked the disappearances and had been through every name missing on Cassia's list, but still they excluded him.

Soft music and the boisterous laughter of over-served guests made Aerin wince. He was in no mood for polite conversation. The wine would help. He tightened the loop that fastened his sleeve as he walked the length of the judicial hall.

Hours ago, this room contained the chaos of the island, but now the three thrones sat empty. The long windows stared down at him with soulless eyes. They pierced through the prince's emerald cloak. In a rush of anxiety, Aerin smoothed his trimmed beard and swept chestnut brown hair away from his face.

Candles glowed and flickered, creating a pathway through the dimness of the room. The silver crown at his brow felt tighter as he walked beneath the gaze of his mother's throne. He paused as the small reflecting pool in the center of the aisle caught his eye.

Twelve years ago, Aerin had stared into this same pool. The day of his awakening, the alchemists gave him a vision from the Void. When the final uprising ended and all alchemists became exiles sent to the End, the awakenings and visions ceased.

He could still taste the bitter yet floral elixir on his tongue. His fingers clutched the marble basin until he felt his fingernails crack.

Fear rushed over him as he remembered the feeling of the alchemists plunging his head beneath the still indigo waters. How a lifetime had passed in a moment before his eyes. He could still hear the splintering sound of rocks and trees being swallowed up by the sea. The Nadr villages burned and crumbled around him while his grandmother called on the mountain to protect their people.

The prince closed his eyes and smoothed his short trimmed beard as he sighed.

Aerin had little faith in the gods but far lesser in the sorcerers that hid behind their runes.

To him, the awakening was nothing more than a cruel trick the alchemists played on children to keep them in line–keep them afraid and keep a generation believing their lies. He did not know if what he saw was yet to come or was their people's past.

Aerin was not proud of the history of his house. There was more between their peoples than the mountain separating them. Aerin was as much Nadr as he was mountain born, the first king of his kind.

He could see his reflection in the waters as he stood over the white stone basin. Aerin analyzed the man staring back at him, his crown and the emerald color of his cloak. A melancholy bitterness twisted in his heart when he noticed how much his face had changed in those twelve years.

Sweat formed on his brow. He felt a heaviness spread across his chest. A second set of eyes appeared beside him in the water, they were lavender irises that narrowed and seethed in the inky pool.

He threw himself backwards as he dashed the deep indigo surface. Ripples erased the image, but it had already engraved itself in his mind.

Nothing more.

He had been too young to fight in the final uprising, but he remembered how their alchemical fire devoured all but the sea.

Thyssia's only salvation had been the gods' gift of Spessian steel. Steel that stood unbent beneath the heat of the alchemist's power.

A gift that the Spessians kept for themselves.

He cursed as he smoothed his cloak and tried to shake all thoughts from his mind. The nine were punishing them for giving the alchemists a place above them. He panted, but he dared not close his eyes.

He straightened as he felt the watchfulness of the room. A cruel trick for children, but he was no longer a child.

The throne of his people would soon be his and what king would be afraid of his own reflection?

Cias

While he slept, the high priest's brow beaded with sweat. His bedding was in torturous heaps as he twisted away from the thoughts that plagued him. Under siege by the solitary burden of confessions, confidence, and secrecy.

That morning, whilst the gathering droned on, the trunk of their mighty oak had split. The golden light of its power simmered through the wounded surface.

Cias fought against the panic rising in him while the attendants watched the growing crack. Their gasps only stoked his flame of doubt swirling in his mind. He had spent his life serving the gods, caring for their bastion of light.

Why had they gone silent?

He questioned his service and searched his memory for evidence of his failing. The life force of their kingdom was dying with no source or cause to its decay.

First was the breaking of the mountain, the bastion of the gods' strength and protection. Then, the river dredged all its provisions and power, and now their tree. The balm of gods was given to mend their people from within.

He heard the gasps of the acolytes that followed him to his dreams.

The secrets he kept and the confessions he heard often visited him.

This night was unlike the others.

His dreams conjured the cracking bark that haunted his waking moments. He could hear the echo of splitting wood between sleep and consciousness.

All at once, he stood within the courtyard of the autumn keep. Smoke swirled beneath his feet, and the scent of ash overwhelmed him. He could hear the funeral dirges wailing from the shores of the Ilsnadad.

The great golden tree of their people lay wasted by fire, and its golden leaves devoured by sparks grappling for something to destroy. Before the ruins of the mighty oak, the flames had blackened the laurel of the Autumn King. The circlet rendered by the heat of the blaze. Its ornate structure winnowed into ash as he touched it. Cias fell and his hands blackened from his fingertips.

His skin began to blight and char. His feet failed him and he could not flee from the spreading darkness.

The stump of the tree remained and fire rose from the cracking earth surrounding the crown. The crags in the soils seemed to claw at his feet and he braced his body to fall into the void it created.

A great beam of light seared through the canopy above him. The blight of blackened wounds on his skin chaffed and fell from his hands. Cias shielded his eyes as the cracks receded from the floor of the courtyard. A frail sapling rose from the stump of the fallen sacred tree.

Sunlight poured down around the young tree, diffusing the whirls of smoke. Its bark was still soft and new. Small auburn leaves emerged from the tender branches. Those fragile limbs reach towards the open blue sky above him.

At the base of the sapling, a crown encrusted with rubies rested atop the ruined stump, fashioned in a white brilliant metal, almost blinding in the revealing light.

Cias stood, the world around him groaning and mending from the fire torn wounds. The temple courtyard seemed to rumble as he moved closer to the new tree. The nine looked on from their pillars with glowing eyes.

He reached for the crown but as he moved to touch it; the dream faded in a chilling plunge through water.

He awoke cold and damp from the wasted sweat on his skin. Sitting up in his bed, the priest moved from his twisted covers. He could not shake the dream from his mind.

Pouring water from his bedside pitcher, he washed his face and tried to find some purpose for the images he had seen.

Through the window of his chambers, the great oak's waning light still prevailed through the blackness of the night but the strength of its silhouette was weakened by the crack at its base.

Chapter Twelve

Gailah

Thousands of fresh spring flowers decorated the ballroom, for every region had brought their best. Streams of blue and yellow garlands hung from the ceiling and snaked around iron chandeliers that dripped with beeswax candles. The floral scent wafted down as Gailah spun breathlessly in a flowing gown that resembled a frost covered flower.

It was a gown that she wore like armor with delicate hues of blush and encrusted with sheer blue, while white gemstones decorated her neck in crystal lines flowing to the hem of her gown.

Each flourish of fabric helped her feel completely and utterly free yet protected in the strength of her beauty as she turned with the chaotic rhythm of the music.

She was lost as the sounds surrounded her and the notes echoed off the arched ceiling.

The room was alive with laughter, conversation, and a dance floor with hardly any room to breathe. Many months had gone by since she had felt this light, no darkness pulling at the corners of her mind.

Spessian music was exhausting to anyone outside of their house, but she began the dancing as soon as the first musicians plucked their strings.

It was expected of her to dance with every eligible lord, no matter how unlikely their chances were. Etilda had fastened Gailah's hair up and swept away from her neck, secured by small crystalline hair pins. A few short strands of her silver hair had escaped and now framed the sides of her face.

The song ended and Gailah felt her mouth go dry with thirst. She wanted more than anything to ignore the failure of her presentation and Oxana's ominous words. Her heart was a tempest of fear and heartbreak at the fate of the priestess. She could not imagine such horror.

A tug at the back of her gauzy sleeve arrested her pursuit of serving trays stacked high with sloshing Spessian wine. Her slippers scuffed against the uneven tessera on the floor, forcing the princess to an abrupt halt.

"You dance so passionately for someone from the Mountain..." Torin said

Gailah turned with the pull of her sleeve to find Torin's grey eyes filled with urgency. He looked down at her amongst the blurry frenzy of the ballroom, and the palm of his hand brushed against her skin as he released the fabric of her sleeve.

She narrowed her brows as everything about the prince had confused her since he stepped forward to escort her earlier that day.

"True and yet hardly anyone from the Riverlands is dancing... including yourself.."

She shrugged off the prince's advances. He sighed, and she noticed his presence as he followed her along the fringe of the dance floor.

"I am pleased with your enjoyment of the evening. It's enchanting to see someone, well, someone like yourself indulge like the rest of us mere mortals." Prince Torin said, and she could hear the teasing smile in his voice, but something in his words felt terse and practiced.

The prince moved behind her with his hands clasped behind his back, highlighting the ornate designs of his chest plate and the sapphire color of his cloak.

Her lips craved a droplet of anything reminiscent of water. Gailah found a servant with a tray full of the deep red Spessian wine she craved. The liquid seemed to call to her as she lifted a goblet from the tray.

She thanked the wine bearer and eagerly accepted the glass.

Much to her dismay, Torin was still following her, dodging members of the court, yet never taking his eyes off of her.

A shiver ran down her spine.

Gailah weaved through the crowd like a hare through a meadow of courtiers, standing so close she could feel their breath on her skin. She searched the fringes for a secluded place to let her pulse return to solid ground, for her lungs to stop burning and her body whole again.

This evening meant endless dancing for her, so respite was a rare and precious thing. Away from the curious eyes of the dancing lords and ladies, she found a column to hide behind. The cold stone felt divine against the fabric of her gown.

Gailah brought the glass to her lips that were dry from the exertion of the dance. The heat in her face simmered beneath her flushed cheeks from the thrum and merriment around her.

Before she could even taste the wine, Torin removed the glass from her hand.

"You must dance with me." he demanded, setting the goblet aside. Gailah heard it again. There was something in his voice that was forced and disingenuous.

Gailah gritted her teeth and stared up as Torin leaned against the column that supported her.

He looked down at her and the width of the sapphire cloak across his shoulders acted like a shield from curious eyes.

It brought a kind of seclusion that offered Gailah no form of respite, but as he leaned closer to her, his scent reminded her of the sea.

"You were enchanting as you danced just then, but the rose color that has settled in your cheeks is something else entirely."

Gailah's eyes widened and pushed away from the column, her heart beat wildly.

She had encountered arrogant princes before.

Flattery was not something that set her heart on fire or made her crumble like a wilted flower.

"It is my duty to dance with every knight and eligible lord this evening, but first I will have my drink, which you so rudely confiscated, then you can wait just like everyone else." She tried to reach around him, but that only moved herself closer to him. She pressed a hand against his onyx breastplate, and it only served as a blockade between her and the refreshment.

He chuckled in a deep breathless sound that sent fire across her skin. His jaw tensed and he shook his head. She paused and before she responded, Torin's eyes were no longer watching her.

They had shifted into a scowl as he looked over her shoulder. Torin did not flinch, but straightened his shoulders towards his line of sight.

The muscles in his jaw strummed with irritation, but the prince simply removed her hand by engulfing it in his. Gailah's mouth dried for a different reason and as he ran a thumb across the top of her hand in a lazy circle, the heat in the room almost became unbearable.

"I will see that you are thoroughly refreshed, your Highness, but first let me claim this dance with you."

Someone else snagged her by the wrist.

Alexi swooped in from the side.

He snatched her like a diving bird and Gailah almost stumbled on her hem as the younger Spessian prince pulled her back to the center of the dance floor.

Where Torin reminded her of the soft blue of the sea, Alexi was as sharp, unforgiving and brutal as the blue of a glacier.

Gailah stiffened in his embrace as she lost sight of the elder prince. Only catching glimpses of his long silver hair through the crowd.

"Your Highness, I must apologize for my brother's advances. He is far less gallant than we expect of him, but there are far brighter stars in the Spessian sky, Princess." Alexi whispered between turns around the floor.

His dagger-point dimples decorated the smirk hiding on his lips. Gailah's mind spun like the couples surrounding them, but between turns, Bjorn stood on the cusp of the dance floor. Her brother's cheeks were red too, either from wine or the room itself.

"Are your people's manners as irregular as your songs?"

Alexi worked hard to earn her gaze, but she tried to avoid the piercing blue shade of his eyes.

Katha watched them with displeasure splayed across her face. Her mother sat like a lioness ready to strike as Gailah moved with the Spessian prince.

"We are a people of action, Princess." Alexi said, leading her across the ballroom. Her mother disappeared from her line of sight.

"It appears you and your people are not content with simply looking. You must touch as well." she said as his hand pulled tighter around her waist.

He smiled, and she counted every step of the dance until she knew she could be free of him. As if the floor rose to meet the soles of her slippers, the fervent music swelled, and they finished out the dance in silence.

"A glass of wine, your Highness?" Alexi said with a simple smile just before he snagged a goblet from the roving servants. "Our wine is finer than any other on the island."

Gailah could not focus on his words, only the goblet in his hands. Her lips were dryer than a Ghobasian desert.

She took the chalice by the stem. Alexi's eyes widened as he looked over her shoulder. He ended their interaction with a chaste kiss on the back of her hand. His lips seared her skin, and she felt unspoken words pass between them, but Alexi bowed almost frantically.

In a swift movement, her shoulder collided with a familiar blockade. Her wine jostled dangerously in its glass like a violent crimson sea. A single drop soared through the air and left a bloodied stain on the high neck fabric of her gown.

Torin reached for the goblet in her hand again, but this time she evaded his arrogant grasp. She quickly considered throwing her wine in the prince's face.

"I will not dance another moment until I can have something to dri—"

Before she could even think, the elder prince replaced the glass with a goblet of her family's wine.

"A mountain wine for a mountain rose." He said with a rigid timbre in his voice, and malice directed at his younger brother. Torin's eyes followed Alexi through the ballroom.

Torin's face was tense and there was nothing coy about his expression. No dimples or clumsy smirks.

Gailah brought the sweet umber drink to her lips. It was more refreshing than a summer's rain–*Nactine*, a strong drink, from the last of the winter stores, pressed from the hulls of young tree berries and left to strengthen until the darkest night of winter.

She drank the glass dry, forgetting all sense of manners. For the first time in weeks, she tasted sweetness instead of sorrow.

Torin narrowed his brows, and it seemed like his first genuine expression of the evening, but she did not care if he judged her. In that moment, decorum was the far lesser god than the thirst that had been threatening her all evening.

She swallowed and her pulse crept into a feverish ripple. His eyes fell upon the wine stain at her collar.

"My apolog—" Torin began, but she thumped the empty glass against his chest. Gailah yearned to dance again.

"You have kept your word. I suppose a dance is in order for the trouble you have gone to for this." Gailah said and he looked down in unreadable silence.

Thankfully, she had not wasted her wine on his handsome, although beardless, face.

She studied the movements of his eyes like the words he wanted to say died before he could speak.

His gray eyes darted across her face, her lips, then back up to meet her gaze. The slightest flicker of pain flashed across Torin's eyes.

The heat of the room warmed her skin again, but the taste of the mountain wine lingered on her lips.

"Dance with whomever you like, but you have no duty to me,"

The severity in his voice startled her. His hand found her biceps, and he dipped his head beside hers.

"Only drink your family's wine and do not trust my brother."

His touch receded, and Gailah's mind rattled with the sensation of his touch.

This face was Torin's true form. There was no deception or pretty practiced words on his tongue. The prince's frame turned and abruptly prowled behind his younger brother.

As he stalked towards the boundaries of the ballroom, a flash of rose-colored skin showed itself on the back of his neck.

Torin's silver hair glinted in the candlelight as he disappeared further into the crowd.

Suspicion crawled across her skin and she dodged a tray of Spessian goblets without indulging in their drink any further. Gailah whisked towards the tables decorated with greenery and ice roses grown on the sunniest mountain peak, she saw how her family looked far happier than she had seen them in months and all unease fled her body.

A single drop of nactine loitered on her lips and she cherished it like it would be her last.

Her brothers lounged beside their mother as she found her seat. Her mother looked down at her with pride burning in her eyes, for she did not return with a Spessian on her arm.

It was the first time her mother smiled at Gailah in weeks.

Bjorn

Bjorn emptied a few glasses of Spessian wine as he listened to his brother carry on about politics and the business of the realm. The duty to arrange Gailah's dowry fell on Aerin and it would be the largest collection of land, horses, and wealth that any lord had ever received in the history of their people. It was all the more reason Bjorn enjoyed the pleasure of being a second son.

He carried fewer matters of state, leaving the safety of his people as his sole concern. His glory lay on the battlefield, not in ballrooms or on the throne of the mountain. He loved his brother, but he did not envy him.

"Let me fill your goblet brother, it is the least I could do." Bjorn rose from his seat and sauntered across the ballroom with near empty goblets in hand.

Bjorn's cheek prickled with their natural flush any time a potent drink met his lips. The rock within his chest felt slightly lighter as the excitement of the room mingled with the wine in his stomach. He took a final swig from his glass just as a voice called out from behind him.

A hearty grip clamped on his arm.

"Your Highness, please, a moment of your time!" Lord Barrock said. "I have someone I would like to introduce you to."

Bjorn turned, and when he saw who stood in-front of him, the prince spit out his wine.

Senna.

Standing beside the ruddy-cheeked general, Senna stood with her small hand in the general's grip. With the other hand, Lord Barrock pushed her forward by the small of her waist. The general's face beamed, and he sidestepped the pair.

"My daughter, Lady Senna Barrock of the Autumn Realm."

Gone were the twigs and fern leaves from her braid. In their place, small yellow gems in the shape of oak leaves formed a circlet crown, secured by white roses at the back of her head. Her copper hair fell freely in tamed waves around her shoulders. Lilac silks draped her frame, replacing her equally captivating hunting leathers.

As if the general had awoken Bjorn from a dream, he blinked rapidly. Senna looked as though she had stepped down from one of the tapestries lining the walls of the ballroom–a goddess of the hunt. He had drunk his fair share of wine, but not enough to deny the fact that she was truly beautiful.

Bjorn swallowed.

Her face was a mix of rosy embarrassment and a hint of frustration.

"You honor me, General, thank you for the introduction." Bjorn said, as he bowed with gaze fixed on Senna.

He tried to hide the effervescent feeling in his chest while his heart pounded like a yearling colt.

"Let me refill your wine," the general said and reached for Bjorn's goblets. He gave them to the general without hesitation. "This dance is a favorite among the forest folk and I am far too old for dancing," the general embellished, "but would you do me the honor of dancing with my dear Senna?"

Bjorn nodded and smiled as he exchanged the goblets with the general and lifted Senna's hand.

"Lady Barrock?" an amused grin spread across Bjorn's face. The warmth of her hand flooded his palm, but he could not help noticing the small archer's calluses on her fingertips.

He enjoyed the weight of her hand more than he would have expected. Panic spread through his fingers as the ballad of the Autumn King swirled in the air.

Senna nodded in response to the bard's call, but her wide-eyed gaze gave him pause.

Lord Barrock had already disappeared, and Bjorn moved to let her go, he would not torture her with a dance if that was not what she desired.

But to his surprise, before his fingers could fall away, her grip tightened and she led him onto the dance floor while the gentle music surrounded them.

The effervescent feeling in his chest only worsened, and he scrambled to remember the dancing instruction he learned from his father.

He leaned down to whisper. "Lady Senna Barrock," he said, practicing the sound of her name and smiled again. "I have many, many questions, and I don't think this song will last long enough for you to answer them all."

"You never asked the right ones." She held his gaze briefly as she turned beneath his towering arm but she did not flinch as he pulled her in by the small of her waist.

His fingers rustled the incredibly soft fabric of her gown, worth over ten woodland cottages.

"Lilac suits you, as do the roses. Why do you hide away in that cottage of yours?" He said softly as not to divulge the secrecy of her hiding place.

"I enjoy finery as much as anyone else, but the forest is the only place I can be at peace. I had no intention of being here tonight." She spoke, and her eyes finally locked with his, lingering for a moment longer than a mere blink while still nestled in his embrace.

They had never been this close before, something they both understood.

"Why not?" He said, his brows meeting at what felt like a slight.

"When a storm is coming, shelter is the safest place to be, is it not?"

"A mountain cannot seek shelter from a storm, my lady." He said, but the weight of his hand in hers occupied every aspect of his attention.

He marveled at how small it felt in his, but then the memory of her knife pressed against his back flashed through his mind.

"Then I hope you are still standing when the storm passes, prince."

"I will know where to find you when it does." he said with a confident smile, leaning in closer as they danced, but the gravity of her voice unnerved him. "Tell me, how did you come here tonight?"

"Through the door, I suppose?"

He stifled a laugh, but Bjorn exhaled through his nose, and it fussed the roses in her hair.

"My father.. He is well intended, but he enjoys meddling as much as most parents do. That is why I am here. Meddling. He misses me and wishes I spent less time in the forest." she said, the corners of her lips in a soft smile as she shook her head. "My mother has been gone a long while, so he tries to fill that role as well."

He gently tightened his hand around hers.

"I understand your sorrow." His parents began the dancing at each gathering, but tonight his mother sat alone.

He looked up towards the flowers dangling from the chandeliers and noticed how far his head poked out above the crowd.

"I know." Senna whispered in response, and her hand tightened around his. "but your wound is fresher than mine. We mourned your father's passing. He was a loyal king consort."

The ballad slowed with the beat of his heart. The next step required him to guide his hand around the base of her neck while they turned slowly.

He swore the music stopped playing when Senna inhaled the moment his palm traipsed around her neck, but as she looked up at him amid the dance, she lost him to the green pathways of her stare.

The music lulled as the dance ended. The couples around them scattered, but he still towered over her in the center of the dance floor.

"Speaking of wounds, how is your arm?" he asked, extending her arm forward, their hands still interlocked.

A soft radiance persisted on the side of her arm where the wound had once marred the skin, leaving a golden glow in its wake.

His brows raised in surprise.

"The priests healed it as a favor to my father. He did not want it to show tonight and raise questions. The gold will be gone in a few days, though thanks to your kindness, it will no longer scar." she said as she unlinked her fingers from his.

The emptiness caused his hand to burn, as if it were gloveless in winter.

"Wait. Why ask for bandages when they could heal you so quickly?" He asked before she could whisk back to her table.

Senna looked him up and down, but fixed on his eyes. "Because I wanted to see if you'd give them to me." A smile sparked across her lips.

He crossed the space between them.

"Don't leave the gathering until we can speak again." His hand found hers, as well as the warmth he had missed.

Bjorn had thousands of things he wanted to ask her, but he needed privacy, something which the dance floor could not accommodate.

His mother watched only Gailah and Aerin, but he could see Lord Barrock smiling almost gleefully from where he sat beside the Autumn King.

There were others watching them as well, and the curiosity of the room tingled along his spine. She curtsied, and he bowed before another song played.

He returned to his seat beside his brother, who was all too happy to resume their previous conversation.

Bjorn watched as Senna disappeared into the crowd and continued to sip on his wine that Lord Barrock had returned to his brother. His heart beat unsteadily in his chest.

Their mother had disappeared from their head table. Bjorn had missed the Autumn King ask his mother to dance and Bjorn's stomach soured as he found her.

The Queen of the Mountain danced with Trejen, but the happiness on her face disquieted Bjorn as they danced happily in some unspoken agreement.

ROMULUS

As heir to the Autumn Kingdom, Romulus claimed one of the

finest rooms in the hall of judgment. He perched alongside Oxana on a large balcony that wrapped around the side of the largest spire.

"What is a man to a mountain?" Oxana asked playfully, and twisted strands of Romulus' hair in her fingers while she sat across his lap. He nuzzled her cheek gently as he nodded at the sound of her voice.

Romulus smiled as he looked over the shadow-covered lowlands. They dressed for the gathering but on his balcony, he held a private ball just for the two of them.

Wine and savory things only for them to relish in. Joy radiated across Oxana's face as she watched the couples dance through the windows of the ballroom.

They had danced until his feet blistered, twirling and gliding to the soft echo of the gathering's melody. She loved dancing, but those gathered would not welcome her presence in the ballroom below.

Oxana caressed his arm as a soft smile graced her lips. She drew her forehead to his with deep affection. A flicker of gold slithered along the cracks on her lips.

"What is a bird to buzzard? Prey is prey?" she whispered.

His breathing paused, and his stomach churned. Her eyes were warm and blue but the marred one was thick with the delusion that lived behind her gold split eye.

"Darling, tell me what that means?" He whispered, cupping one side of her face.

"There are many princes, but only a single mountain, my love." She never directly answered his questions.

The moments of her true lucidity grew rarer by the day. The magic sealing her wounds would not be enough.

He kissed the back of her hand and squeezed it, as if the life beneath her skin was slipping away with her mind.

He fiddled with the green fabric leaves that created the texture on her gown.

His faith in their relic dwindled, not for the sake of the gods or their silence, but because its power seemed unbothered by the people who needed it most. His faith dangled, like the dying leaves of their tree.

His oaken laurel wrapped tighter around his head, a golden shackle.

Romulus' hand gripped the leg that was draped across his lap and focused on the woman that he held.

Why did you abandon her?

Romulus thought in silent anger to the gods.

He drew her close to him. Tears brimmed in his eyes. His jaw tensed.

He could still see her tortured frame as she lay mangled on the desolate stone floor.

"I can't see you," she said. Her voice was weak and wavering.

"There's no light, my love." He said as he peeled her away from the grime of the dungeon. "I have you. Be still, my darling."

His armor was too hard and coarse for something so broken and dying. He had torn his cloak from its place beneath his pauldron, wrapping her in its soft golden fabric.

He had carried her out of the darkness of the cave and into the twilight of evening.

As the memory faded, anger roared through his veins, but he calmed as her fingers gently scratched a soft path along his back.

"*We gave her you.*"

His spine straightened as a silent voice echoed in his mind.

Chapter Thirteen

Bjorn

The night ended in a steady thrum of clumsy drunkenness. Aerin stumbled from the ballroom.

Bjorn rose from his seat to follow his brother, but the candles of the room swayed as he stood. He braced himself on the table, then staggered against a smooth column. He had never been so deep into his cups before. His mind tossed dizzyingly within his skull.

Bjorn took a separate doorway out that led to one of the many gardens lining the inner courtyard of the hall of judgment. Bjorn's cheeks flushed sharply with the sudden chill of the evening.

After the attack in the forest, Bjorn was not himself amid the chaos of a crowded room. The unpredictability and ever changing landscape of faces set his teeth on edge. Threats thrived beneath the shifting of sheer incalculable outcomes. As he looked up, his spirit settled under the open sky.

As he stepped forward into the dark, like ivy, the night climbed the walls of the garden in shades of deep blue, only illuminated by orbs of glowing hammered copper. The metal containers were lit from within while spilling light from the intricate designs on the dangling spheres. Small trees and large earthy smelling hedges offered privacy to those in search of it.

Aerin's sob startled him, and every drunken thought fled Bjorn's mind.

A few paces off, He hunkered with his head resting against a decorative trunk. Aerin's shoulders shook and something twisted deep inside Bjorn.

The heir to the broken mountain lost his footing as Bjorn approached. Then stumbled backwards into a bush that cushioned his fall.

With his head lowered, Aerin's light brown hair tumbled around his face. Bjorn had never seen him in such a state outside of the sparring grounds. They all carried their grief differently. Aerin's method typically included spouts of unproductive brooding, but this was new. Inconsolable anger was not Aerin.

"Aye, go away."

He waved Bjorn off, still struggling to free himself from the shrub.

Bjorn grabbed him by the shoulders and pulled his brother upwards, then steadied him as he failed to find his footing. He swayed again and Aerin's head swung close to his brother's nose.

"You're lucky I'm bigger than you, brother. If you were in my place, I'd have crushed you already." He laughed through his teeth, shifting his brother's weight as he helped them to a nearby stone alcove, then plopping them down on the bench with a grunt.

"Aerin..." Bjorn started as Aerin raked his fingers through his hair while his head rested on his palms.

"I can not be- I am drowning." Aerin sputtered.

His gaze was muddied by too much Spessian wine, but Bjorn's mind was equally clouded. The world was quiet around them, no insects or birds calling out. Only the faint sound of revelry echoing off the walls of the garden.

"I know.." Bjorn rested quietly beside Aerin.

He fiddled with the rings on his large hands. Their gazes fixed on an uninteresting patch of moss, but neither looked at each other.

"They all look at me like I know what to do and how to be but..."

The elder prince rang his knuckles white as Bjorn listened. "I feel like I'm making up everything as I go, ruining everything and praying no one realizes it. I was not ready for him to..to be him.."

"To be Dah? No. None of us were ready for.." Bjorn answered but stopped and chewed his lower lip.

Months of talking around the things neither of them wanted to say surfaced in a thick sadness in Bjorn's throat.

Bjorn draped an arm around Aerin's slumped shoulder.

The silence was a comfort in its own way, a blanket of solitude that wrapped itself around them in the small stone alcove. Bjorn had carried their father's body home, but Aerin had borne the weight of it ever since.

"Mother still washes her hair with ash..." Aerin began. "I saw the maids dumping her bath water."

Bjorn shook his head as he looked towards the sky.

"I still do too.. It did nah' feel righ' to stop until I stopped missing him. Though I suppose I migh' run out of ash." Bjorn's voice trailed off as he listened to a second Spessian ballad in the distance.

The wine was loosening his words and his mountain born accent slipped through. Bjorn had spent the most time of all his siblings among his father's people.

Their kingdom grieved with the ash from the trees high upon the mountain. The same trees used for their pyres. A sign of mourning that the fallen's life lingered in the memories of the island.

Bjorn realized that each gathering would be easier from now on. Grief weaves its healing arts in persisting strands, no matter how often old wounds reopen anew.

The prince knew his grief would dull with time.

Bjorn saw tears in his brother's eyes. Escaping his lid, a single tear raced quickly across his cheek in a burning, angry path before he quickly wiped it from his face. Aerin's jaw flexed.

"You are no' Dah. He never asked tha' of you." Bjorn did not know what else he could say to ease his brother's mind.

Aerin nodded, and he breathed quietly as the comfortable silence hung between them. Nothing more needed to be said, but he would not leave his brother alone when his thoughts crashed upon him.

. . .

SENNA

The first night of the gathering ended once the moon peaked in the sky above.

Senna had no desire to stay that long. She shifted in her seat beside her father as she teased the beading on her sleeves.

The infernal gemstones holding her hair dug deep into her skull. She resisted the urge to comb her fingers through her hair and dreamed of slipping out of the ballroom with her gems and roses flying behind her.

Finery suited her; she enjoyed feeling beautiful, but she needed to be anywhere but here. Everything around her was like a geyser on the verge of eruption. Her uncle's disappearance made her sick with worry, but the increasing attacks only deepened her fears.

Lord Barrock's hand gently covered hers and broke the anxious fog consuming her. She was tapping her fingers against the table in the rhythm of a gallop.

She looked at her father, whose cheeks were flocked with warmth. He looked at her with a knowing glance. His eyes crinkled on the outside. He nodded with a soft smile beneath his graying red beard.

"Goodnight, my dear."

He lifted his chin to the door with a wink.

"Thank you!" She practically flew from her seat, but not before she kissed the top of his head. "Enjoy the rest of the evening."

"Aye."

He saluted with his glass as she darted away from the tables that were drenched in decorative golden leaves.

She weaved through the ballroom, dodging couples that swirled about the floor, blocking her escape.

She yearned for air. The stifling sleeves of her gown itched against the soft sides of her arms. From her hair, she twisted loose a particularly irritating stem of a white rose. A few petals trailed behind her as she freed it from her copper hair.

She held the bud between her fingers and marched forward between the doors that parted into the bustling corridor.

Clusters of lords and ladies clogged the hallway, making it uncomfortably warm. The walls tightened around her, worsening, making her garment cling as if it were a stodgy blanket. The thought of the fresh air on her skin beguiled her.

Hope presented itself in a small iron door that was slightly ajar, while copper light poured through the crack. A night garden waited just beyond.

The night wrapped around her, and her shoulders eased after the hours of maintaining her posture. She closed her eyes and rolled the tension from her neck. Her thoughts drifted to her cottage. She was only a few hours' ride from the solace of the trees.

Shaking the thought from her mind, the cool air filled her lungs with a sigh of relief. She lifted her face to the sky and drank in the garden's quiet.

"Moonlight suits yah'."

Her eyes snapped open and the white bud she held fell to the stony garden floor. Bjorn stood with his arms crossed as he leaned against an interior wall. The lanterns in front of him splashed warm light across his brown beard and soft eyes.

Her startled exhale burned in her chest.

"How long have you been standing there?" She huffed as the prince approached with a warm smile.

Something uncertain scurried across her skin.

"Forgive me, I was on my way to rejoin the gathering, but I stopped when I saw you come through the doorway..." He stood before her, but his head was far above her.

"I felt your absence in the room, and I thought you retired. I was not avoiding you." She lied and held his gaze for a moment, but that feeling crept up again.

"You felt my absence? I'm flattered." He blinked in surprise and his smile turned to a smirk.

Senna brought a hand between her brow and sighed. "We've both had more than our share of wine. I misspoke!"

She stepped into the shrubbery, scanning for anyone that could be listening. She heard his footsteps follow. Maybe the dimness of the evening could hide the color in her face.

The garden was empty.

What had he been doing out here? She thought.

At the far end of the garden, two willow trees hung placidly over a still pond. Their leaves skimmed the surface, tracing faint circles in ripples across the water. She dipped beneath the arching limbs to protect them from prying eyes.

He struggled to stoop beneath the lower limbs as he did the low roof of her cottage. Questions stirred in Bjorn's eyes.

"There is still no sign of my uncle. I fear something has happened to him." She immediately changed the subject to anything but the impact of his presence on her heartbeat.

"As an alchemist, he may be in more danger than yah' know. There are few loyal to them or their practice. Yah' should be wary of anything of their order."

She shook her head as his brows furrowed.

"Trejen was a dear friend of my uncle. Jaius was his chief advisor. He was not one like Haydrian. My uncle is kind, fair, and wants to use alchemy for good. When the judges sentenced the alchemists to exile or death, Trejen built the cottage for him so he could keep him safe and close by..."

"I see... Why would he have gone without telling yah'? He seems like someone who wouldnah' leave yah' vulnerable and alone in the woods." The prince tilted his head and his mountain accent deepened as he ducked lower under the branches above them.

It forced him to stand closer–too close–and she worked harder to still her breathing.

"I can protect myself, but he has been missing for more than a few months now. I'll keep the cottage for him until he comes home. He'd hate to see it in disrepair." Her voice softened when she spoke of him. "He welcomed me with no pretense. My uncle did not care how I behaved or if I asked him questions while he worked. He never left when my father left for battle and for a girl who sorely needed a family. Well, he helped fill the gaps."

She remembered how he walked out of the cottage for the last time. Rabbits tied to his pack but with fear in his eyes. Something was wrong. She had found no trace of him in the woods until Bjorn had found his talisman.

"I see... I cannah' imagine how that feels. His disappearance must be difficult for you. He doesnah' sound much like any of the alchemists I knew."

She preferred this natural lilt to his voice.

"He was not a true alchemist, not really. He practiced its art, but he was not bound to the guild. That's why Trejen trusted him, no one to run back to with information." She said and lowered her gaze to the paving stones instead of Bjorn and instead of the tears that wanted to surface. "Before he left, he said something strange, almost as if he'd never come home again, but I thought nothing of it...He said that the trees were ill."

She wanted to say more, but she choked on her words as she pictured him standing in the doorway with distant, sad eyes.

Suddenly, the warmth of his hands drifted over the gauze of her sleeves.

Her eyes whipped forward as the prince stood closer than before as concern splayed across his features. The warmth from his hands spread through her skin and across to her chest to where her pulse had risen.

"I have no knowledge of your uncle or his whereabouts, but I believe that's why he left the medallion? For you to find him?" The prince's hands remained at her upper arms.

"No, something is terribly wrong. He would never part with that." Her breathing steadied, but still pinned beneath his gaze.

The wind quickened and tossed the branches of the tree in time with music from the ballroom. Despite the dim light under the willow tree, she could still see the green in his eyes. They were kind but sad as he tried to read her thoughts as she stood frozen in his grasp.

Another loose flower fell from her hair.

Her tongue bore a question that she wanted–no, needed–for him to answer.

"What did you see?" she whispered

The Prince dropped his head lower, as if he hadn't heard her, and Bjorn's brows tensed in the middle.

"What?"

His voice was low, and his thumb pressed into her biceps.

"When you came of age, at your awakening, what did you see? When the alchemists made you drink the elixir?"

Her question startled him. His eyes narrowed as he tried to recall the distant memory.

"Oh...." His wine reddened cheeks framed his soft smile. "I saw nothin' but sunshine, warm summer winds across the meadowlands beneath the mountain. It was gorgeous. I'd never seen the sun so bright and I felt... well, I've seen nothin' so beautiful." His smile did not fade as he looked at her. "Why do yah' ask? What did yah' see?"

She heard everything Bjorn had said, but her thoughts crumbled as she struggled to find her words.

Fire roared across the corners of her mind.

"When the alchemists made me drink.... I saw death. The forest burning around me as smoke filled my lungs and burned my eyes." She lied again, but only partly as the vision's heat seared across her skin. Senna wrapped her arms around her body.

There was more to her awakening, but it only lived to haunt her dreams. Senna had seen Bjorn's face a thousand times before. Since her awakening, his face tortured her with those same green eyes that pierced back at her. In those moments, he was there amongst the fires and the smoke of her dreams.

Every time the vision came to her, she saw Bjorn bathed in blood.

His hand gently tightened while the other dropped to her forearm. His thumb ran a comforting circle over her inner wrist, but it was a graze that was almost too much for her to bear.

The surrounding garden grew quieter than it had any right to be.

"Aye, that's a heavy burden indeed. I've never given mine much thought, but they are only warnings or possibilities, they are nah' promised. Yah' still decide yarh' path, nah' some alchemist's elixir. Let us start by finding yarh' uncle?"

Letting go of her arm, He tilted her chin to meet his gaze. Her eyes widened at his touch.

She took in the details of his face that she had never noticed before, the lines by the corners of his eyes from years of laughter and the subtle scars above his brow.

The willow leaves around them brushed through her hair and that uncertain feeling surfaced, overwhelming her.

She leaned forward slightly, but those fire soaked dreams heightened her resolve and she pressed her chin downwards against his hand.

Her mind focused on the sound of his breathing, trying to quell the warmth in her cheeks.

The soft sounds from the gathering grew louder, and the rustling leaves reminded her of what awaited them outside the willow branches.

"We need to leave separately... to avoid suspicion." Senna breathed

Bjorn nodded in response, and she moved quickly to avoid his gaze.

She parted the partition of leaves, but she could not look back at him again without seeing the blood-soaked man from her dreams.

Bjorn did not follow her. His shadow lingered beneath the willow tree and a strange pain ignited in her chest.

The pain told her she was running from more than the terror in her dreams. The sound of her quickening footsteps echoed off the paving stones, and she found the door leading to the outer courts. She would find her uncle and she would never set foot in the hall of judgment again.

AERIN

"Brother! Come and let us retire. I do not think I will make it up the stairs without you." The eldest prince shouted from the garden door.

Bjorn was alone and crouching in the middle of the open garden. At the sound of his voice, his mountain of a brother stood and Aerin's curiosity peaked at the sight of the white rose that he carried in his grip.

Chapter Fourteen

Gailah

As Gailah guided her hand along the cold stone hallway, laughter and giddy conversation followed behind her. The ladies of the mountain court retired from the ballroom in a cluster of happy exhaustion.

Gailah's feet throbbed in her slippers and her weary pulse thudded in her chest. Lord Rorick had claimed most of her dances and clobbered most of her toes along with it, but not out of malice, simply poor skill. He was kinder than she remembered. His freckles still dotted his nose, but he was no longer the villainous page boy that stuffed ice in her slippers. Each step and twirl a gentle mercy while the music helped her forget for a moment.

Her limbs trembled like saplings from being whisked about by every knight, lord, and prince. Well, almost everyone.

Torin had merely watched amid the upheaval with a scowl and did not let Alexi near her.

She had pretended to be the merry and flighty eligible princess, but secretly she had watched the Spessian princes from her periphery. Even as their grandmother departed the ball, Torin stood as a wall between his brother and they disappeared just before the mountain court announced the end of the festivities.

The Spessians shared more wine at this gathering than ever before, but Gailah had not seen Prince Torin or Prince Alexi forget themselves among the crowd, and Torin's warning fluttered through her mind.

The southern wine pervaded every smell and taste of the gathering. Many staggered from the hall and some even slumped on the stairs with gaping, snoring mouths.

As she sealed the door to her room, Gailah chewed on her thoughts, but all of it rattled like a boiling cauldron, shaking and ready to overflow.

It was not the grand chambers of the mountain keep, but it was far more than she deserved for a fortnight's stay in the judicial palace. It held an enormous bed with a four post canopy, a small writing desk, a vanity with a polished silver mirror, large furs draped over chairs before the hearth, and a beautiful balcony facing her treasured mountains.

She settled onto the stool in-front of the vanity and she noticed Etilda had prepared her things for bed: a simple set of clothes and steaming water for her to wipe away the toll of the evening. She had asked Etilda not to wait up and for her to enjoy the gathering in one of the many halls, but she appreciated the effort nonetheless.

Gailah took the warm wet cloth in her hands and rested it against her face. The warm water winded down the side of her face and down her neck. Wisps of hair dangled around her temples after the hair pins slowly lost their battle throughout the night.

The wine spatters along her frost colored gown unsettled her in the silver reflection before her. Too many dropped goblets left puddles of the deep red drink across the dance floor. If blood had spilled that evening, it would have gone unnoticed.

The door creaked as it cracked ajar.

Gailah turned towards the sound and tore the comforting cloth from her still wet face.

Her mother stood in the doorway.

The mountain queen's eyes held a look that any daughter would recognize. Gailah tensed with a strained smile.

"Your hair looks so lovely." Her mother began. "It is a shame to take it down. May I assist you?" The queen gestured from where she rested in the doorway to the brush on the vanity table.

Gailah's uneasiness grew.

Her mother rarely asked permission from anyone.

Gailah nodded and swung her legs towards the vanity.

Her mother crossed the breadth of the room and quickly picked up the brush. Years had gone by since her mother had helped with such a mundane task.

Gailah appreciated her mother's gentle hand, but her stomach did not settle as the queen worked through her silver hair.

"Kissed by starlight." Katha said with a smile on her face, then combed with her fingers in search of ivory hair pins.

After she plinked each one into an antler bone dish, the queen guided the brush in a wave across her scalp. Gailah waited for her mother to speak. When Gailah looked at her mother through the reflection, the glow of victory filled her eyes.

"Gailah, did you enjoy yourself this evening?"

"Yes, I found dancing a needed distraction."

"It is unfortunate that Romulus chose not to attend, but that is of no consequence."

Gailah noted the shift in her mother's tone.

"Do you find him handsome?" Katha asked as she continued to work through her daughter's hair.

"As handsome as any other prince."

"Gailah..." Katha tugged at the braid securing her mountain peak diadem.

"He showed me as much attention as I gave him." Gailah said with a sigh. "I do not set my gaze on a man who loves another. You chose Father. Why shouldn't I get the same chance?"

"I chose your father because I was angry, because I was afraid. I wanted to feel safe. I chose him because I was a queen who needed a king. You are a princess and you are a bridge. Alliances protect our people, they protect your future people. They protect you."

Katha did not lift her gaze, and she did not see the tears forming in her daughter's eyes, but continued to rake her fingers through her loose strands.

There was nothing surprising in her mother's words. Gailah knew her duty.

"What of Aerin?"

"What of *Aerin*?" Katha lifted her head at the sound of her daughter's distress.

"You betrothed him to the Ghobasi princess when he was a baby. Why don't you make them marry? Surely his fate matters more than mine."

Katha sighed again and rested her hands on Gailah's shoulders.

"You know why. She is ill. Her recovery is more important than their marriage. If they betray our alliance, then the loss is theirs alone and there are two other princesses for Aerin to marry in Ghobasi."

Gailah paused and studied the table in front of her. Her anger bubbled beneath her unshed tears.

She would not cry.

"What if that's not true? What if Aerin's betrothed is like me and she doesn't want to marry a stranger?" Gailah said, steadying her uneven voice.

"Strangers are not strangers for long." Katha smiled at her through the mirror and smoothed the silver wisps around her daughter's face.

"What about over the mountain? Send me to Oldema. She would teach me to be a wise woman like her? It would strengthen our bond with the Nadr."

Katha's face froze at the mention of Ellika, the matriarch of the Nadr people.

"Gailah, we do not run from fate..."

"I can not love him!" Thunder rolled beneath Gailah's skin. Her fingers clenched into fists and she tried to still her breathing. "Not after how he looked at her, at the priestess. If she is his, then I will never be! I will not be some dust collecting queen shelved for the rest of eternit—"

"Gailah, It. is. decided." Katha spoke with a quiet force, a decree, with no room for questioning. "Be content that he has any redeeming qualities at all."

The queen resumed brushing and Gailah's stare could have carved into the vanity table.

Aerin's words tapped at the rising tension in her gritted teeth.

A pawn.

"The only thing I knew about your father before we married was that he was kind and that he could kill if I needed him to. Do not disregard a good match over some petty jealousy."

"He loves her."

Gailah had watched them closely at the gathering. The way his hands cupped Oxana's face and how their eyes echoed each-other's souls. Romulus had disappeared for the rest of the evening and Gailah knew they were together.

Gailah was no fool. She knew what love looked like.

"War is coming, Gailah. It does not care who you love."

Gailah swallowed as she closed away the part of her that wanted to scream–the part of her that gnawed at the bridle inside her mouth.

Katha placed the brush beside her and gently kissed the top of her head. Gailah stared into the mirror, unmoved.

The sound of clinking metal drew Gailah's eyes to her mother's hands. In her grip, an ornate hair comb rested in her palm. Golden oak leaves dripped with pearls around the tines.

"The first of your bride price, the rest will follow your nuptials. These ornaments will serve as your currency and status among his people. As Queen, it will be your duty to show favors to the women of his court. Jewels that will buy you allies in your new home."

Katha glided the comb into her daughter's hair and Gailah shuddered as the tines scraped against her scalp. "How you adorn yourself reflects Romulus' generosity and your loyalty to him. You will be the greatest jewel in his crown."

The last twenty years of Gailah's life prepared her for this, but why did it pain her so and fill her with the roar of a lion? She clutched the edge of the desk; the air grew thin and Gailah's pulse beat to a war drum.

The Queen's face flashed a tightened look, and she turned for the doorway.

"Thank you for bearing your duty so well," her mother said with a smile. Gailah gripped the handle of her hairbrush until her knuckles were white.

"Lock this behind me as I leave. I care only for your safety." Katha said as she disappeared behind the large oaken door.

Gailah rolled the title around on her tongue like a briar.

The next queen of Autumn.

The door sealed, and the roar within her clawed out. The brush flew from her hand, struck the breadth of the door and bounced off the carved wood, only to clatter against the dark floor.

As it slid to a stop, a crack rang out, and the ornately carved brush split in two.

A wave of sadness replaced the rush of anger that fled from her body. She ripped at the strings of her gown and stepped from its pile of fabric on the floor before finding refuge in her dressing gown.

Gailah crumbled to the floor before the fireplace and buried herself in the pages of her journal, for she knew sleep would not find her.

Chapter Fifteen

Romulus

THE MOON DESCENDED as the first night of the gathering dissipated into memory.

He sat nestled into the windowsill of his chambers while Oxana slept with her spine propped against his chest. The weight of her warmth soothed the tempest beneath his skin, and he tucked her head under his chin. Romulus watched her breathing, and the sound of her voice resonated in his mind.

His thoughts drifted to the past and how her voice swelled into a song and their first meeting.

As he hunted through the forest, he neared the outskirts of the temple courtyard, lined with circles of trees, where he first heard his wife's voice. More entrancing than any spell, Oxana's song had carried him to her and he nearly tripped on the large stony stairs in his desperation to find the source of such a melody. Embarrassed, Romulus had hidden close by to listen as she sang among the stillness of the leaves, as if the forest paused in awe at her worship. Acolyte's all sang to encourage the health of the trees, but her voice was different.

Her voice brought burning tears to his eyes, and he knew the music from her lips commanded even the nine to listen.

Romulus shook that foggy memory from his mind. The song that had changed his life in the sweetest and cruelest of ways.

Romulus began to loosen all the golden clasps and ornaments from her long, twisting, dark hair while he traced a gentle path through her tresses.

The moon dipped closer to the mountains in the distance and the memory of her capture flashed across his eyes.

His heart tightened, and Romulus stopped breathing as that panic clutched at his heart.

They had planned to wed in secret, and Oxana had gone to find flowers for her crown, but when he came to collect her, trampled flowers were all that remained.

Romulus tightened his grip around Oxana as she slept against his chest and exhaled deeply. His thumb caressed across the fabric at her waist and pulled her closer beneath his chin.

"*She's here.*" He whispered to himself as he closed his eyes. Forcing those memories back to the dark corners of his mind.

A different memory came forward. He smiled, but the tears in his eyes remained.

"*Where you are, there I will be until the light of the gods leaves my body.*" *He promised, as Cias had tied their hands in marriage. Oxana's forehead touching his, her body still healing, and glistening with the light of the priest's work as she lay in bed.*

Cias had sworn not to tell the king. If Trejen asked questions, the soft-hearted priest would say that Romulus swore an oath of protection, which, in truth, he had. He would protect his wife until the end.

Oxana stirred, her hair rustled against his neck.

"Romulus?"

His hand froze as she said his name. Her voice was a treasure to him. So sweet and melodic that if he could, he would wear it as jewelry so she would never leave him. Her cheek rested warmly against his neck.

"Yes, my love, I'm here."

"Where am I?"

"You're here, in my arms." He tightened his grip on her waist.

"Where do I go when I'm not here?" She looked up at him, her brows furrowed as she gently caressed the surface of his knee. Anxiety swirled in her gentle blue eyes.

He swallowed as he turned his face into the warmth of her hair.

"Out there, I suppose.." he gestured to the night sky, but he was only looking at her. "I cannot think of a more beautiful and brilliant star."

His fingers followed the golden fused scars on her amber skin. She tightened her gold scarred hand around his, drawing comfort from his touch.

"Romulus?"

He smiled despite the pain in his chest.

"Yes, Queen of the Heavens?"

"Can we stay here?"

He nodded.

"For as long as you like." He kissed her brow and wanted to believe his words to be true.

"Forever then." She turned, and she found his defined jawline. All sorrow faded from his mind as she smiled at him.

Her lips met his, and he sighed as he drank in the fragrance of her skin.

Her lips dropped from his and shimmering golden flecks of light danced across her scars, the tree's healing power continuously fighting to weave her whole.

"Underneath rivers, underneath rocks, underneath roots, under under under." She murmured into his chest.

Her true self faded in and out like a dwindling fire. He drew her close to him and kissed her forehead. "Forever..."

A loud creak came from the doorway. Romulus instinctively tightened his embrace around Oxana. He snapped his head toward the sound and, without announcing his arrival, Trejen entered the gilded chamber. His uncle was the last person he wanted to see tonight.

Trejen looked shocked as he hid his bashful gaze, fixing his eyes to the floor and shuffling his boots as he awkwardly turned towards the marble fireplace. Then observed the golden figures adorning the mantelpiece with irritating scrutiny.

"My apologies for the intrusion, but we need to discuss matters of state." His uncle said without meeting Romulus' eyes. "Privately."

That word prodded him and the muscles in Romulus' body stiffened.

"It is late, uncle."

Trejen turned towards them with a chiding gaze, and in response, Romulus lifted Oxana's chin and placed a kiss on her brow.

His uncle scoffed and dug his boots into the wooden floor.

"I would rather you learn this information from me instead of the judges." Trejen sighed as he rested his hands against his temple.

Romulus tightened his grip on his wife's waist.

"Oxana will stay then. I will not send her away."

"Romulus." His uncle's voice shifted to a warning.

If his uncle wanted to fight, then Romulus was ready for battle.

He lifted the priestess in his arms and placed her feet on the floor, but he would not trouble her with his uncle's frustrations.

"Sleep well and enjoy the stars, my love." He placed her hair ornaments in her hands with a gentle squeeze. She smiled, and he knew she had already slipped behind the veil of her uncertainty.

As she left the room, her feet almost did not touch the floor, more divine than mortal.

The gods had given him treasured days with her and there was no alliance that mattered more than she.

Oxana disappeared behind the closed door, but not without a final longing look over her shoulder. His hands tightened into fists.

"We have decided, Queen Katha and I, that you should marry Princess Gailah before the end of the summer." Trejen turned from his nephew and he shifted the coals in the fireplace.

Romulus' clenched palms chilled with sweat.

"I did not agree with this arrangement. Did Gailah? I doubt she has anything to do with this."

"As your king, I have decided in the best interest of our kingdom."

"You have gone too far, uncle." His words were stale with the recurring subject of his marriage. A marriage that could no longer stand before the gods.

Romulus stood and snuffed the candles around the room as the smoke coiled around his finger tips. His uncle could make agreements, but he would not abide by them. The gods would not abide by them.

"The crown fell to you and you claimed me as heir, but I fear you are more usurper than regent." Romulus spat and forced his hands through his raven hair.

"Romulus, be reasonable. Oxana will be safe as an Acolyte. She will understand that you need to be with someone... well, someone capable of the role."

Romulus stopped and slowly turned to face Trejen while his pulse hammered in his ears.

"Capable...Is that all you care about?" He seethed. "Every day she slips deeper into that—that fog. I am tethered to her. I keep her here and I will not dishonor the gods by letting that tether slip and lose her to the abyss."

His ragged breath echoed off the walls of the room and into the night beyond the balcony. The air danced in the curtains and ruffled the tapestries embroidered with golden oak leaves curling into the sigil of his house.

Trejen was not alone in this sentiment, and he hated how the world treated his wife.

"You have done so much for her... but you do not owe her your future." Trejen's hands fumbled as his words continued to stumble.

"YOU. WERE. NOT. THERE." Romulus snarled. "You did not see the blood." He whispered, and pain shot through his jaw. "Her blood will never come off my armor. No amount of sleep will take that from my mind." He breathed unsteadily and sank into the chair beside him as his hands supported his fallen brow.

Even now, he could not shake the sight of it. Shackles and so much blood. How he found her and how they left was the only part of his memory that was unsteady. He could not find the cave once again, no matter how hard he tried. He wasted countless hours trying to find the ones who had taken her.

"She is alive because of you, but for you to make her your queen, it is unfair and unkind." Trejen's voice was resolute as he approached Romulus. "The task will devour her and it will only break her further."

"I love her." Cool rage boiled in his voice, and sent fire through his veins.

He did not trust his uncle. Trejen's lack of compassion would lead him to seek an annulment.

"Love does not play a part in this decision. We will speak no more of this. You will wed and Gailah will be your queen."

Chapter Sixteen

Torin

THRILL ROSE in his chest as he crept through the great hall and his heart pounded with the din of distant thunder. It was not the thrill of excitement that powered his movements, but the thrill of fear.

The fear of being discovered consumed him, and the image of his head on a pike tormented his thoughts. In the midst of his campaigns at sea, Torin boldly confronted the fiery destruction of enemy ships drenched in alchemist's fire, his sword never leaving his side.

Yet, this fear possessed a completely new quality to it. Long shadows hung from the grand windows lining the great hall. Even the leather of his soles echoed along the marble floor, and the swish of his cloak made his stomach seize.

Before entering the heavily guarded quarters of the mountain kingdom, Torin found a temporary shelter behind a smooth marble column. The murmur of dull conversations drifted to his ear. He shut out the sound of his pulse and listened for the guard's voices, but in a whisper, his own inner voice taunted him.

"I will see that you are thoroughly refreshed, Your Highness,"

Torin winced as his words stumbled through his mind. Heat flooded his skin. His charms or skill for flattery were not sharpened by years spent boarding ships.

He sighed through his teeth. Tonight was unlike any battle or army he faced.

He knew the guards would be weary from standing and was sure he could smell the stench of Spessian wine. Alexi successfully fulfilled his role as the generous prince, providing ample wine for the entire gathering, but Torin kept it from Gailah at all costs. The entire castle rested in an intoxicated sleep except for a few night watchmen.

He scanned the darkness for any sign of his brother. Their orders were direct and explicit, and Torin was running out of time.

Mercenaries would attack the hall of judgment at any moment. All hope of preventing the attack was gone. Gailah was running out of time. He prayed she was still awake; carrying an unconscious princess from her room was an unpardonable death sentence.

Torin swallowed as he listened again. He considered pounding on their doors and demanding their queen's protection, but he had done as much already. Every warning and letter he had sent to the mountain queen had gone unanswered.

Why would they believe the midnight panic of their enemy?

He steadied his breathing, closed his eyes, and pictured their positioning. He only wanted them out of the way, preferably unconscious. Torin did not need to add to the list of people who wanted him dead.

His figure belonged to the shadows as he crept smoothly along the wall beside the column. The wooden guarded door creaked open. Its squeaking hinges irritated him.

He paused and cursed under his breath.

The largest of the mountain princes stepped outside and Torin could picture the prince tossing him across the room or using his axe to separate his head from his shoulders. There would be no fiercer challenge than Gailah's brother.

His currently attached head rested against the cool marble pillar and he preferred it that way.

He was afraid of more than Bjorn and his ability to go unnoticed; Torin was afraid of her.

He pictured every imaginable way that his plan could turn to disaster. Gailah's unyielding presence in the ballroom caught him off guard. He had not braced himself for the woman who radiated a willful glimmer, a stubbornness that shimmered and flared despite how he shielded her from the poisoned wine. It was a tenacity that made her elusive, yet breathtaking in every sense. His fears gripped him like a clasp tightening around his pulse. Every aspect of her posed unforeseen challenges, each encounter more complex than he had anticipated.

Brutish strength and force would only push her farther from him, but how else would she react to an enemy breaking into her room? Had he lost all sense? Perhaps he had?

Of course, she would not take kindly to him telling her what to do or even go along with what he would ask of her. This was a foolish, hard-headed plan, but it was all he had. It was not the certainty of it that propelled him, but the desperation devouring him should he fail. He was prepared to let Gailah hate him for eternity; and as he thought that, something ached in his chest. If Gailah hated him, it meant he did not sit by while the rest of his house haggled for her blood. That would be enough.

That morning, he had offered his hand to spite his grandmother and the Queen of the Mountain but amid the tension and lingering silence that stretched between his empty palm and the touch of her hand, there was a deeper feeling, there was a greater reason. He was afraid of the woman strong enough to defy the eyes of the island.

The choice to clasp her hand in his became more than an act of spite —it became a flicker of hope that his fight was not in vain.

GAILAH

Gailah brooded in the privacy of her chambers with the door securely bolted.

She fiddled with the silver torc at her neck and her anger lessened with every page she turned in her journal. Ancient texts and ruins covered each page in small scraps of parchments she had discovered in the deepest part of the library.

Old alchemist's notes babbling on about dilutions and titrations.

The blotted lists of ingredients and their purposes, followed by scribblings of star positioning with their seasons in the sky for each ritual to be performed properly.

The light of the fire grew faint with every passing hour, till only embers illuminated the room.

Her silver hair hung loosely around her shoulders as her dressing gown, secured by a golden belt of twisted rope, enveloped her in a pool of sage green. The fur covered floor protected her body from the chill as she sat crossed legged before the hearth.

Shrouded in the dim glow, she scrawled her fingers across the pages. The words in front of her were intriguing and confusing all at once while the curving symbols seemed ready to climb from the pages like spiders.

Her old priests' words whispered in her mind, *Alchemists think of only two things: evil and themselves.*

Even having this collection of pages would be very upsetting to her mother, but there was no turning back. She had this aspect of her life all to herself.

No one could change that.

Well, no one on Thyssia.

The last alchemists were far away, islands away.

A small drawing of a flower bloomed across the pages.

"This seems harmless enough," she thought.

Tracing the runes with her fingers, Gailah closed her eyes and quietly mouthed the long forgotten words in the only way she knew. The pronunciation escaped her and the words sounded clunky and graceless. She pictured each petal and the shape of its leaves, then paused, letting the sound die in the air.

To her disappointment, nothing came from the incantation, no celestial powers, only the sound of candles gently flickering behind her. There was so much she wanted to know, so much the island refused to speak about.

She turned to the brush that lingered on the floor behind her. The crack in the handle made her heart ache, but not for the sake of the brush.

She reached for it and traced the sharp lines along its fracture. A deep and jagged wound severed the decorative handle. Gailah winced. Red droplets sprung from her fingertip as the edges sliced the skin of her thumb, and she brought her finger to her lips to ease the pain.

A loud screech cried out in the dark, and the brush fell from her hand.

A sudden thud rattled her balcony door, and she flinched as she drew her arms around her torso. Beyond her window, the deepest shade of blue stained the velvet sky in the darkest hour of night.

Her pulse trembled in her neck.

Gailah scrambled to the outer door, scattering the ancient texts and pressing an ear to the wood. After a moment, when only silence greeted her ears, she wrapped her fingers around the circular iron handle. The hinges rattled as she sent a prayer of protection to the kindest of the nine.

Her exhale wavered, and she peered around the door.

A large red hawk hunkered on the marble balcony floor. Soft ragged breaths came from its open beak.

Gailah sighed with sad relief and slipped through the opening and into the open night. She kneeled down against the cool balcony floor and lifted the bird in the excess of her robe. The bird flinched as Gailah inspected the hawk's wing.

The bird's eyes were frantic, but not filled with pain. Its feathers amazed her, speckles of maroon and beige along each silken feather. The beautiful bird seemed unharmed by the impact.

"*How odd for it to strike a doo*r.."

She thought as she examined the second wing for fractures. The wind tossed Gailah's hair from her exposed shoulder and a chill ribboned down her spine.

"You poor dear." She soothed the rustled feathers around her neck.

"She's fine, I assure you. We practiced." A deep, timbered voice called out from behind her.

Her heart pounded against her ribs. She recognized the boisterous rhythm of his voice. Gailah spun as she searched the breadth of the balcony.

A hooded figure basked in the shadows behind her outer door and when he pulled back his hood, the moonlight removed any doubt of his identity. Torin's silver hair shimmered beneath the blueish night sky as he leaned against the wall of the keep. She could not find his eyes in the darkness but every muscle along his arms and neck reeked of self confidence.The onyx steel of his breastplate hid him among the shadows and heap of rope rested at his feet. A stout knot was tied to the balcony and a double pronged hook clawed into the stone beside him.

"You!" she spat in frustrated disgust.

Emerging from his hiding place, Torin whistled sharply to summon the bird, but Gailah practically threw the bird back at him.

It gracefully sliced through the air and landed on Torin's shoulder with a look that was almost smug at their mutual cleverness.

"This is Kelligh" He introduced his accomplice, then gave the bird a sliver of meat.

"If you do not leave this very moment, I'll—" Gailah's fury peaked as he ignored her with a side step, then the Spessian crown prince walked through the open balcony doors and into her chambers.

All the while, Kelligh contently perched upon his shoulder while he examined her room with curiosity.

Like falling snow, the journal pages littered about on the breeze that filled the room. She slammed the doors behind her and the pages dropped to the floor.

Torin walked about the room with his hands clasped behind his back, almost admiring the decorations. Gailah stood dumbfounded and horrified at the man who stood before her.

"Your apartments are finer than ours.." His pacing stopped, and he looked on approvingly at the mother of pearl inlaid wood that surrounded her bed.

Just then he toed one of the loose pages from her journal. Torin squatted down to retrieve the leaflet and only the armor he wore creaked with his movements.

Disbelief shuddered through her.

"Does the possibility of losing your head not bother you?!" She aggressively gestured to the closed balcony door. "I don't suppose you would use the actual door like any proper person would. Return to where you came from! Dissolve back into your shadows before anyone else finds you here!" Her voice was an enraged whisper.

She hurriedly gathered up the papers scattered around the room.

"When people threaten to kill you on more days than they do not, those kinds of threats no longer carry the same weight... What is this?" There was an intriguing lilt to his voice and, to her horror, he was examining the book he had plucked from the floor.

Torin's eyes widened, as if he knew exactly what he was looking at.

"*Alchemy...*"

She snatched it from his grip.

"Don't touch that!"

She shoved the papers inside her journal.

"That is forbidden."

He said with an unsettled line between his dark brows. Torin moved for the chair before the hearth. The prince signaled to his red breasted hawk to find another place to roost.

Kelligh landed on a small bookcase and used her beak to preen her feathers. Torin had propped his leather clad feet in front where he sat before the fireplace. She could not believe her eyes and she hurriedly tucked her journal away beneath her furs.

If the tome had not been ancient and precious, she would have considered cracking him over the head with it. With white knuckled anger, she tightened the strings of her dressing gown and stalked towards him. He spotted the cracked hair brush by the entryway and he started to speak, but Gailah grabbed the top of the chair above his shoulder.

The roughness of the wood supported her grip, and she dropped her head low enough so Torin could see the anger in her eyes. Her frustration radiated into his face as her silver hair fell forward and grazed the prince's legs.

In the same way he had blockaded her earlier, her hair flanked him on either side.

"Get. Out. Of. My. Chair." Her voice simmered in a whispered hiss. "I have every mind to call my guards right now and drag your miserable excuse for..." She stopped as the prince raised a finger to her lips and that would have been enough to warrant a bite, but his face shifted.

His grey eyes softened and the muscles around his jawline feathered.

She stared back into a mirror of silver. Their colorings were so similar, save for the tawny shade of his skin and the sharp hue of his eyes.

"Go ahead..." This time there was no arrogance in his eyes."But you have not asked why I'm here...."

"Fine." She spat in a staccato hush. Her gritted teeth reminded her of Karak."Why did you trick me and so rudely invade my chambers?"

The dull glow of the candlelight brought an amber hue to his grey irises. She noticed the lines harden in his face.

"To give you a choice." He said with that same severity she had heard in the ballroom.

The pause that hung in the air amplified the crackling fireplace. Their gazes fixed as they seemed to sift through each other's thoughts.

"What?" Her eyes narrowed.

"My Grandmother and Queen have made a bargain, a contract with cruel people. A bargain that involves kidnapping you." He said this without breaking his stare.

Her mind spun wildly as her chest tightened.

"I've arrived here first simply to steal you away..." Her mouth hung agape, and a sneer rose on her face.

"I'm not sure what's more arrogant? That you thought it would be simple, or that you thought it possible?" Gailah's eyebrows nearly touched as she narrowed her gaze.

Torin scoffed but remained steadfast, a conqueror in her armchair. He shook his head as he looked at her from hem to sternum.

"Oh please, only a few steps left before you're on horseback and halfway back to your beautiful mountain. Though I have never been, I hear it is lovely this time of year. I think *simple* is an overestimation at this point." He stood with self-satisfaction and firmly planted his leather soles as he adjusted his sapphire cloak.

His sea serpent broach practically flicked its tongue at her as she gazed into its small sapphire eyes.

"Let's go!" He tossed a second cloak at her from under his arm. The heap of sapphire fabric nearly slammed into her face.

She held out the Spessian cloak by the tips of her fingers and looked at him in disgust. She found sapphire blue to be such an odious color.

"I do not believe you! But please let me call for my guards or my brothers and you can explain yourself to them? Leave!" She waved towards the balcony again.

Prince Torin did not budge, but crossed his arms across his breastplate.

She exhaled with annoyance, then filled her lungs like a sail of a ship. An unladylike yell rose in her throat, but before she could scream, Torin flew across the room.

He quickly covered her mouth. His grey flecked eyes widened as he stood face to face with Gailah.

His spine hunched slightly as he loomed over her with gritted teeth. Her nostrils flared with angry breath.

In her eyes she hoped he read *"HOW DARE YOU"* as fire rose across her cheeks.

He brought his mouth against her ear.

"They will come either way. Leave with me now, or wait and see if my queen's men will be so well-mannered."

She shivered and considered biting him again, but he lowered his hands as if she were an unbroken mare.

"Well-mannered? Your grandmother is a fiend." She scowled.

"True, but that does not change your situation, Your Highness." He sighed, then rolled his shoulders in frustration. "I need you to find some flicker of a reason to trust me... I will only leave if you leave by my side." Before she could retort with the slew of curses that perched on her tongue, she paused.

"*You have no duty to me.*"

His words from the ballroom flickered through her mind. He spoke to her now with that same pain-filled voice.

"*Please.*"

It was softer this time, a raw and desperate sound that did not fit the man who stood before her.

"Why do you care what happens to me? I am nothing to you?" She asked in an unsteady whisper. Torin's eyes widened and his shoulders sagged.

"If you choose to stay, then you must know they will kill me and they will take you. Your Highness, *please*, I am here because no one else is..."

The honest pang in his voice frightened her.

Shouts rang out in the corridor. Gailah's heart sank as swords collided behind the stone walls. The hope she held within her chest shattered as the sound of bloodshed drew closer.

Death filled the air and Gailah knew fate would force her hand.

The men who came to take her were already here.

Torin's eyes widened and his throat bobbed as he studied her face. He inhaled sharply and drew his sword; the shouts grew louder as Torin walked for the inner door. The door leading to the frey of blood and chaos.

He was telling the truth.

Her thoughts tumbled frantically and her palms sweat against her linen gown. Both outcomes were equally unknown and terrifying. Flee with a stranger or wait for mercenaries to tear her from her room.

What of her brothers? Her people?

"Let's go!" She snagged the back of his cloak before he reached the chamber door.

There was no time for Gailah to think, but out of instinct, she lurched for her journal, its pages still strewn about the floor. Her fingers grazed the pages, but just before she could grasp it, he jerked her hand towards the balcony door.

"Can you climb?" He asked as relief splattered his features.

Torin threw open the door to the balcony, and the breeze tossed strands of his silver hair across his brow.

"Absolutely not! That was your plan?" She masked the panic in her voice with sarcasm, then took one last look at her chambers before he pulled them into the night.

The sound of bloodshed only echoed louder against the stone hallways. Kelligh's screech drifted through the starlit sky as the bird spiraled ahead of them.

Taking the cloak from her hands, he swooped it around her shoulders as the warm linen rippled across her skin. As he secured the cloak in a frustrated knot, she noticed how his fingers tied it with a shipmaster's grace.

"I expected as much..." He pulled at the leather straps across his chest. "Something for you to hold on to."

"Absolutely not!" The mortifying notion spread across her face in shock as the prince steadied himself against the railing. They were going to die.

He tugged on the rope to test his weight on the pillars he secured it to.

This was a terrible idea.

"Death is indifferent to propriety, Your Highness." He waved her to come towards him, towards the railing, where he swung his leg over the side. "I cannot toss you down.."

Her feet dug in again as the crisp air rose through the delicate white and sage fabric of her dressing gown.

The broken mountain carved a shadowed silhouette against the stark and clear horizon. Her home called to her through the moonlight. Waves of shadowy blue fields rippled in the distance. The pang of wanting anything familiar filled her heart with loneliness.

She took a single step forward.

A foolish and trusting step forward. She looked at Torin as he finished tying a rope to his waist. Warning churned through her.

Please.

A shrill groan seeped through the walls of her room and through to the balcony.

There was no time for doubt.

Torin blinked rapidly in surprise as she quickly lifted herself over the railing like a deer in flight. She clung to the balcony with hands that fumbled and shook while her robes beat wildly above the darkness.

Gailah's silver hair coiled in swirls around her while she shuffled toward him along the stone lip at her feet. She reached for him and again, his gentleness surprised her, the strength of his hands instantly stopped the shaking in her fingers.

He guided them to hook beneath the leather straps that held her tightly against him. The belts dug into the softness of her hand. She did not care. She would hold to them as if they were a second skin if it meant not tumbling to her death.

She rested her head on his armored back. The metal's cool surface felt like ice against her cheek. He planted his feet on the stone wall beside them, then wrapped the rope around his arms.

“Keep your eyes on the mountain, Princess, it is a long way dow—” Torin’s words died as splintering wood and shattering hinges screamed through the air.

As the wind rushed to greet them, her stifled scream burned behind her gritted teeth. Gailah’s fingers tightened and her heart beat wildly as he dropped them from the view of the balcony.

Chapter Seventeen

Bjorn

A TRAIL of blood dripped from Bjorn's axe as he forced open the doors of the great hall.

Bodies of mountain born and the men who attacked them littered the corridors of the royal apartments. At his feet, two of their guards, two honorable men, stared past him with their throat's slit. The rush of the attack burned under his skin in an unshakable hum.

He retired shortly after inspecting the night watch, as his head still thumped from too much wine. After collapsing onto his bed, Bjorn had fallen into a thick nightmarish slumber, so when the attack began, there was no difference between his nightmare and his reality.

When his door was forcefully kicked open, he thrashed awake with an unprecedented level of disorientation, feeling strangely detached from everything around him. His eyes rolled around in his head and the torch light seared with pain.

Bjorn had neglected to don any armor, for there was no time, barely time to reach for his axe as the men from the forest, from his dreams, descended upon him.

Even now, as he stood amid the chaos of the hall of judgment, the glint of his axe was enough to force his eyes closed. Bjorn rubbed the temples of his brow as every sound pierced through his mind with the gentleness of a dagger.

As he spat, the metallic flavor of blood marked his lips, though it wasn't his own. He had survived simply because his muscles knew battle better than anything else. His mind may have abandoned him, but his body only needed the touch of his axe to understand.

Gailah was gone.

Panic and terror churned behind his eyes. Bjorn arrived in her room before everyone else, a room filled with wild men tearing Gailah's belongings to pieces. He could still see the milky eyed shock on the raider's face as he stumbled through the doorway. On the battlefield, Bjorn fought with purpose, but here he fought to quiet the hammering rage in his skull.

The guards meticulously combed through every corner of the castle, praying that Gailah might have discovered a hiding spot, but Gailah was nowhere to be found.

With each passing search, the realization settled furiously in his chest.

His sister was gone.

Selfishly, when Katha asked, he volunteered to bring Trejen to his mother's quarters. He knew Aerin and his mother were safe, but he did not know of the fate of the Autumn Kingdom.

Senna could fight, but the odds were not in the favor of the fiery forest dweller. Bjorn had struggled to take down the mercenaries that broke down their doors. They all bore the same markings. He had seen them before on the men who had slain his father, the same runes from the cemetery. The markings of an alchemist.

He wanted her safe, but he needed more answers from her.

Courtiers hurried about the great hall with their bedside oil lamps in hand and he parted through them like flocks of nervous birds. Discerning moonlight poured in through the giant windows, casting darkness around the columns. He scanned the crowd for bright copper hair or even her burley Lord Father, but Senna was nowhere to be found.

The muscles in his jaw tensed.

The mercenaries had made confusion their weapon as they split their attack amongst all the wings of the castle.

"Your Highness? Is it safe?" Someone cried out from the crowd.

He paused as all words of comfort escaped him.

Safe.

He no longer knew its meaning. Their frightened faces looked at him, but he did not stop.

His feet lead him to the chambers of the Autumn kingdom. Their doors hung broken as pools of blood stained the floor, leading to gold cloaked guards.

Their watchmen laid slain in the same pattern as their knights–a direct and lethal slash.

A lone knight stood in the hallway, his eyes wide and face pale. He was young, too young to be comfortable killing and his sword hung awkwardly in his hands.

"Take me to your king," Bjorn called.

The guard watched with frozen eyes as he stared at the red running down his blade. Bjorn felt a tug in his chest.

"Boy, are you injured?'

"No.. No, Your Highness." The boy's voice shook as he struggled to sheath his sword.

"Good, your king lives and you live. Your sword will need tending." He slowly eased the sword back into the sheath at the young guard's side. "Show me to your king."

"This way, Your.." He said distantly as he nodded further down the hall.

His hands shook beneath a cloak that was too large for his shoulders.

Bjorn placed a hand on his shoulder. "You protected your people and they will never know what that cost you."

Trejen stood surrounded by generals, dressed in simple trousers and a loose tunic.

No crown of golden oak leaves contrasting the silver at his temples, including Lord Barrock, whose eyes were puffy from sleep and bewilderment showed in every other aspect of his dress.

The older king's eyes widened as he saw Bjorn enter. If he were not the son of a queen, Bjorn would have looked more madman than a prince.

Blood adorned every part of his body, from his beard to his boots. He did not bow. There was no reason for formalities. He saw the same panic rise in the king's eyes.

"Your Mother?" Trejen pushed through the men surrounding him.

"Unharmed, but she requests your presence. My sister is gone. The entire palace is to be searched." Bjorn said. His words commanded the attention of the room. He turned to face Lord Barrock. "Are all your kin alright?"

The general shook his head. "Senna fled when the fighting broke out."

Bjorn hid his sharp inhale as tension spread through his limbs. Her body, he hated the thought of it, was not among the fallen. He returned his attention to the king, but his mind crumbled and dread filled his stomach.

Where was Senna?

Trejen turned and placed a hand on his shoulder, but the king paused.

A strange expression flashed across his face, and he braced himself against the prince. The lines around Trejen's eyes creased in a painful wince.

"I know our people are safe and I will see to the people of the mountain. Lord Barrock, you guide them in my absence" Trejen returned his attention to Bjorn. "Show me to your mother."

Once he delivered Trejen to the mountain court, Bjorn dismissed himself to continue his search throughout the castle.

Bjorn stood in the silence of the stables while the sticky scent of grain and musty animal fur dulled his senses. There were no signs of struggle or missing horses from their stalls.

Gailah loved horses more than any other animal, even Karak. Horses in dull slumber filled each row of stalls. No torches remained, and he scoured the darkness for any sign of his sister. He hoped he would find her here, hiding amongst the animals. Hiding from the bloodshed that followed their family like a winter hungry jackal.

Delusion stirred the embers of hope in his mind–hope that his sister was *safe*.

With his father's dying breath, he promised he would protect their family.

There were fewer and fewer places left to search, and with every empty room, the prince felt that hope grow dim.

Ahead of him, in the cold blackness, the stable gates were wide open, with only eastern wood filling the horizon beyond its threshold. Crouching down, he noticed a single set of horse tracks that led from a separate row of stalls.

The stables belonged to the Spessian Riverlands.

"Just the prince I was looking for," a voice called out from the dark emptiness of the stables behind him.

"Show yourself." Bjorn said and slipped a dagger from his belt, instead of the axe heavy across the width of his back.

"I am not your enemy." The voice was male, young, but old enough to be a man. Bjorn could see the slim outline of his figure. "I have valuable information for you, but please, kill me before I tell you where they have taken your sister." Prince Alexi, second son of house Spessia, emerged from the shadows.

Alexi's raised hands seemed to mock Bjorn as he wagged his fingers.

"How would you know that?" Bjorn seethed as he rose from examining the dirt.

He loomed over the shorter silver haired prince with his dagger still tightly gripped in his fingers.

Alexi's smile sickened Bjorn.

"My brother has her. Your sister is in more danger than you can imagine." Alexi's face was cold and calculated as he stepped around Bjorn and into the hallway of the stable.

A smoldering rage burned beneath Bjorn's skin. He pictured Torin's face as the eldest Spessian prince had watched Gailah dance the entire evening.

Bjorn grabbed Alexi by his collar and with rage-filled ease, he lifted the smaller prince's feet from the floor.

"Take me to her and if your brother has harmed her, then I will kill him where he stands." He pinned the prince beneath his dagger. "If you're lying, then you will know a worse fate for wasting my time."

"I agree, and I'm happy to be of help in that effort." He wheezed and Bjorn shifted his weight as he dangled him against a stall doorway. Alexi used his fingertips to push Bjorn's weapon away from his chest.

Bjorn froze.

He noticed Alexi had had time to dawn a chest plate and gauntlets. Something no one else in the castle had the luxury of and something no one else had been sober enough to do.

"You would slay your own kin?" The cunning schemes of the Spessian prince did not surprise Bjorn. Their people were not to be trusted.

"Slay? No, but a happy accessory to his demise. Let me help you find your sister and I will let you do all the slaying. However, if the opportunity presents itself..." Alexi said with smug confidence, his hands still raised in defense. Bjorn lowered the prince's feet to the floor.

"And how does betraying your own brother benefit you?" Bjorn lowered his dagger cautiously

"I thought you, a fellow second son, would understand? Torin is an arrogant, empty-headed shell who thinks of nothing but himself. He stole your sister and will take anything that he wants." Alexi was no longer speaking to Bjorn but to the air.

The Spessian cooled his anger and resumed his usual bravado.

"Now, with Torin out of the way, I will get what I want."

"You would be king." Bjorn whispered as he shook his head.

He wondered if Aerin knew how lucky he was not to have a kinslayer in their house.

"Now you understand..." Alexi said with an insulting smile. "Let us help each-other get what we both want."

Alexi extended his arm to seal their bargain in a warrior's promise, as a horse whinnied in the dark.

Bjorn whipped his attention to the stables of the Autumn king. In the quiet of the shadows. A horse and rider shielded themselves in the darkness, unaware of the men watching them.

"Stop!" Bjorn called out, and the sound reverberated in his ears.

The rider froze at the sound of his voice. He thundered towards the hooded figure while his pulse beat in cadence with his steps.

The rider frantically climbed into the saddle and urged the horse from a walk into a canter in a direct charge.

"Stop!" Bjorn extended his hands, finding a mix of horsehair and leather as his body slammed into the horse's thick neck.

Alexi, far more concerned about his own fate, threw himself backwards. Bjorn's body shook as the horse continued to press forward.

"I am not your subject to command!" The rider cried out.

"Senna..." He exhaled and shook his head.

Horse riding leather had replaced her lilac gown. She was here, she was *safe*, but she was running.

His heart tightened.

"Let go!" She commanded from her horse. Her hood remained in place as she tugged at the reins.

"Who is this flighty spirit?" Alexi asked. Rising from the cloud of dust, he winced at the cuts on his hands.

"I don't deal with Spessians, let alone one of their princes." Senna sneered at the silver-haired prince. Her horse shook its head at the tension on the reins, but Bjorn held his grip.

"Senna, it's not safe. We've only cleared the castle. I cannot protect you from what awaits you out there," Bjorn said.

"I have everything I need and I will not waste my days waiting to die for royalty." She urged the horse forward, but the horse's neck fought against the resistance.

Bjorn's hands fell from the horse's bridle as the beast cried out in confusion.

They held each-other's gaze for a long moment. His eyes did not leave her face, but from beneath the hood, he could see the fear in her eyes.

What about him was more frightening than what awaited her in the darkness?

"Senna, *please—*"

Senna's heels found her horse's side and, without looking behind her, she galloped out of the stable. The wind threw back her hood as she rode into the night. He watched that shimmer of auburn until she disappeared beneath into the trees of the eastern wood.

He closed his eyes and prayed that the nine would protect Gailah and Senna both.

Chapter Eighteen

Torin

Gailah rode before him, and his arms wrapped around her on either side as they raced towards the Broken Mountain.

The muscles in his neck ached as his head rested above her shoulder while the last biting chills of winter hung in the air. Each draft stung the skin across his face and his inner desires moved him to her like a moth to an open flame. His head sheltered in the warmth of her hair. Fragrant oils lingered on her skin and they clouded his sense of direction with every gust as the floral scent washed over him. Her fingers gripped a tuft of mane and she ducked with the wind like any true rider would do.

He pulled his head back from her as his boorishness twisted with guilt. Torin let the cold wind knock some sense into his skull. She never intended to be here, let alone anywhere with him. Gailah deserved to feel safe somewhere, and he wanted her to feel safe with him.

The moon slipped lower into the trees, and shadows formed like arching hands across the ground.

Each pounding thud worsened with the hours that passed as they fled from the center of the island. Torin hated horses. Ships were the far better form of travel.

The strained breathing of their horse called out into the night, and it worried him. Torin braced Gailah's waist as he slowed their gait. Her breath shuddered through her frame just before she turned her shoulder into his chest. Only enough to look up at him through the pitch black of the forest.

He could feel the vaporous warmth of her exhale in the bitter spring air.

"Are you warm enough?" He withdrew his arms from the reins and began loosening his cloak.

"This.. this is warm to me. My family's castle drips with ice on the mountain, so the cold tells me I'm coming home."

A second puff of warm air fluttered behind her words.

The longing in her voice ached through him. How her voice weakened at the mention of the place she belonged, something the prince himself did not know.

He resumed his grip around the reins and fought the desire to draw himself closer to her while the wind drained the life from his skin. He let his mare continue at a walking pace, for both their sakes.

"Are you warm enough?" She asked, as the hood of her cloak rested around her shoulders.

Torin was relieved that the princess could not see the color of his face.

Of course he was cold–as a prince from the Riverlands, snow never came and winter was simply warm rain. The intensity of her stare, piercing through the shadows, sent shivers down his spine. He pretended the chill did not gnaw at his exposed skin and that the warmed air from her breath was not a beckoning embrace.

His miscalculations were obvious now. All of his planning had not anticipated the distracting potency of her presence.

They moved forward through the quiet. Torin fixated on anything besides the floral scent of her hair or the warmth that tormented him, smothering the part of himself that relished in them both.

"I do not trust you."

He stiffened in his saddle, but her words did not surprise him.

"Tell me the real reason you wanted to kidnap me? If you can even call it that? But I do not trust you."

He wondered if she would laugh, if she knew that her mother had rejected his proposal months before the gathering, or if that would make her more afraid.

Perhaps it was out of mercy for her daughter that Katha did not concede her to his protection? Who would entrust someone so lovely and alive to the house that carried the banner of death?

He had traded the knowledge of his grandmother's schemes in hopes of an alliance, but Katha did not believe him. The queen had accused him of jealousy and that his warnings were a simple trick to win Gailah's hand. Torin was many things, a scoundrel's excuse for a prince but never a liar.

He would see Gailah safe within the walls of her castle and with that, he hoped that would be proof enough to the mountain queen she was wrong about him and they would topple his grandmother's reign. How he wished time had granted him the chance to know her during happier times. She would never forgive him now.

Lost in the labyrinth of his thoughts, he did not realize that Gailah still looked up at him. He swallowed as she blinked her eyes with curiosity, and he stumbled for an answer to her questions.

Her borrowed, oversized cloak devoured her. Torin tightened the grip on his reins before he spoke.

"I am a prince in need of allies, powerful ones and preferably wealthy ones. I can find both conditions under your family's banner." He retorted quickly and more defensively than he would have liked. He shifted on his saddle, leaning forward to read her gaze. "To let mercenaries steal you away is hardly a way to make allies, Your Highness."

"Why is the *noble* house Spessia in need of allies?"

"Spessia needs no allies, but I do, and so do you. My grandmother refuses to step aside, and her choices have jeopardized the safety of my people."

They stopped for a moment at a crossing in the woods.

"Like this, for example, I'd prefer not to be fed to your mother's bear. My grandmother's choices have jeopardized my safety as well." He smirked as he pressed forward along the wooded trail, but shuddered inwardly at the thought of her beast.

The breaker of bones, a title the bear had earned alongside the king consort of the mountain. Torin knew the battle fame of King Freyden well. Every child raised during Sefti's wars did.

She waved her hand in the air in frustration.

"Your grandmother did not force you to trick your way into my chambers, coerce me, under duress I might add, to leave IN my dressing gown and ride off with someone I only just met yesterday. Am I missing anything, Your Highness?" Gailah said angrily, and he wondered if her cheeks flushed like they had earlier, but he quickly silenced the thought. The dense forest hid the sound of her voice and it did not carry into the night saturated trees.

"Only the part where hired mercenaries were about to forcefully and, most likely, violently kidnap you. I merely skipped the violent kidnapping and got things over with." He flicked his reins as he made a turn off the heavily worn trail. "We both get what we want."

"Oh, and what would that be? What do I get for all of this?" Honey coated sarcasm dripped from her words.

"Not violently kidnapped."

He kicked his horse into a faster gait.

"Oh, so only the nonviolent kind, then?"

"I saw only two outcomes...Please know this is far better than what could have happened." He shook the thoughts from his mind.

"I still could have you hanged," she snapped.

"You could, but I'd hope that you'd think better of me." His stomach soured.

"Bring me home, and perhaps I will forgive you." Gailah narrowed her eyes and brushed the horse's neck. Her silver hair fell forward in tumbled rings around her face.

Torin found her stillness unraveling with each inhale and exhale of her breath.

Chapter Nineteen

Katha

Katha rang her hands in the fabric of her nightdress as the dressing gown flowed over her shoulders in feathery plumes of fabric. Her pulse pounded in the veins of her forehead.

She paced the floors of her bedroom as heat drained from the soles of her bare feet. Fear calcified in her tired body with every frantic step. In the seconds that followed the ambush on the hall of judgment, Katha had raced to Gailah's room, but at the sight of the fractured door, the queen fell to her knees.

Among the furniture scattered about her daughter's room, the wind billowed through the balcony doors as it tossed the bedpost curtains in unfurling waves.

Katha's inner voice cried out to her husband.

Freyden, I've failed her.

Bile rose in her throat as her eyes welled with tears. Katha wrapped her arms around her body and returned to her rooms in a lifeless trance as knights stormed in every direction. Karak padded in anxious circles around the breadth of Katha's room.

The silken touch of Gailah's hair burned in her memory, and the sweet scent of rose oil lingered on Katha's hands. All of it mocked her as she stared into the fire with sodden, restless eyes.

A single set of footsteps entered the room. She looked up and Trejen's almond-shaped eyes found her. Her heart ached at the familiar shade of brown that knew her soul better than any alive.

"Are you injured?" He asked, taking her arm in his.

She shook her head as despair buried her voice.

Trejen's face shifted, and his eyes scanned the room. His touch confused her, but there was no space for anything other than the fire that burned behind her eyes–a fire that had been lit long ago, a fire from the depths of the mountain.

"Gailah is gone." Her voice surfaced in a fury filled sob. She gripped the fabric at his chest and Trejen's eyes widened.

Her heart tightened as her fingers clutched the linen of his tunic and shook against his collarbone as her mind descended into freefall.

He cupped her face as tears flowed beneath his fingers.

"Katha," his voice hardly a whisper.

He was her oldest friend, but he had never felt more a stranger to her. Twenty-five years was enough to distance him, but not enough to erase what he had meant to her. She could not utter his name, for the sound would be unbearable, and she had nothing left to break.

Her bones ached with a rage that knew no bodily escape. That anger reawakened a side of the queen she had not known in decades: the Queen of the Chasm.

"They took her. She is gone." There was something hoarse and feral in her voice. "They have murdered my husband and now they have taken my daughter."

Trejen's calloused and time worn hands cupped her face.

"Katha,"

Her eyes searched his face as panic overwhelmed her in dredging waves, pulling her deeper into a vortex of fear. The world was too close around the periphery of her vision. The sound of her short, ragged breathing clawed at her mind.

Trejen framed her face with his hands, keeping her eyes on him.

"Kat,"

Pain seared through her heart. He alone called her that.

"We will find her, and your nightmare will be no more. We will bring them to justice. Do not let them break your spirit my…"

His words disappeared into the night as she felt years of lost time flood her senses. Old memories followed by years of unresolved hurt filled the space between them. He chose a life apart from her; she would not cling to him. She pulled away from his embrace and wiped the tears from her eyes.

She pulled herself up from the floor and smoothed the fabric of her nightgown, and drew her furs around her shoulders. The despair that clamped onto her heart gave way and, in its place, that fire poured out in molten ire.

Her posture shifted, and her joints stiffened. The path before her was unmistakably clear.

"Bring Regulus to me."

Romulus

His wife was safe. Trejen stormed through his bedroom door with madness in his eyes as Romulus returned from Oxana's chamber. The attack had not breached the twisting halls of the tower where the Autumn court resided.

"They have taken Gailah. We must join the hunt for your betrothed." Trejen caught Romulus by his sleeve.

"Do not speak her name." The prince jerked his arm free, bringing his face within a breath of his uncle.

The muscles in his uncle's face burned with exhaustion. Romulus wondered if Trejen had ever slept a day in his life.

"I have sacrificed everything, everything to protect your throne. Many rose for your crown, but I have protected your legacy. This is how you thank me?" Trejen's jaw hardened as he dropped his voice into a whisper.

The room emptied of any source of life.

Not even the birds sang in the darkness of night beyond the window. His uncle's resentment moved through every twisted word and unspoken glare. Torch light illuminated the hardest lines of his king's face.

"Who asked this of you, Uncle? I surely did not." Romulus sneered.

Trejen gawked at him and threw his hands in the air.

"I do not ask this of you because I want to hurt you Romulus, I am protecting you."

Trejen's hands found his nephew's shoulders.

"Protecting me? You're asking me to set aside the woman I love. The only person who means more to me than all else," Romulus spat, and he pushed Trejen's hand away.

His feet stumbled backwards against the stone floor while the distance between them only grew as he moved further towards the empty hallway. Trejen followed him as he struggled to keep pace.

"Romulus! Romulus, wait!" Trejen called out as his voice wheezed.

"I am protecting you from my mistakes." The king whispered, and he gripped Romulus tightly by the wrist.

Romulus's skin rose in thistle pricks across his flesh. The prince rolled his shoulders as he fought against the lion's roar beneath his skin.

"Your mistakes? Or the life you did not get to live? I cannot live it for you."

Romulus stopped, his heart filled with apathetic ice.

Trejen's body heaved as he supported himself on the circular handle of the decoratively carved door.

His uncle's eyelids hung low against his cheeks, with too much white showing beneath his irises.

"Romulus, I am dying." Trejen rasped. With shaking hands, he loosed the side of his tunic and, to Romulus' horror, Trejen bore a raised weeping lesion across his ribs.

It was a wound visibly angry and ugly. Purple veins of torturous dying tissue spread from the wound at his side.

"Poison."

Romulus felt something for his uncle, but it was not love but pity in its crudest form.

"Then let the priests heal you."

His brow softened at the sight of the desperation in his uncle's eyes.

"No, Cias has tried everything. It draws its power from an unknown source. Our magic cannot fight it when the tree is already weakening."

"Who would dare poison a king?" The prince responded. His tongue was thick with confusion.

Had the poison gone to his mind? Romulus thought.

"My mistakes have brought this upon me. The tree is dying because I am the poison of our people." Trejen spoke quickly and something eased in his uncle's face.

He covered the wound at his side as he moved them into a corner, out of sight.

"No one must know, do not sully your legacy with my failure. If anyone knows about this, then our alliance with Katha's people will dissolve into fields of blood."

That ice extended from Romulus' heart to every corner of his body.

"What have you done?"

Romulus pulled away from his uncle.

"It is what I could not do." Trejen was no longer looking at his nephew. His memories had clouded his eyesight. "The day King Freyden came to discuss the boundaries of the forest." He paused and struggled with his words. "Our trees are taking more and more of their land." The king's fingers rested between his eyebrows. "We argued and could not agree on the new borders. He left with no resolve, but in my anger, I did not warn him. Before he arrived, the scouts had alerted us to an encampment of raiders on the edge of the forest. Freyden did not know this, and I knew the raiders would outnumber them. I directed the king there, I sent them to the gaping jaws of death!" Trejen's continence fell. "Jealousy blinded me. The guilt I felt overwhelmed me, but I arrived too late… far too late as the king consort's heart had already stopped beating, but my jealousy earned me this.."

He gestured to the wound at his side.

"A raider laid dying but not yet dead. His dagger found me out before anyone else could."

Romulus' stomach dropped, and he could no longer breathe.

"Your jealousy would have me marry to absolve you of your sins?"

Trejen stared at him for a long moment as his lips drew into a firm line.

"Yes. To protect our people, should Katha discover the truth of her husband's death, you must protect our people."

The prince wanted to strike his uncle down, to throw the dying man in front of him to his knees, but he stayed his hand. It was not for himself, but for the man he once loved as his father.

"You have imprisoned me, Uncle, Gailah and Oxana too. You may trap me and force me to do your bidding, but I cannot free your conscience."

Chapter Twenty

Gailah

Dawn eclipsed in the distance, small rabbits and song birds scattered along the edge of the great forest. Sluggish thuds of exhaustion rocked her forward in the saddle as their horse prodded along the trail winding ahead of them.

Soft beams warmed the earth in hues of red and orange, bathing the forest in waves of fiery daylight.

Torin's rigid frame softened as they approached the Broken Mountain and the moon disappeared below the horizon. His arms held her in the saddle as she supported herself against him. They swayed silently in the morning light, and her eyes yearned for sleep.

Torin's silence unsettled her. His eyes were tired and his shoulders slouched forward. She ransacked her mind for something to say to shake the silence from the forest.

"Whose horse is this?" Gailah called out, startling the prince.

"What?" He asked, turning in the saddle enough to see the princess's face. "Oh, not sure, really? He belongs to my people, so assuming we get you back to your mountain, the horse will guide me home. They always do."

She nodded, but tried to assure the beast of his safety as she guided her fingers through its mane. She was sorry for the beast but also experienced a strange sense of camaraderie with the horse she patted, they were both stolen away in the night.

Torin tightened his grip on the reins and Gailah felt it through his arms around her waist.

The prince cleared his throat.

"I must ask, when your mother has forbidden alchemy, why do you carry pages with their markings?" Torin asked as he scanned the horizon of the glade in front of them.

But as she looked back at him, she caught a hint of suspicion in his eyes.

"How would you know what alchemy runes look like if it's forbidden?" She replied with a hidden smirk.

He sighed, and he tried to wipe the exhaustion from his face.

"Because I was the first prince to receive their awakening. I remember them well. Alchemists are not to be trusted. Spessia will never forget what your grandfather created."

The mountain born would not forget what house Spessia did to her great aunt, but she would not hold him accountable for the actions of his predecessors. She chewed the inside of her cheek and regretted her words.

"What do you intend to do with your markings? Please wait until I am long gone from your mountain to summon anything."

"No. No, you misunderstand me. I cannot do anything with them, but I want to help people, to make the suffering I see out there less, I suppose."

A twinge of loneliness rocked through her chest as the rocky chasm looked back at her through the trees.

"There is more to it than all that. I want to have a purpose. I do not know what, but I want something else besides all of this." She gestured to the bits of finery that still clung to the twisted golden belt of her dressing gown. "To create a legacy greater than the land and gold attached to me."

"Something else... hmm" He sounded almost amused as he watched her smooth dust from her bedclothes. He looked down at her and paused as he studied her eyes. "Well, let me know if you find it."

She arched to see the look on his face.

"Have you ever thought of something beyond putting a golden crown on your head?"

"Golden? Our crown isn't a golden one, Princess. Onyx is the only color I dream of." He said with a brief chuckle in his tone. "No, I have thought about life beyond kingship, but it terrifies me. What is a king without a crown?"

"Just a man." She said as she looked over the hills and valleys leading to the mountain keep.

Her home.

Thick dew clung to the grass in crystals of light that gleamed in the softness of morning. Closer to the forest edges, frost cowered in the shadow covered leaves.

"I don't believe you've ever been 'just' anything."

Her heart stopped, and she looked back up at him. Gailah thought he wanted to say more than he did, but Torin leaned forward, closer to her as the saddle creaked behind her.

Torin took in the sun's warmth on his face. She stared at the colors that shaded his skin as his silver hair absorbed the brilliant sunlight around them. He stared at her with the same curiosity in the pink glow of daybreak.

His eyes darted in a triangular pattern across her face, but only rested on her lips for a moment. He reached above them and plucked a white blossom from the spring trees basking in the dawn. Before he handed it to her, he twirled it between his fingers and dropped the flower into her palm.

"Thele's tears," Gailah muttered as the cool petals molded to her skin. Dew drops pearled in shimmering blues and pinks as the flower's yellow center stared back at her.

"I'm home." She said in a softer voice than she intended, and his eyes widened as she looked up at him.

Torin blinked rapidly and looked towards the mountain. She

unfixed her shoulder from where it pressed into his sternum, faced forward, and her heart resumed its steady beat.

They could be in the halls of the mountain keep before the cooks cooled the ovens. The thought of a warm meal made her fingers tighten around the reins. Her memory weaved the smells and tastes of those mornings into a fabric of longing. Gailah often stole to the kitchens before the rest of the house arose to steep in Orlas' presence. Gailah was not above kneading dough as she spoke with the woman who she knew better than family.

In the kitchens, Gailah was seen and understood, so she haunted them as a happy apparition. Her heart ached for a gentle hug. She dreamt of the tantalizing aroma of warm, flaky bread and a pewter cup of mead after enduring the longest night of her life. She smiled and imagined the steam rising from the freshly baked loaves.

"When we arrive, the eastern gate will be open to farmers selling to the steward. We will draw less attention that way," Gailah said. "They will not expect us, but I know we will find something to eat. Would you stay to break your fast?"

A twig snapped in the distance, Gailah's heart thundered and her eyes snapped to find Torin's gaze.

His arm tightened around her waist and it almost crushed her to him as he crossed their bodies with his other arm to unsheathe his sword in a swift flourish. With the eyes of a hawk, he scanned the shadows of morning forest down the width of his blade and held her flush against his chest. He kept her hidden behind the profile of his shoulder as his blade glinted in the sunlight.

Gailah could not breathe as fear crept up her spine but Torin's exhale feathered the wisps of hair along her hairline while her head rested beneath his chin.

The bushes behind them rustled and a lythe winter fox bounded towards the meadow.

All the muscles in his body eased and as his palm loosened around her waist as she gasped with her burning exhale.

Torin shook the tiredness from his face, but the soft smile that bloomed on his lips weakened something in her chest. She never imagined treasuring such a sight.

"The last thing that filled my stomach was from the gathering..."

"I would like to introduce you to a few—"

"Oh, no. That will not be necessary." The prince started quickly. "I will eat, but nothing more. Any more could bring you more attention than a princess would desire."

His refusal filled her with a soft sadness, a new and entirely unfamiliar feeling.

"And what do you know of my desires?" She said with a sly smirk across her lips as she stretched her sore arms.

The hood of her cloak fell slowly around her neck as she breathed in the scent of the trees.

"What is that?"

Gailah tilted her chin towards him, and Torin's face suddenly shifted. Confusion spread across her face as he glared at her hair.

She ran her fingers through her tresses, and her stomach dropped–the comb. It hung loosely in the tangles of her silver hair, the golden leaves poked out in sharp clusters.

"The first of Romulus' *bride price*. It is a custom among their people."

A flicker of betrayal flashed across his face. Torin cursed as he turned his head away from her. His accent heightened with anger, but in a dialect quicker and smoother than the lilt of Gailah's kin.

"They made an agreement and signed the contracts as of last night." Gailah spoke truthfully, but she did not know if the marriage contract bore her mother's seal.

"This complicates things. Greatly complicates things." He sighed and rubbed his brow.

Kelligh circled far above, and her colors blended beautifully with the sunrise. Gailah could not fathom why Torin would care about who she married.

"But you do not wish to marry me?" Gailah hated the pitiful way her question sounded.

There was something in his face that filled her with embarrassment, and it only made her feel worse.

"Indeed, Princess, I do not."

His words stung some place tender in her mind. She wondered if this sham kidnapping would save her the embarrassment of no one actually wanting to marry her. She had fought the idea in every way but did not realize the gods had been so moved by her prayers to actually answer her.

"Why does Romulus matter, then?" She said with a twinge of bitterness.

"Because in the eyes of the island, the judges, and your mother. I have not only taken the only daughter of the Mountain, I have also taken the prince of Autumn's betrothed. They will think I stole you to spite him and he will demand justice."

"You did not take me. I left. The judges will believe me or they.."

"Romulus has the right to ask for a duel, or have the judges decide my fate by trial."

Torin did not remove his gaze and stared at the comb like it was a viper.

She wondered if he regretted intervening.

"I... All of that would be true if Romulus cared for me. He does not and he never could. I belong to myself, and I'm tired of everyone trying to convince me otherwise."

Torin's gaze softened, and he turned to face her. She did not know what part of that revelation changed him. That Romulus would not fight for her or that he might not have to clear his name for protecting her.

"Ah, so neither of you petitioned for this arrangement?" There was something smug in his face that annoyed her.

"No, he loves another, the priestess."

"Yet you wear a token of his affection? You do not wish to be Queen of the Autumn Kingdom?"

"Unfortunately, that is not for me to decide."

"In your heart, I know you do not believe that." Torin shook his head. "You would sentence yourself to a very slow death."

She watched as his brows tensed and he studied her. The prince moved closer to her in the saddle and as she looked behind her; she liked how the gray flecks of his eyes shifted with the sun.

Torin reached around her until his hand found the jeweled ornament tangled in her hair, but his eyes never parted from hers. A chill ran down her spine as the teeth of the comb grazed her skin. She understood every word from his mouth, but her mind failed to comprehend the man beside her.

Gailah watched as he studied the golden piece as if it were an insect he pulled from her hair.

"I do not believe gold to be your color, Your Highness." There was a subtle smirk in his expression as he spoke.

He feigned a sense of calm, but it only masked the tension beneath the surface of his tensed jaw. He bore a pink scar across his wrist. The new skin that bridged the gap told her he still felt the dullness of its sting.

She paused as an intrusive question nagged at her thoughts. Before she could ask, he spoke in a quiet voice; in a tone so soft and contradictory to his being.

"When I first saw your face at the gathering, you bore a look that all creatures wear when trapped in a cage. It didn't suit you." She expected him to smile, but he did not. There was no sarcasm in his voice, just a sadness in his eyes. From where he sat, the prince turned his face away from the sun, hiding his expression among the trees.

He held the golden hair comb in his hand, but as he reached around, he placed it against her palm, curling her fingers around it.

"Be rid of it or wear it with pride."

His hand lingered for a moment.

She turned the oak leaf comb back and forth against her skin. Her mother's words echoed in her mind.

Bride price.

In a swift visceral motion, she pitched the golden comb, glinting as it tumbled through the foliage. A soft thud sang back as it struck the forest floor.

Torin looked at her and she forgot anything and everything else. Her heartbeat lost its rhythm.

From where he sat behind her, Torin moved to touch her face, and Gailah froze. Her pulse tumbled again, and she could not silence the thrill her heart had found as he looked down at her.

She held her breath for far too long, waiting for the graze of his fingers.

It never came.

His touch did not meet her skin. Instead, Torin lifted the hood of her cloak. Gailah swallowed as he tucked her silver tresses out of sight. She fought against the warmth spreading in her cheeks.

She looked forward and the blue sky had conquered the pink shades of the morning.

"Shall we press on?" Torin whispered.

She nodded and rustled her shoulders beneath her cloak.

He extended his hand to the sky and gave a sharp whistle.

His bird landed aggressively against his forearm.

"That's where the scars came from," Gailah thought.

Kelligh's eyes tilted with the scanning movements of her head.

"Tell me this..." She swallowed and tightened her grip on the reins. After her senses had settled, she needed to know something more about the prince, but more specifically his brother.

"What did he do to the wine?"

Torin froze, and his shoulders sagged forward.

"It was my grandmother's idea to make you sleep. Before they arrived to take you, she commanded that you be made agreeable."

Gailah's stomach churned.

The scent of the Spessian wine persisted in her memory.

"I do not know what the casks contained, but it was enough to produce the desired effect. Enough for the mercenaries to have the advantage."

She should have warned her brothers. Is that why they had not found her? Her heart sank as she realized her guards were dead. Bjorn? Aerin? They all could be dead...

She blinked rapidly as shock settled against her skin.

"You have my thanks .."

Torin flinched.

"Do not thank me for preventing him from poisoning you...You thank me for having a shred of decency, Princess? Do not thank me for choosing not to be despicable."

"You are far from despicable..."

"You do not know me." His chin bowed, and he did not meet her gaze.

Suddenly, his hair flicked her cheek as his gaze whipped towards the distant snapping of twigs in the tree line.

Pain seared across her neck.

"TORIN!" Gailah cried as her body rocked forward.

She heard Torin unsheathe his sword as she fell from the saddle.

A whoosh rushed through the leaves.

Torin grunted with pain.

All air fled from her lungs as she collided with the ground. The forest around Gailah grew cold and quiet. Darkness crept in from the corners of her eyes. The smell of ash and rotting flowers filled her senses. She clutched for anything to hold on to as her fingers grew numb.

The sky was no longer pink, nor blue. Everything around her became shadow.

Chapter Twenty-One

Bjorn

Bjorn and Alexi carved through the forest. The Mountain Born and the River Snake–two titles Bjorn never imagined being paired together. Never conceding his back or any weaknesses to Alexi, Bjorn let the younger prince guide them forward.

They rode as the moon fell and until dawn emerged from the east. Alexi was certain he knew where Torin would take her, and his urgency to spill his brother's blood unsettled Bjorn.

"TORIN!"

Gailah's cry pierced through the thickness of the leaves. The pain in her voice terrified him. Bjorn's heart erupted in panic and they galloped towards the sound of her scream and the chaos that followed it.

His pulse kept time with every thundering gait as his horse barreled through the trees. There were other cries, too–loud, monstrous war cries that sickened him, cries that belonged to the pearlescent eyes of his dreams.

The dread building in his throat made it difficult to breathe and the darkness of his heart prepared him for the worst. He had seen them kill and knew what awaited them if they were too late. Bjorn would not hold Gailah just as he had eased his father into the hands of the gods. He could not bear it.

He prayed to the God of the Mountain for strength, for there was no time to pray to the other eight.

His dread forced him to ready his axe. He held it close to him, poised to attack as he dodged limbs and leaves that tried to blind him. Bjorn raced forward, but he was no closer to her. The forest swallowed the sound of the skirmish.

"Over there!" Alexi's horse surged past him.

The smallest of saplings swayed and bent as they hurried to the tree line just beyond.

Bjorn's rage swelled like the tide when he saw Prince Torin's silver hair peek through the undergrowth, but as he readied to dismount, Bjorn paused.

Torin lay bloodied on the ground. If he were dead, then he would have died where he fell from his horse. Alexi and Bjorn circled the clearing. Bjorn searched Alexi's face for any sign of despair or agony, but only malice mixed with his pale indifference.

Cracking and snapping limbs echoed around them.

"I will keep moving. Gailah is gone. I will waste no time on your traitorous kin." Bjorn huffed from where he sat with his ax still readied. "The gods have had their justice. I do not need revenge on a dead man."

Bjorn looked skyward as a red sparrow hawk circled above them. Its screech was sharp and panicked. Gailah's scream was clearer than the thoughts that raced inside his mind. She was near, and he would not rest until his sister was far from the men who would hurt her. Alexi knelt beside his elder brother.

Bjorn's stomach seized. Alexi would confirm his death. If any life lingered in Prince Torin's body, Alexi would relish in it. Bjorn could not imagine such hatred, but he would not interfere with Spessian treachery.

He searched the tree-line until he spotted a path of crushed green thicket. They had dragged her. A single lilac slipper remained beside the clearing. His teeth ground down against his jaw and he took off towards the deepest parts of the Great Forest.

Alexi did not follow.

Racing through the trampled pathway, he followed the crumpled sticks and footsteps in the soft soil. A wounded animal shrieked close to the mountain prince. Old leaves crunched in the distance as it stumbled through the forest. He listened for its ragged breathing as his hand dropped to his axe and the blue sky pierced through the canopy.

As he drew near, the swish of fabric preceded frantic exhales.

Like a drone lost from its hive, a wild-looking young man with ill-fitting leathers limped through the trees. The young man bore the same blue painted runes of the men he hunted. Bjorn could not see his face, but the paint on his pale skin shone through the greenery. He followed the tuft of brown hair with fire in his heart. This man would be his only hope of finding Gailah.

The prince galloped at a speed that rattled his joints.

To torture someone was not in Bjorn's nature, but there were other ways of forcing desperate men to speak. Awkwardly, the man hobbled through the undergrowth with an injured leg.

Each thundering stride of Bjorn's horse sent terror through the wounded man as his head snapped towards the prince. Bjorn's heart tumbled through his chest and he drew back his arm, ready to knock the raider off his feet.

His jaw tightened as the flat of his ax connected with the young man's legs. Bjorn's horse continued forward, and the prince urged his beast to turn back towards his prisoner. After colliding with the ground, the young man gasped breathlessly on the forest floor.

When he struggled to rise, his chest heaved in desperation. Even as the prince drew closer, the man thrashed in the leaves and could not stand. Bjorn's stomach dropped.

The wild man was no stranger. He was the son of a mountain blacksmith; a young man who had disappeared during the winter's thaw.

Frantically, the boy's eyes mimicked his body, rocking from side to side in his head. There was nothing familiar in his maddened, milky gaze.

He was lost behind what held his mind captive.

The young man's face turned feral and his neck arched upwards. He rose to his feet like his limp no longer mattered.

Bjorn's stomach soured, and his hand tightened around the handle of his weapon.

The runes that painted his body gleamed in the afternoon sun in a sky shade of blue that covered every part of his anvil hardened frame. After he found his balance, the young man drew a jagged knife from his belt.

He lowered his milky white gaze at Bjorn and growled in a guttural roar. Swiftly, the prince drew back his ax and charged forward.

The wild man lunged and Bjorn's horse cried out as his knife dug into its shoulder. As the beast reared onto its legs, Bjorn dismounted and clung to his axe as his feet pounded into the soil. Bjorn needed him alive for more than Gailah's sake but for all the others that had gone missing, and for his nightmares to end.

Bjorn dodged his attack and the prince's armored leg collided with his attacker's wounded knee. Like a breaking twig, the man's leg dropped out from under him.

As he fell and screamed, the young man's foot no longer faced forward. He cocked his head up, and with his muscle corded biceps, the man stood as if death only mattered.

Something whispered from the depth of the forest, and the attacker reached for his knife. Bjorn stared into the terrifying paleness of his eyes and the surrounding whispers grew louder.

As the young man slashed for Bjorn's stomach, the prince stumbled backwards and struck with his axe. Steel chopped into his axe handle as they grappled between the trees

The axe handle saved Bjorn's neck as it caught the sharpness of the blade. The raider's body tumbled forward under his momentum and Bjorn's footing slipped and the forest fell around them.

Suddenly, frigid shallow water surrounded his shoulders. His head nearly dashed in the bed of a shallow ravine. As he threw his body upward, Bjorn pinned the man beneath him with the weight of his trunk and his axe handle held the man under the water.

His hands fumbled against the current as Bjorn pressed him further below the surface. Water ran down the prince's face as his white knuckled grip tightened around his axe.

As he bore down through gritted teeth, the water ebbed higher around Bjorn's knees and saturated his cloak. Bubbles sputtered amid the rapids beneath him. As he pressed against the pebbly riverbed, the man thrashed like a trout. Bjorn's eyes pounded with his pulse, but he saw the man's rune covered arm reach for a rock.

The blue paint covering his skin floated to the surface of the babbling ravine. Suddenly, the rock fell from his attacker's grip and soon his skin was bare.

Under the water, his eyes drained of their milky color. To wait any longer seemed foolish to Bjorn. He needed him alive. The wild man's scraggly stubble surfaced, and he drew a starving breath with brown irises shifting in panic.

Bjorn eased and grabbed the man by his collar, yanking him from the water. The large prince slammed the young man against the bank of the ravine, but his guard and his ax did not fall.

After spewing water from his open mouth, the blacksmith's son blinked back against droplets rolling on his lashes.

Birds chirped happily in the distance, but Bjorn only heard the pounding of his heart. While Bjorn glowered over him and steadied his feet within the current, the young man looked up at him like a water-logged hound. His brown hair glistened with water as confusion racked his body.

"Where am I?"

ALEXI

After Bjorn disappeared between the streaks of morning sunlight, Alexi stared at the wreckage of his brother. A thin barb protruded from the side of Torin's neck.

He thought to shake him, to pound his fists against his chest, but what would that do? Nothing could satisfy the hate burrowing in his skin. Even now, as he knelt beside Torin's body, his chest tightened and every muscle rigid with contempt.

Alexi shook as he brought a hand to his brother's neck. A weak heart beat tapped against his finger, but when he felt it, Alexi's pulse roared behind his ears. He lost himself to the sounds he hid from as a child.

The scraping of his grandmother's staff, her ragged breath, and uneven steps. There was a knot inside of Alexi that cinched itself tighter the longer he looked at his brother

He wanted to scream at Torin. He hated him for leaving him behind to find glory while Alexi covered his ears, closed his eyes, and prayed for a reprieve; for leaving him to suffer the scorn, disdain, and resentment as the lesser of them. He hated Torin for never seeing the bruises that perpetually bloomed across Alexi's shoulders, spine, and anywhere clothing would hide. As Torin's ships left the harbor, Alexi's beatings began.

"*It will make you strong like your brother,*" she would say after each lashing before her throne.

How Alexi hated Torin for setting a standard in which he paled in comparison. For every strike that told him he would never be enough, he would never be Torin. Alexi's hand moved from Torin's pulse to the dagger at his side. He no longer shook.

"*Show me how strong you have become.*"

He could hear his grandmother's whispers in his mind. As Torin betrayed them before the gathering, she promised Alexi everything he had ever wanted in return. He would be king, and he would never cower before her throne again.

The Riverland crown would belong to Alexi now.

Alexi's palms sweat against the hilt of his dagger. Torin had all but sealed their fate by revealing their plot to the Queen of the Mountain.

Why would their oldest enemy aid him when Spessia bought back their crown from Tiranus with Ahtalah's blood?

Alexi scoffed at Torin's naivete. That tightening knot within him fastened around the pulse in his throat. He held his breath and unsheathed the needle point dagger from the hilt at his side. The onyx steel muted all the shine from the blade.

Lifting away Torin's cloak, no blood had pooled beneath his armor. Alexi knew where to strike, where it would be quickest.

Alexi had learned to clench his teeth instead of weeping, to swallow tears before they shed, to bite back against screams that would only bring more pain. The dagger rattled in his grip as he brought it against Torin's throat.

"Why?" He seethed through spittle and gritted teeth. "Why didn't you protect me?"

As he steadied his hands, he exhaled against the frosty morning air.

Worst of all, Alexi hated Torin for knowing what it meant to be loved by their parents, and for being old enough to remember them.

He had no memory of their faces or the kindness of their touch. If he could steal that memory from him, he would. The tightening knot within him snapped.

His eyes burned and he let the dagger fall from his hands while every stifled scream escaped his lips and his blade clattered beside him.

Alexi hated himself most of all because their grandmother was right.

He would always be weak, afraid, but the fear that stayed his hand was the fear of what the world would feel like if he were truly alone–alone with her.

He wanted to vomit as tears rose in his face.

He buried his head against his brother's torso. Torin breathed deeply and, as Alexi panted against the echo of the forest, a soft, warm voice resonated deep within his memory.

Chapter Twenty-Two

Jaius

His tongue lapped at the moisture that clung to the grime covered stones. A bitter watery mix of dirt and the faint metallic tang of blood. The dry skin on his lips cried out for the only relief he found on the stones of the dungeon.

The socket of his shoulder burned as he strained against the biting irons on his wrist. His body hung by a single shackled arm to the wall behind him as iron broke flesh and ground against bone.

Water sang out from the corner, dripping as it pooled beneath a crack in the prison wall. It beckoned him with a temptress's promise to quench his thirst. The pain that wracked his maimed body worsened with every torturous drip.

The deep, aching throb of infection radiated along the tattered remnants of his legs. He pulled at his shoulder again as the drip seemed to scream from the corner of the cell.

His tongue scraped across the roof of his barren mouth. The memory of water tearing across his mind was summoned by every rippling drop collecting far beyond his reach.

To his right, behind the bars and down the corridor, footsteps approached.

His eyes knew less light than a cave creature. Jaius winced at the crackling torches the guards carried, startled by the sudden light filling the cell.

"No! No! Please!"

"Silence, retch!"

A glimpse of silver hair caught his eye as the guards laid an unconscious woman on the floor of the cell. Her body slumped forward on its side, with her limbs splayed out in front of her.

She appeared to be only wearing a dressing gown and night clothes. A single slipper remained, and her bare foot dragged along the stone. That long silver hair now splayed across the pool that had been collecting in the corner. Before long, her hair would bear the same mud and the scent of blood that permeated the prison floor.

Death claimed everything in this cell.

"No irons. He will have need of her before you could fashion them." The head guard called out as a sentry crouched, ready to chain her to the floor.

Without looking in his direction, they left as quickly as they arrived. In their minds, he had become as much a permanent feature of the cell as the dripping wall.

Darkness reclaimed the cell, and the pain in his eyes eased.

She laid there, almost lifeless, as her chest raised slightly with each shallow breath.

It was if she were sleeping; he envied her, but only for that reason. His body had not known true sleep in days or weeks. In this prison, time did not pass. His only rest had come when pain and exhaustion racked his body of its consciousness.

Dread filled his mouth like bile. He knew who she was. They spoke often of the queen's daughter.

He had never seen this woman before in all of his travels over the years, nor during his time a chief alchemist to the kings of autumn, but he knew they hunted for the mountain born heirs.

The dripping crack in the wall continued, but it now fell on her head in a much softer, less maddening thwack.

She did not stir as the water continued to collect around her hair and dripped down her scalp. He watched as her brows furrowed and pain flashed across her face, though her eyes remained closed.

He could not imagine how deeply one would need to be unconscious to shut out the cruelty that had digested them.

The pain in what remained of his lower body returned and demanded his attention. The pain was impossible to ignore, causing him to bite his lips until they bled. He pressed his free palm against the oozing wound above where his knee had been. A cry escaped him as the throbbing pain only worsened at the touch. A single prayer escaped his lips.

Long ago, he had forsaken the gods, replacing them with alchemy in his heart. The order had pledged an easy life of abundance, a promise he had accepted willingly.

Now he prayed for death–a prayer that came out of a drowned scream.

At the sound of his stifled cry, the woman flinched, and he let his head fall back and land heavily against the stone behind him. He closed his eyes and waited for the gods to answer his prayer.

"WHERE AM I?" Her voice was soft and muddled with confusion.

Jaius rocked his neck forward and locked eyes with the woman, who was now very much awake.

She stood before him. If he had not seen the guards leave her there, he would have thought the gods had sent her to bring him to the afterlife. Her long hair fell around her shoulders like the branches of a willow tree. Despite the dampness of her hair, she was an ethereal vision of beauty. All except her eyes. Cold and filled with fear, her eyes betrayed her emotions. Her regal posture hinted at royalty.

Suddenly, shame clawed into his skin as she took in the sight of his wounds. Her eyes filled with horror and he only wished he could cover what remained of his tortured limbs.

She was not his guide to the halls of the gods, for they would not welcome him.

"What have they done to you?" She cried out, her hands flew to her mouth and nearly tripped over her dressing gown as she stumbled backwards. Shadows parted around the brightness of her hair as if the dungeon itself struggled to assert its darkness in her presence. But that was not so, only fever clouded his mind.

Tears would have budded in his eyes if he had not lifted his gaze upward. His voice faltered as he coughed against the pain in his chest. With each exhale, he sensed water in his lungs.

"He has taken my bones..." Weak and raspy, his voice emerged as he clutched his thighs with his free hand. Betrayal and embarrassment clouded his mind as he stared at the mangled heap of limbs beneath him.

The horror on her face only deepened as she dropped to her knees before him. The purulent grime on the floor claimed more of her white gown rising through the fabric in streaks of filth. Her delicate fingers gripped the stones, and the realization sank through her spirit like a stone in deep waters.

Her knuckles whitened as if she could claw her way through the ground. In the prisoners who had come and gone, he had witnessed that familiar despair. Another young girl had once shared her shock, but that seemed like an eternity ago.

Regrettably, Jaius did not know her fate, but she was kind.

"Where am I?"

He did not speak, he could only hunker against the wall and he thought to say,

"What an awful host I am... This place once belonged to me."

Jaius remained silent, his mind clouded with both shame and infection refraining him from uttering a single word.

As if the stones pulled her down, the woman slunk back on her heels with defeat rising in her blue eyes.

"Can you tell me who they are?"

A laugh, not of mockery or contempt, but of bitter regret, escaped his lips.

"They are me, I am them... We are many."

The first words of the alchemist's order fell from his lips, for the muscles in his tongue could not forget them. He shook his head as he watched her eyes narrow in a mix of frustration and distrust.

Delirium crowded his thoughts. He thought he could see the sky above him.

She moved closer and tried to find his face in the darkness of the cell. Her hands crumpled into her lap as she found his gaze. The despair that hung in her eyes buried deep in his chest.

He could face his end alone, but to see it in another's soul made his hope crumble.

"Why have they hurt you? How can I ease your pain?" There was no disgust in her voice as she examined the harsh angle of his arm.

He closed his eyes. He did not have the strength to deny the only request that ate at his mind. He was a broken man with no dignity left, and could not quell his desperation.

She sat back on her heels.

"Your hair. There's water there. Just a drop, please..."

Beneath the darkness of his lids, he heard her move closer.

"Hold out your hand."

He blinked and sat forward.

The woman stood and let murky droplets fall from her tightened fists as she rang her silver hair of what little moisture it held.

The droplets fell into his outstretched palm, a balm filling the crevices of his hand. The scabs on his lips broke free as he drank dry every drop from his hand, savoring the saltiness of his tears as he cherished the water she had wrung from her hair.

Avoiding her gaze, shame climbed the walls inside his mind, and he curled himself away from her.

If she was indeed the Princess from the Mountain, then she awaited a fate far worse than his. He wanted to help her, to get her far away from the people he had once considered his equals. Jaius had not known the depth of the order's schemes until they had taken all from him, and now not even a shadow of his old self remained.

His hands shook as he felt the infection rising in his pulse.

The impending moment of judgment before the gods drew near, and he clung to hope, offering fervent prayers for mercy. He saw the relics of every island contorting into the shapes of their divine forms, beings seated and ready to pronounce him condemned.

Jaius raised his eyes.

He beheld her, arms wrapped tightly around herself, braced against the dungeon wall in a stance of palpable fear. Yet, within the contours of her face, he discerned a lingering shred of hope, a fragile ember in the darkness that mirrored his own desperate plea for their pardon.

He asked the girl her name to confirm the gnawing behind his eyes.

"Gailah, Princess of the Broken Mountain."

He knew now that the nine owed him no sympathy.

"Jaius,"

She tilted her head as he spoke his name.

"My name is Jaius. I served as alchemist to the Autumn King."

Her continence shifted, and her eyes fixed on the floor.

"Why did they hurt you, then?"

"I betrayed their order. I believed our work to be greater than the depravity of men, but when I tried to warn my king when their need for revenge became .... became all of this.." he swallowed, savoring the last taste of water on his tongue. "And they hunted me like a dog,"

Senna.

He frantically pulled himself from the wall, but only as far as the chain would allow before it tore into his flesh.

"My niece, she's alone in the woods, on the farthest side of the forest. She's alone, and she doesn't know about what's coming. If you...." He did not finish his sentence.

The hope drained from the young girl's eyes. He extended his free hand and held it out to her. His hands were filthy, but so were hers. The mud of the cell claimed everything in its clutches.

She took his hand and he could not help but feel unworthy.

She looked down at his hand in confusion.

"Know this, I cannot amend what I have done and I will never expect your forgiveness, but Your Highness, do not become them. Do not tread amongst the fires of their evil. Fight like you will never see the sky again because they will fight to keep you in darkness." He could not help but shake as he clutched her hand, but if there was any will to resist left in him, he wanted her to have it.

She nodded, dropping his hand with ice in her fingers as she slid downwards along the wall beside him.

Gailah drew her knees to her chest. She bore no chains, but shock shackled her to stone.

Her eyes fixed on the locked cell door.

Fever danced through his mind and began chattering in his teeth. This was no ordinary fever, this was the touch of the Void. It would be the last thing he would feel before the eternal dark.

"Tell me about your home. Tell me about the mountain." Anything to take their minds far from here.

She spoke, and a softness returned to her face. He felt the snow of the mountain on his skin as he listened to her describe the pointed peaks.

He had only traveled to the Mountain Kingdom once, but while she described her home, he felt as if he had known it for a lifetime. Jaius did not know if it was the infection in his blood or the girl's story, but he smiled, closed his eyes and something loosened behind his ribs while his breathing slowed. His body sagged under the weight of his desperate need for sleep. Under his closed eyes, golden leaves rippled beneath the open sky and his heart lept knowing that would be his last glimpse of its blue expanse.

If this were to be his end, he hoped that his life's work had not damned him for eternity.

Gailah

Gailah flinched as she remembered the strike of the poison dart.

She could still feel the effects of the poison as it raced beneath her skin.

Her hand instinctively went to her neck, where the dart had embedded itself in as a briar under her skin. It left a tangible wound that assured her this was not a cruel trick of her imagination. She leaned against the wall, pressing her hands against the stone to relieve her aching back.

Torin.

Where was Torin?

The sound of thundering footsteps echoed through the halls of the prison. Rising from the floor, she backed toward the darkness of the corner.

Three guards stopped before her cell.

"Looks like he finally gave up. Suppose they'll want the body?" A gristly voice sneered between the bars.

It belonged to a stout man with crude blue alchemy ruins on his face. They all bore the same markings, some darker, some even the deepest shades of blue. Its power filled all their eyes with a milky shade of blue beneath the orange brazier light.

"Let's burn 'im"

"No! Not yet! Not till he takes what's left!"

The iron door wailed as they pushed it open on its hinges. The three guards entered the room and everything inside her wanted to run for the opening.

Her inner voice screamed for the chance at freedom but before she could rise, she saw Jaius' face and the pain there.

He was still alive.

The guards spoke as if Gailah were invisible. Through a chorus of disregard, the guards guessed at which parts of his body the alchemists would use for their sorcery.

Their cruel laughs rippled under her skin and she knew she could not leave him.

"I will not let you touch him."

Gailah stepped out from the darkness of the cell.

They turned, their laughter grating like whining jackals. Undeterred, she blocked their path, hands extended, and gaze lowered with a mix of frustration and defiance.

At that moment, a spark of self preservation urged her again to run, to look to the opening once more.

Gailah silenced that voice. Every twist of fear commanded her body, but as she steadied her feet on the stones, she knew what her father would want her to do.

The largest of the guards hushed their laughter with a wicked grin and he still bore a helmet that framed his hate-filled eyes.

"So you're finally awake. We can't kill you, but he said nothing about showing you a little pain," He sneered and turned towards the guards behind him.

Her legs began to shake.

"Fond of corpses, are you?" He said, taking a step closer, and jerked his chin at her.

Removing his helmet, his head tilted with a malicious stare and the milky white of his eyes made her stomach drop.

"He's dying! Leave him be!" she growled at them between outstretched hands, refusing to lower her stance. "I won't let you touch him."

His shoulders seemed to ease and his eyes softened.

"Fine."

The large guard turned to leave and Gailah exhaled.

In a swift flare of his arm, the guard's helmet collided with her skull.

The cell spun in a dizzying circle as she dropped to her knees. Her mouth filled with blood. She brought a hand to her lip, and it sang out in pain. Her blood dripped from her broken lip to the floor of the cell. Each drop unfurled in the muddy mortar rivers between the stones and as the guards' laughter faded, Gailah buried her head in her hands.

Chapter Twenty-Three

Alexi

The late morning sun warmed the ground around the princes while Alexi lingered by his brother, counting every swell rising within Torin's chest.

Small wandering creatures rushed chaotically through the glade, but each time, frozen fear erupted in the animal's dark eyes, but not before they tore off in bounds of scampering fur. He had never seen such small animals before.

Alexi closed his eyes, and his thoughts twisted in maddening circles.

Torin had betrayed their family, if he could even call their small cluster of bloodbound kin such a name, but Alexi had betrayed everyone else. Alexi no longer knew what he wanted or who he wanted to be, but he was certain he no longer wanted to be himself.

He would not die a traitor.

A dry snap cried through the brambles beside them, and Alexi's eyes shot open. Soft, cautious footsteps moved with intentional placement and crept ever closer to them.

Alexi reached for his dagger and spun it in his hands, ready for whomever hunted them. Torin continued in his unhelpful unconsciousness and he felt his brother's pulse one final time before he looked up.

There were eyes in the trees, and his skin prickled as he scanned the glade. After a moment crawled by painfully, the prince paused as the tip of the blade grazed his bowstring-calloused fingertips. Nothing moved beyond the small clearing.

The footsteps had stopped.

Amid the quiet of the forest, he heard the muffled footsteps again and as his head snapped up; he found the gaze of the striking woman he had seen only hours ago in the stables.

"I knew you were following us..." Alexi sneered as he lied.

Clutched tightly in her talons, she carried a silver amulet that swayed about in the air. Almost protecting herself with it, as if the small bit of metal warded away the evil in the trees.

If Alexi had not sat silently and listened on her approach, then she could have killed them both. Sly was an understatement, and he admired that. He believed her to be the very personification of the foxes that darted through the heather, but when she stared back at him, her green, copper flecked eyes welled with a malice that Alexi understood.

"I doubt that considerably," she said, removing her cloak. Alexi could not look away as she let the morning blaze through her auburn hair in a waterfall of fire.

"Where is he?"

She did not need to say who. Alexi knew instantly that Bjorn was the force pulling her towards them.

"They took his sister. Dragged her through those trees." He pointed towards the crushed undergrowth.

The woman promptly crouched and scanned the forest floor for hoof prints.

Drawing both of their attentions, Torin's eyes fluttered, and he gave a watery gasp.

Alexi sprung to his feet, then cupped his brother's neck.

"I have more pressing matters at the moment." Alexi spoke through gritted teeth as he examined the wound at Torin's neck.

Lodged just beneath the skin, a barb protruded from his brother's neck. He plucked it and translucent liquid poured from its barb. The huntress kneeled beside Torin with furrowed brows.

"Please, give me that. I can help." She said, reaching for the dart without pause.

She clipped it from Alexi's hand and brought it to her lips. Alexi winced, and one of his eyes twitched in disgust. Her expression soured, but her eyes widened before viciously spitting on the forest floor.

Next, she dragged a finger across the wound, lifting the viscous fluid in her fingertips. She examined it like it was an insect wobbling across her hand. She was unafraid of its venom, as it glimmered in the forest's light.

"It's not fatal. He'll survive, but make him drink this."

The woman dug through her satchel and produced a small vial of viscous purple liquid.

"An elixir of Dead-nettle and crushed poppy."

"You want me to give him something called *Dead-nettle..?*"

She must think him incredibly stupid or incredibly ignorant. Perhaps both.

She shook her head in disbelief. With the hands of a healer, she tilted Torin's head enough so his lips could meet the vial.

"Just enough to take the poison down. Too much and he won't ever sleep again."

Once Torin's head returned to the ground, she rose from the forest floor and tucked away the purple liquid.

"Stay with him. It may take a few moments for him to wake up." She said before her tresses disappeared into the hood of her cloak. "Oh, and princeling...I was not following you. I was trying to catch up."

She said with self satisfaction as the shadows swooped in around her face.

He began speaking, but the huntress had already disappeared into the awakening forest.

Alexi looked down at Torin's deathly colored cheeks, but as he shook his brother's chest with the width of his hand, a groan escaped through Torin's closed lips.

. . .

KATHA

Katha's jaw ached terribly from her teeth-grinding that kept rhythm with her feet as she paced the breadth of the great hall. With every hour that passed, more demands and orders poured from her lips. She had not slept since the attack, but her eyes burned with spent tears and anger.

Her fingers plucked at the skin beside her nails as the queen weaved between each of the wide stone columns.

Riders from every kingdom scoured the island for signs of her daughter. Though her son Aerin was not among them, she commanded Aerin to call down upon the mountain clans and for her uncle Regulus to guide him.

As the heir and future king, he alone could raise their armies on her behalf to summon every banner man that remained guarding the meadows and the mountain's chasm.

Katha would raise every piece of their island until she found her daughter.

Even as the thick layers of her velvet gown surrounded her, the queen felt bare to the eyes of Thyssia. The tension beneath her skin pulled at the base of her skull as she failed to ease the pain between her eyes.

Karak blocked her path and began nudging her with the stub of his snout. She scratched between his rounded ears and braced herself against a column as the gigantic bear rested the weight of his body against her skirts. The comfort she took from him was far greater than she could ever repay her loyal friend. He was the best of the Island.

Trejen was there, standing with his hands clasped behind his back as he watched her from afar. Each time, averting his gaze when she found him staring a little too long. He waited patiently, smoothing his black beard that stood out from the silver of his armor and the yellow of his cloak.

Queen Allagria's staff shook from side to side as the Matriarch of house Spessia entered the room, clacking loudly as she made her way along the marble floor.

The She-Snake of the River Lands, the longest reigning monarch of any house in history, a longevity bought with bloodshed, approached in a cloud of annoyance.

Her fibrous grey hair coiled tightly around the base of her onyx crown. Allagria masterminded the idea to mine the river beds for its ore. She swore that the gods had given the instructions only to her in a vision, demanding she claim the river's power for their people's house and fortune. Her onyx crown contained the first extracted ores before their mines became Spessia's glory.

Katha and Trejen had not yet been born when she ruled in her prime.

As Allagria scanned the room with a predatory gaze, a snarl pursed on the matriarch's lips before she spoke.

The early morning light did not favor her, and the inconvenience of this conversation seethed from her person.

"My grandsons are missing, yet you do not see me pacing ware marks into the marble." She sighed. "Do you wake me from my slumber to slander my house? You accuse them of treachery, do you not?" She slammed her staff against the tile and the sapphires coiling around its stem rattled in their facets. "Perhaps your daughter compelled them? We all saw how she danced through the gathering last night. Who could blame them? With such a display for all the island to see?"

Katha stopped breathing as her teeth ground down again, and a sharp pain shot through her jaw bone. There is no greater threat to a woman than those who deem beauty as an excuse for cruelty.

Katha quieted a hateful laugh despite the pain in her chest. Her voice was hoarse from the tears that had burned a path down her throat. Only Allagria's crown spared her neck from the thoughts that spiraled beneath Katha's steady gaze.

"By what reasoning?! Gailah would not disgrace herself by running off with either of them. Why would she dangle her honor so precariously when she is to be Queen of Autumn? She has nothing to gain from ruining herself with the company of Spessian Princes."

Allagria's lips tightened into the sharpness of a dagger and her hands fiddled along the center of the driftwood staff. Fingers well acquainted with misery and inflicting misery upon anyone happier than she.

The queen of the River Lands lifted her chin and stared back at Katha with bitter contempt.

With the eyes of the one who betrayed Ahtalah, her dearest friend.

"All for the better than, sensitive women do not survive in the River Lands."

Trejen was the first to move. The first step between the rival queens just as Theor entered the room.

The war chieftain marched towards his queen carrying a scroll of parchment between his armored fingers.

"They found it among the bodies, your majesty! It's addressed to the Queen of the Mountain."

Katha's heart beat furiously as the ground rocked unevenly at her feet.

"I could not question the mercenaries, your majesty. They grew stronger and wilder until... until they snapped their bones and they crippled their own bodies, trying to fight free. I've not seen anything like this. They wear the runes of the old Nadr, but that was never their way."

He placed the scroll in her open palm and in Theor's eyes, there had never been such uncertainty in a war ragged face.

"My Queen, they are the disappeared ones, after they die and beneath the runes on their skin, the men see their friends and fathers in those faces... They are our people."

Her stomach pitched and her finger nearly crushed the parchment between her fingers, but a sticky seal prodded her thumb.

A seal Katha had never seen before, and not from any other island's house or Lord. A seal barring a golden, crescent-shaped alchemist's rune in a cold pool of black wax. The Queen ran her fingers over its sharp golden angles and round half circle. She gasped as its curved edges singed across the pads of her fingers like the hiss of embers.

No.

She tore through the seal that pinned the edges shut. A soft pale blue dust plumed from the paper, filling the air around the queen's face.

How?

Her eyes darted across the page like starlings. Each letter and word echoing the twisted pleasure of the author's voice. Her fingers squeezed the parchment until her knuckles matched its color. Silent screams plummeted through her mind.

She could see his face.

Haydrian's calculated eyes black with hate. The patient kind of vengeance grown in a garden of rage. Seeds she had planted and buried with his corpse deep within the mountain.

How?

The world darkened around her. The room swayed and Katha saw only Trejen as she fought against the shadows in her eyes.

Everything dimmed and her knees buckled as she fell.

The chill of the marble kissed her face and as gray fog billowed in from behind every column and doorway in the great hall, she knew she was not alone.

He was here too.

Haydrian stood before her with instinctual ease as he occupied the floor before the three thrones.

"Katha, Your Majesty..." he bowed with an elevated bend in his neck. The scarred slice at his throat smiled in a mocking grin across his flesh. "Queen and Protector of the Mountain. How I have missed you?"

She could not speak.

Her flesh crawled as her heart thrashed against her ribs. Her body became completely frozen and limp as the floor drew her tighter towards the ground with an immovable force.

That chilling crescendo followed him as he moved towards her. Unable to move, speak or flee, the creaking of his bones drowned out all else as he crouched beside her. Then the pulse-less touch of his hand snaked around her collar as he drew his face close to her.

No.

She frantically scanned the tense angles of his cheeks. All elegance was gone from his face, his raven hair tumbled in slick inky waves around his once green, now yellow eyes.

No.

"How you tremble?" He whispered and with his other hand, his thumb curled around the warmth of her wrist as he lifted her arm upwards. "Before your oldest of friends? You wound me..."

He raised her fingertips to the lethally straight scar on his throat. The raised and calloused wound bumped beneath her touch as he forced her to feel the deathblow. His skin was like ice, yet she could not draw back her hand. Her eyes widened, and his grip tightened on her wrist.

Katha could not cry out or fight him, only watch as her body panicked in every paralyzed muscle.

His laugh was as piercing as jagged crystal, and it rumbled beneath her hand at his neck. His yellow eyes twinkled with the glow of immortality, and a sickness churned in her gut.

She had done this to him. She had let him fall for the sake of their misdeeds. Her advisor was once all too eager to test the patience of the gods and somewhere in the darkness, evil had forged him whole once more.

"You're far less frightening when you look so afraid, My Queen." He released her hand and let it slap against the marble.

Forgive me.

Haydrian's face was closer now. The rotting decay of his body dominated her sense of smell. If she had retched, she would have heaved across the floor, but she lay paralyzed and his head tweaked to look directly into her eyes.

"You would not yield even when death tried to deny you. You thought we would forget? The Void does not forget."

Haydrian brought his nose against her cheek. Ice filled her senses as he nuzzled her skin and inhaled her scent.

"How I missed this..."

The shadows ebbed and, like sparks, Katha felt her hands tingle.

She could see Trejen in the outline of the murky gloom. He could not hear her scream, no one could, for she made no sound.

Haydrian merely shifted his gaze to the shape of the Autumn King. The alchemist's laughter sliced through the room, and Trejen's face paled.

He could hear it, too.

"Does it comfort you to know that she loved you enough to damn me?" Haydrian spat at Trejen.

Warmth from her hands trickled up her arms in tingling waves of bee stings across her skin. Haydrian's eyes twitched as he looked from Trejen to Katha.

A smile burned across his face.

"Oh...?"

He chuckled and as if he kept something from them.

"What if I could separate you from them, from Freyden, from the gods forever? A waif, nothing but a wisp made flesh left to wander the wastes of eternity with me.. with.." He sneered and grabbed the Queen's face. "You should have told them, told Gailah. She could have run if she had known she was prey."

Haydrian and his shadows fell away.

Sunlight pierced through the room and the Queen felt her body return to itself as if he had plunged her into frozen waters.

His whisper lingered in her ears, and Katha's eyes burned. Her pulse could not still, it galloped in frantic and wild beats that raced through her neck.

Trejen lifted her from the floor. His arms shook as she drew from his strength. Her legs were still burning and unsteady as she noticed the same pale powder covered the arms of Trejen's tunic.

All the eyes of the room focused on them, and Katha's tongue clung to her mouth as dry words formed on her lips. In complete disbelief of the sounds she uttered, she rasped:

"Haydrian is alive."

Chapter Twenty-Four

Gailah

Time did not move in the dungeons. Gailah huddled in the cell's damp night. She did not know how long she had been asleep. She stared into the dark corridor, waiting for the end or a horrid beginning.

The only thing that changed was the pitch of Jaius' weak breathing. After She had crawled back to the darkness of her corner, she counted the sound of the solitary drip crawling through the cracks above her.

Each watery "*thwack*" dropped in tune with her aching pulse. Despair challenged her every hope-filled thought.

"*You are lost*." The drip seemed to say. "*Abandoned, Forgotten.*"

Gailah bit into her swollen lip and brought her knees to her chest. She knew her brothers would not abandon her.

Her chest tightened as she thought of her mother, how worried she would be. That tightness in her bones switched to tears in her eyes.

"*Lost,*" the drip called out again.

Despair conquered the walls in her mind with the maddening "*thwacks*", but Gailah covered her ears and buried her head between her knees.

For a moment, she was no longer in a cell. The stone at her back was the stone surrounding Thele's keep, and the mud beneath her nails belonged to the babbling creeks running from the glacial springs, not the filth of the floor.

"Hello" a high-pitched voice called out.

Gailah whipped her head towards the iron bars of the cell. The door stood ajar, yet no keys jingled, and the awful screech of rusted hinges did not bite at her ears.

Within the gap, a girl stood and stared back at her. Her face was remarkable, but something ethereal radiated from her lavender moon-ish irises. Moonlight, everything about this wisp of a girl, reminded her of the moon. Soft and beckoning moonlight flitted from her hair and soft ivory skin. There was something childlike about the way she stood upon her tip-toes, but everything else seemed so out of place. Her head tilted strangely, as if keeping herself upright was almost painful.

"Come with me?" The girl said as she motioned towards the open door. Her voice was as effervescent as a song. "I need to show you something."

The poison had seeped into her mind. She thought. None of this could be real.

Gailah rose to her feet and knelt at Jaius' side. His brow was soft and without pain. She breathed with a tight pain between her ribs, then asked the nine that he would meet them in that way, free of pain.

She scanned the darkness of the prison walls and the emptiness of the corridor behind the moon spirit. For "girl" seemed too mortal a word for her description.

"Where are the guards?" Gailah said before she lifted herself from the sogginess of the floor.

"No matter! They are not here now, I need you to follow me." She called out again in a melodious lilt.

The muddy fabric of her gown clung to her skin and old blood flaked from Gailah's chin as she wiped her face with her sleeve.

The moon spirit at the cell door walked away with her eyes still fixed on Gailah.

Eyes that made Gailah's stomach turn.

She motioned again just as she disappeared into the shadows further down with only her small tip-toeing shape outlined beneath the torchlights.

The chance at freedom pulled Gailah with such force. They would find a way out, but they would leave together. She would not leave her in such a dark and horrid place. Gailah paused as her hands froze on the iron door.

"Wait!"

She no longer saw her silhouette in the hall. Only soft, distant footsteps.

Without a glance in either direction, she rushed from the cell, dodging puddles of unknown filth with her singular bare foot. Her silken slipper was no longer lilac but a dingy sort of brown. She rounded a second abysmal hallway and caught sight of the moonlit girl who swished ahead at a hurried, willowy pace.

"Do keep up."

"How do we get out of here?" Gailah whispered in a voice so soft that she hardly heard it herself.

They passed by the cells of other creatures and human remains alike, and shadows seemed to reach out at her skirts. She stifled a gasp as glowing yellow eyes followed them from empty cells that prickled her skin with horror.

To scream would only ruin their chances of escape, but Gailah saw only walls of eyes lining the stony dungeon corridor before them. The oppressive heaviness that surrounded her squeezed her from within, so much so that her vision blurred.

Just before she lost control of the scream bubbling in her chest, hope showed itself in a soft, dim halo around her guide. There was a brighter light ahead.

Her footsteps quickened with the growing light and as the hem of her stodgy nightclothes clung to her ankles, her eyes narrowed at the glow of the room.

Her heart dropped through her chest.

The prison corridor led to an overwhelmingly vast circular room, where shadows circled overhead and intensified the emptiness beneath the towering dome. Feeble lights hung from round iron chandeliers, looking over the room with flickering blinks. Above them, higher still, were faint golden cracks that fractured the ceiling.

Tables of crude glassware lined the sides of the room, sheltered beneath nine stone arches that supported the weight of the ceiling. On each pillar, a statue decorated the column supporting the dome, and on their faces, she inhaled sharply. They had carved alchemists runes over where the faces of the gods should have been or never were. Bubbling crucibles over small flames sputtered at various stations. Dust covered moths hovered and scurried about from one candle to the next. Thousands of colored bottles sat shelved along the wall. Tools hung around the columns and the angle of the blades and pronged instruments made her shudder. The room smelled of damp soil and vinegar.

The moon spirit stood in the center of the room. She commanded Gailah's attention on a raised disk that glinted with a golden radiance but she looked different now—older—under the glowing light, but all of it drew Gailah to her.

Why was she comfortable in such horrible circumstances?

"Please, I need you to help me! We can get out of here together. I do not know what you have suffered, but please, I will get us out if you show me the way."

As Gailah made her way across the room, her eyes darted around, searching for any signs of twisting shadows that may have crept forward while she had her back turned. She reached for her hand, but her guide flinched and simply shook her head with a soft smile, almost chiding Gailah as she focused her gaze.

She was not of this world, but if the spirit had brought her this far, Gailah would not leave her behind to rot in the darkness of this prison.

There must be another doorway, and as she found two large ornamental doors, her heart leapt.

"It would be rather rude to leave before I have the chance to show you what we do."

Just then, she noticed thin alchemy runes etched into circular patterns across the floor that seemed to slither as the spirit spoke.

Ice engulfed Gailah's body and the girl's voice shifted and possessed a strange crystalline quality that plinked off the glass vials dotting the work tables.

"Where are we? And what could you possibly show me that would get us out of here?"

The shadows of the room convulsed and all at once converged on them in a pack of claw wielding beasts. They rushed past her in a wave of darkness and as the room disappeared. Fire nipped along her skin.

The room transformed as the moonspirit stepped back, allowing the shadows to rearrange its features in swirls of death. The fractures in the domed ceiling pulsed with a feeble light.

In the center of the dimly lit chamber, a long, dark table adorned with the most exquisite items Gailah had ever encountered captivated her stare. Two seats opposed each other whilst dancing flame oil lamps rested between them. The golden place settings reflected fragments of the light above them. The aroma of sliced figs and roasted fowl weakened her senses and called to her from the towers of food spread along the lush red fabric. Jewel encrusted goblets perched near both seats and stray shadows filled each of the goblets with blood colored wine.

Gone were the alchemy instruments, crucibles and work tables.

Only the chandeliers above them remained the same.

In a terrified blink, the shadows receded, and the lights around them reemerged like a sunrise.

No, not a sunrise, for that did not belong to the underground. The sun would not find her here.

The girl's face was pleasantly smug as the shadows fled to wait on the edges of the room. Her eyes were no longer lavender and large, but the deepest shade of yellow.

Gailah's hope died on her tongue as she watched the spirit's fingers elongate as it walked towards the farthest seat.

"We have starved you. What poor manners, my apologies, your highness."

The moon spirit, the girl, stood beside the high-backed chair and motioned for Gailah to sit.

No. No. No.

Her body fought to the point of breaking to disobey the spirit, but this room did not belong to Gailah. It belonged to the monster that crossed its spindly legs and glowered at her with narrowed eyes.

"Sit."

Gailah took a barefoot step forward and felt utterly awkward as nothing but air threw her into the high-back chair. Her silver hair tumbled down in heaps around her arms, speckled with mud. The enticing smell of the feast washed over her in a dizzying haze of desire.

"Thank you, your highness..."

In a gust of frigid northern wind, all warmth drained from the room. The candles shuddered, nearly extinguished by the chill, and the moon spirit turned monster was gone.

Gailah screamed because the man who sat across from her was a man more dead than alive. His ashen skin and yellowed eyes crinkled as her scream filled his mouth with a jagged smile. A scar encircled his collar as he pushed back his raven slicked hair from his gaunt features.

Gailah scrambled from her seat, but instead of falling backwards, the chair forced itself against the table. Her fingers slammed into the wood with a yelp that seared through her skin.

"Who are you and what have you done with her?!" Gailah snapped back!

His laugh rippled through the wine, and crawled across the table and traipsed along her skin.

"She never was...." He smiled with his rotting gray lips that lacked any spark of life. "My apologies for the delay and for the pretense...I needed to speak with you, and what better way than over dinner? It has been many years since I entertained royalty, but please pardon my presentation." He raised his goblet in a self-satisfied toast. "She was simply a way for me to see you lower your guard. To see what trust looks like on you. A beautiful shade of stupidity."

"What are you?" She demanded as disgust drowned out all else.

"Tsk. tsk." He took a sip of wine then smoothed his maroon colored cloak.

Gailah could not hold his gaze. His gaze was too pointed and hollow. Even from across the breadth of the table, his presence made her stomach rot. His flesh moved against the cheekbones and protruded from his skin.

Instead, as he poured himself a second glass, she slid a knife from the table and let it disappear in the bell shaped opening of her sleeve.

"Answer me," she said without lifting her eyes. "I demand to know with whom I speak."

The shadows clamored along the walls. Ready to seize the room the moment he commanded them.

"Spoken as a true-blooded princess. Just like your mother."

His appearance contorted and his skin was no longer a lifeless gray. A golden mist masked his skin and smoothed away the black strands of hair. The wound around his throat was almost a pulsing pinkish hue. The yellow hue had vanished from his eyes, and a youthful quality embalmed his skin.

"There, does that make me more palatable?"

She cast her gaze downward to the reflection swirling back at her on the golden plate before her seat.

"Look. At. Me." He barked and his anger sizzled through the room.

Gailah dug her nails into the wood of the lavish seat. She lifted her eyes to meet him. All the while, her heart surrendered to despair.

"How dare you speak to me this way? What do you want from me?"

He smiled, illuminating the sharp golden lines of his face, lines that shuddered beneath the glimmer of his facade.

"Who am I? I come on behalf of the emperor, a man whose destiny the void has intricately woven with yours, Princess."

"I have no need of you, and Thyssia knows no emperor. Tiranus died because he sought to claim us. There is nothing you or some useless usurper could offer me."

"A queen you would be indeed, a good, quiet, well behaved, silent wife of a husband who wanted nothing to do with you. What a lovely fate indeed." He smirked and sliced into the food before him. He lifted his gaze. "Please, we've spared no expense." He gestured to the goblet. "The Emperor will arrive once I send for him and I do not wish to present him a starving bride"

A goblet now rested in her hand, but she had no memory of lifting it from the table. She sipped the wine and stiffened her spine. She was not in full command of her body. Every piece of her strength fought to keep her fear behind her eyes.

No, that was not what he was watching. His gaze narrowed and as if he read her thoughts, his smile became a blade thin smirk. He enjoyed her pretend bravery.

The wine was horrid, thick, and metallic. She had never tasted such a foul thing, but she swallowed, refusing to give him the satisfaction of her disgust. Every drop burned its way down to her stomach and soured against her tongue. She could not bear another mouthful, but thankfully the goblet was empty.

Instead, something, a shadow perhaps, had ladled a portion of the sweet smelling figs. Her arm shook against the force that pulled her hand towards the two-tined fork. She was not afraid of the food, but afraid that her knife would fall from her sleeve. There was nothing she could do to stop the tines as they slid into the honey covered fruit. Nor could she stop as it lifted it to her lips and compelled her to bite into the nectarous fruit. As its fibrous skin touched her mouth, her tongue became ash. Gailah wanted to retch. The forceful hold left her body, and she snatched the now refilled goblet to wash the taste from her mouth. She locked eyes with him and drained it of the metallic, odorous liquid.

Gailah was many things, but stubbornness was her preferred weapon. She seized the arm of her chair and bit back against the disgusting aftertaste of the wine.

He smiled again and his eyes winced, almost in pain. The force of maintaining his false beauty waned and his yellowed eyes flickered through the mirage. She wondered how much of his power he wasted on such a display.

"Why would you make me an empress? I am of no benefit to you?"

She slid the knife from her sleeve into her lap. Burying it in the folds of her shift.

"This fleshly cage cannot sustain me. I need someone, something more..." His long and slender fingers gestured across the table. "We shall call it an anchor, simpler than the alchemical explanation, but the emperor has promised me an anchor for my devotion to his order."

Gailah could see the thoughts swirling behind his yellow irises. Thoughts that played out in the sinister expression that spread across his lips.

"Imagine. There would be no one who dared question or disrespect you. Empress of Thyssia and any island you wished. The entire archipelago resting as your footstool."

Gailah could not deny the desire she recognized in her heart. The desire for even a taste of the freedom he promised, but Jaius' warning rang in her ears.

"Those are bold promises for a man whose existence hinges on my acquiescence. I will not be your empress, nor will I tolerate any threat to the freedom of Thyssia."

She lifted her chin and stared beyond his shoulder, hoping someone, anyone, could find her in this forgotten place. He laughed, and it rattled in her teeth.

"You? You are chattel. You will go to whichever warden takes the keys from your mother. You are nothing more than any other empty-headed princess before you. Need I remind you? Your great aunt learned that lesson too late. You are a prize of conquest, a prize that was promised to us long ago."

She wanted to scream, to tell him how her family would rip him limb from limb. That those that loved her would present her with his treacherous tongue, but what would that do? She understood that if she succumbed to the allure of his offer, allowed the words to twist through her mind, she would cease to be herself ever again.

She had no swords or savior. The sparring swords she had played with as a child were no match for the shadows that hovered with waiting claws. She would play his game. There was no field where she felt more equal than in a battle of words.

"Tell me where I am." His brows shifted, and he took another long drink from his glass.

"Look up," He spat and she noticed he did not let a single crumb touch his lips.

Golden torturous lines ran across the broad domed roof. She had noticed them earlier, but now they shimmered delicately, some even dangling in thin ribbons from the ceiling.

"Roots, they are beautiful, are they not?" He smiled.

The tree.

Her heart sank. She felt the weight of the tree above crushing down on them.

How would anyone find her down here?

"You hide it well, but the distress in your eyes betrays you. These halls...." He swept his arm across the table. "They belonged to Jaius. I believe you are acquainted? The alchemist of the Autumn King, well former, I suppose. However, they are all but forgotten by those above us. So very far above us... A dungeon that no longer exists in the mind of man, just how we wanted it to be." He sneered and refilled her goblet from the invisible vapor in the air. "Your mother painted over my legacy with the blood of my order, but we hid what belongs to us with our charms and enchantments. No one will find you. Drink."

She did not lift her glass, but the longer she looked at it, the more irresistible it became. Her eyes. She closed her eyes. The feast was a spell that compelled her to partake. Gailah locked eyes with the carvings that covered the walls of the chamber. Alchemists pulling down the stars and crushing the sun within their fingertips.

She needed to keep his thoughts away from her. If he would examine her mind, she would pick him apart as well.

"Why did you hurt him?"

She ran a finger along the rim of her glass but did not look into the wine.

"Jaius."

His face twitched and exposed the chink in his armored facade. More graying flesh exposed as his face jolted.

"Jaius befell the greatest weakness of all. He had compassion for the man who died at your mother's behest."

He pointed his chin upwards, exposing the marred flesh of his throat. A reddened crescent moon, the kiss of an executioner's blade.

"In that compassion he festered the desire to right her wrongdoing. To bring our people home from the End." He rose from his seat. "He pulled me from the void. I am Haydrian reborn. A name you only know in whispers. In the stories of our mountain and the songs of our uprising, but you do not know the truth."

"I know nothing of you but your deceit."

Gailah tried to push away from the table again, and it did not budge. She did not believe a word from his mouth. She knew their history well.

"From the wreckage of my failure, Jaius perfected the rite. He brought me out of the chasm. He possessed the knowledge and the power I did not. So much more careful and calculated." He pointed upwards to the roots glistening above them. "This tree is life itself. It is a pity, though, that when he saw his magnificent work draw breath..."

Haydrian gestured to his body, draped in black Ghobasi silks.

"Well, Jaius was not willing to sacrifice himself for... for me. So I took what I needed."

Haydrian pushed away from his seat and rocked the chair back on its feet. He side-stepped around the table with a flourish of his maroon cloak.

His fingers tapped along the table's edge and with the width of his hand, Haydrian sent a pitcher of wine clattering to the floor. It hissed and evaporated the moment the liquid seared the floor. His eyes glowed like a crocodile, unblinking and steady.

Gailah swallowed and kept herself from the flickering gold in his eyes. Her heart thrashed in her chest. She could not run, she could only reach for the last nagging question that perched on her tongue.

"...and you'll take what you need if I say no? Did you capture the prince's acolyte? Did Oxana say no?"

A guess, but to Gailah, everything seemed clearer now.

Haydrian surged forward until he stood flush against the seat of her chair.

Dominating every angle and aspect of her gaze. Gailah's hand dipped beneath the table and clutched onto the knife that burned in her grip. He stood so close that the scent of rotting flesh made her eyes water. She fought against the rising panic in her chest.

He drew his lips to her ear and the shadowy restraints tightened against her skin.

"Many times."

A single tear slid down her cheek.

She clung to the shreds of bravery that slipped through her fingers and let the tear that burned across her skin propel her hand to bury the knife in his chest and before he could pull himself from her; the blade sliced through his soft, decomposing flesh.

Haydrian's breathing hitched, and food tumbled from the table. Gailah shoved the knife deeper and felt the blade strike bone as he stumbled backwards. She did not know if what remained of him could die, but he deserved a thousand knives to the heart.

His power no longer held her to the seat.

She scrambled from the table and her body fell back against the stone floor, grinding into her palms as she rushed away from him.

He clutched the dagger and panted as he wrenched it from his chest. His bones twisted and popped with the force of his pull.

Rising from the floor, she threw herself towards the doorway. Each step exploded with the glimmer of escape.

She did not know what awaited her beyond the door, but every stride meant that she would not succumb to the Void or twisted words from Haydrian's lips. The cold metal handles of the great ornate doors greeted her frantic hands.

Before she could lift their heavy circles, brutal palms clapped against her thinly covered shoulders. Hands that smothered the flicker burning within her. The guards tore her from the ironclad doorway as she screamed.

Gailah clawed at the arms that pinned her against rough leather armor. Her nails became daggers, breaking skin and ripping hair from his forearms. She could not bloody his lip, but pain came from many places. Her teeth found a chunk of flesh to sink into, and the guard cried out as the taste of blood filled her mouth.

His hand loosened for a moment, but not long enough.

Haydrian stood, his breath labored, leaning heavily on the table for support. His once-imposing posture now bent, his strength fading, and the mask that had concealed his face for so long no longer provided its veil.

The guard's awful hands clutched her chin in a crippling squeeze.

A bridle, payment for the blood she had drawn from him.

"Hold her still!" Haydrian commanded.

She screamed out against the sweat of his palm.

Haydrian reached for her and her screams no longer mattered. He extended her arm with a caress that made her stomach drop while each smothered cry only brightened his smile.

Every kick became a misstep as panic flooded her mind.

The knife she had lodged in his chest now rested in his hand. Its point dripped a black liquid in small pools at his feet.

Haydrian's narrowed eyes followed the fear in her eyes, and he raised the blade before them.

"Shhhh.. tis but a pinch."

In a precise cut, the golden blade seared the flesh of her arm.

Her cry died beneath her closed teeth as he carved into her skin.

Gailah clamped her eyes shut and thrashed against the sob that burned in her throat. Beneath her closed lids, there was nothing she could picture that could take her far from here.

"I shall give you time to reconsider.. I am more patient than our emperor, but he is eager and will not wait long. Now that my work has begun, he need not wait." He whispered, then ordered the guards to take her back to the dungeons.

Gailah's senses plummeted as pain and rage fought for dominance in the pit of her chest. She did not yield. They would not take her without having to fight her every step until her body failed her.

Just before they dragged her into the dark, she flashed her eyes towards the alchemist.

He stood with dilated eyes and, as if they infatuated him, the drops of her blood rolled down the blade.

"What a beautiful shade of red."

Chapter Twenty-Five

Oxana

Oxana trembled as the hall of judgment billowed with fervor. Her vision blurred as those that hurried around her passed in streaks of gold and green. Shouts cried out between the squabbling regents, but their words jumbled into shapeless heaps in her ears.

Haydrian was always behind her eyes. Haydrian's voice was in a serpent's hiss behind every syllable. His words compelled her from consciousness and daylight, from the surface of her world.

Deeper into the maze of her mind, she stumbled through the chaos of her thoughts, pleading for freedom, for someone to listen.

The sound of Haydrian's voice created a swirling sensation, a whirlpool that spread feverishly across her skin. In a muddied wash of water, her reflection was forever unclear and inconsistent in the rippling current.

Even in her own mind, she did not trust herself.

Oxana's existence, as she knew it, had her trapped beneath a lake-like surface where she watched life through the crashing tide–a window within the cell of her mind.

Golden veins of sunlight pierced through just enough to keep the darkness of the deep at bay but not to free her from his grip.

Try as she might, no magic or healing could break through the barrier.

She watched the movements of their realm trapped within the corners of her mind, a golden fractal of a window into the world to which she had once belonged.

When her lungs felt like bursting and she could not bear the darkness, the gods brought her air.

Air came as raven, tousled hair and the gentle touch of his hands. Romulus always lifted her above the surface of her nightmare. His voice silenced the words that tormented and cornered her spirit.

It was always his smile that told her she was awake, no voices or darkness.

There were so many things she needed to tell him–to warn Romulus, to warn everyone–but each time she came up from the deep, all those things were gone.

She was vanished beneath the boundary that remained behind her eyes.

She loved him.

She clung to that, to the tether that kept him close to her. The love that held her to the truth. That was all she knew when Romulus' touch came to steady her.

She reached for Romulus, for the sound of his voice that protected her from Haydrian's whispers. His cruel words always waited for her to return to the darkness of his labyrinth, welcoming her to the deep.

Each time she remembered herself, she saw Haydrian lingering below like a monster, ready to drag her back to the depths of her mental prison.

As she drifted down again, the teeth of his voice sank into her skin, followed by the delusion that suppressed all hope of escape. She was drowning her in despair.

But this time was different. As the tide of his power rose to claim her, something shifted.

Blinding, searing golden light pierced through the surface above her.

He was in pain.

Someone wounded him.

As Oxana sunk within his grip, she felt his pain. An image flashed through her mind, a golden blade cut through the waves above her. The wards collapsed in a terrifying, thunderous crack and the watery prison in her mind fractured.

All of it fell away–despair, the pull of his voice, and the bite of his pain.

In an instant, she could breathe as the watery veil vanished. The oppressive weight of his power receded, and Oxana awoke with her face pressed against a cold marble floor.

Like the sky and the ground itself had risen to meet her, every sense came alive.

Warm air filled her lungs.

She could see through both her eyes with no golden slit for a window. The golden streaks around her hand slowly fused in sore and snapping movements.

Her entire body ached from the space he had taken up in her spirit, leaving her somewhere between alive and dead. The freeing emptiness of her mind rolled through her neck and all stiffness fled her body.

Her mind was no longer underwater.

It was clear, like a sunrise over an open glade where flowers bloomed as blue painted the sky. She alone inhabited the space behind her eyes.

The only voice inside belonged to her. Tears brimmed in Oxana's eyes.

As she pressed up from the ground, familiar hands cupped her face.

Good and kind brown eyes enveloped her as she saw her husband's face. Every fiber of her being wanted to dissolve into him–to weep, to cling to him, and to disappear from the world around them.

Romulus' eyes were frantic as he pulled her close with fear in his fingertips as he held her tighter.

"Oxana," he whispered, "My dear, what's wrong?"

"I can see you." She wept as he held her face. "I can see you."

The aching wounds in her arms and legs continued to provoke the magic in her veins.

As he held her, Oxana looked up, and they were surrounded.

His uncle stood a few paces off. Trejen's eyes were sickly and his usual color was gone from his cheeks.

The chill from the floor clung to her skin, and it reminded her of the first frost of spring. From across the room, the mountain queen observed Oxana with an ashen face and terrified eyes.

Her momentary peace shattered.

All the warnings she had screamed behind the prison walls came flooding back.

Spessian guards surrounded their ancient queen with their swords drawn. Yellow piercing light illuminated the room, exposing the dust that swirled in the air.

"The tree," she gasped. "He has her beneath the tree."

"She is mad." The Spessian queen cried.

"What does she mean Romulus?" Trejen spoke to Romulus like she was absent from the room.

"I will not waste my breath on the ravings of a madwoman! My people will return to the Riverlands until your men find the princess." Queen Allagria backed away with enormous eyes and cautious steps.

Her guards followed as the Spessians hurried from the room.

Romulus' grip tightened around her waist and tucked her shaking frame beneath his chin. Her heart swelled as he helped her rise from the ground.

"Speak my love."

"I am not mad! Haydrian has Gailah in the same dungeon in which they held me prisoner!" Oxana's pulse dropped out from under her. She gripped him harder as she fought against the memories that overwhelmed her. "He has her beneath our sacred tree. In the dungeons of the alchemists." Her voice choked on the words rising in her chest.

"That cannot be! Those were sealed!" Trejen turned to face Lord Barrock.

Something passed between the king and his commander. Their faces mirrored each other, blanching in horrid realization. Lord Barrock called for his men, for horses to be readied and weapons gathered.

She would not waste a single second of her true self.

She clutched onto Romulus with frantic fingers. The words rising in her throat came out in the panic of bees.

"He is using the old alchemy dungeons beneath the tree! That is his lair! He siphons life away from its roots. He is stealing life itself! Go to the tree! That is where you will find her! He will do to her what he has done to me if you do not find her! He will pois.."

She could no longer master her shaking hands. Her limbs followed and her head fell to her husband's chest.

"I'm so sorry" Trejen's voice was but a whisper.

He held out his hand for the Mountain Queen. "Let us ride and bring Gailah home."

The queen took hold of his hand and he led her through the doors of the great hall. Oxana watched as all but Romulus left the room.

The comfort of his attentiveness surrounded her, but it did not shut out the blow of indifference from anyone else in the room.

Her body continued to groan and heal shut, though only parts of her body seemed to respond to its freedom. Her fingers and hands still bore golden streaks, desperate to fuse her skin.

"He will take all he can from the tree until it is no more, Romulus..." her voice burned as horrifying visions danced across her mind.

"Once he takes what he wants, I will be gone."

Torin

The gentle afternoon sunlight pierced through his closed eyelids. His lungs expanded, but Torin's inhale seared through his chest. Everything hurt. His eyes snapped open, and a deep groan escaped as he lay against the soil.

Dirty, crumbled leaves greeted him as Torin's hands flew to the ground beside him. He rocked forward with the heels of his hands, but someone stopped him by gripping his forearm.

"Easy brother, you've been nearly dead for sometime now."

Alexi?

Why was he here? Where was Gailah? A tidal wave of frantic urgency coursed through him, each heartbeat echoed the memory of their ambush and the acidic taste of fear lingered on his tongue.

Alexi's blurry silhouette overshadowed him, and everything around him was a bright splotchy green.

"Where is Gailah? What have you done?" Torin seized his brother's biceps, and his words echoed in his ears as he gripped Alexi tighter. The horizon bobbed like the bow of a ship. "Where is she?"

"The better question, brother, what have I not done?" Alexi brushed off his hand bitterly, and he rose from the dirt beside Torin.

He bent his knees, but pain swiftly scaled his body. In a sudden reflex, he ran a hand along his side, and as his breath caught, Torin spat.

His ribs had cracked.

Years of fighting at sea had gifted him many broken bones and his body held onto the memory of each one. While his onyx armor offered impenetrable protection, the unrelenting force of the fall paid no heed to what armor he wore.

A familiar screech tore through the dense canopy, and the unmistakable cry sent a jolt through his heart. Torin quickly extended his forearm.

Anticipation and hope coursed through him.

In an instant, Kelligh collided with his arm, the impact reverberated with a powerful force that nearly set him off balance.

The hawk cocked her head to the side and yanked at his cloak with her beak. Her distress saddened him, but he smiled at the cacophony of chirps following her movements like the sound of a disgruntled, brood hen.

"I'm sorry, I gave you quite a fright didn't I?" He whispered as he brushed a hand against her rust-colored feathers.

"We found you half dead, and the gods would have you right now if.."

"We?" Torin responded and searched the forest beyond his brother.

Alexi shook his head.

"The second-born prince of the Mountain. We found you, and thinking you had died, the prince left in search of his sister. He left you to me."

The words rolled across his brother's tongue in a deft mumble. Alexi did not look at him and Torin knew there was more behind his frozen gaze that bored into the forest floor.

The heaviness in Torin's pulse struggled to find an even rhythm.

Flashes of their attack blazed through his mind. The forest teemed with voracious white eyes, descending upon them with an unforgiving hunger. Pain and poison consumed him before he could even grasp his sword, but not so fast that he did not see them take her.

He closed his eyes as her scream echoed in his memory.

Torin!

A shuddering exhale raced through his lungs and jolts of lightening ran along his spine.

"Where was he headed?" Torin sputtered.

Alexi's eyes snapped upwards, and his brows furrowed.

"Why didn't you tell me your plan before you tried to get us killed?"

Distrust rose in his stomach and Torin steadied himself as Alexi stared back at him with his ice-blue eyes.

"When you agreed without hesitation to be the one to poison Gailah, I knew I could not trust you."

"It was not poison, it was a small mercy."

"Mercy! Do you hear yourself? You would have had her wake in Haydrian's cells, terrified and alone."

"None of what you or I did matters. They still found her and took her. There will be no stopping the armies of the End. You know that as well as I!" Alexi spat, then snatched his dagger from the ground. "Why do you think these men intercepted you? You never stood a chance, brother. You only gave her a fool's hope of escape! Not when our grandmother all but gave our crown to that thing..."

Torin exhaled as the pain settled between his joints. His teeth clenched in his jaw as ran his fingers through his dirt covered hair.

"Don't you see?" Torin barked back, "That's why I stole Gailah, why I begged her mother for an army. If Haydrian's fleet arrives upon the ships, our grandmother gave him, wearing our Spessian armor." He pounded a fist against his chest plate. "Our people will be the first to fall on their path of retribution. I have not seen their sails on the horizon, but they could arrive any day now. So many will die because she has betrayed Thyssia. But brother, I stole her because of you, because of everyone else who would stand by as our island falls to them!"

The breeze twisted Alexi's hair around his face in the sunlight, and something in his younger brother's sour expression cracked.

"Which way did he go?"

"Away from the Mountain, back towards the keep in the forest." Alexi paused. "There's another archer with him. She's the one who saved you. She passed through just after the last frost melted with the sun."

Torin cursed and retrieved his scattered sword. "We need to move if we have any chance of—"

Torin paused, with Kelligh still perched on his arm. He fumbled for a pouch secured to his belt.

"What are you doing?"

He tied something small around the ankle of his hawk. Torin then pulled a small chunk of dried meat from his belt. Without further explanation, he raised her skyward, and the hawk barreled through the canopy.

Torin stopped. Alexi was not looking at him, but staring into gaps among the tree line.

Alexi grumbled under his breath.

Far in the distance, bleeding from the mountain, a mass of knights spilled into the meadowlands. Churning war horses rode together with their green banners and steel glinting in the afternoon glow.

"Your chance at greatness and war marches this way brother..." Alexi turned for his horse, tied a few paces away.

"Brother, wait!" Torin caught Alexi by the sleeve. "If they see us flee, then I am as good as dead. We need them on our side."

"If you wanted the next King of the Mountain on your side, you should not have stolen his sister." Alexi pulled loose from his brother's grip. "You can let him kill you now or bring Gailah back to them and perhaps he will let you keep your head."

Torin sighed, and Alexi rolled his shoulders in irritation, then looked at Torin as if he waited to know which way they would go.

As each moment swept by, Gailah slipped further into oblivion and his failure delved as a dagger between his ribs.

Memories of the night before flooded back to him; of Gailah moving gracefully on the dance floor, as beautiful as sunlight over the sea. From the outskirts of the ballroom, he observed, torn between awe and terror, wondering what it would be like to dance with her. The same dagger of regret stabbed him again, as the fear of never knowing the feeling of dancing beside her writhed beneath his skin. He had wasted that chance.

Torin stumbled through a labyrinth of choices as armies that hated him flanked them on either side.

There was no turning back, no retreat from the path he had set for himself, for Gailah.

Torin braced his hands on his knees as the pain in his ribs worsened with his quickened breathing.

He had promised her the safety of home, to be far from those who would harm her. Empty words and promises that had all turned to kindling.

He had all but handed her to Haydrian.

The trust she had placed in him, fragile as glass, shattered despite all he could do to protect her. What delusion led him to believe that someone as reckless as himself could safeguard delicate things?

Now he knew how his name sounded in her blood searing scream but not the hope of her smile. The sight of her silver hair disappearing through the trees as she clawed at the ground.

That image tortured him above all else as the last thing he witnessed when his skull collided with the relentless soil.

Sweat beaded along his neck and he knew Aerin would not heed his words. He stood suspended as the mountain armies gathered in a storm of retribution.

Alexi gripped Torin by the collar of his cloak.

"Brother, you have no need for their legions. Our people would rise to your call if it meant that you would ease their torment. We can lead them together when the time comes, but that is not now. I ask you to speak the truth? Did you take her because you wanted to protect our people or because their queen rejected you?"

His brother's question jabbed him in the chest as Alexi shook the front of his chest plate.

"I..." Torin could not take his eyes off the mountain calvary as their numbers swelled into storm clouds, "I arrived at the gathering with the heart to earn the right to fight for our people's freedom. To convince the mountain queen I deserved to be the one she chose for her daughter's hand. But all that changed as I beheld her, as Gailah..."

He had never said her name aloud before and it burned on his lips.

"As we stood there before the Island, we were surrounded yet so alone. She looked at me like a star in a sea of a thousand lesser lights. But as I stood beside her, while every soul looked on, she placed her hand in mine and I knew I would spend my life fighting for the right for her to do so again. We were alone together, and she saw me as no one had before. Like every choice had brought me to her. It was not solely for the sake of our kingdom that I would not let them harm her, but that something so lovely understood the same loneliness that burns beneath my skin. I wanted to be better for her, for our people, and for her to know that someone else could see her and that she was not alone."

Torin's mouth ran dry.

"But everything I have done has only solidified the hate they bear for our people."

Through lowered brows, Alexi rolled his eyes and shook his chest plate again, but not out of anger.

"Why must you be better?" Alexi snapped and spoke through gritted teeth. "Our people are devious and far more clever than any other on this cursed island. That is our strength, brother. We are the serpents among our kingdoms, but let us choose who feels our venom. If Gailah is to be kept safe, our people kept safe, then let us use the best of our cleverness to bring her out."

Torin stood in stunned silence, and there was an undeniable truth to what Alexi had said so close that their noses almost touched. They would face the darkness together. Torin nodded and Alexi shoved off his breastplate and released his fingers from his cloak.

Whisking through the air, an arrow fledged with green feathers sailed over the prince's heads. The cracking sound of bark buffeted through Torin's skin as the arrow plunged into a tree behind them. His jaw ticked as the muscle responded, ready and conditioned for battle.

"Fate has decided for us, brother," Alexi arched his beast's head towards him. "I doubt their next arrow will be so forgiving."

Torin swiftly secured his blade. The metal clicked into place, and then he firmly clasped his hand around his brother's forearm.

With Alexi's support, he mounted the horse, feeling the coarse texture of the animal's fur beneath his fingers. His pulse quickened, syncing with the rhythmic beat of its hooves, as the distinct twang of an archer's longbow reached his ears.

Chapter Twenty-Six

Aerin

Aerin sat astride his father's war horse on a saddle crafted anew from Nadr leather, passed down by his ancestors. They had painstakingly cleaned and cut away bits of the saddle to eliminate his father's bloodstain.

Aerin's chest ached and the clouds above fled the sky, leaving a bluebird sky above them and the chasm staring down at them. Aerin faced the men gathering in his name, twisting against the tension in his jaw.

The knights of the Broken Mountain moved like floodwaters through the meadowlands, trampling sheaths of grass and roiling in herds of calvary. Rumors of war and retribution had captivated their kingdom for months. Their people craved answers and so did Aerin.

Perched high in his saddle, Aerin scanned the horizon in search of Regulus and his knights.

His thoughts caused his breath to labor, straining with each exhale. He was unable to rid himself of the grogginess that lingered in his fingers. His exhaustion starved him of his patience.

Aerin knew that their rejection had insulted house Spessia, but this kind of treachery was more than a slight.

Despite his pathetic attempts to persuade them with made up schemes, Torin had surprised him.

As an heir, an act so brash and thoughtless could cost Torin his title and his life, if the judges so deemed. He would not give the Crown Prince the satisfaction of pleading before the judges. Aerin vowed to kill the next Spessian prince that crossed his path. This was his answer.

Torin wanted war.

Among the gathered knights at the mountain's base, Uncle Regulus emerged on the horizon, with the Chasm's knights following. They were only called out in a moment of absolute need and spared only a few men from the Chasm's defenses.

His father's shadow rode beside him as the knights saluted Aerin in Nadr fashion, an homage to their king, to remind all of who fought beside them. The best of the last Nadr clans.

Regulus urged his horse towards Aerin, separating himself from the rest of the gathered forces. His uncle's black thistly beard protruded over his dawned silver steel chest plate.

His stomach knotted as Regulus approached.

"Greetings, Uncle, thank you for your urgency. We can waste no more time. Soon it will be nightfall."

"Thank you, my Prince. Your loyalty to your sister becomes you." His uncle drew his horse closer and so close that only Aerin would hear. "I would be remiss if I did not confide in you, my Prince, that there is far greater treachery hidden on our island." Regulus whispered beneath his breath.

Aerin flinched, trying to hide the confusion rising with the hairs on his skin.

"What greater matter do you wish to discuss, Uncle? My dear sister's life hinges upon us."

"Indeed, my Prince, but do we know who has taken her?"

"I saw the Spessian heir riding off into the night with her uncle. It is his head that we will be hunting."

"I do not doubt you, Your Highness, but please listen to the truth that only I have seen."

Aerin watched his great uncle's eyes flicker with a golden malice.

"Go on.."

Regulus smoothed the gray edges of his long beard.

"Many years ago, a young man who reeked of wine came barging into your mother and father's wedding feast. He was raving and wild with drunkenness. However, my men caught the fool before he disturbed your parents. How unfortunate that I knew this boy well, for he was raised among our people. He made violent declarations and threats against your father. Words that would only lead him to the noose or the blade. The young man wept before my men released him back to his people."

Regulus did not hold Aerin's gaze, and he watched the green banners swirl through the meadow.

"We released him because of the young boy he once was. I spared Trejen's life that day before he made himself the laughingstock of the mountain."

"Why are you telling me this?" Aerin asked, for he could not picture the stoic king of the forest in a besotted, drunken fury.

His uncle released a tired exhale.

"Because I owe your father a life debt. I held little regard for your father, but he was my king." Regulus' movement was subconscious as he withdrew his mutilated arm closer to his chest. "When your mother called for my head, your father spoke on my behalf. He bore me no obligation, yet he reminded her of the queen she wanted to be. I can still remember the sound of your father's footsteps as he stepped before my executioner's stone. He saved my life, but she wanted something in return for my treachery. A stark reminder of my involvement in Haydrian's uprising, even if my choices were few in those days."

Aerin watched as Regulus lifted his gaze towards the sloping burial mounds.

"I have worn many faces, but I will not die in your father's debt."

Aerin shuddered.

Haydrian had died well before Aerin's birth. His parents had sent them far over the mountain during Azoth's uprising, the longest time Aerin had spent with the Nadr.

"I understand, but please, Uncle, you are wasting your breath if you cannot tell me how this will help me recover my sister."

"The words I speak will be your declaration of war, Nephew."

"Everything you say creates a war inside my mind, uncle. Speak the truth or be silent."

Regulus coughed.

"I believe the man that murdered your father is in league with those that stole your sister. By our laws and the goodness of our gods, I confronted him. I gave him time and opportunity to clear his name, but alas, he has merely confirmed my accusation by implicating his nephew."

Anger coiled within Aerin's chest with the heat of dragon fire. Sparks of blue and green flared across his eyes and blurred his vision.

"Do not reawaken my grief if you do not intend to share your secrets. If you wish to bring my father peace, speak his murderer's name and I will end him."

"My Prince, it is no secret that..." He gave a suffocating pause. "Trejen plotted against your father for the love he bore for your mother. He envied your father from the moment he became king. I saw how he wept at the gates of their wedding feast. Jealousy does not die, young prince, it only burrows deep and bores roots into your soul. I was there that day. I was with your father as he died. While our knights circled to protect your father, and your brother wept, I saw him, Trejen, between the trees. Did he trail us to relish the satisfaction of witnessing your father die? I cannot say. What remains clear is in his hasty retreat, he left behind proof of his treachery."

Aerin's thoughts consumed him and took the form of hate-filled beasts that crashed upon the gates of his mind. His knuckles tightened on the reins of his horse that chafed in his palm.

He pictured Trejen's eyes, and he saw that hate there, too.

Leaning forward in his saddle, he summoned the courage of a king.

Though he did not wear the mountain crown, Aerin understood that history would record today as the beginning of his reign.

"We will meet them before they have the chance to hide behind their wall of trees. Let us fight him before their forest." Aerin said

Regulus' expression did not reveal his thoughts, but he raised a hand to command the legions below the hill they crested.

"What is of utmost importance is that we control the evidence–the truth. They will come for your mother's honor, they will paint your sister the harlot for running with the Spessian heir, they will do everything save confess they murdered your father under those trees. His blood is the proof that we have, and they cannot deny that. We will hold them to the fire and make them produce your sister. If they are in league with the Spessian princes, then we shall find their justice as well. Aerin, your father knew the power of stories. That is why no one speaks ill of him. Why mourners lined the hillside for miles when we burned and buried him? He knew that his power rested on the tongues of his people. Who could despise the King that forgave his enemies? He gave me land, armies, more gold than I can spend. He knew the power of debt. Let all of Thyssia know that as king, you will bring justice to our island and you will avenge us, avenge Gailah, with the swing of your father's sword."

Before he replied, a soldier cantered towards them.

"An archer spotted the Spessian princes in the trees."

BJORN

The prince crouched before the young man as he arched from the pain coursing through his fractured leg.

Bjorn braced the boy's dislocated joint, and the young man breathed rapidly through his teeth.

Bjorn could set the knee right, but the severity of its angle made it impossible to straighten.

"If I were to set your leg, I would only harm you further. You need a healer. What is your name, boy?"

"Tomas" His eyes were closed, with pain creasing his brows.

Bjorn fashioned a splint using a fallen branch and the belt that secured Tomas' sword. Having witnessed ample battles and injuries, Bjorn was well aware of his healing capabilities.

He yanked the belt taut between his fingers as he tightened the branches, then searched for something to bear Tomas' weight.

"You will walk again, Tomas. Many a soldier has come home dressed in such a brace." He adjusted the ties on the boy's joint.

Tomas' face became ashen.

"I am no soldier. How can I face my family as a traitor? My hands run red with blood, yet I have only a nightmare's memory of what I've done."

Bjorn exhaled and held Tomas' gaze.

"You are no traitor. Help me find my sister, help me free our brothers, and I will knight you myself, Tomas. I promise you this." He extended his arm. A warrior's promise. Bjorn saw himself in Tomas' frightened gaze.

Through wisps of his brown sheep's wool hair, Tomas looked up at Bjorn's hand with skeptically hopeful eyes. Tomas paused but clasped Bjorn's forearm as the prince lifted him from the ground. Tomas yelped and winced with each movement upward, mindful of his extended leg.

Bjorn's skin prickled. His heart stopped as leaves rustled in the distance.

The white-eyed ghosts of his dreams often followed such ominous sounds.

"How can I help you if I cannot walk?" Tomas' voice knocked against the panicked haze in Bjorn's mind.

He lowered his hand to his ax, his pulse raged beneath his fingers. Before he had the chance to respond to Tomas, a familiar, feminine voice cleared the haze from Bjorn's eyes.

A frigid shiver traced its way down his spine as he pivoted to behold Senna weaving through the depths of the forest.

Relief tackled him, and a spring of hope bubbled within his chest.

She was safe.

Fear came second.

He wanted her far from the knife wielding shadows hiding behind every branch but if there was one person capable of battling the terrors of the forest; he knew it was Senna.

"Do you always leave wounded men in your wake?" Senna parted the thicket and crossed through the creek, hopping from stone to stone with only the sounds of her boots tapping softly. Knives decorated every curve of her body and a bow string peaked over her shoulder. Senna's smirk dissipated and her brows furrowed when she found Tomas beside Bjorn.

A faint streak of smeared paint still stained his brow.

"My name is Tomas, my lady." The boy tried to bend into a bow, but almost lost his balance against the prince.

Senna smiled cautiously, but the curiosity in her eyes was something Bjorn had never seen before. Her thoughts moved furiously behind her eyes.

"How did you..." She raised Tomas' dangling arm, pulling back the tattered wet layers to see the remnants of watery paint.

"They poisoned his mind. He is free of the runes that impressed him. Senna, He belongs to a family on the mountain. All of them are men of the Island." Bjorn spoke, linking his shoulders with Tomas.

She was silent for a moment and her eyes fluttered with incredulous beads of curiosity before she leaned forward to study the remnants of paint on his skin.

"We've slain our own people..." Her auburn tresses shook as she stared back at them with pain-filled eyes.

Bjorn breathed deeply as he supported the young man beside him, but also for the sake of never again wanting to see pain in her eyes.

"Senna, I.." Bjorn stumbled over his words, but suddenly she looped an arm around Tomas' waist. She took on a portion of the boy's weight and met Bjorn's gaze.

"Someone ransacked and tore apart my cottage. They are hunting his talisman. My uncle is in danger and if your sister is with his captors, I would never forgive myself if I stood aside while they needed rescue."

"Tomas, tell me who painted these on you?" She asked as she turned her head inwards to see Tomas' weary face.

"A man more dead than alive. They came during the night while I carried oil for my father's forge. Something pierced my neck and then all my thoughts became feverish and vile. I had forgotten what it meant to be alive and what life was worth living for. I felt so angry that only hate mattered, and that I needed to make someone suffer for it."

Indeed, there was a circular pink scar at the base of his neck.

"All of that faded when we fell into the ravine."

Senna gasped and her head snapped towards the bubbling ravine that had soaked most of Bjorn's lower half.

"This ravine is a branch from the mountain, where Ilsnadad begins..."

Her eyes flicked up and down the trickling river bank. Senna looked at him and, without hesitation, he understood why the enchantments had lost their grip on him.

The river, the relic of house Spessia, wandered the length and breadth of the island as the conduit of the gods.

"The others! If Tomas can lead us to their encampment, then we may save more than my sister and your uncle. We can bring our people home," Bjorn said. He harbored fragile confidence in their success, yet found himself with no other anchor for hope.

He watched a muscle flex in Senna's jaw, but her mind began to churn again until her eyes widened with something that burned brighter than the hope he held onto.

Senna straightened her spine and looked at Bjorn with a piercing gaze and suddenly, he knew he would follow wherever she led.

"If Tomas can find his way back, I will summon them. I will draw them to me and lead them to the river. Their fate will be determined by the gods, and their runes shall be erased. I cannot promise you I will spare those who chose to fight me but—"

Tomas shook his head.

"That won't be enough. The longer the runes stay on our skin, the more we lose ourselves to him. Blue fades to the darkest colors of night. Permanent runes that will not wash away. Those who guard the deepest parts of the cave have runes that are no longer paint but have become their flesh. I may never walk right again, but I know the nine showed me mercy by letting me live a while longer with my mind." Tomas said and hobbled away from them then braced himself beside a tree trunk.

Tomas stared into the trees the same way Bjorn did, untrusting of everything that surrounded them.

"They're hidden in a cave?" Senna asked, moving to face the boy.

"Aye," He nodded. "The deepest kind I've ever seen. It turns to stone and damp cold air. My memory is poor, but not so poor that I cannot take you there. I know we are close by."

Bjorn sighed with relief, knowing they would find Gailah soon and that he had wasted no time trying to find her.

The fear of being too late sunk deeper into his stomach.

Bjorn shook drops of river water from his hair and beard. Senna caught sight of him. Her eyes rolled with a hint of exasperation, yet a fleeting, nearly imperceptible smile graced her lips and vanished as quickly as her eyes dropped to her satchel. A smile that burned into his memory like a blazing star.

Senna retrieved a tonic from her satchel and brought it to the boy's lips.

In the maze of greenery and saplings, Bjorn found a sturdy branch and snapped it across the width of his thigh. He smiled secretly at his handiwork and handed Tomas' the crudely shaped wooden crutch.

"Show us the way. I'll carry you if need be, but we must hurry."

Chapter Twenty-Seven

Bjorn

Tomas guided them to the cave with little difficulty, for he swore he would never forget the paths that hatred had etched into his memory. Among the spring torch heather, Bjorn carefully tampered down a comfortable spot for Tomas to conceal himself while they explored the cavern.

Despite his willingness to accompany them below, Bjorn decided against it. The prince knew it may come down to a fight while protecting himself, Gailah, and Senna's uncle.

He did not want to add one more person to his list of those he promised to keep safe.

Tomas had endured enough in its depths.

As the yawning rocks came into view, he was grateful for any help the boy provided at all. They approached the mouth of the cave, Bjorn fervently prayed that Tomas would remain hidden.

Senna clutched his wrist.

With the flare of a sunrise, her grip pulsed through him and his feet stopped in their tracks.

Her green eyes shot left and from beneath her cloak, she drew a finger to her lips. She had spotted a wandering raider beside the cave.

Neither of them dared breathe as moments passed in the dawdling suspense of their target.

He staggered forward and the ragged, wild man dipped his head under the arching entrance.

The lines tensing Senna's brow eased, and they released their breaths in unison.

Senna lingered in the trees beside the opening of the cave, looming overhead like the gaping jaws of a monstrous beast. Its mouth was greater than the beasts of old that soared through the sky and spewed fire for breath. Senna's eyes studied every tree and root before the cave.

Fear did not haunt a single angle on her face. He watched in awe as she dipped behind every trunk, searching for any signs of threat. His skill in battle rested between the strength of his shoulders, the fire in his heart, and the sharpness of his blade.

He did not think as she did, but he found her entrancing as she scanned their surroundings.

But when she returned to his side, Bjorn's spirit rebelled as Senna secured the knives around her waist.

The idea of a horde of men pursuing her was a burden too heavy for him. Bjorn's heart swelled in his chest. He grasped her arm before she stepped out from the shelter of the trees.

"Senna..."

Her eyebrows snapped upwards at his touch, but he could not let go of her.

She would be fast; he knew she would be careful, and he never doubted her aim, but he doubted the trees, the river, and every changeable thing standing between her and safety.

She reached her free arm behind her and Senna passed him her quiver, saving two arrows she plucked from its keeping. She did not smile, nor did she speak, as she pressed the leather quiver against his chest.

It forced him to release his grip, but he took it from her with a pleading look.

"Hide it here, near these trees. I'll move better this way." She said, as if she had read the creases between his eyes like the pages of a book.

He took the weight of it in his hands.

Her weapons were precious to her, and that responsibility rested heavy against his palms.

Senna nodded and raised her hands to her verdant cloak. With the deftness of a spider, she unfastened the knot, and the cloak descended to the forest floor. Her hair fell around her shoulders, burning brightly as copper flames among the trees.

He scooped the fabric from the ground and her warmth still clung to the wool beneath his fingers.

In the next moment, she shed anything that posed a risk to her escape. He stood there in silence, battling the panic surging through his pulse. She reached for her bow and tensed the string twice before she held in tightly in her grip.

"Be fast."

She turned to leave, but Senna looked back.

"Wait," From beneath her tunic and leathers, she produced her uncle's talisman.

She came back to him, pulling her hair away from her neck. Uncertainty flared in her emerald eyes as they flashed up at him. She untied the leather band from behind her head and dangled the triangle between their bodies.

In a swift snap, she rendered the thin brittle metal in two and the magic hissed.

Both pieces bore the light of alchemists' work, but she slipped the smaller piece within her leathers.

The larger piece still dangled from the strap.

"So the cave will accept you."

She stepped onto her tiptoes and reached her arms around his neck.

Bjorn bent lower and his pulse quickened. Senna's forearms rested on the width of his collar and her hands rustled the edges of his beard. She tied the knot behind the nape of his neck.

He scoured for something clever to say, but for just that breath, he stayed silent to enjoy the closeness of her presence.

The crisp scent of the forest surrounded them, and the leather cord pulled against his neck.

"Be safe." Was all he could think to say as she stepped into the clearing with the grace of a deer and the certainty of the stars.

His heart pressed against his sternum, just below the talisman, with the magic that prickled against his skin.

Senna's spine was unbearably straight as she stood undaunted before its entry.

The darkness of the cave crawled forward in a fog. The muscles in the curve of her calf pulsed and her foot bounced, making herself ready to fly through the trees.

She drew back her bowstring and the muscles in her shoulders responded in harmony to the tension, a tension that mirrored the tightening cords of his heart.

As Senna released an arrow, he felt the strain within him. He could not exhale against the tightening in his chest.

Every breath was a battle.

The cave devoured the arrow, and a stir emanated from deep within the cave. A sound rose like the hum of a hive. Undeterred, Senna drew her bow once more, and time slowed around the spiraling arrow as it disappeared into the rocky mouth.

The thrum grew louder and her leg no longer bounced but shook. That change was enough to crack his resolve, and he drew his axe.

If Senna needed him, he would charge from the trees before anyone could harm her. If she fell, then she would not fight them alone.

She wanted a swarm; she wanted the entire throng of hate enchanted men to follow her.

Bjorn tightened his hand around the handle of his axe. He readied himself for those that awaited him underground.

Senna bent at the waist and screamed into the mouth of the cave. Her voice echoed in taunting arrogant waves against its stony surface and it only worsened the fear in his heart.

Senna's cry echoed through the dimness of the forest just before war cries, accompanied by the clang of steel, erupted from the cave's entrance.

Thud.

Thud.

Thud. Thud. Thud. Thud.

Their wolf-like footsteps sprinting against the cavernous floor was her signal to run.

From where Bjorn stood hidden, the need to protect her almost ruined him. In a swirl of auburn, she turned towards the trees, but paused just long enough to let them see her.

Bjorn bit back against his tongue, commanding her to run. Everything in his body was ready to betray his hiding place. Bjorn had watched Senna disappear time and time again, but not like this. Bjorn forgot everything as he watched the men stumbling against each other. Wild flesh clamored against stone.

Their milky eyes and tortured bodies reeked of bloodlust. Their hunched posture and snapping jaws lurched forward along with their onyx swords.

Senna ran, and Bjorn's eyes burned with anger as the throng of men tore after her. She moved through the trees like the forest revered her, almost as if the trunks and undergrowth were making way for their queen.

The men continued to stumble from the cave and followed the rest that ran after her. Their painted runes glimmered in every shade of blue among the dimness of twilight. Senna dissolved into the long shadows of the trees.

Only her hair glinted in the dwindling rays of sunlight. She weaved between the narrow trunks, then vanished into the evening. That last sight of her weakened him as she disappeared behind the horde that pursued her.

Bjorn's hand tightened on his axe and as the last of them tore through the trees, he waited and then he stepped forward before the mouth of the cave.

Chapter Twenty-Eight

Gailah

They callously hurled her against the stone, displaying no sign of remorse. These men behaved worse than animals, like men without mind or feeling. As Gailah pulled herself from the mire of the dungeon floor, the ache of her body's exhaustion crumpled the strength in her arms.

Cold frost spread along her bleeding, wounded arm. The angry and burning pain subsided into a strange dull sensation, deep almost to the bone.

She could no longer hear Jaius' weakened breath, but she could still see the silhouette of his helpless, wounded body. He had not stirred since her return to the cell. She prayed he was no longer in pain.

Gailah did not hate him, but a shade of her own cruel voice flickered inside, and told her she should. That this was his fault, all of it, but this was bigger than him, bigger than her. Jaius had payed for his misgivings with his life. Hate would only rob her because he had nothing left to give.

The burning slice of the blade roared through her mind. Tears beaded in her eyes. The symbol engraved on her skin stared up at her. It resembled a near complete crescent with a line at either side.

She had every right to fear the rune he had carved.

It was more than a symbol–it was a name.

The last island, the island of exiles, the island that no longer belonged to the gods but to those who had claimed it, an island that had become the end. Its name and symbol was the sigil of death.

She crumbled against the wall of her cell as if she could become one with it, as if the stone would hide her from this waking nightmare.

She knew the frigid stone like the embrace of an old friend, no, her father's embrace. She remembered cold air rushing against her chapped lips as she chased him through the forests near the castle.

How he had carried her after hours of teaching her to create kingdoms from clumps of snowflakes.

Gailah wrapped her arms around her weakened torso, clutching her bloodied arm to her chest, trying to find his memory and give it life. Smoke. The comforting aroma of burning firewood always accompanied her father's presence.

The smell was a delightful concoction of laughter and goodness that instantly lifted her spirits.

She hated that anger crawled across her skin, loosening her arms from her body. The memories of him became thinned and translucent.

Grief bit into her flesh like a gathering of insects.

She had felt that anger before.

It stood beside her like chiseled stone before his burial mound, as she mourned in fury filled silence.

She had wished for the ground to swallow her as they heaped the last stones over what remained of his pyre. Burned and buried.

As Gailah curled against the prison wall, she realized the ground had listened.

Her heart burned with betrayal.

Warriors like her father did not die.

Her chest pounded at her own foolishness. A foolishness that always expected her father to stand at her side with the sword of the mountain drawn at ready to defend her.

Of course he could die.

The smoke from the pyre ruined the smoke of her memories.

She tried to smother the biting gnats of anger that whispered, *"He would have been here already. He would have carried you home."*

"I'm so sorry," she whispered aloud.

Praying that her words would slip between the stones and find the sky so he could hear her from so far deep beneath the ground.

But there was no one to hear save for the bars and dripping wall.

She had lived with her fingers interlaced with grief. They traveled together through her recent days as companions.

She looked down at her hand and at the ring on her small finger.

Her eyes followed the triangulated swirls along the width of the band–a ring, carved from bone and painted with sky blue swirls.

Runes, but not the kind that enslaved men to their own hatred. They were the carvings of her father's people.

They had come down from the mountains that day.

Gailah watched as the clans paid their respects, passing by with words and duty filled nods.

She had never felt so alone.

Each one mourned by placing small stones in the gaps of the larger stones on his grave.

A small Nadr girl, with mahogany braids, slipped between the crowds and placed the ring in Gailah's palm.

The weight of it was hardly more than a pebble.

The young girl pointed backwards to her mother and father standing a few paces away.

"Dah made me this ring so I can talk to my grandah when I miss him but when Mah told me our king was your dah, I knew Grandah wanted me to give it to you." She spluttered.

The priest's had dipped Gailah's hands in ash that day.

The white bone ring shined brightly against her second skin of cool dust.

She remembered his last day.

He had cared for them so well, but she had not even thought to say goodbye as he departed for the great forest.

She let the muddied crown of her head rest against the wall.

Her eye swelled with tears as she pictured herself. She had stayed in her room that day, alone, and curled up in her usual places. She wanted to beg her former self to go down, to wish him a safe journey, to feel his embrace one last time, to feel the warmth of his sunny beard against the chill of her neck. She had no memory of him disappearing past the gates of the courtyard.

Slipping the delicate band from her hand, she held it close, pressing the ring against her heart.

She wanted to believe the gods had endowed some sort of sympathetic power to the small token.

Maybe all this torment would bring her to him, and that their parting would not be long. Her throat thickened with tears and her fingers tightened around the small ivory circle.

She prayed that the nine would welcome her.

From the corners of her memory where her father lived, the warmth of his voice echoed in the quiet.

"Gailah,"

Gailah felt her spine stiffen and Jaius' words shuddered through her mind.

For they will fight to keep you in darkness

Why would the gods welcome her? Because she was the daughter of a good and faithful king? Perhaps, but she could not think of any other virtue they would find worthy of their venerable halls. The legacy of someone else's triumph? Why could she only see herself through her father's eyes?

Her existence hinging on the pride that filled his eyes and how loudly she could make him laugh.

Gailah, daughter of Katha and Freyden.

Is that all her life would be worth when they came to bury her?

A few ink blots on the pages of their history. A branch caught between the rapids of the world around her. A twig beaten and broken beneath the weight of the water crashing in on all sides. A pitiful, transient wisp of a soul torn to pieces for being her mother's daughter.

Gailah's fingers raked through the matted strands.

No, that would not be all. There was more, far worse, staining the stories that would be told of her.

Torin was dead because he believed her worthy of saving.

Torin, the prince who died.

Torin's face appeared in her mind, and she saw the sunrise in his silver hair, the grey of his eyes and how hopeful they had been.

She wanted to wretch as her fingers dug into the skin at her scalp.

Fight to see the sky again.

Jaius' words pierced through her chest and her tears made it difficult to swallow.

How?

How could she fight to see the sky when the ground had swallowed her among the damned?

She wiped a tear from the quiet stream on her cheek. She wanted to hide her tears from the world and from the walls of the cell. Everything around had eyes.

All she knew to do was hide.

"Do not be afraid."

She heard the kindness of her father's voice and it flickered within her like a candle left to burn through the night.

There was nothing but fear in Gailah's body as she shook against the smothering lump in her throat.

She saw her life like the shores of her island, hammered repeatedly by the thundering waves. Each passing current took more and more of her spirit.

Something deep within her whispered to curse her mother, curse her for all of this, and for the rune carved into her skin.

Gailah did not hate her mother for the duty she owed to her people. She did not hate the idea of marriage or being queen. She wanted marriage, but a marriage that meant feeling whole alongside someone else.

She pulled her knees close to her body. Gailah saw life ahead of her as queen of the great forest, like the empty darkness of her cell.

"Why did she stop listening?" the question rattled her clenched teeth as she rested her head upon her knees.

Why had her mother stopped hearing her daughter's words, as if her voice belonged to nothing more than the wind? Why had her silence become more valued than her desires?

Gailah wept because, though her mother still drew breath, she had lost her as well.

She tried to resist, but exhaustion had stolen her strength and her ability to stay conscious. In a crumble of fabric, mud, and tears, she fell asleep.

TREJEN

Katha rode at his side as their golden cloaks moved along the great forest pathway, while the late afternoon sun lowered in the sky. Each hour passed like a thousand, and any hope of recovery dwindled with the dying sun.

The poison at his side was nearer now to his heart, like an ever present shadow. He could even taste its venom with every swallow and it clung like a thick sap as it pooled within him.

He knew it would not be long now.

His sword arm ached with pain deep in his bones.

Her restless night was clear in the sunken and bloodshot appearance of Katha's eyes.

It was a mystery to him how she kept her dignity, despite facing so much torment. Her remaining guards accompanied the royal retinue as they thundered back to the keep of the Autumn court. Trejen had defied her decree and indulged Jaius out of well-intentioned hope.

He was weaker than the pain ravaging his body.

Trejen knew that war rested in his beloved's eyes. If they could not bring Gailah home, that hunger for war would fall on him.

The world was crumbling around him because he was no match for the man within him who still loved the Queen of the Mountain.

Chapter Twenty-Nine

Gailah

THE SCATHING PAIN spreading across her arm shocked Gailah awake. Her lids were stiff and sore as they shot open.

As the rune's powers diffused through her skin, the wound swelled with red, fiery anger. Beside the mark of the end, her skin was taught, and the heat spread upwards like burning rose thorns.

With feeble and unsteady hands, she pushed herself away from the wall. She needed a healer, and she needed one now.

More than a healer, she needed a way out of this nightmare, out of this dungeon, and out of her sham marriage to Romulus.

She would not die down here when there was still so much of life that she had yet to live for herself. She would not be an empress to a faceless tyrant.

Gailah shredded the fabric of her hem, her frantic nails ripped the pieces into a bandage.

She had no water to wash the mire from her angry wound, but she did her best to clean the area surrounding the rune with the fragments from her gown.

In the cell's darkness, she fumbled with the ties around her wrist, bracing her arm against the floor.

Her skin was now pulsing and warm with a budding alchemical fever. She struggled to secure the scraps over the wound. With the pressure of the fabric against the rune, she fought against the tears in her throat as she fastened the knot with her teeth as she bit down on the scraps.

She felt herself cracking as it tightened against her flesh in a blinding, nauseating wave of pain. It was a bandage that ached but seemed to hold her together all the same.

It would buy her time.

Her vision spun as her stomach tightened with the sickening throb in her arm.

Suddenly, she realized the drip in the wall had gone silent for a moment.

The iron doors absorbed the torchlight, but from the corner of the cell, a gentle glow emerged from the darkness.

It vanished in a burst of yellow rays but left in its wake, cracks fissured the mortar and stone. A violet five-petaled flower bloomed from where the cracks began–a flower in the shape of a star.

In a blink, the drip resumed and splashed up its gentle face. The plant's stem was delicate and twisting beneath the blossom. Its frail light seeped in a deep lavender into the center of the flower. Its petals were far brighter than any flower she had known on the mountain.

Sweat beaded on Gailah's brow.

Day and night had become one. She could no longer distinguish between what was true and what belonged to her dreams.

With the lifting of every finger, a prickling tension fought under the muscles in her hand. She reached to touch the flower's soft petals, but she did not trust that what she saw was real.

Her finger grazed the lip of the petal, and she recoiled.

Soft golden spheres erupted in plumes from its center.

Gailah gasped and fell back onto her hands, but she bit down into her lip as her wrist buckled against the stone.

The orbs danced in the air, and she pushed against the floor. They bobbed on invisible strings and circled her finger tips. She dared not touch them, but they found her.

They melded to her skin like dew drops made of honey. Something strange traveled through her, making her skin shudder and chill. Gailah blinked and all of it was gone, the flower, the orbs of light.

Gailah had suffered the hallucinations of fevers before. Her head was too heavy now. She closed her eyes and let her head fall back against the stone wall.

Gailah blinked as the dim glow of the room greeted her. She was no longer in her cell.

No.

No.

She panicked as, above her, the golden roots of the oak tree weaved in shimmering vessels across the ceiling. They had removed her crude bandages.

The rune carved into her wrist and stared up at her. She felt it burrow against her bones, deeper with every fevered chill.

Her pulse echoed in the radiating throb that consumed all her limbs. The fever was swift and left her skin burning like parchment.

Gailah pulled herself up slightly, just enough to lift her head from the floor. She could hear the scratching of metal and something burned.

The smell of rotten oak leaves overwhelmed her.

There was no feast on display or any sort of finery. The shadows had returned its contents to the original alchemy tables. There were scrawny runes carved across the floor filled with shards of glass and streaks of paint. There was glass on the tables and glass on the floor.

Where had they found pure bright glass?

Her thoughts collided with the fear in her mind. She could see the runes better now from where she lay on her side.

That was how he controlled the shadows.

He commanded the room to obey him with the spells etched into the stone.

“Ah! There you are! I apologize for moving you before you awoke, but there is no time to dawdle!”

Haydrian craned his neck from where he sat as she rose from the floor.

"My preparations are already underway and I will not keep our emperor waiting."

In front of him, a sizable table displayed an array of tools and peculiarly colored liquids, all unfamiliar and intimidating to her. Small iron racks of candles stood ablaze, stationed around the room as sentries.

Once again, he was draped in a cloak of rust-colored velvet, but this time, adorning his chest was a plate of deep onyx armor. She did not know if he knew pain, but now she knew her knife had struck him deep enough to be afraid.

He was vulnerable, and now they both knew it.

Like a forgotten final stair, her heart tumbled.

Spessian armor was unlike any other. Another facet to the treachery that had festered in the Riverlands. His mercenaries and the Spessian queens were the same.

Her feet stumbled backwards. Behind the alchemist, the enormous ornate doors rested ajar.

Her nightdress was stiff with filth, but as she ran for the door, it clung to her legs. She grabbed for her skirts, but it was not enough. She was too slow.

"Bring her to me!"

Two guards seized her by her upper arms. Their hands bruised deeper as she reared back, throwing her body weight down, her bare feet dug into the floor.

He clicked his tongue with pretentious condemnation.

"Let go of me!"

Haydrian did not flinch as she cried out through the domed chamber. Instead, he focused on something small and delicate in his hands.

"Did I not instruct that you were to be gentle with her?"

Their fingers eased with reluctance. Gailah could not cease the burning in her chest or her ragged breath as she seethed at him through lowered brows.

"You ask them to be gentle, yet you carve into me like a dead animal?!"

Gailah's teeth ground upon each other as fire danced through her veins.

He sighed and looked up at her from his work.

She stifled a cry as their eyes met.

She would not cry, no matter how much fear fermented in her stomach.

Gailah's knees began to shake.

His face had taken on a more ashen hue than before, devoid of any attempt to conceal his appearance.

He was more ghastly than any corpse, with yellowed eyes and loose lids sagging around them.

"I will make no apologies for my appearance. My work is far more important than appeasing your delicate nature." He paused, but continued his fervent fixation. "I will assure you that the pain you feel is only temporary. However, it will worsen the longer you are apart from the other who bares your mark." As he spoke, despair plunged its knife into her spirit. "The void has chosen you and it will not be satisfied until the mark you bare finds its equal."

"The nine damn you!" She pulled her head backward again.

He blinked back and cocked his head sideways.

"They already have."

He placed what he had in his hands on the surface of the table, then returned the tools to where they belonged. His fastidious fingers snaked around long iron pincers, and he looked down from where he stood at his desk.

"He will make you empress of the entire archipelago. You will say who lives and who does not. The sun will rise when you tell it to. I can grant any favor you ask. We offer nothing but honor, Your Highness."

She stood silent, hardening herself against the sound of his voice. She closed her eyes trying to picture her father, her family, their mountain, anything besides the gold covered lies he was weaving with his voice.

"You would be the empress the people long for. Our people will finally have some sense of reason to govern them and think of the World you could create at his side? All you must do is surrender to your destiny and you shall never be afraid again. All I ask is for the rest of your kin."

"No!" Gailah's eyes shot open. "I would rather rot in your cells than give you even a fragment of my mind. You're a fool to believe I would surrender my family so you can preserve even a second of your miserable existence."

"Oh? You sound so lovely in that tone. Airth will enjoy that." He smirked, lifting a small golden ring into his focus. "Do you even know what misery your family is capable of?"

Her ragged breath heaved in her chest, and the rune at her wrist scabbed over in a searing wave of magic. She fixed her eyes on the floor, refusing to acknowledge the mockery in his voice.

The guards jerked her head up and the tension from their grip burned in her shoulders.

"Did she tell you what she made me do to their king?"

He rose from where he sat before his instruments. She tried to fight how her arms trembled beneath the guard's fingers.

"Did she tell you how she came to me, weeping, how she begged me to let her keep her beloved? How desperately she needed Trejen by her side, no matter the cost or no matter how much it would cost me. How much it would cost Decius or Lyssia?"

"You lie!" she spat.

Something shattered inside Gailah's chest.

"Do you know what happened? Do you know what she did when your mother saw Decius as I am now? A wretch from the bowels of the void?"

A muscle in his jaw twitched with sick excitement, almost laughing as he stepped away from the desk. His inky strands shook with the movements of his head as he sighed.

Gailah's throat burned with acid, her mind drowning as the words he spoke threatened the foundations of all that she knew.

"I can still see the horror on her face as the king wept for his queen, how he cried and how he called for his boy."

Haydrian's voice rippled in a mocking shift.

"Lyssia! Lyssia! Decius cried. That watery rotting piece of flesh, Katha, Oh Katha had begged to make live again. To be king again so that Trejen might not have to leave her."

His laughter became erratic, like the sound of wild dogs.

"That, that is the true cruelty of this fate, princess. I may have conjured Decius back from the gods, but he was not a man, he was only sorrow. All he could feel was sorrow. And for me? All I feel is hate. The same hate I held in my heart as the gust of the executioner's blade kissed my skin. It now lives and burns aflame inside me."

"She was a child." Gailah sputtered, her hope capsized beneath the weight of his words.

His eyes widened, and he flew across the room, only a breath away from her face.

His teeth blackened and snapped with rage.

"No!"

A wild finger collided with her cheek. He snarled at her through his lowered brows.

"No..." He whispered and his breath reeked of decaying wood.

"She was a queen. A queen I was forced to obey, and she betrayed me! When the judges and priests came for the man who broke the mountain," He snaked a hand around his throat. "She let them take me. She let my blood absolve her before the eyes of the world."

Everything Gailah knew about the uprisings, the mountain had all been a lie. Gailah felt the barriers in her mind beginning to weaken. She could no longer picture her mother's face.

His haunched posture retreated and in an instant he rolled back his shoulders like an uncoiling snake.

He lifted his cold, ashen hands to her cheeks and whispered.

"Who could refuse the chance for such power? To shake the gates of paradise? How could the nine taunt us when death is no more?" Haydrian laughed bitterly, and his fingers gripped her skin.

"*Now all they do is taunt me!*" He screamed against her cheek and his hands shook her skin.

His voice rattled through her teeth.

His fingers tightened around her chin, pursing her lips, nails digging into the softness of her flesh..

"Let go of me!" Gailah screamed back and felt something monstrous rise within her, something within her that frightened her. "No matter what you accuse my mother of, I will join my father beside the gods before I let you or your emperor have a single stone from Thysia's soil."

He smiled, his hands fell away and warmth returned to her face.

No, not warmth, fire.

"Are you certain? You sound so alive when you promise this kind of violence. You are certainly a well-matched pairing. Your declarations are admirable, but there is little choice left in the matter. The pain you feel, Airth feels it too."

Haydrian took a few paces backward and took in her figure.

"I must admit, I made a mistake. When I had them take the priestess from the forest, she looked so much like your mother. When the mark rejected her, well, I had no other alternative but to make her useful to me. That's how I found you." He tapped a finger just beneath his eye and shook his head with a chuckle.

"I don't understand."

"The girl, the priestess, the one who wept for the autumn prince." He waved his hands as irritation filled his words.

"I was searching for you, but she has made a beautiful informant for me, albeit unwillingly, but she helped bring you to me."

Gailah's legs weakened and she could picture Oxana's gold split eye.

"No!" She threw her weight against the men holding her.

They countered.

Gailah cried out as they forced her arms behind her back. Then shoved her head forward in a contorted bow.

Gailah's fears mixed with spit at the apex of her mouth.

She heard him moving across the breath of the floor. The rustle of velvet against his plated armor.

"You wretch." Gailah snarled and let her head fall forward.

Her shoulders ached against her body weight, but her eyes fixed on the runes carved into the stone floor.

"Even if you had all the islands in your grasp and the power of the gods in your veins yet all you would be is a hate filled corpse. I pity you! You who know only hate! Yet you wish to take everything from me when I was not the one who stole your eternity. I did not take your power or your soul from your body. I commanded nothing of you! You think your vengeance would move my mother? That she would beg your forgiveness? No! I do not even have her affection, so then why would she pay you mind? She would only move to silence you again, like a mere fly buzzing in her ear."

Haydrian's spine was straight and unmoved as he stood over his alchemy table, but the muscles in what remained of his face did not lie.

"You mistake me. I do not want all."

He lifted the golden trinket once more.

"I am but a singular insect. She cannot silence the host that draws near. Their cries for justice call from the sea, from the End itself. Even if I am lost as a martyr for our empire, my work is already complete."

Lifting her head, coursing heat slithered in waves from the rune at her wrist.

Her teeth silenced her cry as she bit into her swollen lip.

"When your brothers come for you, which should I kill first? The big one or the coward?"

Every boundary in her body snapped.

All hope and courage faded at the image of her brother's dead and grey, like her father.

"Please! You have what you want, but do not take them as well! No one else must die!"

He smiled as he walked towards her, rolling the circlet in his hands.

"I told you I would be fair. I told you, you would decide."

He lifted her hand with ice for fingers and slid the smooth metal band down her forefinger.

The cool metal scraped against her skin, and Gailah's vision blurred.

As he forced the too small band painfully over her knuckles, the rune awakened in a smoldering orange glow. Her legs failed her and the guards released her biceps as knees struck the floor.

In a pendulum swing, she struggled to keep her head from the ground. The pain in her wrist crept in torturous circles across her flesh. Gailah did not have the strength to keep herself from the cool stone, as if the crusted, crescent rune pulled her downward.

Her mind was awake, but her body was unresponsive.

She alone could hear the scream that fell silent on her tongue.

She saw the soles of Haydrian's boots.

He knelt down, tilted his gaze to meet her's. There was a cruel laughter painted across his features. The burning in her arms had spread further, it charred behind her eyes.

"You fought beautifully." He cupped her face as he spoke.

Her head ached as if he had placed a knife between her temples. She was shaking as if every fiber and bone had abandoned her on the floor of his dungeon.

She would have cried, but her tears had fled long ago.

Gailah searched her mind for something of herself to cling to, to hold on to whatever remained of her.

She could only breathe, there was no strength left in her eyelids. She pictured the warmth of her bed, the smell of burning firewood, the sound of her brother's laughter, the softness of Karak's fur nestled against her cheek, the touch of her mother's hand through her hair.

No, that memory was poisoned now. Like fingers slipping from a ledge, she felt her body being lifted from the floor.

Gailah lost herself in the darkness behind her eyes.

Chapter Thirty

Alexi

As weakening daylight crept through the trees, the princes paused beside the edge of the river.

Torin breathed heavily as he drank obnoxiously loud for a prince, from the banks of the Ilsnadad. He stood, and shook the water from his hands as he stood above the mossy stones.

Alexi sighed and ran a hand across the shelf of his brows.

"Brother, I must speak with honestly. I know where they have taken—"

Torin's face blanched, and the disappointment in his eyes festered. Alexi paused and he could not meet his brother's gaze.

In a painful moment of truth, Alexi unraveled the depth of his involvement in their matriarch's schemes–plans he had agreed to, including the retrieval of their compensation.

Three vials of an elixir were made from Gailah's blood.

Torin's anger erupted from where he stood.

"You knew.... You knew what they would do to her and yet you still..." He processed it in a whisper. "...brother, I knew you were going to kill me, but you have damned yourself." Torin's voice echoed through the trees and that disappointment plunged into betrayal behind his brother's eyes. Torin's hands trembled beside the leather bands that hung from his waist.

"...and I did not kill you."

Alexi raised his hands away from his sword.

"The air you breathe should be proof enough. Brother..." He said that word with bitter emphasis. "Let me show you how deeply I regret playing any part in her schemes."

Alexi sighed.

Torin looked at Alexi like he was a spider and Gailah had been a fly on his web. His brother crossed the distance between them, and Torin spoke with gritted teeth.

"Bring me to her and if Gailah is lost, then so are you..."

His brother's voice rolled like thunder, and in that moment Alexi knew when silence was wise.

He nodded.

Torin resumed his grip on the horns of the saddle.

"We are losing precious time. But brother, we can handle a few guards, but beyond merely killing our way in, how will we get through?"

Alexi smiled and shook his head.

"You will do what you do best." Alexi made a gesture with his thumb across his throat. "And I will remind Haydrian of the debt they owe us. I can keep him preoccupied long enough for you to find the girl and get her out before everything goes to.. Well, let's not find out."

Alexi walked toward the river.

Then, suddenly, he remembered Bjorn and Senna.

He spun on his heel, stormed through the leaves, and jabbed a finger in Torin's chest as he stood beside their horse.

"If we cross paths with the Mountain Prince," Alexi held his hands mimicking prayer, "Please explain to him as quickly as you can that you mean his sister no harm and then maybe, he will be gracious and decide not to kill us. I would not like to have my head pulverized!"

. . .

BJORN

He ducked beneath the cavern's entryway. The rocks hanging above him dripped with sediment, like the salivating jaws of a wolf. Bjorn felt the arching walls of the cave pressing in as he descended into the depths of the ground.

Each stride pulled him further into the cave while twilight disappeared behind his shoulders.

There were no torches lit.

The ground echoed as his boots met the muddy clay.

Senna had placed her uncle's talisman around his neck, and he could still feel the softness of her touch. As fleeting as the tail of a comet, but equally impossible to forget.

He wore the alchemist's pendant against his chest, knowing his fate rested on the words carved onto its surface and raying the cavern's doors would open.

Begin at the End.

The weight of his axe chewed against the callouses in his hands. He tightened his grip as the ceiling continued to lower. The prince moved down the slope like the halls of a forsaken tomb.

The sound of his footsteps shifted as mud turned to dark carved stone. He squinted against the darkness of the corridor.

Bjorn could taste the dampness of the walls–metal and the suffocating odor of alchemy. He knew its scent well from his childhood.

The foul yellowish powder that always clung to the alchemists and their robes. He remembered the uprising from the eyes of a frightened child. He could still see the flames dancing across the meadows and the ships carrying away the exiled.

Bjorn quelled the sound of his breathing as voices whispered in the dark. Torchlight flickered ahead and iron bars took shape through the dark.

"Water!" a weary voice called out to the shadows.

Bjorn could not find the voice.

Stairs surrounded him on either side. Stairs that led deeper below into the darkest shades of night.

Something slammed against iron and the creaky metal bars sang out through the halls of the dungeon.

"SILENCE!" a guttural voice roared back. "I will cut out your tongue should you speak that word again."

Bjorn swallowed.

He tried to meld with stone and shadow. The prince's feet became heavier and every muscle tensed as he crept towards the sound of the weary voice. Further down, torches lined the walls, casting circles of orange light.

He could not make out who the voices belonged to as he approached the corner of the hallway.

He did not lower his axe. He braced himself against the wall, facing the impossible task of making his profile smaller, but found his mind drifting to Senna.

He envied the clandestineness of her being, appearing always when he needed her, like the gods had sent a relentless shadow that would haunt him if he did not keep it beside him, a shadow that moved with devotion. He wished he could divine the world as objectively as she could.

Perhaps it would hurt less than seeing light in every corner of darkness. Bjorn knew Senna would find him again. That was her way of things.

The guard's footsteps disappeared.

He could breathe again as they faded into the dungeon.

Bjorn stepped into the corridor of the prison. His senses heightened as he ducked around the jutting torches. He no longer heard the voices as they cried out for a reprieve. Each cell that he passed was empty.

There were no guards, no prisoners, just cold dark walls. As if the ghosts of tortured souls called from the memories they left on these stones.

Not far ahead of him, the prince heard the faint sound of dripping water. He crept forward, conscious of every step. Bjorn rounded another corner and came upon a second set of cells. The stench of charred death filled his nostrils.

Gristle painted the floors of the cell. Fire had claimed this prisoner. Amidst the shadows of the cell, a shadowed heap caught his gaze. A heap of bone turned black. A single skeletal arm still chained to the wall above him.

They had flung the iron door of the cell open and left it ajar. The talisman rattled against his chest and Bjorn's breathing stopped.

Bjorn entered the cell, and then the stench struck his face. The scent of death and bodily fluids made his eyes water. The heap was the silhouette of a man who had surrendered himself to the flames of his captors.

Alchemist's fire. Senna's uncle.

His heart fell downward and sadness sunk against his chest while the talisman continued to rattle for its owner.

The dripping sound that had brought him from the hall was quiet now.

It belonged to the same cell.

The prince traced the source of the sound. He found the water along the wall, droplets racing along the mortar. Tracing their route, a small flowerless stem sat beneath its incessant drip. White petals rested at its base, each one crinkled and scorched by the blaze that had claimed the prisoner on the opposite wall. He squinted against the dark.

What a horrid place for something so fragile to bloom, he thought.

Bjorn moved closer to investigate the stem, but then mud soaked silk caught his eye.

His sister's slipper. Gailah's slipper lay discarded behind the open prison door.

Bjorn lifted his axe from the floor. His pulse hammered against his neck to the tempo of a smith's anvil.

Blood stained oak leaves, the sound of steel, sputtering sounds from his father's lips–all of his memories attacked from the corners of the prince's mind.

His hands shook and the curve of his blade glinted in the dark. His grip tightened till his fingers dug into his palm. Every shadow that surrounded him became the wild men among the trees. His body stiffened, trapped within the paralyzing dread that stalked his every breath. The gurgling of his father's final breath as blood overcame his voice remained longer than all other memories.

He felt like he was falling, as if all his strength had abandoned him. His vision rocked as the tension in his neck strangled his breath. He fought for control of his mind, of his body.

"I will not let the mountain fall."

Bjorn heard his own voice.

The oath of the mountain king. A promise he had whispered as his father's spirit ascended to the gods. He had never meant to utter the words, but all thought escaped him in those moments. He did not speak of their people or Thele's keep. He spoke those words as a vow to protect his family.

A rage-filled scream from his lips shattered the hold his memories had on his body. The sound of his axe against iron startled him as he slammed his weapon against the width of the door.

It was a reckless move, but all of it reawakened the warrior within the prince's bones. His fear of loss could not defeat the vow he had made beneath the sky and before the gods.

A hoard of thundering footsteps collided with the dungeon floor, echoing snarling voices filled the air.

His breathing stilled, and he raised his blade.

Chapter Thirty-One

Katha

They rode in silence through the meadows between the hall of judgment and the Great Forest. Trejen breathed heavily beside her as their horses galloped together in unison.

Visions of him in his prime flooded her eyes. They had ridden the breadth of the island as hunters, beloveds, and allies.

Yet, the man beside her was a stranger that occupied the warmest memories of her girlhood. The lines that time had etched across his brow only mirrored the one's longing had left beside her eyes.

The horizon darkened as horsemen approached against the fading sunlight.

Her army descended with more banners than she could capture in her eyesight. The clouds above them reflected hues of the sky, but galloping ahead of them, she saw her son as the strength of the mountain roared behind him.

Aerin led them on Freyden's horse, and her heart swelled at the sight of the mountain sword in his hand.

Hopeful tears sprung beneath her lashes. Bittersweet pride filled her chest as she beheld the privilege of watching their children grow for the both of them.

Aerin was more fiery of heart than Bjorn or Gailah, and even more than Freyden. He was so like her in every way, and that terrified her.

Regulus and the knights of the Chasm moved in a dark stream of green among the calvary, but as the prince and her armies crested the last hill and descended into the valley, her pride evaporated at the sight of Aerin's eyes.

The vitriol blazing across her son's face resounded with the vengeance in his grip. Katha saw herself in her son as their armies flanked Trejen's legion. Aerin was unaware of the priestess' revelation.

"Aerin! My son, we ride for the Autumn keep. Its relic sustains our enemy's existence, and we may yet recover your sister in the dungeons below."

Aerin was not looking at her. Her words were inaudible against the storm in his eyes. She stared wide-eyed at her son as he circled Trejen's horse.

Freyden's blade still poised in his grip.

"You coward!"

Trejen spoke to defend himself, but Aerin did not let him speak.

"King Killer! Do not speak of any treachery other than the one that stains your hands!" Aerin's words cut like knives across her skin.

Her body swayed in her saddle. Her blood thickened and chilled as Trejen's knights drew their swords.

She failed to master the rhythm of her heart.

"Aerin!" Her voice was shrill through the din of steel. "Think of your sister! Think of your oath, do not do this! We must not waste time. We must recover her."

"Recover?" He sneered. "You speak of her as if she is already dead."

Aerin's head whipped towards her, his sword still high in his hand. He exuded rage from every angle of his body. Staring down at any who would approach him.

Katha's heart felt the anger in his gaze. The anger of a fatherless son. She could not fathom that Trejen had become a man capable of such accusations.

Her thoughts tumbled into an avalanche of fear. Fear for her son, fear for her people, and fear that she had allied with a murderer.

"Your Highness, if I may..." Regulus rode forward. "As the gods bear witness, this man killed your husband."

Like a starling shot from the sky, Katha felt her uncle's words pierce her with the strength of an arrow in her chest.

"Spare me the bloodshed of your people and bring me your head!" Aerin barked at him.

She looked at Trejen. His face was whiter than the mountain's peak. His hands were white as well as were his hollowed eyes. Katha stifled a cry from her lips as she no longer saw him but Decius' face instead–the face of death.

Trejen's silence only deepened his guilt.

The creeping thought that all of this was her fault filled every corner of her mind.

She could only watch as her heart fell, and the alliances of the island fractured before her eyes.

Her hands shook against the reins of her mare.

Trejen moved from his horse like a man twice his age.

He held a hand to his side as he drew his sword in a feeble grip.

Her breath failed her, and Katha's eyes burned with a clouded fury. Trejen kept silent and stood before Aerin's horse with his head bowed in surrender. Trejen's cloak moved in the breeze and suddenly she saw him again as he had looked down upon the tourney for her hand, but now he looked at her.

His sullen brown eyes hung low against his gaunt cheeks. Katha felt a crack shudder through her.

"I will only ask for the forgiveness of one."

She held his gaze, suspended in pain and disbelief.

Her voice failed her as she pictured Freyden's shroud–the ice of his skin as she removed his sword from the pyre, the sword of his people, the sword their son now wielded in the name of vengeance.

Aerin dismounted in a blur of rage.

Katha saw Karak hurry towards Aerin. He brushed her bear aside without a second thought, and she saw the pain in Karak's eyes.

Aerin drew back his sword.

The blade reflected the golden light from the winnowing sun before the violet clouds splayed out across the sky. The Broken Mountain watched in the distance.

Everything around her became still.

The frenzied roar of Trejen's armies echoed through her heart as they charged to defend their king. All of it was frozen in the horror behind her eyes, as if the gods had let her see their descent into war and chaos.

They would not honor Freyden this way.

She had lost Trejen a lifetime ago, but she would not lose Aerin. She fell from her saddle, the hem of her skirts only tripping her through her hurried steps.

Aerin stalked towards Trejen.

He did not flinch or cower.

Trejen's eyes found her. The girl she had been all those years ago screamed inside her mind.

Trejen bared his neck to her son.

She moved before the Thyssian grasslands could dissolve into a garden of bloodshed.

Amidst the cries for war and clamor of death, she threw herself between them.

"STOP!" She cried, she could feel Aerin's breath on her neck.

Aerin stood with his sword, ready to claim Trejen's life. Her face was only moments from the blade in Aerin's grip.

Only a breath away were the swords of Trejen's knights. Their forces had mirrored the response. All prepared to die for their king.

Katha's blood seared through her veins as she clutched her son by the collar like a pup. Her white knuckled grip shuddered against her shaking hands, hands that were no longer afraid but enraged for her husband, her family and her daughter in desperate need of rescue.

"Do not do this!" she commanded her son.

The sound in her voice was that of a lioness. Karak looked at them with confusion in his large, sad eyes. "Let him stand trial before the judges. That is our law!" Katha felt the heat of her son's pulse.

Releasing her hand, she brought it to Aerin's cheek. "I know the pain that drives you, my son. I feel it too, but know this: our mistakes, the mistakes made by the Nine's appointed kings, will last for a thousand generations. How many fathers and sons must die today in the name of vengeance! Save your anger for the man who has taken your sister. Do not spill our people's blood while your sister may yet draw breath."

Aerin fought against her hand that cupped his cheek.

Katha froze as his blood-shot eyes pierced her heart.

"Father is dead because of him!"

Katha felt every pain-filled word through the wobble in Aerin's voice, her son's voice.

She weighed every syllable before she spoke it, and with every burning exhale.

"Then he will answer according to our laws or face your father before the gods themselves, but do not start a war with *my* army.." Her voice fell to a whisper only Aerin could hear.

"Aerin, I will not bury you, my son. Give me my sword."

Aerin dropped the mountain sword from his hands. The emerald encrusted hilt shimmered as the meadows swallowed it at their feet. Her ragged exhale burned in her lungs.

Aerin's cheek filled with red, embarrassed anger. The heir to the mountain continued to seethe as he stood frozen in the twilight of evening.

The gentle sway of grass was the only sound that surrounded them as both armies looked on beneath the rose-colored sky.

Aerin threw her hand from his collar and anger radiated from his footsteps as he stormed towards his mount. The Crown Prince whispered something to her uncle, but Regulus then motioned to the knights of the chasm to heed their queen.

Katha felt her skin pebble as he climbed onto his steed.

"Aerin!"

Her son galloped away, but not before he snatched an ax from the knight beside him.

She called out to him again, and her voice ached through her with the setting of the sun.

Every eye followed her movements as she retrieved the sword of her people. She felt the jewels press into the softness of her skin as the golden sword receded from the grass.

With the armies of her people assembled at her back, she inhaled deeply and faced Trejen and the ones who stood beside him.

The silver steel of his breastplate glowed above the green sea at his feet, but as the sunlight reflected onto the time carved lines of his faces, she saw him.

She looked at Trejen and knew.

Katha knew he had killed her husband. Guilt consumed every fleck of the weary king's eyes. As the sword's weight strengthened in her hand, all the love she held for him began to fade with the sun.

She lifted the blade between them, and with iron in her voice, she asked him a question.

"Answer me, who's blood stains your hands?"

All at once, Trejen's grip on his sword weakened, and a groan escaped from the king's lips.

"Kat..."

Trejen reached for her, and both blades fell away. He gripped her outstretched hand–not in a lover's embrace, but with the chill of death in his fingers.

He sputtered for air and she felt the steel of his armor as he pulled her hand to his chest. She steadied him, but with a frail breath, Trejen fell to his knees.

Katha reached for him, but as her hands found his face, Trejen's eyes widened and he did not look at her. A watery gasp was his only plea, and that sorrowful sound ruined her. It was a sound that she had only heard once before.

Katha called for his men, but as she did, Trejen's skin chilled with sweat. With his hand holding his heart, the Autumn King dropped to the soil.

The queen's knees buckled as the world passed too quickly around them.

She knelt beside him, and she supported his head on her lap.

The queen's gaze turned from the armies assembled on either side. Trejen's breathing hitched and his speech continued to waver.

"Save your king!" she shouted to the Knights of Autumn. Lord Barrock dropped beside her and searched for Trejen's pulse. "Bring a healer! Make haste!" His commander's voice fractured as he tried to speak to his king.

Her body trembled as she lifted a gentle hand to Trejen's cheek.

The gray streaks through his beard surprised her. She had missed seeing him grow old. She could not deny the part of her that refused to let him go. He was the last being who knew her and understood her soul.

The Trejen she knew was kind, noble, and even-tempered. Tears pooled in her eyes. She had been the rash one. The one striking with her heart, letting the pieces fall where they may. That was why her grandfather had paired them all those years ago. They had sent Trejen to tame her, but despite her best efforts; she had fallen for him with the strength of a winter storm.

Shouts rang out among the banner men, and riders galloped towards the keep and the temple of the Autumn relic.

"They have sent for Cias. You must hold on a little longer. Do you see? The tree is just there," she pointed to the great oak. It's light, frail and weak as her voice wavered. "You will be home soon."

Trejen's grip tightened, and his eyes narrowed with pain.

"Kat," He said again, but his voice was a bogged whisper. "Do not leave me here. Do not let them bury me in the trees. You have always been my home, Kat. Bury me on the mountain."

She held his shaking hands that were as frigid as the steel of his armor.

"Romulus... Tell him..." He began, but his voice faded. The king's skin had become ash and bulging purple lines grew from under the collar at his neck.

"I know," she said, lowering her forehead to his, their crowns touching. "He loves you."

His voice was soft as he looked up at the queen. His eyes became unfocused and distant.

In that moment, he looked at her as the raven haired boy who had only ever yearned for a home.

"It's snowing, my love."

The muscles in his face eased. His gaze looked towards the mountain.

She felt the part of her that loved him slip beneath her fingers as his hand fell away to his side. Trejen's head fell back in the queen's lap. She would let that part of her die with him and as her heart released him, his body followed, and the king surrendered himself to the gods.

Katha's hand rested beneath Trejen's neck and she drew his head to her heart.

She held the last of him.

Lord Barrock kneeled beside her and placed the king's sword upon his chest. Purple veins proliferated across the breadth of his hand. Her heart wrenched as she guided them to the hilt of his sword. He would face his justice in the next life.

As the heavens faded to the darkest of blues, she knew her husband awaited him there.

Freyden would face him before the seat of the gods. She looked to the sky, and a silent prayer fell from her lips.

"KNEEL!" Lord Barrock roared as he rose from his king's side.

The knights moved in waves of gold and green, but only Romulus remained, standing between the hills of sagebrush.

The prince's eyes were sodden, and somewhere far away, his priestess remained perched on her saddle, but she solely fixed her eyes on the oak tree in the distance.

Lord Barrock's hand was steady as stone as he removed the golden laurel from Trejen's brow.

Sweat still dampened his hair as she cradled him in her arms. Its oak leaves glimmered the light of dusk as every knight beheld their commander.

Katha knew the ways of the Autumn people. Their crown could not rest on the departed, a crown destined and protected for the son of Decius and Lyssia.

Lord Barrock carried it with outstretched hands as knights parted before the young King of Autumn.

Katha knew best of all that the secrets of the dead were loudest among men.

Trejen had paid for them, and so would she.

Oh, how she wished she could take her younger self by the hand, plead with her not to seek Haydrian's help. She had the power to dissolve the alchemist order into vapor, yet she had given them the heart of a broken queen.

She did not mean for the dead to cross the Void, and yet the Void was coming for her, hunting those who held fractals of her heart. Promises weaved in the mountain's darkness that now crawled freely from the depths of the Void.

A debt was owed and as Katha looked upon the amber sunlit forest, she saw the beginning of the end.

Chapter Thirty-Two

Senna

The roar of the falls guided her to the river, and her heart hammered against her ribs. Senna prayed to every single one of the nine as she sprinted through the trees while her breath sliced through her teeth.

She did not bother with their names but only pleaded with them for what they stood for: strength, peace, hope, love, provision, protection, justice, kindness, and healing.

Each word sprang from her lips in panicked gasps as she swerved and leapt through the forest.

Her feet skidded across the ground as she turned towards the rush of the Ilsnadad. Their pounding footsteps were so loud that she could hardly even hear her own as their guttural cries rippled through the forest behind her. Senna's hair moved like a torch, guiding the men to the banks of the Ilsnadad.

She knew these paths better than she knew the hallways of their keep. Even in darkness, she would always find the river. The copper sunlight poured through the white tree trunks in streams of orange. She tumbled through the uneven pathway, knowing there was no time for pause or failure. She launched over every root and rock as the horde of men rushed after her.

The falls were close.

She could see the waters in the darkening evening light. Their thunderous calls beckoned her. The glimmering surface reflected the twilight like fireflies darting across the wide river.

Senna's lungs spasmed with every heaving breath as she arrived at the bank. The Ilsnadad's wide path was littered with slippery, moss-covered stones. She waded into the frigid water as the current rushed just below her knees, but the torrent dredging around her only quickened her pulse.

The water wrapped around her and she urged her legs harder and deeper towards the edge of the falls.

The evening around her froze as she watched the painted men tear through the trees like wolves. Their runes appeared almost black in the golden glow of dusk. With precarious footing and steady hands, Senna reached for the largest of stones.

Climbing from the threatening pull of the river, she raised herself to her feet on the precipice of the falls. The vibrations and spray of the falls made her stomach drop. Just beyond her feet, the frothing mouth of the river prepared to swallow her. The water crashing below suppressed the sound of the men's feet colliding with the river, but they trudged through the current with blades at the ready.

She resisted the urge to jump as every fiber of her instinct told her to flee. She needed them closer, so close they could not resist the temptation of her flesh. She locked eyes with their leader. His clouded and ravenous gaze narrowed with hate as he drew a dagger from his belt.

That was all she could see in their empty eyes, men devoured by hate. The rest of them sloshed a mere paces behind him. Her body screamed for the water below, for shelter, but her feet stood still. Senna mirrored his advancement and unsheathed the dagger at her thigh as its familiar hilt steadied her pulse.

The sun was lower now, casting their shadows like jagged teeth across the water. Cold darts of mist from the falls pricked against her skin and, as she had hoped, her barred teeth and threatening stance only encouraged them. She watched as the leader snarled, pressing forward through rocks and undercurrents, undeterred by any instincts of self preservation.

Senna turned and fixed her eyes on the rocks below. Throwing her arms outward, she closed her eyes. She heard the sloshing of his boots against the rock. The pulse in her chest pounded against her resolve.

She knew the water beneath her would be so cold, breathing would feel like fire.

"*Wait.*"

She commanded herself and placed the dullness of the blade in her teeth.

"*There is no one coming for them, save who you can.*" Bjorn's words weighed heavily on her chest.

Senna wanted to turn and disappear into the thick of the forest.

Let the gods have their justice.

"*Senna...*"

She shuddered. Even the way he said her name was infuriating. She tried to shake his gaze from her mind, but he looked at her like he could open every locked and secret place within her. The softness in his eyes made her afraid–afraid of what it meant to feel soft again, a softness she pruned back every day as it tried to grow and fill the cracks in her heart.

The kind of softness that made her do foolhardy things like this.

The ragged snarls of the men at her back were so close now. Her body would wait no longer. Senna dove as the falls whisked her auburn hair behind her as she pierced through the air. Wind and mist enveloped her, and the deafening roar of the falls silenced everything else.

The surface rose to meet Senna's hands as they sliced through the icy depths of the pool that devoured her. Arcing downwards, she let the force pull her away from the rocks as the water crashed above her. Her dagger fell from her teeth and before Senna could reach it, it disappeared into the rocky caverns below.

She cursed and drew a second from her belt but dove further down and away from the falls.

She blinked against her water-clouded gaze, then turned onto her back. Despite her blurry eyes, her plan had succeeded. Shadowed figures collided into the blueish green surface above.

Through the shadowy depths of the water, they struggled in a mass of frantic men, each one grappling for air as the icy shock made them forget their bloodlust.

Pushing off from the rocky floor, she shot towards the surface as her lungs burned for breath.

Her arms tore through the water, far from the men who had pursued her, and pulled her closer to the darkening sky above. She gasped as the evening air filled her chest and her head bobbed just above the current.

She looked behind her and the clamoring mass seemed to quell while sky blue ink rose to the surface. The effervescent foam highlighted those eerie streams of paint as it floated among the bubbles in the water. She watched as the paint dissolved in swirling pools amid the rocks at the base of the falls. Blood pooled there as well.

She could see the dullness of the great oak tree in the distance. Shining high above the four cascading courtyards of the keep but her heart tightened as she had never seen the golden light so dim.

Senna swam her way towards the closest bank and clenched her chattering teeth, and without warning, a hard grip took hold of her. She screamed as water poured into her mouth. Forceful hands snatched the scalp of her hair.

She could not see, could not breathe. Senna fought against the fingernails digging into her flesh; She cried out through the water and bubbles rushed from her lungs. She slashed with the dagger, but without success, as another yank pulled her deeper.

They tumbled downwards, and in the water, it was too dark to see. As pain radiated through her, her foot connected with the roundedness of a skull. There was a second below her, clawing at her legs.

With fire that matched the hateful men that held her, she swung her knife upwards. Behind her shoulder, the hands at her scalp loosened from her body.

Senna swam deftly towards the surface, kicking and swinging her knife towards any shadowed shape. Air. The only thing she could think about was air and darkness crouched in the corners of her eyes.

The water pulled at her limbs as every stroke towards the surface siphoned her strength.

Fire erupted through her body as she breached the shallows near the opposite bank. Sputtering, she threw herself onto the muddy rock covered shore, her hair obscured her view in cords of soaked locks.

Flipping onto her back, Senna saw several men clamoring from the ravine.

They were dazed, like fawns on their first morning. The runes were gone save for a few streaks on their clothing and hair, but there were many shadows beneath the water, lifeless, drifting shadows beneath the waterfall's current.

A few breadths down the bank, a man struggled to move against the swirling water. Blood seeped from his temple.

She spat as she lifted herself from the pebbled shore. Senna sheathed her dagger.

Her ankle sang with a biting sting, fingernail scratches had drawn fresh blood down her skin. She waded towards him and, from where she stood over him; she grabbed a fistful of hair.

Untrusting of his eyes until she saw his unclouded blue irises.

Fear was the only thing painting his body, no runes, only pure terror. Locking her arms beneath his, she dragged him to the steadiness of the bank.

She had seen fish more comfortably above water.

His gasps turned to sputters, then spews of river water. She eased him onto his side, but kept her eyes fixed on the waterline. His breathing softened, and he slowly calmed.

The man's eyes locked on the water tumbling in-front of him.

His leathers were in tatters and waterlogged, but no weapons dangled from his belt. They likely rested with one of her daggers deep below the falls.

Senna saw another, a few paces away, still struggling against the pull of the current. He cradled his arm against his body and treaded dangerously only an arm's length from the bloodied boulders.

"Stay here," she commanded, walking away from the man recovering on the bank.

His eyes did not blink, and he did not meet her gaze. His mind was far from the river.

Senna trudged through the murky waters as she made her way towards the survivors for a second time.

Some of them stumbled through the trees, cowering and pleading for mercy as they fled. She felt the muscles in her hand twitching for the dagger at her side.

"Please!!" the drowning man cried out as he struggled to keep his head above water.

His eyes could hardly keep still, and she could not see their color, but the runes from his face had disappeared. He desperately splashed through the water as it threatened to creep over his lips.

Senna dove towards the center of the pool, gliding quickly through the water.

She dared not look below at the shadows sinking further into the depths of the Ilsnadad.

In two strokes, she looped an arm around his waist, but he thrashed against her, against the water as if she was the one dragging him down.

Senna shoved him towards the shore as his hands forced her head down. He gripped onto her and panic sliced through her as his fingers scrambled over her face.

She saw through the last wisps of the dying sun that blackened runes stained the tops of his hands. His eyes were white. He was lost. She had no time for a final breath. Water filled her senses, and his fingers dug into her arms.

With any air she had left, she planted her feet against his body and as the water rushed against her spine; she broke herself free towards the shore.

Still, he scrambled for her, his eyes filled with a hunger for blood. She clawed for the shoreline until her feet found solid ground.

She stood and turned to see him moments behind her.

In a fervent, wordless prayer, senna plucked her dagger from her belt and rushed towards his outstretched arms.

His thrashing ceased as she withdrew her dagger from the soft place at the base of his neck.

She watched as his eyes changed color, no longer a soulless white. His eyes were green. She let go of him and his body sagged as he drifted facedown, pulled away from the shore by the sway of the river.

Senna fell backwards against the cold, rocky shallows. Her lungs burned as she gasped. Her thumping pulse subsided when her eyes fixed on the gentle blinking stars of twilight.

The roar of the falls was all she heard as she steadied herself against the boulders of the riverbank. The man she had pulled from the water was gone. He had fled like all the others. He fled because he was afraid of her.

A mix of pride and disgust welled within her as she wiped her blade clean in the now blood speckled grass. At least ten men had survived the fall, and she prayed the only men who drowned were men that bore the permanent runes, but she could not be sure.

She sighed and as she climbed, the surety of soil welcomed her to solid ground. She rang the river from her hair and the coolness of the night fell among the trees. There were no beams of sunlight visible through the branches.

She sheathed her blade and raced through the undergrowth, ignoring the stinging pain radiating from her ankles. Her body still rippled with shock from the fear she felt beneath the water.

Senna, all at once, believed Bjorn, every piece of him, was the first prince she knew that actually loved his people.

She now saw why Bjorn was the kind of person who men followed to war. They knew he would not abandon them but die beside them. She felt a cord within her heart tighten.

Senna's mother had been that same kind of person.

Chapter Thirty-Three

Alexi

ALEXI KNEW where to find the entrance of the alchemist's dungeons. This knowledge weighed as if a sword dangled above his scalp.

He marched ahead of Torin for the first time in his twenty-two years. Alexi had no word of what to expect beyond the gates that guarded the entrance. An entrance was an exaggeration for the black stone slabs that obscured the opening.

Each was marked with a seal that commanded all who looked upon them to turn away by order of the nine and the king of autumn.

The broken seals remained on the slabs, but the chains that once held the alchemist chamber's entrance shut lay at the feet of the great stone slabs.

Alexi's orders were simple: end Torin's life and return the vials with haste.

Alexi had already defied one order.

He would scarcely comply with the second. Not when their queen longed for Haydrian's promised elixir, the payment he owed her. She was more afraid of death than any soul in the archipelago.

The carved slabs rested upon each other with an opening so narrow that only one might enter at a time.

"Brother," He paused as the word marinated on his lips. "After we go down, if you cannot find her."

Alexi clenched his teeth.

"Do not wait for me. I'll find my own way out but..."

Torin's eyes widened, and before Alexi could utter another word, his brother gripped his forearm. Alexi felt something crumble beneath his sternum.

"If I cannot find Gailah, I will not leave you in his lair." Torin said. "We leave together."

The warmth of his derision made Alexi smile. Torin unsheathed his sword and moved to stand beside the slabs.

"Wait until you can no longer see the color of my hair." Alexi said.

Their plan was to draw away the attention of the guards further down, to give Torin an opening at the depths of the dungeons.

He shuffled between the jagged slabs, and as the forest disappeared on either side, the shadows welcomed him.

Alexi inhaled deeply and began his descent to the alchemist's temple. It was a temple hewn in stone that delved beneath the ancient glowing relic.

A short distance down, two guards positioned themselves before an enormous set of doors.

On the face of the stone doorway, covering each panel, runes glared back at him in menacing shapes.

With faces glazed like pottery, the guards' bore the mask of death. Shadowy runes marred their skin, men that had become one with stone, for they were no longer truly alive. They did not speak, but they moved in acknowledgement of his presence.

Alexi cleared his throat, which ran dry and breathless.

They would not attack their master's guest. Haydrian was expecting him.

"Bring me to your master." Alexi's voice dripped in superiority and entitlement.

He dipped into the part of himself raised to enjoy treachery.

"I am here for what is owed to *my* queen. Our payment is due."

Alexi could not tell which guard spoke. A voice called out to him, but their mouths did not move.

"What are your words?"

Alexi swallowed, and without hesitation, he uttered,

"Begin at the end."

His orders ended there. Beyond retrieving the elixir, he did not know what came next. He quieted the shakiness in his hands and rolled back his shoulders.

The guards shuffled away from the doors as they parted almost freely and scraped over the stony floor. The loud bellowing doors quickened his pulse, and the torches flickered with the gust of cool air sweeping through the doors.

Between the doorways, empty, soulless hallways curved through the darkness of the dungeons. Torin would need as much time as Alexi could waste to scour the dungeons for the princess.

The listless guards led him further down and more painted men gathered around the others, but they did not follow them. Their eyes were equally distant, and the same night colored runes covered their skin.

Replacements.

His stomach tightened. Torin would have company.

The stone doors closed behind him with a hollow echo and the cavernous walls dripped with moisture, then Alexi realized they were beneath the great river.

The prince clenched his teeth as the guards led him to a second set of doors. They were larger and more ornamental, with golden markings depicting an alchemist standing above Thyssia with the sun in his hands.

"Begin at the End."

The doors parted with the same grinding sound, and Alexi did not have time to prepare himself for what he saw as his eyes found Gailah's body.

Alexi's stomach fell and his mask of feigned indifference became near impossible to maintain. He breathed through his teeth as Gailah lay sprawled across a waist high marble table.

No, an altar to the Lord of the Void.

Blood and filth drenched her body. There was nothing regal about the woman before him. With Gailah's chin tucked against her chest, her exhale was barely visible from where he stood.

He swallowed again and guilt struck him like a lash from his grandmother's men. Biting his tongue, he silenced every part of him that threatened to reveal the pain in his chest.

He could not quiet the flame of remorse gnawing at his mind, roiling at every choice he had made that helped bring her here.

He was complicit in this and he felt it squeeze the air from his lungs. He deserved every cruel pang that made him want to vomit.

There would be no hope for Torin to take her undetected from the cells. She was here. She lay before Haydrian on a shrine to his temple.

Like a buzzard picking at carrion, Haydrian straightened from his craned posture. His eyes still lingered over the princess' body.

The alchemist's black hair obscured his decaying skin. His eyes flickered curiously over the prince. He bore the tongue of a serpent; he licked something from his ashen lips. Disgust churned in Alexi's gut as he watched Haydrian, the reanimated corpse.

Alexi ground his teeth and stiffened his quaking joints.

"Ah, yes, the parchment prince," Haydrian's smile made Alexi's skin pebble. "Well, Crown Prince, I suppose if you're here and still alive, then your brother no longer lives... Please reassure the beautiful Queen Allagria that we will deliver her payment when the emperor allows it."

He gestured to Gailah's hands. Her finger tips looked as if they had been dipped in ink.

"My work is almost complete and further delayed by your brother's betrayal. She should have been here hours earlier. If my men had not found them, then your grandmother would have no hope at all."

The alchemist's smile deepened as he scanned Alexi's face for a reaction.

"She thought he would kill you instead once he found out about your little bargain. I'm quite surprised you bested him."

Haydrian laughed, and Alexi's body recoiled from the sound of his voice.

"*The Terror of the Carridean*. What terror does your brother inspire now, dear Prince?" Haydrian moved away from Gailah's body and glided towards the prince. Alexi subconsciously stepped towards the alchemist and Haydrian's wolfish hunger, but not to speak with him.

Alexi needed to get closer to her.

He moved from the doorway and entered the darkened antechamber. Torches illuminated either side and glowed with a golden, otherworldly hue.

Alexi drew from the bitterness that simmered within him. He resumed his posture of the scorned prince.

"That will not satisfy her! I cannot return empty-handed without payment." The prince turned his lips into a snarl. "Your master begged for our ships, the safety of our ports! Our armor suits you, does it not?"

He gestured to the onyx breastplate secured to Haydrian's chest, "My grandmother will not stand for your excuses!"

The alchemist sneered.

He turned towards the princess and lifted her listless arm.

"Indeed, the princess was an unpleasant guest. I would have sooner completed the rite, but alas she arrived less than subdued... unlike what *your* matriarch promised me. We had to imbibe her in our own way."

Dropping her wrist, he moved to stroke her cheek with his arched fingers.

Alexi could not fathom what had transpired between them, but his imagination filled in the gaps. That same guilt clung to his insides like honey, dripping and claiming every piece of him.

"Her blood is precious. Blood older than the Agamites. Blood of my enemy, royal blood. If your blood was worth anything at all, your Queen, your grandmother, would have had you on this table. Not an ounce of what flows beneath your skin is royal."

Haydrian paused, letting his words burn through him like ice.

"How does it feel to fool the world? To be a prince in name only? A fraud with silver hair."

Alexi flinched.

His head swam as he tried to make sense of Haydrian's words.

"You may disparage my grandmother, but the royal blood beneath my skin is alive and real unlike..." He let his eyes finish his sentence as he reviled the alchemist's undead corpse.

"Oh?" The alchemist's eyes widened, and he looked at Alexi with pity. "Tell that to the Iosi mother who pleaded for her children, as a Spessian knight tore two silver-haired boys from her arms. Your grandmother killed them, the true princes of her house. You and your brother replaced the real Torin and Alexi before anyone could blink. She's very thorough, that matriarch of yours. A hurried accident, how she ordered the death of her son, but she never meant to kill all of her heirs of her house. Only her son."

"You lie!" Alexi spat

"You are not the first to mark me so, but how sad, for all I speak, is the pain of truth." The alchemist sighed and fluttered his eyes.

Unbothered, Haydrian returned to his place beside Gailah. He lifted a strand of her ashen hair and took in its scent.

Alexi's hands ached for a blade.

"*Silver for Silver*, I believe your queen compensated the Iosi family well. Now please, I have matters at hand far more important than your grandmother's payment."

Alexi's head spun with the dizzying words he had just heard. As the alchemist searched for something along his workbench, in the same breath, Alexi suppressed a bitter and pain filled laugh.

Disbelief soured in his stomach. He wanted to squelch the hope rising in the deepest part of his heart. The part of him that knew someone existed in the world that wanted him. The part of him that always knew his grandmother was nothing more than lies.

He tried to bury the hope threatening to capture his focus. The hope calling him to the shores of Iosi. He dared not believe that they, his true family, still waited for two sons to come home.

Looking past the busy alchemist, from the far side of the room, Alexi saw a flash of auburn. Then something green eclipsed the shadows of the room. He steeled himself at the sight of Senna's hair. She moved like a hummingbird–beautiful, swift, and a knife at the ready.

In her wake, a single guard's body fell, but before he could collide with the ground, someone silently pulled the guard into the shadows of the corridor.

Alexi did not see him, but he knew Bjorn was always in her orbit.

He cleared his throat and sighed with clenched teeth. They needed time, more time than Alexi could create for them. Everything was unraveling around him and they were dancing on the blade's edge of failure.

"Do you think your ships will find a safe harbor without payment? Do you think we will allow your exiles and emperor to flood our shores without assurance of what you have promised us?"

Like the cracking of an egg, Alexi heard a faint rumble above his head.

The glowing constellations in the ceiling produced a quick flicker. A few specks of dirt danced down from the ceiling while the stones continued to grumble.

Haydrian's face acknowledged the disturbance as well. Something glimmered across the alchemist's face. Irritation flared across his eyes as the enchantment in the room seemed to ebb with the flickers above them.

He moved away from the altar towards a rack of vials along the wall.

Alexi could no longer find Senna or the Mountain Prince, but a second guard had disappeared from the room. They had moved so quietly it seemed the guard had evaporated through stone.

"The emperor and his men sailing towards your shores await my signal. Some might even call it a beacon. I had hoped to wait to present them with an empress and the head of her mother, but the latter will happen in time." Haydrian said and drew a amethyst bottle from the shelf nearest the wall. "Smoke makes an excellent signal by day, but night requires a little more illumination, don't you agree?"

He had left Gailah alone on the altar.

Alexi moved towards her, but as his foot caressed the threshold of the golden runes carved in a circle around the floor, the prince hissed as he removed his foot from the stair.

He could not ascend, merely stare as his legs burned with a tingling pain that pounded through the bones in his feet.

Haydrian chuckled as he looked on.

"Not too close, princeling, you'll share your brother's fate if you cross that circle.... Although, I doubt you will be apart for long." The alchemist looked down at the onyx chest plate he wore. "Your armor is invaluable, but I doubt it will offer you much protection in the days ahead."

Haydrian was smug as he mixed black clumps of powder and blue liquid.

He lifted the pestle from the mortar, a thick liquid dripped down the rocky hand piece.

"A fire that clings to the bones. A creation of my imagination. It will make an excellent beacon for the ships waiting in the *Carridean*. The smoke will carry across the isles and the flames will heed no master. It was a risk, to make the trees my balefire, but I will be the first to admit the roots of the forest drank it up far better than I had calculated. The forest above us will erupt with fire, and the emperor will know he may begin his conquest."

"You would burn half the island!?"

"Yes. It's beautiful, do you not agree? A fresh Thyssia to begin our emperor's reign." Haydrian's words were rapid and filled with scholarly excitement. "And better yet, the trees will do it themselves, their hunger for water only strengthening the decomposition churning beneath their bark, and I have already..."

The alchemist's face sagged with disappointment as he looked at Alexi's confusion.

He sighed.

"This is beyond your capability of thought, but you will witness it nonetheless." Haydrian moved between Alexi and the princess.

His hands moved with hurried and precise movements flitting about where he worked. Small candles lined the edges of the altar as candle wax wept down the sides in soft streams.

The ground rumbled once more and a dull thud continued to the beat of a war drum. More dirt loosed from the ceiling and the roots struggled to maintain their light. The canopy of constellations weakly shimmered above and the ground continued to shake as the sound of falling stones rang out through the halls.

Haydrian's scowl vanished, completely revealing the alchemist's true face. String's of black hair hung around the exposed muscle and peeling skin around his neck; he bore no color beneath his ashen skin, save for the yellow of his eyes.

Alexi's body told him to run, to tear through the forest like a frightened animal, but there was nowhere to run.

Gailah needed more than distractions, more than he could give. Only the gods themselves could free her from this torment. His feet stood firm against the stone as he warred against the fear in his body.

He commanded himself to stay. To face the hand that his treachery had dealt him.

Perhaps the gods would forgive me if I stayed. Perhaps this is my atonement.

Haydrian moved towards the prince and Alexi felt powerless as a familiar cold paralyzed his body.

"You should not have come, prince."

Chapter Thirty-Four

Romulus

Evening bled into night.

They had crowned Romulus king before the armies of both kingdoms. Oxana had come down from their horse and stood beside him and laced her fingers with his, as the duty to his people rested in his commander's hands.

Lord Barrock had wasted no time upholding Trejen's wish for him to be king.

Romulus felt a thousand things at once.

He had watched the poison claim Trejen's body, and his uncle was gone. Old memories washed forward and the days of Romulus' childhood at his uncle's side welled up in his throat. He felt his childish hands tugging at a bow string as Trejen steadied him. The sound of wooden sparring swords galavanted through the courtyard.

The cool air on his skin hunted beneath the trees.

Romulus felt those memories calcify and turn to stone as he held Oxana's hand. Romulus' eyes watered at the conflict that intertwined beneath his skin.

Trejen's head still lingered in the Mountain Queen's lap and his uncle's rigid frame made his stomach turn.

His only blood, his only kin, was now attended by Cias and his novices as the Queen of the Mountain never left his side. Her pause confused the prince. There was no urgency in her eyes. Her only daughter's fate was still unknown, yet she smoothed the draping of Trejen's cloak.

Was it shock or adoration that kept her beside his uncle?

He felt sorrow for the man who raised him, but that was all he could feel for his uncle and king–a king who had spent his life pining for a crown he would never wear, a crown that had been his undoing.

Romulus felt the heaviness of the Autumn King's laurel on his brow as its golden leaves pressed against his scalp. He rested his heart in the grip of his wife's hand. Their interlaced fingers filled him with strength from the passing months that had depleted so much from him.

"My people, I have kept something from you, the only thing that I treasure more than the forest itself—"

Before he could announce her as his wife and queen, Oxana winced. Romulus found only fear in her eyes. The glistening crack across her eye seemed frantic as it narrowed slowly through the blue of her iris.

"My dear, what is it?"

She gripped his hand so fiercely he knew she was in pain. She parted her lips, but before she could speak, the pounding slice of an axe sang out across the meadow.

Its blows resounded through the early evening like a plea from the forest itself.

Oxana felt it, too.

Her fingers clutched his, and she shook with every slice of steel. He looked down and saw only a few golden streaks remained across the trunk of her body.

He turned his head towards the relic of their people and its branches rattled in pulses of golden light.

Aerin.

He had fled the meadows with a horse and an ax. Romulus' skin pebbled at the realization and his knees threatened to fail him.

Above the sloping tree tops, the golden leaves of their relic quaked and its limbs convulsed and reached for the blood colored sky.

As it shook, glowing leaves fluttered like feathers in luminescent spirals and extinguished before they reached the ground.

He watched in horror as the island shook with every groan from the tree.

Romulus found Cias at his uncle's side, and the sight of the weathered priest's face wounded the prince and Oxana dropped Romulus' hand. She moved for her horse before he even felt the loss of her warmth.

In a swift climb, she found her place in the saddle, and his wife kicked her horse into a gallop before Romulus could sprint to his steed and take after her.

Lord Barrock shouted for him to stop–to wait–but Romulus pressed forward behind her as they raced for the keep.

Torin

Darkness prowled behind the prince as he stalked every corner of the dungeon. He left only bodies behind him as he felt the roar of the sea beneath his skin. Each pulse sent waves of fury through the strength of his blade.

He crept through each nightmarish cell with the hilt of his sword in a bloody knuckled grip. Each hallway led him deeper underground as whispers and groans surrounded him. Yet, as Torin searched every cell, they were empty save for the gnashes of the invisible dead.

In a flourish of swift steel, Torin engaged every guard with the same question.

"Where have you taken her!?"

His voice graveled through barred teeth as the width of his blade coaxed blood from their neck. Heaving breaths burned in his chest as he stared into the white irises of hate.

Like a rabid dog, in the face of unwavering loyalty to their master, their bloodlust-clouded eyes seared behind their snarling teeth. He saw them dragging her by her hair and her scream tore through his ears.

The edge of his blade obeyed him.

Each guard met the Void in the same manner, collapsing into the stone, felled by a single slashing blow.

In the quiet of death, Torin feared he would lose himself among the walls of malice and decay, both in body and mind.

Everything muddied itself in the mire and blood of the never ending corridors. The further he searched without a sign of hope, the more his futility breathed life into the ruthless desperation that gnawed at his heels.

Blood ran down his body and dripped along his fingertips in streams of warm madness.

Every drop that trickled along his fingers was a memory that would follow him for the rest of his days.

Fear slithered in, weaving through dense tangles of doubt and failure, while every vacant cell taunted him. It was as if any trace of Gailah had fused with the very stones surrounding him.

Torin found himself alone in the depths of the prison, alone with the dead and the ghosts of his defeat. There was no torchlight to chase away the shadows that reached for him.

Beneath his armor, a bead of sweat traced his spine, and he tasted the bitterness of ash and blood. His heart galloped beneath his ribs and he felt the ache from his fall sing out.

Only Torin's exhale resounded in the blackness of the underground. Each step in the darkness echoed a reminder: every wasted moment meant Gailah would be lost to the Void forever. While the blood of his violence clung to his fingers, he prayed it was the price he paid for her freedom. That all this death and darkness was not in vain.

From the corners of his memory, he heard the song of his house. It was the melody that Gailah had danced to and inscribed deep within his heart.

The ache in his chest drowned out the cry of all else.

In that instant, as though the song beckoned to him from the very stones above, he knew exactly where he would find her.

. . .

ROMULUS

Ahead of him, Oxana raced through the forest, leaving chaos in her wake as the mighty oak tree continued to tremble. The resonance of clashing steel echoed through the air, surrounded by pulses of golden light that flared with each strike. Each flare resembled bolts of lightning that convulsed through the early night sky.

Romulus trembled as he raced towards the keep.

Priests fled from the large wooden walls of the castle, carrying urns of golden leaves with frantic hands. Golden leaves that fell freely like embers, abandoned as they tumbled through the darkness. Romulus' body ached with uncertainty.

The angular ornate wooden gates of their keep shook with the rumbling of the ground. The guardsmen lay dead beneath the yawning portcullis. His body abandoned all thoughts of doubt, only anger burned in his veins.

He surged past Oxana as he urged his horse into a gallop. The groans from the tree drowned out the sound of their horse's hooves as it continued to grumble through stone.

As fire burned through his veins, everything in his being told him to take Oxana far from here; to abandon all of this, yet who could follow a king who deserted his people?

Undaunted, they charged together through the first two courtyards. Oxana embodied the essence of a queen in every way.

The sound of an axe lopping through bark pierced through his thoughts as they raced to the inner courtyard protecting the tree and its temple.

As the walls of the castle braced against the shaking giant, their golden banners tore from the stone in tumbling piles of golden fabric, marked with the sigil of their house.

The air was thick with chaos.

The forest itself shook and his heart filled with despair as the ancient tree was near the bare of its leaves.

They crossed the threshold of the inner courtyard, and the relic of their people overwhelmed all else. It towered above the forest and a man became an ant as it stood beside the width of its golden trunk.

Romulus' gaze met the Prince of the Mountain, and his heart plummeted through his chest.

Aerin swung the large steel ax wildly at the tree, and the fractured oaken trunk emitted otherworldly shrieks akin to the shatter of broken glass.

Fear flooded his body as he jumped from his horse before the beast came to a halt. Oxana raced in behind him, her blue eyes filled with sorrow. Romulus drew his sword, and his pulse ignited with rage.

"Strike once more and I'll kill you," Romulus demanded in a guttural yell.

He glanced upward, and the tree continued to shudder. Oxana hastily dismounted from her horse.

Aerin glowered back at him, and the madness in his eyes burned from where he stood at the base of the great tree. The Crown Prince of the Mountain raised the weapon without breaking his stare.

"Your uncle must pay! He stole my father's life because he was a coward! I will have my satisfaction!"

Oxana did not hesitate as she climbed the large marble steps leading to the tree, as she had done a thousand times before, agile, as she moved over the large tortuous roots. Each marble step was cracked and fissured, overcome by the weight of the tree's roots.

"If I cannot end him, as is my right, then I will let him feel my wrath another way." Aerin seethed as brought down his axe.

"I beg you, stop!" Oxana called out from the lowest steps. Romulus hurried behind her.

"My uncle is dead!" Romulus yelled to Aerin, and those words sank against him as the truth of Trejen's death soured in his stomach. "What satisfaction do you want from a dead king? The only King of Autumn speaks to you now! I wear my father's crown as you one day will. Strike that tree again, and I promise you, you will never get the chance."

His words echoed through the courtyard, and as he began to climb, Romulus fell. A root sent him spiraling towards the marble steps, but Oxana did not stop. As the golden light of the gods enveloped them, Oxana, draped in a cloak of sky blue, ascended the final stairs in a swift flash.

Fury devoured him as Romulus returned to his feet. Each pounding step against stone rippled through his body. The hilt of his blade burned callouses into his skin.

"Give me the axe." Oxana's voice was soft, but steady.

The sound of her voice made it difficult for him to breathe. The surety behind every word she uttered terrified him. He climbed quicker still.

Panic rose in his throat as she approached the prince.

Aerin's hands shook as Oxana drew closer. The Mountain Prince's eyes were wild and confused all at once. His brows flexed as she eased her hands out, her palms open for the stem of the axe.

"No, my love, you cannot!" Romulus shouted as his lungs burned inside his chest.

Oxana ignored him.

"Give me the axe." She said, but Romulus had found the last step, and his sword longed to find its mark.

Aerin breathed like a ravenous animal, and Romulus could not shake the growing terror that ran along his spine.

Oxana's body was not yet healed and with every strike of his axe, the tree's power waned.

Aerin did not speak as the priestess approached him.

She lowered her hood, and the ebony waves of her hair fell around her shoulders. His wife cleared her throat.

Romulus watched as the tree's light warmed Oxana's skin in honeyed hues and illuminated every stray strand of hair in the fading light of the gods.

She barred his path without taking her eyes from the wolf-like prince at the base of the tree.

Romulus' pulse crashed against his ears as she spoke with a voice that haunted him. He had fallen in love first with the sound of her voice–a sound that weakened the knees of men and compelled the will of the gods.

Aerin's eyes flicked to him, then back to Oxana.

"I feel it, your anger, for you did not have a choice in your father's death, but I did not choose to be melded and entangled in the fates of kings. This tree was to be protected, not butchered. I can hear its voice just as I heard Haydrian's taunting your sister."

Aerin's eyes widened. She ran her fingers delicately over the relic's glowing bark.

"Neither of us had a choice. His corrupted touch burns beneath my skin and its trunk...I feel it dying. I feel its agony." She turned to face Aerin. "You would cut it down to spite my people. You would end its life for your own satisfaction, but let me do so out of mercy. You have robbed me of any hope of healing alongside the relic of my people, but do not crush our people by letting our tree fall upon the open city. Many will die. If it must fall, let me guide it towards the trees, towards the forest where it will do no harm."

Romulus heard her words, and the stones at his feet fell out from under him. His sword dangled loosely in his hands as his mouth turned to ash.

Oxana reached for Aerin's axe as his knuckles still held the weapon in a falcon's grip.

"The loss of your father was desperately unfair and your grief will not ease by ending life in anger. Let me free us from Haydrian's touch. Let me end his reign of suffering as one who has suffered because of him. You will find no peace in vengeance."

Her hand covered Aerin's, and Romulus could only watch as his wife spoke.

"Let me protect my people. Give me the axe."

Aerin's gaze fell to the blade. He rotated the handle once more and golden light glistened off the blade's edge. Romulus' sword cried out for Aerin's blood, but he stilled the beast within his skin.

He longed for his wife more than his need for bloodshed.

"Let it be her." Romulus spoke with his heart in his throat.

Aerin's shoulders eased, and he released his grip on the axe. There were tears in his eyes. Oxana accepted the weapon.

As she grasped it, Romulus felt the weight of the blade against his own neck. His wife walked forward and Aerin fled.

Romulus silenced his gnashing hunger for Aerin's head, as he knew the prince could not escape what awaited him. Romulus would not forget this.

Justice would not forget, but only Oxana mattered now.

Their time together became one with the tree and the light that waned in groans through the forest.

He reached for her, and he could feel the cracks in and along her hands beneath his thumb. Cracks that spread from his touch to his heart and would forever separate them.

Romulus watched her as she pressed her forehead to the base of the tree.

She whispered a broken apology as the ax dangled in her hands. Oxana spoke to the tree like it was a wounded animal–frightened–a life that lingered in agony.

A tear ran down Oxana's cheek and it shimmered, crossing the gold cracks like sunlit rain.

She was his wife, his queen, but she was an acolyte long before and she did not belong to him.

She came from the shores of Misenia, the island of those who devoted themselves to the gods.

Romulus was her sworn protector, and now his oath would be to the end of them: the end of holding her, hearing her sing, basking in the quiet of their love.

He stood transfixed and afraid of the end. He wanted to take the axe from her hands. He wanted to command the tree to live. He wanted his queen to see another sunrise.

"There must be something we can do," Romulus' voice broke into a thousand pieces.

Oxana shook her head and looked at him with eyes that held the love of his lifetime.

"He has taken too much. We cannot let him take it all."

Within the hewn bark of the tree, the trunk bore the scars of black rot at its core. Its inner rings, once golden, had turned brown. The entire tree exuded a nauseating musk. Insects crept along the soft ancient wood, drawn to the massive bite carved by Aerin's axe.

The trunk swayed in the night breeze, hinting that it would take little more than a gust of air to bring down the decaying relic.

Oxana closed her eyes, and he watched her mutter a soft prayer. He could not help himself.

He wrapped his arms around her from behind her and drew her to him, just to feel the beat of her heart against his hand. He felt her anger, too, in the subtle movements in her body as she clutched the axe with both hands.

She struggled to lift it from the ground, and he moved to bear it for her. She shook her head, and a second tear stained her cheek.

Oxana's chin tilted upwards and as he looked down, a burning tear raced towards his jawline as its searing path dipped down to his neck.

"I will not have you feel any guilt from this blow." She let go of the ax with one hand and cupped his cheek. "I will end him, end our torment. He will not claim another while my heart still beats." She whispered, her eyes pleading with him and he could not refuse.

He kissed her with the force of a man starved of water, a kiss that etched the memory of her lips into his consciousness. A part of him would forever belong to the only queen he would ever claim. As they parted, he tasted the sea in his tears. The waning glow of the tree enveloped the young king and queen in golden embers that ascended around them like fireflies. Oxana inhaled and closed her eyes.

With a strained effort, she lifted the axe, bearing the weight with the honor befitting one who served the gods. Silence hung in the air and eternity passed in the pause before the blade fell. He felt it sever something within him as the steel and wood collided.

Claiming the silence, a wounded bellow echoed through the forest and the young king felt it in his bones. It was a sound so great that the entire island could feel its resonance. The shaking limbs arching above him paused, swaying gently like the end of a dance, and then the forest was still.

It cried out again, and the sentinel of their people began to fall. The splintering of its base sliced through every sound of the Great Forest. The remaining leaves tumbled around them in golden wisps of dying light.

Romulus saw himself in the crumbling bark that shattered above them.

Like a toppling statue, the body of the ancient tree collided with the walls of the keep, but it did not fall upon the city below, only towards the river and the forests beyond.

Roaring, shattering wood erupted in waves of ebony bark as the ground itself split from its impact. The stony courtyard rumbled with a hunger unheard by any in his lifetime as the thrum of the gods' voices faded into vapor and the golden haze of light receded from its branches like the sun beneath the horizon.

Oxana's gold, scarred skin mirrored its ebbing light. She clutched his hand. His queen's breath wavered, and her eyes unfocused as her chin dipped to her chest.

As the last threads of yellow light disappeared into the night sky, darkness surrounded them. The air was stale without the ethereal glow of their relic.

Romulus had no time to think.

He held her against his armor as the softness of her hair brushed against his cheek.

"Romulus," her voice broke.

"I'm here," He uttered, clutching onto every fleeting second of her presence.

His hands trembled in the darkness as he sought to find her face.

"I can't see you"

"I'm here. Feel my hands."

He cupped the softness of her skin, and she gasped.

"Your hands.. They are like ice."

Her words plunged through him like a sword. The only chill he knew was the ice on her cheek. The priestess could no longer stand. Oxana dropped as her knees buckled towards the ground.

"My Queen of the Heavens, do not go."

He clutched his wife to keep her from falling. No golden light lingered in her scars.

Fragments of shattered bark surrounded them like spears. Sweeping her upwards in his arms, he pulled her close to him. He could not see her face, yet her tears weaved across his fingers. Shouts rose across the courtyard. Cries that echoed the distant roar that grew in his bones.

"No," His voice dissolved in his mouth. "No my love, not like this".

His forehead rested against hers, and as he did, her body released its spirit, not in the hollow give of a warrior's defeat, but the soft, gentle rising of the song of Thyssia.

Something infinite and unexplainable collapsed inside Romulus' chest. It left him in a muddied plea as he stroked the curve of her neck.

The darkness enshrouded them as he held her at the splintered base.

He had known no greater pain than the feeling of her listless hands resting at his chest. The young king could not loosen his grip.

He could only hold her tighter.

His mind unraveled as he desperately clung to his wife and the Queen of Autumn.

Chapter Thirty-Five

Alexi

Haydrian smiled as he scanned the room, but no guards remained along the walls or beside the doors. The roaring of the ground had hid their stealthy attacks, but it was not enough. The iron chandelier hung precariously and oil lamp stands had fallen all along the room.

Haydrian had discovered them, perhaps even felt their presence.

Even though he did not stand on the runes carved into the floor, something gripped him. Alexi could not feel his body save for an icy hold running through his veins.

"They are close. I hear them breathing...Especially the big one." Haydrian sneered as his power left Alexi immobile.

The alchemist moved from the tables and prowled towards the gaping doorway at the end of the shadowy domed room.

The groaning from above returned, and the warmth rekindled in his blood and fought against the power holding him captive. Every guttural sound from above the stone walls caused the Alchemist's power to ebb.

Fear flashed across the Alchemist's bony face and Haydrian's fingertips became claws. Although he had not left the room, the quaking walls grew louder, and the lights above them grew dim. Alexi's fingers burned as they fumbled like daft, graceless stones.

The prickling in his skin climbed higher and with each moment, he felt his body again.

As the Alchemist scoured the room, he knew Haydrian realized it, too. Alexi studied the blackness in his eyes and the prince saw no fear there.

Martyrs were not to be underestimated, and Haydrian had already died once for his beliefs. He had done what he came to do and even now, if he died here, there was no undoing what waited for them beyond the Spessian harbors.

Haydrian stalked the width of the room, and then, behind Alexi, shouts rang out beyond the ornately carved door.

Torin.

Alexi's stomach churned with panic, but he could move his fingers again.

Haydrian cocked his head towards the sound of his brother and a deep rumble shook the room, so loud that weapons clattered to the ground as more dirt fell from the ceiling.

Alexi waited for the walls to fall down around them, but when the groaning stopped and the lights flickered brightly, it grew quiet all around them.

The icy feeling completely receded from Alexi's body.

As Haydrian searched the room, Alexi knew this was his opportunity.

He stepped towards Gailah's body, keeping watch for the runes on the floor. The altar dripped with wax from the candles that pooled beside the princess, and as he crossed the rune barrier; he felt no magic clawing at his skin.

The sound of steel against steel rang out beyond the door and in a moment, the large doors crashed open as they slammed against the interior chamber walls.

The dull drag of leather against stone caught Alexi's attention.

A guard with black painted runes stumbled through, his throat cut and his body slammed against the floor amid the open doors.

Torin yelled in a ragged and visceral voice. Alexi could feel his brother's rage in the echo of the room.

Torin strode into the arched alchemy chamber and stood above the body with a monstrous disposition.

Alexi had never fought alongside his brother, but as his brother's sword dripped with blood and the Spessian blue of his cloak took on the darkness of the room, his hammering pulse stopped. As terror crawled across Alexi's skin, he now understood how Torin earned his epithet.

Alexi found his brother's eyes first, and his heart found its rhythm again.

The alchemist clapped his hands, and Haydrian almost seemed impressed, but his disbelief bled into annoyance.

"You are weaker than even I expected," Haydrian spat at Alexi. The alchemist's words were nails against his skin. "My senses betrayed me.."

Alexi did not take his eyes off his brother. In Torin's fury-filled stance, his brother had focused on the threat before him, but as he exhaled, Alexi saw Torin's eyes find Gailah.

They widened with horror, and his body echoed the pain that spilt across his face.

Despair rattled Alexi's body at the sight of Gailah's blackening hands that grew necrotic with every moment. Her breath still bobbed in her arched neck as her head lay backwards on the stone slab.

Her eyes darted beneath her closed, creased lids. She was in pain.

Torin roared toward the Alchemist, his sword raised high above him. The icy build of Haydrian's power soared through Alexi and he shouted for Torin to stop, but his warning died on his lips as a surge from the Alchemist's wrist threw Torin across the room.

The room rippled as the maelstrom gust extinguished the candles in fine ribbons of smoke, but the Alchemist heaved with the effort.

In his wake, a wraith-like scream pierced Alexi's ears.

Haydrian gasped loudly and his body recoiled as his power shuddered with the rumbling ground above them.

Alexi winced, watching his brother slide across the floor. Torin rolled and cradled his side in agony. His groans were breathless as he struggled to rise from the floor.

Haydrian moved closer and Alexi steeled himself against the pull in his chest to defend his brother. Instead, he moved for the princess. Still, the floor bore the glowing marks of the Alchemist runes.

Alexi paused and heard the loud thunder of footsteps.

The darkened hallway was no longer empty.

The mountain prince commanded the frame of the archway, save for the vengeful sprite beside him. Her eyes were tearfully red and overflowing with rage.

"Your head belongs to the Mountain, abomination!" Bjorn bellowed, rolling the handle of his ax with shadows in his eyes.

Torin drug his body from the floor, and with a sputtering breath, he gasped against the stones of the Alchemist temple.

"If only Aerin were here, then I would truly shred your mother's heart just as I broke your beloved Mountain." Haydrian smiled as he lifted his hands.

The alchemist's hands were sure but unsteady. From the tables in the room, like weightless feathers, he lifted three Spessian bolts with the force that lingered in his body. They hung in the air above his body like buzzards, and Bjorn's eyes widened.

Haydrian's icy hold no longer clung to Alexi as he drew on all his power to suspend them in the air.

"Oh, noble Prince of the Mountain, do you remember what sent your father to the gods?" Haydrian taunted.

This was his time. Alexi ran for her. He tested the ground with shakiness in his limbs as he slid his boot across the enchanted circle.

Bjorn's face enraged as the arrows flew not at him but for the woman beside him.

Alexi leapt over any rune on the altar's stairs, not risking even to touch them.

As he climbed towards the slab, seconds turned into a lifetime as the arrows embedded into Bjorn's back.

There was no time for Senna to scream, but as the bolts found their target, the Mountain Prince buried her in his embrace. The sound of their thudding impact mixed with the agony of the prince's defining scream, a sound Alexi felt in his bones.

The alchemist stared at the mountain prince with a hungry gaze, but as Torin rose from the stone floor behind him, Haydrian had forgotten the third prince laying on the ground.

Torin surged for Haydrian again, offering Bjorn a moment of reprieve and the time Alexi was desperate for.

Alexi ignored the clatter of engagement. He could hear a string of curses fly from Senna's lips.

Each step filled his body with a frenzied strength and as Alexi climbed the last step, he did not waste a moment to guide his hands around the nape of Gailah's neck.

He could feel her breathing, but her flesh was damp and feverish.

Cruel and barbaric instruments surrounded her, and vials of strange liquid lined the table. The glowing cracks in the ceiling illuminated the darkened bruises growing under Gailah's skin as if the nine forced him to witness every detail of his betrayal. Blood split through her lower lip and darkness blossomed around the collar of her neck.

"Your Highness..." He urged and the panic in his voice frightened him, but the princess did not stir.

Her arms were limp.

He had no time to examine her for wounds, but his gaze fixed on a golden band on the princess' finger. The origin of the spreading blight along her fingers.

The hairs on his neck stood on end.

His knowledge of the Alchemist's schemes ended at the price of their betrayal, but not this. But what had he thought they would do? Treat her with kindness? Perhaps Torin had been the wisest of them. There would be no undoing the part he had played.

Alexi no longer knew the man beneath his skin.

Alexi draped one of Gailah's arms around his shoulder and as he lifted her from the altar, he found whispered pleas for forgiveness tumbling from his lips.

His movements felt rushed and precarious.

Gailah's bed clothes snagged on the surface of the altar and as he pulled her from the table, instruments clattered against the floor, and his heart stopped.

Alexi found Torin's gaze as he panted, and his sword dangled in a tired grip. Blood dripped freely from his brother's nose.

His eyes rested on the princess in Alexi's arms. Pain flashed across his brother's face and when Torin looked up at him, blood matted the silver hair around his face, and then his grey eyes commanded Alexi to run.

Alexi nodded and felt his heart tighten as Torin rushed the Alchemist again. Alexi hurried with her in his arms from the dais. The runes were still dormant and quiet along the floor.

He held Gailah close and rushed for the golden doors of the entrance.

Alexi did not look back.

The sound of Haydrian's phantom screech overwhelmed every voice in the room, a crystalline and scraping scream that dizzied him as he stumbled forward with the princess. The constellations above them burned so brightly it erased every shadow from the chamber and before Alexi and Gailah could flee the Alchemist temple, Alexi's feet felt it first.

Beneath his boots, a circle of runes burned like embers.

A final snare that sent a wave of energy weakening all of his joints. His legs crumbled as he moved for the door. He cupped her head against him, desperate to keep Gailah's head from striking the floor.

His body swarmed with pain as if a wasp stung at every muscle. He moved to right himself, but his arms failed him next. The princess fell from him and Gailah rolled onto the stone floor beside him.

Alexi could no longer hear the others moving in the room.

Only a singular set of footsteps scraped across the floor, coming towards them as Haydrian's laugh grated across his mind.

Alexi swallowed and could not silence the fear bleeding under his skin.

"The gods do not take kindly to betrayers, young Prince. Neither does the Void"

Haydrian loomed above him. His yellow eyes did not blink as his inky strands of hair dangled around the scar across his throat.

Curses died on Alexi's tongue.

The Alchemist crouched down.

Haydrian's skeletal hand slithered around the base of Alexi's neck, and his narrow, bony fingers began to squeeze.

Alexi inhaled desperately, but as nothing filled his lungs, he could not even lift his arms to defend himself.

Torin.

Alexi felt his heart call out to his brother just as he had in those days, in the voice of the beaten boy who knelt before the Spessian throne.

A splintering crack shook the ground once more. The roots dangling above them seared and crackled like branches in a fire, then receded like dying stars.

Haydrian's lips snarled as if in pain, but his grip on Alexi's throat only tightened.

Each squeeze made his lungs burn, and bright flashes of light danced across his eyes.

From the corner of Alexi's vision, the runes in the floor diminished their red glowing light in symphony with the roots dangling behind the Alchemist's head.

Haydrian's eyes fluttered with his arching, snake-like neck.

Footsteps stirred across the floor and they rocked through the stone at his back. Torin ran for him.

"Let me tell you a secret," Alexi wheezed. His eyes were wide as the Alchemist pressed against his throat. "Spessian armor has a weakness..." the prince sputtered, but he could not finish, for he felt darkness beginning to drown his mind.

"Let go of my brother!" Torin growled above them.

The alchemist's eyes bulged, and his face blanched.

"*No,*" Haydrian whispered, not in defiance but in bitter disbelief.

Torin's sword pierced Haydrian between the clasps along his spine. The only fragility in *near* perfect armor.

The force of his brother's sword bore down upon them.

Black purulent liquid overflowed from Haydrian's lips and poured out on Alexi's breastplate.

The apex of Torin's sword was only moments from Alexi's face as Haydrian's lifeless black eyes fell backward into his head and he fell forward onto Alexi in a disgusting heap of flesh and steel. The shadowed essence of his presence evanesced from the room and the roots in the ceiling were no longer constellations but empty dark eyes above them.

Alexi could feel his body again, save for the lingering shocks that sent fire through his fingers. Alexi shoved the Alchemist off of him.

Torin gripped his forearm and lifted Alexi from the floor. The younger prince felt a heaviness fall off his shoulders.

His thoughts swam with the rush of it all, and the hardest places in his heart began to ache. As Alexi steadied himself, Torin was already lifting Gailah from the floor.

The tension in his brother's face evaporated as he found her pulse and he exhaled with relief. Torin searched for any sign of injury under the filth that coated her skin, but as he lifted her in his arms, the rune carved into Gailah's wrist made Alexi's breathing stop.

The mark of the End.

Alexi's stomach dropped. They had come too late.

Bjorn and Senna crossed the breadth of the room. Gailah's brother gasped for breath, but moved with a fire that sent fear through his skin.

"Torin!" Alexi called out, but as his brother looked up, Bjorn's axe was already steady at Torin's throat.

"Touch her again and you'll be as dead as him."

Bjorn stared down at the Spessian prince and his breath wavered as the bolts still protruded from the hide of his back.

Alexi grimaced as they moved with the Mountain Prince's exhale.

Torin knelt down and slowly lowered Gailah into Senna's waiting arms as she supported her body above the floor. Torin raised his hands, removing any trace of him from her body.

Alexi watched with his hands on his knees, his throat still burned from the Alchemist's grip.

"I warned your mother three times..."

The muscles in Torin's jaw flexed as he began to speak. Bjorn did not lower his blade.

"I told her everything. I begged her not to bring Gailah to the gathering. I may be dishonorable but I did what I could to protect her and if I must die, then I will know I have given all!" Torin seethed like the blade at his throat was a feather. "I even offered to marry her to keep her safe and to some that may condemn me, and that I was a fool, but I will die knowing that I did more than those who claimed to love her. My failure is no excuse for the suffering she has endured, but why did you and your people refuse to listen?"

Bjorn flinched.

"I had no warning! They kept anything you shared with my mother a secret! If you wanted my help, then you should have come to me!" Bjorn snarled back, his axe still flush against Torin's neck.

"If my life must be the payment for my failure, then know I only desired to keep her safe." Torin said, lifting his chin to Bjorn's blade.

Alexi scrambled from his knees, and his heart pounded against his chest, trying to support his unsteady limbs.

"If I may,"

Alexi stepped between Bjorn and Torin.

"Let us bring Gailah to the healers, to your mother, to your mountain. Let her speak, and if her words clear my brother's honor, then he goes free, but if Gailah demands retribution, then you can take his head? Does that suffice?"

Bjorn looked at him with glimmering confusion in his eyes; Alexi could feel his anger cool like rain.

Torin closed his eyes and exhaled. Alexi could feel the exhaustion in his breath.

The Mountain Prince nodded and secured his ax in his belt.

"Gailah will decide your fate, but if..." Bjorn's voice swelled with emotion. "If she does not wake, I will haunt you. You will never know peace."

Bjorn knelt beside his sister and lifted her from the floor.

Alexi saw tears in the large man's eyes, and his brows flexed to keep them from falling.

Every joint in her body was limp, and all the color had faded from her skin.

"Dah, I'm so sorry." The Mountain Prince whispered.

Torin retrieved his sword from the Alchemist's corpse and, as Alexi's mind settled, he remembered the beacon.

He clapped his hands together to draw their attention.

"We must leave now before this entire dungeon goes up in flames. He's done something to the forest, and I do not wish to be here to find out what."

Alexi still felt the fiery jolts running through his fingers. As if he'd dipped his fingers into hot coals. His body would not forget the touch of their magic.

Senna stood behind him, scanning the doors for any signs of attack. An unfamiliar sound sent vibrations through the dungeon columns, shaking the ceiling, and the iron hinges cried out.

Falling in a heap of iron, the chandeliers crashed against the stone floor.

Senna looked between them and, without a word, she rushed for the doors on the far side of the room.

Bjorn's face flared, and the prince panicked. Bjorn lumbered after her, but the weight of his wounds and Gailah in his arms stopped him.

"Senna! We must leave! We cannot go that way!"

She turned to him but did not stop as her feet raced forward. In a swish of auburn, she yelled back a name Alexi did not recognize.

"Tomas!"

Chapter Thirty-Six

Senna

Bjorn's voice bellowed behind her.

Her still damp clothes trickled with water down to her legs. She was not thinking, only responding to the broken place in her heart that refused to believe her uncle was dead.

She would not leave Tomas to face the fires alone, but more than anything, she wanted to say goodbye.

Senna raced through the halls of the dungeon with no fear for herself. Senna careened through the dark, stony hallways and her heart pleaded for her to stop.

Before Bjorn had discovered his sister, she had found him ready for battle in the depths of the dungeon. But when she arrived, she realized he stood over what remained of her uncle. The talisman in her pocket called out with the magic he enchanted it with and, as it did, her heart had shattered.

He had promised to find him, but there was no way to take him from the cell. Senna stood before the cell in complete sorrow, for the island would only know him as a traitor, a monster, an alchemist. Another thread of her family's tapestry extinguished by the Alchemist's fire. Even now that grief weakened the strength she held in her shoulders.

Gripping the bars of the cell, the thought of leaving him burned with betrayal. The fire had melded him with the stone, and there was nothing she could do to take him from here.

The stone above her head shook as the ground continued to warn her she needed to move, to find Tomas, but as she stood in the doorway of her uncle's cell, tears resurfaced in her eyes.

Jaius taught her the ways of the forest and loved her enough to dull the cruel memories of her life. He deserved so much more than to be condemned to the Void. Words rose to her lips and with a deep pain in her chest, Senna spoke the funeral rite of Autumn over her uncle's body, for he could not travel the Ilsnadad.

"Sleep no more."

As the last words fell from her lips, she fled from the cell and angry tears carved paths down her face. Her cold hair whipped behind her and her pulse pounded in her neck.

Senna ran because that was all she knew.

She fled because running promised so much safety without ever having to stop and face the hurt and the horror that snarled at her back. Senna ran until the mud crept between the paving stones and back towards the sloping mouth of the cave.

In the darkness behind her, a whisper crawled from the depths of the dungeon.

A whisper from a shadowed and crumbling staircase, spiraling downward into the thriving blackness, it spoke in a groggy and broken voice. She stood dumbfounded at the top of the stair and could not distinguish it from nightmare or reality. She looked down the winding stairway and knew it only lead to despair. She lingered for a moment, but only silence yawned from the darkness at her feet.

As she started to run again, her wounded ankle simmered with pain when it planted against mud and stone. She hurried through the hallway behind her and tried to shut out the biting ache in her foot.

Tuhhh...

Tuhhh...

Tuhhhh...

The ground shook above her. The roots of the forest whistled beneath the dirt as fire spread through them like intertwined fingers. They sparked in streams of fire across the ceiling as it chased her forward.

Senna saw nothing but the darkness ahead of her.

The heat from the growing fire roared after her along the walls of the dungeon. She cursed. She had stayed too long, but as her heart hammered her forward, she saw stars.

The incline of the cavern slowed her steps, but she ran faster than her body had ever pushed itself to do. Her mouth frothed with spit, but as she looked up, the night sky bloomed ahead in small clusters of stars.

Smoke unfurled through the opening of the cave. Rocks collided with her feet, and she steadied herself against the muddied wall and her lungs struggled against the smoke, fighting for breath.

Senna covered her mouth and eyes before she tumbled out into the coolness of the night air.

Crisp air welcomed her at first but then, with her face covered, the haunting scream of cracking, smoldering bark cried out through the forest. The trees shrieked as their wooden skin boiled beneath the Alchemist's fire.

She gasped as the place she called home, her peace, now blazed before her in walls of falling fire. Run. Her body demanded in screeching terror through every muscle in her body. Senna frantically scanned the horizon for any sign of Tomas through the trees.

He had promised to stay close by, to stay out of sight, but now she only screamed for him to come out.

"Tomas!"

She coughed against the smoking slithering across the ground and tore through the saplings that huddled beneath the trees.

Her feet hammered against the forest floor as fire exploded from trunks and roots around her.

Vines of fire climbed the trunks of the Great Forest with a hunger unlike anything she had ever seen. Its flames devoured the ancient timber in swaths of gnashing gusts as it dripped freely from limbs in weeping trails of death.

Flying through the smoke and flame, Senna fought against the torrid haze of smoke with her arms shielding her face. Nothing seemed familiar and she could not find the trails amid the wildfire.

"Tomas!"

There was no sign of him and as she spun in search of the boy, her pulse pounded in her ears. She could not stop.

Hesitation always brought failure.

The roaring falls of the Ilsnadad filled her ears and she pictured its banks welcoming her with a frigid embrace.

Senna's heart pounded, and she ran towards the river, but as she lept over a fallen limb, she landed and her body erupted with pain. The force of her body on her weakened ankle turned it inwards with a nauseating snap.

The ground betrayed her, and her face collided with the soil. She gasped for breath as the fire scourged the world around her. From all sides, a herd of deer launched themselves in terrified bounds, soaring above the fallen trunks as she clutched the unscorched soil to steady herself.

Their hooves pounded against the ground and as they ran ahead, Senna's ankle swelled with pangs of heat she knew could not run beside them. As she writhed in pain, the herd disappeared towards the open meadowlands ahead of her, and Senna knew she was utterly alone.

Ghostly embers rose around her in hungry clouds of swirling fire. The growing flames chewed through the forest and Senna's sweat evaporated in periling steam. Her eyes burned from the heat as she wiped the smoke from her face. Her pulse soared with panic and she slammed her hands against the ground to force herself up.

Her body trembled as she found her footing, each step shook her entire body as she wobbled forward. Her ankle throbbed and each pain-filled step shot terror through her heart.

Roaring through the canopy, trees crumbled to ash. A large cracking sound tore through the air above her and a tree as old as the island began to fall. Its trunk was rendered in two as its roots seared and charred beneath the ground.

The heat from the fire gusted around her and the trembling giant swung towards the ground in a pillar of fire. Its limbs split away, falling through the canopy, and crashed around her.

Senna shielded her head, but time stopped moving, so did her feet and her heart too.

The trunk of the fiery giant rattled the forest floor as its body blocked her from any chance of finding the river.

Senna's thoughts abandoned her.

She spun and hobbled in every direction while the forest toppled with outstretched arms of death. The falling trees cornered her like a fox among wolves. She could not run, she could not breathe.

Her eyes flooded with smoke filled tears.

The fire held her prisoner in a cell of smoke and flame.

The lapping heat kissed her skin. She devoted her life to running from fire and those who would threaten the walls she lived behind. Yet all of those guarded years still brought her here.

The bursting tree trunks resounded in shattering waves of deafening shards of fire.

She looked up towards the sky to shield her face from the searing breath of the blaze. The moon looked down at her, and she could feel the coolness of its night on her face.

"*Mother, find me now and bring me to you...*"

Beneath closed lids, she pictured her mother's face. Soft Auburn curls framing sky-blue eyes, and tawny skin warmer than a sunrise. She felt their embrace, both her mother's and father's arms enveloping her body. But it that moment Senna felt her heart crack as she had forgotten the sound of her laugh.

Suddenly, her eyes shot open. A warm, calloused hand found the column of her throat. Hoped fluttered through her chest and she moved to find Bjorn's face.

How had he found her?

She turned to find him, but all at once she knew they were not Bjorn's hands.

White eyes starred back at her and a man covered in blood snarled at her. His face bore the smears of shadow painted runes.

She could not scream as smoke smothered her cries, and his hand tightened around her throat.

He had climbed from the depths of the Ilsnadad.

Haydrian was not his master.

Senna's stomach pitched as he forced her to look into his dead stare and rotting teeth.

Senna reached for her dagger. Her fingers fumbled for its hilt. Her other hand clawing at his arms and face.

The dagger tumbled to the floor of the forest, and before she could reach for her fourth and final blade.

Her feet lifted from the soil. As her body weight dangled from his grip, she gasped for air and for a moment; he suspended her above him, just before he slammed her to the ground. Leaves and branches crunched beneath her back.

The shock rattled her teeth, and she felt a dizziness in her skull. He pinned her beneath the weight of his body. His rune painted arms flexed and his fingers dug into her neck.

He had no blades, but his strength was just as lethal, a strength she did not have.

Senna scratched at his wrists and reached for his eyes, but as he tightened his grip, her skin tingled and smoke overwhelmed all else. Her pulse pounded in her chest, but there was nothing she could do to stop her hands from falling away.

The forest grew quiet, and embers rose around them like flower petals in the spring breeze. Her vision darkened, and she fumbled daftly for the dagger on the ground.

She saw the moon again.

She saw her mother, her uncle. She was not ready.

She had fought so long to keep going, yet fate and fire still chased after her. The sight of his milky eyes and gritted teeth burned itself into her memory.

Senna's hands stopped fumbling in leaves. She could no longer command them to move. The shadows in her eyes came forward and her head lulled to the side.

What remained of her vision fell upon the trees, and now she knew she would die alongside them. She would only look at them, not into the face of death as it squeezed the life from her body. Her pulse hammered inside her eyes.

Air flooded her lungs as his hands flew away from her throat.

Pain rushed through her skull as her need for breath overwhelmed her.

She could not think.

She could hardly move, as that same pain devoured her being. Waterless tears bloomed in her eyes and the smoke engulfed the only sound she uttered.

Despite the throbbing in every muscle and bone, her heart found its pulse again as she rocked herself upwards.

Amid the sea of fire and fractured trees, Bjorn held her attacker by his scalp.

The Steel bolts still decorated Bjorn's back like the spine of a dragon and blood seeped from every shaft that pierced his cloak.

They fought like bears. Hands that grappled for limbs and faces. Tearing and roaring in the beastliest form of man.

Senna's body whirled on the precipice of life and death. Her mind clutched at the pain, but it was a pain that meant she was alive and a pain that drove her hands into the ground and shoved her upwards in a spiraling, disoriented stumble.

The rune-covered warrior grabbed a protruding bolt in Bjorn's back and he twisted it further into him with a guttural cry from the prince that rattled in Senna's mind.

The shaft of the steel tipped arrow split and with Bjorn's roar, he threw his attacker to the ground.

Her wobbling, fawn-like limbs frantically scoured the fallen leaves for her dagger. Her heart leapt as she found it.

The metal of her blade warmed her skin as it took on the heat of the forest, and the familiar dagger became an extension of her body.

Bjorn cried out again and the sound that followed pierce through her heart.

The brittle snap of bone drowned out all else.

Senna paused as everything in her body became afraid, and she tightened her grip on her dagger.

She was half terrified to turn and see the prince dead upon the ground, but if she did not, he would come for her next. She faced them, ready to plunge her blade into the runed warrior's chest.

But as she spun on her heel and lifted her knife from the ground, it nearly slipped from her fingers as her hold stuttered along with her heart.

The warrior knelt before the prince of the mountain with no strength left in his neck. His body swayed and toppled at Bjorn's feet, with eyes that no longer belonged to his master.

Bjorn's gaze found her, and his face ran with blood. His torso, his beard, all of him drenched in blood.

She quickly sheathed her dagger as he stood before her, and every haunted dream flashed through her mind. The Alchemist's awakening on full display and the need to retch threatened her above all else.

The pain in her head only worsened and her ankle did not relent, but after all those years of fear and hiding, she ran to him.

Her body found its strength as the flames climbed higher.

His brows lifted in relief as she stumbled towards the prince's embrace.

Senna's heart found its rhythm.

She knew they would not die here. There was no sign of terror engraved in his flesh, but suddenly, his green narrowed with pain. The fire would not be their end.

Her vision had not been an omen but a promise. A promise that he would always come for her.

She coughed and held his head in her hands. The smoke continued to climb their legs.

"Senna, we must go now!" but as Bjorn lifted his arm, his eyes shot open, and his face blanched.

Senna looked down and found a wound worse than any pain in her body,

Just above his belt, a shard of wood buried itself deep into the prince's flesh. Blood seeped around the splintered wood and as the prince swayed, his eyes relaxed like they were far away.

"Senna."

His hands enveloped her shoulders. His fingers dug into her skin.

"No. no. no. no."

He fell forward with Senna's face buried in the width of his chest. Bracing against him, she dug her feet into the soil.

She would not leave him, but she could not move him. If he fell, they were dead.

"Hold on to me, move with me, but you will not fall! You cannot fall!"

Her hands framed Bjorn's unsteady face. His green eyes glowed orange in the endless hunger of the flames. The prince shook his head.

"Senna..."

As smoke stole the strength of her voice and the tears from her eyes.

"No! I will not leave you!"

His breath was weak, but he nodded. Senna wrapped her arms around him.

Each step became the weight of an army.

Senna guided them forward with shaking, pain-filled steps and looked to the map of stars above them. Each bend in the constellation's belt pointed them west.

Smoke churned in throws of crashing waves as devious roots became unavoidable in the forest's chaos. Each path became fraught with treachery and impassable with fallen trees.

As they struggled between the flame filled trees, Senna's body teetered forward and Bjorn's blood pooled against the fabric of her tunic. Their steps slowed, and her hands shook around his waist while she pushed upwards to support him beneath his arm.

"There!" Senna's voice carried what was left of her strength.

To their right, the beckoning call of night opened to the deepest shades of moonlight. The blue meadow grass shifted in a ripple of hope.

Senna's pulse surged, and she felt a desperate force rise within her heart, and she saw that same hope in the prince's eyes.

He looped an arm behind her back and, with an agonizing charge, they crashed through the licking flames of the undergrowth and fell into the cool, wispy night swollen meadows.

Senna could only cough as she felt the chill of the grass on her hands and braced herself against the ground.

Air overwhelmed her as the pounding behind her eyes eased. Every bone in her body screamed as Bjorn dropped to his knees beside her. Her neck ached, and new bruises rose across her skin.

Soot and ash covered her body like wilted flowers. Smoke held her mind in its grip as she tried to wipe the scent of the fire from her nose and mouth.

She had never been so grateful to see the gaping darkness of the meadow.

Chapter Thirty-Seven

Senna

She slammed her fist against the ground as a loud crack shook through the air. Senna trembled as the life she knew disappeared before her eyes.

Every branch and twig between the mountain and the Ilsnadad dripped with alchemist's fire. She forced her body to breathe, for her heart to steady, and to keep the panic behind her eyes from claiming every piece of her mind.

You are safe. You are not burning.

An arm's reach away in the grass, Bjorn rocked forward and his head lulled over. Senna rushed to his side and as pain shot through her body, the rune warrior's face flashed through her mind.

At her neck and under the bruises, the memory of the warrior's hands around her neck racked through her mind. She had felt the closeness of the stars in those moments, the patient hands of death, but in the jaws of the flame-filled trees, Bjorn had come for her.

"Bjorn!"

Senna stood before the prince of the mountain, and her breath caught in her chest.

Her hands found Bjorn's shoulders, and her body supported him as he knelt before her. She held him upright, his body on the verge of failing, but as she looked into the prince's face, her eyes welled with tears.

She saw how much he had given of himself to stay alive, to keep both of them alive. Senna had told herself that she would not live to die for royalty, but as an ache settled in her chest, she never imagined that a prince would let himself die for her.

His weary eyes looked at her, and his pulse patted beneath her fingertips at a frightening speed. The colors of the fire behind them illuminated the wounds lining his back and the seeping streams coursing down his no longer green cloak.

Blood drenched the expanse of his back and the wooden shard in his side was no longer brown, but coated in crimson. They were wounds he had taken for her. Senna shut out the pain calling out from all over her body. She would fight to keep him alive with everything she had left.

If the prince were to fall forward, and it plunge any deeper, he would die. She would not remove it, nor the arrows. Bleeding would only worsen his wounds and drain him of his spirit. Bjorn closed his eyes and rested his enormous frame against hers.

Her knees shook, but she would not let them give way. His shaking hands clutched her waist, while her fingers curled in the softness of his hair. Senna's eyes and throat still burned from the smoke as it coated every part of her tongue.

The sacred oak of Autumn no longer towered above the forest's canopy. Where the golden light of Autumn had once guided her home, now only darkness claimed its space.

Senna found it unbearable to listen to the taunting crackle of the ravenous fire consuming her home. Out in the dark, above the intensity of the flames, the faint flickering stars beckoned to her with voices crowned in sorrow.

"Senna,"

"I'm here."

She scrambled for the satchel at her belt, but all the loops along her side were empty. She swallowed tears before she spoke.

"I don't have my elixirs. We need help."

"Just hold me."

She nodded and tightened her grip on the prince's shoulders.

"Gailah?"

"She's here, she's safe,"

The muscles in Bjorn's face softened and his head grew heavier against her torso.

Not far off, Senna had spotted the eldest Spessian. In the safety of the meadows, Torin embraced the princess of the mountains, while Gailah's silver hair shimmered over the crook of his arm.

Just beyond the prince and princess, Tomas lay in the grass unburnt and unharmed.

Senna's breathing eased a little. A voice caught her attention. Torin whispered into the night as the prince looked on as the wall of trees dissolved among the flames. Each line that carved through his face reflected the hopelessness that twisted in Senna's heart.

Where had the younger gone? Senna thought as she studied the crest of the meadow.

Alexi was gone.

A thousand questions coursed through her mind, but none of them were more important than what she saw riding towards them.

"Help's here. They're coming, We'll be alright."

She saw war on the horizon of their burning island.

Her father's men assembled in golden columns along the tree line. Their hollowed faces reflected the light from the climbing flames. Black smoke soared through the sky, smoke that would be seen for miles even after the sunrise.

"Lord Barrock! Father!" She cried.

Senna dared not move, yet Bjorn's head did not stir against her stomach as she called out into the night.

His stillness frightened her.

"Feel me breathe," she whispered, wrapping his soot-covered fingers around her lower ribs. "Breathe with me, keep breathing, and do not stop. I command this of you." her voice cracked.

His fingers squeezed back with ghostly strength as every movement echoed with pain in his grip.

"Father!"

The reverberating sound of hooves striking the ground drew her attention. A frenzied assembly of green and gold-cloaked knights on large war horses encircled them.

She watched as knights of the Chasm surrounded Gailah and Torin.

Through a chorus of guttural insults, she watched as they spat at the Spessian Crown Prince. All they knew was that he had taken the daughter of the queen, but as Senna looked on, the prince remained stoic and unmoved. Gailah still lay protected beneath his arm. There were no knights from Spessia among them, and Senna's stomach soured.

"Have Mercy!"

Senna shouted to defend him, but Torin disappeared between a thunder of calvary. Trejen's knights created a barrier of fire painted gold.

Senna strained to identify her father's silhouette in the shadows.

Bjorn's breathing faltered, and she gently cupped the corner of his cheek. Though her body trembled, the pain behind his eyes tore at her heart.

"Senna!"

She recognized her father's voice, and the familiar whinny of his mare, Thea—a beautiful horse the color of moonlight. Thea emerged first among the horses, her coat now auburn from the glowing fires. In a matter of seconds, the commander locked eyes with his daughter.

In the unspoken language of father and daughter, the words splayed across his face brought tears to her eyes. She had spent so long running from a life without her mother. Even as the forest burned, her tears were for the home that now rode upon a war horse.

Her father dismounted and raced to take her in his arms, but shock rushed through his face upon spotting the arrows in the prince's back and the blood on his daughter's body.

"Father!"

Her words failed her. The smoke still burned in her throat and her ankle threatened to collapse.

"Cias!"

Lord Barrock shouted into the night. His hands found her and he drew her forehead to his.

Gently, he took Senna's place. Her father looped his arms under the prince's shoulders and bore the weight of him. Her father cleared his throat, summoning a second desperate yell.

"Cias!"

She scanned the crowd for the priest, but as she did, her legs gave out, and she collapsed into the meadows. At that moment, as her knees struck the ground, Bjorn's eyes fell closed.

"Cias!"

The priest attended to those who had fled the fires; villagers and knights alike. His arched spine set him apart from the rest. The acolytes of Misenia surrounded him. Their hands filled with salves and bandages.

She did not see the King of the Forest or his nephew amid the legions of Autumn.

Cias moved as quickly as his body allowed. There was little magic now, only sparingly a few godly elements left to add to his poultices.

Cias found her father, and in a strange pause, the priest stared at them in disbelief.

"Auburn..." the priest muttered, shaking his head, clearing an invisible fog from his mind.

The blood against her skin dried, and the stickiness of it pulled at her skin. Her heart tumbled erratically through their chest as the healer looked at Bjorn's wounds.

Cias held his fingers to the prince's neck, and he called for a wagon. Lord Barrock's eyes mirrored her despair.

"He may live, but we cannot tend to him here."

The priest singled out a sunny-haired knight of the Mountain to help move Bjorn. Cias removed a vial from his belt that swirled with fragments of golden leaves.

"For the pain," he said, opening the prince's lips.

Bjorn's lids fluttered at the touch of the liquid, and that glimmer of life in his eyes was enough to keep despair from consuming her entirely.

Knights of Autumn lifted the prince into a creaking wagon. With great effort, they laid him on his side, keeping his wounds from worsening. Bjorn's eyes lulled closed again, and she watched as his inhale rose shakily in his stomach.

"Senna..."

"He'll be alright, my lady," the sunny-haired knight said as kept Bjorn from shifting on the wood.

"Who are you?"

"Lord Rorick, my lady." She saw the freckles across his nose gleam in the firelight and he could not have been old enough to be a lord, but the hope in his face helped her heart settle.

"Senna..."

As Bjorn groaned her name, her instincts screamed for her to climb inside the wagon, but before she reached for the wooden rail, a loud cry echoed out behind her.

The cry of the Queen of the Mountain.

A knight of the Chasm locked Torin's hands in irons behind his back.

Beneath the eyes of the Broken Mountain, Senna saw movement past the circling armies.

Emerging like apparitions from the darkness behind them, a lone rider led a third group of horsemen.

The leader, a woman of advanced age, with a long snow-white braid, rode with the vigor of a young woman. Perched on her shoulder, a red hawk bobbed and scanned the trees.

Senna's attention was drawn to the woman's posture as a white banner floated in the breeze.

On its face, sky-blue swirls danced in a cloud pattern. Nadr horsemen gathered behind their matriarch. Their leader's eyes focused on the wall of fire engulfing the great eastern forest. Grief filled the woman's face.

Senna recognized her immediately. This could only be one person: the mother of the fallen King Consort, Ellika, Chiefess of the Nadr and mother of Freyden.

They rarely descended the Mountain, revering the relics more than any other people. Ellika had walked the isle of Thyssia long before Tiranus sailed from Ghobasi.

The last of old Thyssia.

The armies of Autumn and the Mountain parted for the Nadr.

Queen Katha now cradled Gailah's unconscious form and rocked with a panicked madness. Senna observed the Mountain Queen's face pale to ash as the Nadr horsemen approached.

Horror filled Ellika's face as she beheld Gailah lying in the meadow grass.

Chapter Thirty-Eight

Gailah

Gailah winced at the piercing sunlight that filtered through the windows. Beyond, the sky was blue and shining like the sea. The rustle of fabric greeted her ears. Soft swaths of linen covered her body and tightened around Gailah's aching joints.

The bed embraced her on every side, but as she attempted to lift her head, her bones cried out, threatening mutiny if she moved.

"Easy, child."

Her grandmother's voice washed over her in a wave of comfort. Her Nadr accent chirped in the cadence of a songbird. Gailah's heart swelled with emotion at the timber of her voice–warm, perfectly uneven, and sensible.

Gailah blinked against the light, and the room gradually came into focus. Her grandmother's soft but shaky hands supported her neck and helped her sit up against the white wooden bed frame. Her grandmother's almond-shaped blue eyes stared back at her as they crinkled with her smile. She cupped her chin and brushed back Gailah's hair.

"There are those eyes. How do you feel?"

"I pictured death differently," Gailah said and her heart beat with uncertainty.

Her grandmother laughed, squeezing her hand with the soft pads of her fingers.

"I have not gone to the gods yet and neither have you, my dear. Although, I know they will celebrate us when we arrive, but I think we must give them something to talk about for just a little while longer?"

There was pain in her voice, but it was not the physical kind. It was the kind that longed to see her husband and sons again.

Gailah leaned into her grandmother's touch and tears slipped down her cheek. All the tension within her body dissolved like the spring snow. Moving onto the bed, her grandmother wrapped her arms around her and kissed her head.

She had never felt such a desperate need for her sureness and solace–to feel the touch of someone who wanted nothing from her and only held her to keep her above the fear rising in her mind. Gailah did not know how her grandmother was here, but was certain the gods had called her down from the mountain.

"Did you save me?" She tried to hide the disbelief in her voice.

Her grandmother laughed again.

"No, child. I have worked my talents on the enchantments in your skin, but I was not the one who saved you. I will answer all of that, but you must rest."

Ellika shifted slowly from the bed. There was a firmness in her gaze, followed by a chiding look before she spoke.

"I do not want my efforts wasted by your inability to rest."

As her words hung in the air, Gailah sensed stiff bandages wrapped around her hands. Memories of the dungeon, of Haydrian, the rune, and the ring flooded her mind in a thick panicked fog.

She frantically pulled her hands from under the blankets. Small ground herbs and salts rolled from the strips of cloth, tight and overlapping like burial clothes, against her fingers.

Sadness etched lines on her grandmother's face, and she pressed her lips firmly.

"Time. You will heal, but time is the only cure for such wounds. I let the knowledge I carry for our people guide me, and it keeps you as you are, but I do not know the depth of this marking, my dear girl," Ellika swallowed. "I must tell you, the rune will not heal until you satisfy its enchantments. I can minimize the pain, but Gailah..." She pulled her close once again. "Know that I did not let his power reach your heart. This rune will still call to the Void, but you will always be the Daughter of the Mountain. I cannot take this burden from you, but if they had all failed you, if he had burned our mountain to ash, still I would have come for you."

There was a shakiness in her hands and tears in her eyes as she held Gailah close.

Gailah longed to fade away beneath the tender embrace they shared, to escape the visions that danced before her eyes.

The door creaked gently, its sound invaded the walls of their privacy. Gailah held her breath as the door's hinges reminded her of the iron prison cells.

Her mother entered the room, followed by Cassia, the judge of the Mountain, who had kind but calculated eyes.

"Oh, my dear, it's so good to see you awake," Katha's voice carried a hint of tension with her hands clasped before her usual green velvet gown.

Gailah's joy vanished at the sight of her mother. She could only see Haydrian's words painting an irreversible image of a woman she did not know. *Liar. Murderer. Traitor. Warden.*

Gailah attempted to shake his words from her mind, but the whispers lingered. Coldness enveloped Gailah as her grandmother withdrew from her side, only to be replaced by her mother's tight grip.

"Let this conversation be amongst only necessary members." Katha said and directed gaze to the chiefess. "We can never repay your wisdom and gifts, but I will remember your service to my daughter."

"She is my family. There is no debt."

Ellika bowed at the waist and exited the room.

The skin beneath her mother's eyes was swollen with heavy circles, and she seemed more tense than usual. The Queen's hands rubbed against Gailah's sleeves, each movement sent aches along her bones.

"Cassia is here to take down your words." Katha spoke emphatically. "I told them it would be far too strenuous for you to attend the trial.

Graciously, they have understood and have agreed to a written testament."

"Trial?" Gailah's voice echoed off the marble. "Where is Bjorn? Where is Aerin?"

"Bjorn is being tended by the healers, and Aerin..." Katha sighed heavily. "Your uncle has plans for your brother's future. That is all I will say for now, but regarding the prince, yes, there will be a small assembling of the judges. The Spessian prince must stand trial for his actions. That is why Cassia is here."

"Alexi?" Gailah said.

His name stung like a wasp on her tongue.

Her mother sighed as she lifted Gailah's chin with her finger.

"My daughter, you are far too frail to be in such a position. We believe Alexi to have perished in the fire that has claimed much of the eastern forest. The elder is who will stand trial for his treachery."

"Fire...?"

She stumbled over the word in a whisper.

Lightning struck through Gailah.

Torin was alive. The conflicting emotions surged within her; she wanted to weep and run from the room all at once. A wild desire to fly through the hall of judgment gripped her, just to feel the pulse beneath his skin, to confirm his existence. She pictured the pink hues of sunlight staining his cheeks just as her world went dark. Gailah pushed the blankets from her bed and swung her feet over the edge.

"No, you must rest, my daughter."

Every joint felt stiff from her fever and the lingering infection. Despite the physical discomfort, she longed to find him, to know that he had not died alone in the trees. Her heart thundered beneath her linen shift. The effort of moving herself from the bed stole her all of her strength and left her weaker than a wisp of smoke.

Cassia studied Gailah and ignored their queen's instruction.

"How old are you, Your Highness?" Cassia spoke with an inquisitive lilt.

The Queen responded.

"She has seen twenty-one summers and will see her twenty seco.."

Cassia held Gailah's gaze with a strange intensity. Her green eyes narrowed as she waited for Gailah's response.

"Twenty one." Gailah responded.

Her mother's face twitched, and a heavy silence coated the air.

"Thank you." The judge settled into the chair beside Gailah's bed. "As our laws require, your testimony must remain unbiased. Your Highness is of sufficient age to respond for your own account."

The judge placed a small scroll upon the desk, followed by a quill and bottle of ink. Gailah nodded.

"Your Majesty, in keeping with our laws, I must ask to speak with Gailah privately."

Katha's face ruffled with color and as the queen swallowed and gathered her skits, she said, "I will see to Aerin."

Cassia waited until the door closed before she spoke.

"Your Highness, are you well enough to speak the truth as you know it?"

"I am well," Gailah responded, her inner voice branding her a liar as she attempted to get comfortable on the bed. "But, Cassia, I will not see Torin tried. There is nothing I blame him for, and I will not see him harmed."

The knowledge that Torin was alive surged through her and a new energy fluttered within her.

"He is not my enemy. If the Alchemist who captured me is to be believed, then our true enemy moves across the Carridean. The fire was a signal to bring war to our island."

Gailah's words spilled out on top of each other, and what she said sounded like pure delusion.

Cassia's wide-eyed stare unsettled her.

"You are aware that anything you say to me now is included as part of your testimony?"

"I understand. I must speak with him. I must know if the princes knew of the emperor and his army. May I speak with him, please?"

"My apologies, Your Highness, but in order for the truth to be found out, your words must align perfectly. We cannot risk further.." Cassia exhaled deeply. Her eyes were tired, too. "Further stress for Your Highness"

Gailah stared at the sunlight streaming across the mosaic floor. She remembered what grieving for him felt like, how she pictured the cold shroud of death over the lines of his face. She would not do so again.

"Cassia, we must not waste another moment. We cannot prepare for trial when war is looming. If I say I am well enough to speak on his behalf, will I be able to talk to the prince?"

The judge looked up as she adjusted her quill and ink. Cassia tilted her head and rested her hands on her lap.

Gailah had surprised her for the second time.

The judge blinked rapidly.

"Not directly, but he will hear everything you say. Your mother believes that Prince Torin orchestrated all of this — that he is the one who plotted against you."

Her pulse rose.

Gailah felt the softness of his touch as he removed the oak leaf comb from her hair. She remembered how Torin strode beside her, carrying her hand before the entire gathering, under every watchful stare. She remembered his voice and the draw of his sword as death descended upon them, and the sturdiness of his back beneath the moonlit sky on her balcony as her arms encircled his shoulders. How he tucked her hair beneath her cloak and pulled it close over her shoulders. To an outsider, those brief moments would seem like nothing, but to Gailah was enough hope to hold on to. If he had wanted to hurt her, he would have let her drink the wine.

"Please."

She heard his voice in a melody that lingered deep within her bones.

Torin was here, he was alive, and they would kill him if she stayed silent.

Gailah swallowed, and every angry joint reared against her as she struggled to push herself upright.

"When is the trial?"

"Tomorrow, at sunset."

"Cassia, please tell the other judges I will give my words before the courts."

Cassia's gaze steeled on Gailah as the judge's eyebrows raised for a third time. She gathered her things and rose from her chair.

"As you wish, Your Highness."

Bjorn

Bjorn stumbled through the dungeons as his eyes longed for the light above. The scent of alchemist fire filled the air. Senna's scream shattered through his mind, reverberating through his teeth. He crashed forward, his feet useless, trapped and alone amidst the torch-less dungeon.

Her screams turned to weeping–thick and watery sobs beyond the length of his reach. Then, as his fingers carved through the darkness, he found her huddled in the dark. She could not see him, and her weeping only dug itself deeper into his chest. He could feel the shaking in her voice. As he held her arm, warm liquid greeted him, and all at once blood painted his hands. Senna's blood.

Bjorn's mind failed him, and then his body next.

He could only see the red that spilled from the wound on her arm. Senna vanished. Then the dungeon disappeared, with her cries fading into endless night. He was falling and his breathing stopped. He looked up into the never ending starless night, and orange fire erupted through the silhouette of the forest. His eyes burned, and fire surrounded him in crashing walls of falling trees. Walls of smoke swallowed him, and as death drew near, Bjorn could only scream–screams that turned to silence on his tongue.

Light seared his eyes, and his body shook as sweat dripped down his brow. He moved his fingers and soft linens pressed against his skin as bright sunlight sent a dull pain through his skull.

Something warm surrounded him, heavy sleep-filled arms draped across the width of his body. Between the narrow slits of his eyes, auburn hair tickled his cheek.

If this were nothing but a dream, he would have wept.

Crueler than any nightmare if this were not real. Any moment he would wake, cold and alone in the darkness of the trees. Tears pricked at the corners of his eyes. If he had conjured this, then he would cherish it. He brought his hands to her and pulled her close. As he moved, his shoulders roared against the pain lining his spine, each pulling ache from the arrows that no longer pierced into his back.

He was awake. This was real.

His heart tumbled, and he breathed sharply through his teeth. He knew for certain the warmth he felt belonged to flesh and bone.

When Tomas had stumbled from the fires alone, every muscle in Bjorn's body ignited with fear. He left Gailah in Torin's arms and threw himself back into a maze of fire and death.

The thought of Senna lost among the trees, as fire claimed every limb and trunk, forced him to forget all regard he had for himself. He charged toward the river, guided by the pull in his chest that demanded the Alchemists were wrong. Her vision was wrong. She would not die this way. It was not Senna that he spotted first, but the rune painted warrior as he crushed her beneath his weight. Rage was too soft of a word for the fury that had taken hold of his body. He had blinked, and the man was dead between his fingers. That rage saved Senna's life and was worth more than any nightmare that might follow him.

Movements stirred in the periphery of his gaze.

His eyes stiffly widened as acolytes in sky blue drifted between the rows of beds.

His cheeks flushed as he realized they were not alone. Healing beds lined the walls of a secondary chamber in the hall of judgment. With trepidation, Bjorn tilted his head to see her.

First, he felt her fingers.

Senna had woven her arms around his chest, and her skillful hand cradled the width of his jaw. Her other hand rested softly against the nape of his neck, as if she had fallen asleep counting the movements of his chest.

"Breathe with me, keep breathing, and do not stop. I command this of you."

Before the flames, as every fiber of his body demanded him to surrender, she commanded him to breathe. The emotion that erupted within his chest was too much for him to bear.

Senna had embroidered herself to him, almost falling off the edge of the cot. Her body was balanced and wedged against his arm. Senna slept, and he could smell the smoke that haunted her hair. Ash smeared every exposed part of her body from her freckles to the backs of her hands.

Her ankle was splinted and wrapped in tight bandages. Her breathing was slow and shallow, and he dared not move.

He closed his eyes and rested for the first time in what felt like an eternity. Content to remain enveloped and smothered by her warmth.

He did not wish for death, but if he fell into the embrace of the gods like this, then he would know his peace.

Chapter Thirty-Nine

Torin

The knights of the Chasm had thrown him against the stone with indifference, and Torin knew if they had held him captive in their own cavernous mountain, he would be dead. His ribs sang as he wheezed for air.

He knew the history of his bones, and those old wounds were now reopened, bleeding. The hairs on Torin's neck bristled at the sound of fabric shuffling and the steady voice of the Mountain Queen.

"You cleaved down their relic."

Torin tried to arch his neck between the bars of his cell, but all he could glimpse was the green of her skirts as his dirty silver hair hung between the bars.

"Romulus will.... We must tread carefully, my son. His mistress died in the collapse of the Great Oak. He is raw and unpredictable."

Aerin scoffed.

"It had to come down! I will not let them treat me as a traitor when they should greet me as their savior. Do you think Bjorn could have succeeded if that rotting giant had not come down?"

"My son, you must keep these thoughts to yourself. When they bring you before Romulus, you must repent. Repent and be ready to move. Your great uncle will come for you before tomorrow's end. He will see you on to the shores of Ghobasi."

"No! You cannot send me away! I belong here with you, with our people."

"Aerin... War is coming and I cannot risk keeping you here if you will not obey me. Bring your bride home to our mountain and show yourself ready to fulfill your duty as King."

The walls hid Aerin's face from him, but Torin could hear the heaviness of his breath.

Footsteps rang out in the distance.

A boldness flared in Torin's chest.

"Why did you not answer me?"

His fingers tightened against the bars as he demanded answers for her silence.

Torin swallowed as Katha's spine straightened. Her shoulders shifted and Torin felt the ice of her stare. The golden mountain crown sat heavily upon her braided coils. Katha's chin tilted and she studied him from a distance. The disregard in her face was the same shown by her knights.

To her, he was not a threat, but an inconvenience, an unruly thread to be cut out.

"Answer me!"

He snarled as the bars pressed into his cheeks.

"Why have you made me your enemy?" He hated the breathlessness of his voice, but the unrelenting pain in his ribs prodded his lungs.

"My mother owes you nothing, sea snake!" Aerin's voice called out. "You killed my sister's guards and stole her for your own gain. I would kill you now if the stones did not separate us."

Torin stifled a laugh as they stood parallel, partitioned by the cell.

"Ask Gailah what happened that night. Ask her and she will tell you that my hand spilled no mountain blood. I vow my word before the judges and the gods that no harm came to your sister while in my keeping."

Katha stepped away from Aerin's cell.

"Then how did Haydrian find her?"

The Queen's words scalded him and he heard his name in Gailah's scream. His head dipped between his hands as he held the iron before him. The tension in his shoulders threatened to drive him mad.

"They found us because you did not listen to me! I warned you they were coming. I told you everything I knew and still you dangled her before the Alchemist's snare. You could have spared her from all of it, but yes, Your Majesty, if you must make me your vessel of hatred, then know they found her because I alone was not enough. Haydrian is dead. I put the sword through his back, not you or this pretender beside me. You failed Gailah the moment she left your fortress."

Torin's hands shook as irons gnawed at his wrists. The truth from his lips burned a path towards his heart. In the forest, he had failed her, but only because he had stood alone.

The queen's silence taunted him. His pulse soared, and as she stood unblinking, she traced the intricate beaded embroidery on her sleeves. Her unmoved stoicism was more terrifying than any of the beasts he had faced in the dungeon.

"Alas, how unfortunate that such words are of no use to your brother. Sorrows for your house, but know your lies will reunite you, Prince. That is my promise."

The bars pressed harder into his face and the prison walls crowded in. His stomach tightened. He quieted his shaking hands and refused to lower his eyes.

"I offered Gailah my sword and my fealty, and for that I deserve to die?"

The queen glided towards his cell, the shadows of the mountain crown passed over his face.

"You lie well, Prince." She whispered

Torin shook his head. As disbelief mixed with the bitter rage in his hands, he could have rendered the bars.

"Your true enemy will come, Your Majesty, and you will fail her again."

Alexi

He had ensured Gailah and Torin's safety, but before anyone could arrive to collect the princess, he had slipped away to the river. The Kingdom of Autumn burned around him as he let the memory of Prince Alexi die among the flames.

As the fire laid waste to the eastern wood, Alexi let the Ilsnadad carry him to the sea. He dove into the thrashing current and let the smoke that coated his body dissolve on the surface of the water.

Alexi would let the world forget him. While Gailah might forgive Torin, he was aware she would never erase guilt from the prince who had stood by as her enemies haggled for her body. There was no future left for him under the banner of house Spessia.

As the river's path coursed through the island, he clung to a single word.

"Iosi"

He emerged from the water into the coolness of the night air. Alexi stood and observed as the fire coursed towards the Autumn King's watery border.

He had no reason to believe the Alchemist's story, save for the cord within his heart that drew him to the isle that dotted the horizon of the Spessian harbor.

To that island, he ran with everything in his body. They had been so close, and it tormented him to realize that as he gazed at their blooming cliffs each night, someone might have been staring back at him. From their peaceful shores, had his parents also kept vigil at their windows, yearning for any sign of their stolen sons?

As his feet pounded against the pebbled beach, the need for truth filled him with pain and hope. He could not endure Haydrian's words festering in his mind.

Night seeped into day as he traveled along the wooded coast. Two days passed as the prince moved in the shadows of seaside villages, following the rocky shoreline until the colors of the sea shifted from cerulean to turquoise.

He strode beneath the light of the stars as the cliffs climbed from the sea and until the rivers of his people carved through the soil at his feet.

There was a moment as he stood beside the Carridean. Alexi looked out into the night, and rising above the surf, nine dark spines sliced through the waves and were gone in a blink. His chest burned from running, but now his heart galloped as its scales twinkled in the moonlight. The beast was silent as its back arched through the water, but Alexi had seen it. The Spessian sigil disappeared to the deep below, but the ripples in its wake were proof enough. Gone for a century, but now, the monsters from the depths were hunting along the surface.

The spires of the palace twisted through the sky in the distance as the moon descended. Soft glowing lights twinkled in the fishers' villages. Night swallows darted through the air in chirping swells of air as their wings beat down amid the silence.

Alexi did not fix his gaze on the palace. His heart pounded as his eyes rested on the smallest cluster of lights that climbed the singular hill on the island of Iosi. He dreamed of what home might feel like away from the cold alabaster walls of the palace.

Blisters gnawed at his feet. His stomach cramped at its emptiness. His only food had been what he could forge for from the coast.

Haydrian spoke of many things, and Alexi's sole focus had been on his parents. He had overlooked the Alchemist's promise of vengeance.

As a crimson dawn crested the throes of the Carridean, Alexi's heart stopped and nausea overwhelmed him.

His knees fell to the sand.

Night slipped away into the darkness of morning and before his eyes, a wall of onyx colored ships swayed in Spessia's harbor. Their black banners bore a golden crescent rune at its center. Behind them, the red morning sky bloomed with columns of smoke from the towers of the palace.

Spessia burned before the prince's eyes. The devastation did not pierce his chest out of love for his house; he no longer regarded them as anything but thieves. Alexi mourned for those caught in the infection of their queen's making, a sickness he allowed her to spread with indifference.

The alchemists assembled in unwavering legions along the sea walls of the palace. The dread building inside him intensified with every battalion that arrived on the shore. On the face of the ramparts, black banners unfurled, claiming the seat of house Spessia for the Lord of the End.

The prince moved closer along the rough sand and saw the Spessian steel guarding the heart of every soldier. Their queen had traded her city for its destruction, all so that Allagria might outrun the outstretched arms of death–a destruction that sailed on ships crafted by Spessian masters. Those same craftsmen now lay dead along harbor docks. All of them slain and drenched in morning sunlight as they awaited the return of their crown prince.

The largest quadrireme rocked in the tidal rhythm of the harbor.

The isle of Isoi was just beyond the blockade. Its lush greenery and white stone cliffs sang to him in words only his bones remembered. He fought the urge to swim the breadth of the channel, to dive beneath the crystal surf and do what came naturally to him, to protect himself alone.

No, he would not hide.

He had signed his name on the ledger of fate with his people's blood, Gailah's blood, the blood of every soul claimed by Haydrian's touch. Alexi's stomach soured as he looked at the unmarred Iosian villages. How could he come to them now with only traitors blood to his name? What father would claim him as their son?

Alexi understood that he would never find peace while evading shadows. He would find their queen in the city. They did not slay rulers like cattle.

It would be a spectacle.

He would wash the blood from his hands with the blood of vengeance from the woman who stole the kindness of a frightened boy with every blow, from the woman who pitted brother against brother in the fighting pits of their own self doubt. Only her blood would dissolve the treachery that burned his skin. He could not stop the armies that bled through the city's wounded gates, but he could silence the heart of the one who sold them to the Void.

He could not rest as a son of Iosi while the last vestige of Alexi still toiled in his chest.

He almost laughed as he realized there was no need for disguise when he already wore the armor of his enemy.

An onyx helmet lay discarded beside the ruins of the smoldering walls. Only she would see his silver hair and know that he could not forget, that the past would not be forgotten. He secured the Spessian helmet.

The eyelets merged and left space for his mouth and nose. The cold steel was not the ornamental protection of a prince or a king, but the simple hammered steel of any soldier.

Alexi moved through the ranks of the men gathered along the shore, blending in among the Alchemists in onyx armor.

These men bore no runes or signs of impressment. In their unenchanted eyes, he saw their collective anger burn brighter than the heat of the Alchemist's fire.

Chapter Forty

Cias

He stood waist deep in the river's current and the water moved around him, tugging him in its gentle pull. Cias had taken this stance on numerous occasions, far too many times, but only once before for this many souls.

He found a hidden strength deep inside as the mourners gathered beneath the broken and scorched trees of their forest. The night was quiet, save for the sound of those standing on the riverbank. Each voice pressed upon his heart.

Cias had a duty to them, to the families of the souls lost to the flames and those slain by Prince Aerin.

He had sat with each family, learning their names, their stories and the joy that had been their life.

Over three hundred boats lingered in the water, floating in the same current that moved around him now. His hand rested on the smooth wooden hull of a boat that belonged to a girl, a young woman who had no one to claim her and give her name.

No stories to be told and no one standing in mourning alongside the bank. The acolytes had prepared her body for the journey and still they had no name. As each boat passed him, he lifted their names to the gods and blessed their journey to the sea.

The tragedy of the tree's collapse ached inside him like it had fallen upon his heart. The absence of its light pervaded the darkness that surrounded him.

His aged fingers clutched the helm of the vessel and he began his prayer of blessing–old words, words uttered across lifetimes, words only shared between the priests and the departed, but as he recited the incantation, Cias' eyes began to burn.

As the boat swayed beneath his fingers, a tear streaked his skin. He could not utter a blessing without a name to attach it to.

The river's current moved against his back, pulling the edges of the vessel farther down, tugging the boat towards the sea. His feeble hands could not bear the weight of the current and as they lost their strength, he released the side of the boat.

He watched the river guide it softly forward in a maternal sway that carried the girl and her boat to the sea.

In his mind, Cias heard a voice, one he knew better than his own. He had dedicated his life to it. The voice uttered a name, calling her home.

A slight blossom of light stole his gaze from the shrinking boat. He turned to see a woman standing among the gathered on the bank. She carried an outstretched lantern for those cloistered around her as each person took away a small lit candle upon a frame made from reeds.

Those candles flickered like starlight at the water's edge as families dotted the surface, placing them upon the river.

In shimmering clusters, the lights traveled beside the boats that continued to drift down for his blessing. As the lights rested in the river's current, he knew their gods did not live in the rivers, trunks, or mountains, but as the glow fell upon those that mourn their loved ones.

He felt the gods among them grieving alongside them.

The last boat to receive his blessing lingered farther back along the river.

A boat carved from an unmarried oak was filled with purple flowers carrying their young queen, a queen not yet crowned or known by their people. Beside the queen's boat, their king stood waist deep in the water.

In his hands, Lyssia's laurel rested between his fingertips.

As the water rose higher around the king, Romulus' golden cloak ebbed and drank in the river at his back.

Cias felt his heart give way for a second time that day.

Romulus' forehead pressed upon the bow stem, and as the young king leaned forward, he placed his mother's crown upon Oxana's brow.

Romulus would not let her sacrifice end with the sea. She would be known by the departed and the living as the wife of the king. Lyssia was waiting for her. Their people would know that their queen had given all, so they might see another sunrise.

She had understood earlier and more profoundly than he did that hatred and healing could not share the same heart.

Cias took the young king's head in his hands.

"Do not bow to the darkness. Our hope is not lost, even if we do not live to see it."

Chapter Forty-One

Gailah

Maroon clouds framed the dawn as sunlight crawled above the horizon. The Agametian windows of the hall of judgment drank in the light of the early morning sun.

They had moved her to her original chambers to convalesce among her own things and the comfort of the familiar.

She tried to find rest throughout the night, but fear kept her candles aflame in the dark. The shadows watched and hissed behind every flicker of its wick. Its beeswax ebbed with the night, and she lost herself in wisps of fire.

Gailah curled into the window seat as the maroon sky swelled into billows of orange and yellow. The sentinels of the sky grieved the scorched Thyssian soil as the moon and the sun traded places. Gailah could see the ruins of the Great Forest.

The Ilsnadad had acted as a wall protecting the keep and the largest of villages. Black shards of tree trunks protruded through the ground while ribbons of smoke lingered in the air. She felt strange and overwhelmed, knowing all this had transpired while she fought the nightmares of alchemical sleep.

Gailah held her knees close in the cloister of cushions as her mind ruminated on how close she had come to losing everything she loved in one day.

Her bandages frightened her.

They were tight and restrictive, with a strong herbal scent.

Each wrapped finger reminded her of someone prepared for burial. She flexed them one at a time and felt a pain in her heart when she realized her Nadr ring was gone. She knew her grandmother would have kept it safe, but the bump on her forefinger filled her with weakness, a deeper and darker pain.

The ring Haydrian forced onto that finger still rested on her hand.

They could not remove it. If it had been possible, then she would not have it trapped against her skin. The thought of seeing the carved rune made the walls press in and her breath weaken.

The tightly wound knots fought against her thickly wrapped fingers as she tried to untie them. The panic rising under her skin whispered,

"they are coming".

Her grandmother's healing gifts held the pain beneath the rune at bay.

But for how long? Gailah wondered as the dull thrum beneath the wound pounded in a war drum's rhythm.

Gailah's eyes found the horizon once again and as she did, a dying star flared across the night soaked corners of the dawn.

The tail of the fleeing star faded in a blink and exhaustion overtook her just as the sun broke through the fog covered meadows.

"Good Morning, Your Highness" Etilda curtsied, then entered the room with a golden gown draped over her arm. Its beadwork formed the shape of oaks leaves down the sleeves, and its train grazed the floor as Etilda approached the bed.

"It will take some time to dress you, but Her Majesty specifically instructed that you must look your best today."

Gailah's eyes fluttered open at the sound of her attendant entering the room.

"Thank you, Etilda, but I would love a bath more than anything in the world." Gailah's body ached for the refuge of the warm water. She imagined slipping beneath the water and letting this dark dream wash away with every sore muscle and throbbing limb, but there was no water that could wash the filth of fear from her skin.

Etilda nodded.

"I will send for them to draw you a bath, Your Highness."

She flared the gown out on the bed, and Gailah marveled at the precision of the embroidery. A dress that would have taken weeks to make.

"Her majesty will be here in just a moment, Your Highness. "

Etilda curtsied again with a smile.

Gailah felt the warmth of her smile and crinkles of kindness in her eyes, but just before she left the room, the young woman said, "I prayed the gods would bring you home. I know I was not alone, Your Highness, but I wanted you to know that you never were."

Gailah could only smile, as any words threatened would come out muddled and weepy. She recognized the dress now sprawled across her bed. It was a gown commissioned by her grandfather and worn by her mother at her betrothal to Trejen, an engagement that ended with years of bloodshed. Gailah's hands shook, both from pain and ire.

The door creaked again, but this time, her mother entered the room.

"Ah, how good to see you standing." Her mother smiled from the doorway, but it did not reach her eyes. "Your strength rises with the sun."

"Good Morning, Mother,"

"Etilda tells me you requested a bath. A wise choice, for today you must glisten." Katha crossed the threshold and glided towards the bed. Katha's eyes admired the dress from a distance as she stood over the fabric with her hands folded at her waist before she lifted the sleeve with reverence.

"I loved this gown. It broke my heart not to wear it again."

Gailah slowly lowered herself into the seat beside the fire as her legs moved like a fawn. Her anger rose in furls of steam from the boiling rage deep in her heart.

"Why must I glisten when all I feel is pain and fear?" Gailah wrapped her arms around herself as the flames danced among the embers. "They are coming for me. I can feel it."

"Sweet lamb, your enemies are dead or will be soon. We must think of Aerin."

"*Aerin?*"

"Yes, Romulus wishes your brother to face justice, but with you as his wife, perhaps he will spare him, so we might move forward as allies."

Gailah's body stiffened against her seat before the hearth. Her words spun dangerously on her tongue, in taunting whispers from Haydrian's lips.

She felt them flutter between the truth she feared and the lies of her childhood. Gailah wrapped her bandaged fingers around the arms of the chair. As she stood, her joints protested in slow ginger movements.

Her mother faced her in pooling swaths of emerald green fabric, regal and poised as the Mountain itself. The calm expression she wore was that of the morning fog–distant, cool, and apathetic.

Gailah gathered her pebbled words, ready to dash the still waters of her mother's face. A question gnawed behind her eyes ever since the darkness of the dungeons.

"Where lies the King of Autumn?"

She wanted her to guess. She wanted to dangle the question like an innocent snare.

"We will burn him on the Mountain, but then they will bury King Trejen in the Hall of the Noble beside Tiranus and his descendants. A compromise."

Katha fiddled with the rings on her fingers. Gailah shook her head with Romulus' mother's name heavy in her throat.

"Will they bury him beside Lyssia?"

Her mother's face blanched and her spine became painfully straight. The Queen's eyes widened further, and her jaw muscles tightened.

"What did you say?" Katha's voice was a whispered rumble. Her hands stopped fidgeting and fell to her sides.

"Why should they carve a tomb for him when Decius' tomb lies empty?" She savored every syllable as she watched the brows in her mother's face twitch.

Gailah attempted to press on, but her mother swiftly positioned herself directly in front of her, bearing the gritted teeth of a bear.

In a torturous moment, she scanned Gailah's face. Her mother's eyes cooled and became almost death-like.

"Gailah," she spoke soothingly and smiled at her daughter, cupping her chin and Gailah felt spiders run along her skin. Haydrian's fingers had felt the same and Gailah's body could not shake the pressure of his grip.

Her mother's throat bobbed as she cleared her throat.

"You will put on this gown. You will defend your honor to the judges. You will tell them how the Spessians plotted all of this and insist on Torin's execution as per *my* request. He stole you to spite us. He is a wrathful, foolish man. Torin is a servant of the Void."

Gailah narrowed her eyes and scoffed at the absurd accusation.

"Torin did not carve this mark into my flesh!"

"Torin wanted you for himself, and now your brother must stand trial as well. Ensure the judges do not squander their mercy on him when Aerin deserves it more than anyone else." Gailah had never seen her mother's eyes so unattached. "Remind Romulus of what he owes us, what he owes you. As king and your betrothed, this is an insult to him as well. Perhaps he will even duel Torin himself.... What a sight that would be? Do this. Let him die as our enemy and the rest of his house will follow."

Gailah's eyes darted to the gown on the bed. She could sense the gown's ties cinching around her waist and along the ribbons of its sleeves. The diaphanous oak leaves along the neckline glittered in the sunlight and her lungs ached as the rune pulsed in waves of pain, as if each ripple pulled her towards the sea.

Any restraint that held her tongue in check snapped, and with her exhale, every suppressed word poured out.

"Dah would hate you for this! He would have never let me come here if he knew I was in danger. He would have never married you if he knew what you had done. Haydrian may have broken the mountain, but you lied, lied to everyone, to the judges, to your family, to your people. You exiled thousands to cover up your lies and executed the rest. You led our people to war so you could bury any proof that you were the one who defied the gods. You broke the Mountain, you let Haydrian taste the Void..."

Katha was no longer looking at her.

Her mother's gaze rested beyond Gailah's shoulder. Fear roared across her mother's face as her body followed in an avalanche of panic. She fell to the floor in a heap of velvet.

Her body heaved in rapid breaths, but her eyes did not move from the corner of the room.

"STOP!" she cried, covering her ears and closing her eyes like a frightened child. "PLEASE! I BEG YOU STOP!"

Katha wailed as she opened her eyes. Her mother pointed to a trembling hand.

Gailah looked, and they were alone.

A wintry chill emanated from the emptiness of the room and brushed across Gailah's skin.

"Mother."

Katha did not hear her.

She only shook as she slammed her hands over her ears.

"Forgive me, forgive me," Katha wept and rocked.

"Mother.." Gailah knelt as her hands found her mother's shoulders.

Sweat dampened Gailah's fingers through the velvet of her mother's gown. She found her frenzied gaze and as they connected; it was as if she woke from a dream. The worried lines of her brow straightened.

Katha's frightened eyes darted to the corner and sighed with relief as her mother saw they were alone.

"Gailah... I," her mother's voice broke. "I know what I have done and there is so much more that you will never know, but trust that everything I have done was to protect my people and my family." Her mother paused and her face became stone. "Gailah.... Please remember that as your mother, I am not requesting that you choose your words carefully before the judges; I am commanding you as your queen." She drew closer to her daughter and lifted a few loose pieces of her hair.

"Where is the hair comb I gave you?"

Gailah tasted salt and fire on her tongue. The cowering heap of her mother had sublimated into a callous, regal shell.

"It is gone. I hope it burned in the fires!" Stinging pain erupted across Gailah's skin as the back of her mother's hand struck her cheek. Something flickered across Katha's face.

All of Haydrian's knives and runes did not burn her as harshly as her own mother's hand.

"Guard your people. Safeguard your brother. One life taken is an act of mercy compared to a thousand." Katha did not linger for Gailah's response.

She did not witness Gailah's cheek as it bloomed in the aftermath of her palm. With composed grace, her mother gathered her skirts and departed the room.

Without glancing back, she missed Gailah's legs as they gave way, the tears that welled in her daughter's eyes, and Etilda as she returned to her daughter's room. The Queen nearly collided with Gailah's attendant in the doorway.

Etilda's face betrayed every thought behind her eyes. Gailah knew her lady saw her tears and the streak of red that added to the toll of bandaged limbs, wild hair, her garden of bruises, and the bloodied wound at her neck.

"Your Highness..."

Her words failed her as Etilda's face softened.

Gailah resisted the soft voice inside that urged her to give in, the one whispering for her to let the crashing waves of fear devour her beneath its tide. She wanted to curl into the floorboards, bury her head in her hands until the storm passes.

That same voice coaxed her to simply slip her shoulders through the bodice of the shimmering golden gown, a voice that urged her to obey. She felt those stays tighten again until her hunger for air overtook all else.

She gasped and gripped the bedpost beside her.

She studied every leaf and golden curl of beaded lace before her eyes. Gailah looked towards the doorway. Her heart found its rhythm again as she locked eyes with the softhearted woman before her.

"Etilda, I need your help."

. . .

Alexi

He weaved through the city streets as every paving stone led him to the walls of the palace. The urgency in his veins hastened his movements, as if each breath was poised to betray him to the Alchemists flanking his every side.

No bodies lined the streets. The only evidence of bloodshed lay between the harbor and the city gate. Under the scraping of his sandals, his footsteps ignited the path before him with the ghosts of his childhood. Amid the rows of onyx armor, their column slithered forward with shields barred together like scales through the alabaster gates of the palace.

The armies of the End moved in unison, yet there was a frantic quality to their steps. The rush he sensed drifting among them was not born of fear, but of vengeance.

Crumbling walls narrowed around them as they moved closer to the heart of the city. Piles of ash adorned the streets as inky clumps of alchemist's fire burned like pitch clinging to stone. Alexi's stomach churned. No one walked on the deserted streets.

Upon entering the great square, the emptiness followed them as every stall stood bare, and the sapphire banners of House Spessia lay charred in a smoldering bastion.

The fountain before him bubbled in its same effervescent melody, but only the flowering trees kept any semblance of their house. The statue of Queen Allagria was gone, and no longer carved through the sky. Her marble facade lay toppled in a fractured rubble of the palace courtyard.

The black banners of the end hung beside the large doors at the end of the courtyard, replacing every sigil of their house. Voices grumbled and shouted beyond the walls of the palace. Spessian voices filled his ears as the sound of their accent fluttered in his mind.

Their battalion did not halt before the palace, nor did they enter it.

As they crossed the outer walls of the courtyard, Alexi was certain that they headed towards the amphitheater beside the sea. If they were to make a spectacle of Spessia's defeat, it would be there.

The clamor of the crowd intensified as he descended the green but rocky hillside just beyond the crashing surf of the Carridean. Amid the gleaming helmets of Spessian steel, Alexi caught sight of commoners and nobles alike, their beige and sapphire tunics drenched in sunlight.

Stone pines surrounded the upper lip of the amphitheater. They were trees he had climbed as a child and tossed rocks into the sandy arena below. They all stood arranged in rows on the graded soil. Like a cluster of fish, their armored battalion stood side by side and descended the stairs of the theater.

Spit coated Alexi's neck.

Insults and curses rang out from the captive Spessian citizens, accompanied by their shaking fists and snapping jaws that surrounded him on either side. Each pounding stone step reverberated through his body as his feet led him downward.

The spit rolled down his skin, and as the sand of the arena shifted beneath his sandals, a minacious figure claimed its center. His broad back faced the crowd as he took in the crashing chaos of the sea.

The commander's helmet rested at his feet, but his honey colored hair curled and billowed in the shore's breeze.

Night colored runes blared across his arms in contrast to the bronze sheen of his skin. The arena basked in the glowing morning sun, but the Spessian armor on his chest absorbed its rays in a darkening thirst. The black fabric of his cloak moved in harmony with the wind and as he paced the ovular area floor. He spun a short sword in his grip and tossed his head back in such a swagger that let the light warm his face. Shadows carved along the height of his cheekbones as he stood undaunted before the sun.

Impatience framed his posture as sprays of sand collided with the onyx armor that guarded his shins.

Alexi took his place among the soldiers encircling the arena while his unwavering gaze remained on the commander before the crowd. Alexi held little faith in the gods of Thyssia, but now he believed the commander who stood before him was the Void made flesh.

Chapter Forty-Two

Torin

The sunlight arched across the floors of his cell as the afternoon crawled across the bars. He knew the knights of the Chasm would come for him soon. Dim yellow light painted shadows across the width of his barren cell, falling just beyond where he sat against the wall.

To prepare for his trial, the guards had loosened the irons that chained him to the floor, giving him a wider path to tread. As Torin soothed the burning chaffed skin, he knew escape was never an option.

The thought did not even bother to taunt him, as the prince knew it only delayed the inevitable. Every distant footstep set his teeth on edge. His body sagged against the stone.

There would be no clemency.

The only Spessian still quartered within the halls of judgment was the eldest judge, Sherat, who spoke for the people of Spessia. He was a mere extension of his grandmother's hand, a puppet upheld by a tyrant's string. Torin would stand alone before the judges and the people of Thyssia.

There was no one from his house to speak for him.

No one was coming to his aid.

Surely when the Spessian courts returned without him, his men would have noticed.

Why had they not come? Lehgan and Atraxis would not have given up on him.

Bile burned in his throat as he imagined the great sword of the Mountain careening through the air. The grooves in the floor ready and waiting to catch his blood before the executioner's feet. The instant he stepped onto Gailah's balcony, he foresaw this end.

So many things had been far from his control, yet he willingly threw himself into this situation, fully aware that his destiny now lay in the hand of those who hated him.

When he asked for a word of the princess' condition, they met him with silence and disdain. Gailah was alive, and that was his only comfort besides the pulse in his chest and that his head still rested on his shoulders. If she were dead, then they would have killed him by now.

His memory of the night only days ago roared through his mind. The flames scorching his face pulled on the fibers of his heart as he remembered their flight from the forest. He held her as his sapphire cloak enveloped Gailah in the stillness of the meadow.

The memories of his clumsy confessions spilled from his lips, a silent prayer that she might hear him as she lay unconscious in the soft grass. He pleaded with her to wake as the soot from his fingers smudged her cheek.

Torin never begged, but he had done so for her twice just in the days of them knowing one each-other.

As the grass in the meadow hissed from the heat of fire, pleas were the only words that fell from his lips. Each pleading word echoed in the crackling night and he could still hear how it had broken his voice. Her closed, listless eyes had not seen the despair collapsing in his gaze, but he had felt it ache behind his armor.

Gailah had gone into that darkness without knowing they were coming for her, without knowing if she would ever wake or if she was lost to the Void. Torin carried no regret save for this, that he was selfish.

He wanted to be enough for her, and it had nearly cost her everything.

He fought for her, for Thyssia, even if it meant facing death or the descent into madness. Yet death seemed the more merciful option compared to the torment that awaited him. An unsettling sensation tugged at the corners of his thoughts.

Emptiness burrowed in every corner of his body as doom tensed each corded muscle and commanded his mind to prepare to face the judges, to face the gods.

They had stripped Torin of his sword and his armor. He had nothing to defend himself, save for his threadbare tunic and his tongue. Thoughts of Alexi filled his head. He excelled at manipulating words to suit his needs, a skill honed through a lifetime of self-reliance, and now he needed his brother more than ever.

He held onto his last glimpses of Alexi.

A pang of anguish shot through Torin as he envisioned his brother vanishing into the fiery chaos of the forest. Torin's bruised ribs felt tighter as he exhaled. He could justify all his actions except for those involving Alexi. The guilt of not loving his brother better haunted him, and as he rose from the ground, his restless pacing only intensified the swirling thoughts.

Even the bears in the fighting pits of Ghobasi seemed more composed than he.

Even if he managed to survive and live to see another day, there was still so much awaiting him beyond these halls. His grandmother, nestled within her lofty alabaster walls, would prepare herself and wait for the impending war. The weight of this realization rocked him backward, and he nearly stumbled.

Torin had to brace himself against the wall, his thoughts thundering so loudly that he missed the sound of the creaking iron doors, the sound of Aerin being escorted back to his cell. Torin would be heard last and then their sentences called out to the realm. His pulse beat like a war drum in his neck. The judges were ready for him. The gleam of the guard's silver pauldrons caught Torin's eyes, and he took a deep breath. Each breath silenced the voices pounding between his ears as the guards approached his cell. He closed his eyes and felt the storm in his chest cease as they slid the key through the lock.

One guard held a set of smaller, tighter irons in his gloved hand, and Torin had to steady himself once more.

They exchanged the ones he wore for the ones they would parade him in. The sensation of smooth colder restraints against his skin sent fire through his veins. The chains were vines constricting and strangling his wrists.

He steeled his gaze and did not resist as they shoved him forward into the hallway. Stone scraped against his soles and Torin saw Aerin first as he passed the prince's cell. Aerin's eyes flared wide and the Mountain Prince's silence spoke volumes.

He only glared at Torin. Just before he disappeared upwards to the winding stairs, Aerin nodded in farewell.

Alexi

"Thyssians!" the onyx cloaked commander called out. "Grant me your audience so I might show the great people of house Spessia what I offer you."

The crowd was stubborn but gradually settled into a grumbling silence. Those gathered in the theater were crammed together like cattle, shoving and shouldering each other in the tightly packed rows.

Alexi scanned their faces, and the turbulent whispers rose with the hairs on his skin.

"I am Airth, Son of Azoth, Lord of the End, and I will end your suffering. Our islands long to be united under one banner, and I will cease your torment with my father's sword." He extended his sword to the crowd, and as he did, soldiers opposite the crowd parted.

"I give you a choice." He shouted.

The eyes of the crowd followed the movement of the soldiers, but Alexi's eyes never left Airth. Victory claimed every aspect of his muscular frame, and the sunlight beaming down upon him filled Alexi with dread.

The dragging sound of sand made Alexi's stomach churn. Next, he heard muffled cries amongst the soldiers and his attention snapped as they approached the commander of the End.

Between the rows of citizens, they carried the woman he no longer claimed as his grandmother between the iron grip of two alchemists.

Devoid of her staff, only the Spessian blue of her robes and the Riverland crown atop her bristly hair set her apart from a tragic peasant. They had silenced her with torn strips of the royal banners and forced her to her knees. The Spessian queen scanned the crowd with frantic eyes.

Alexi's hand fell to his sword.

The swarm of bees in his chest demanded justice as Alexi's calf muscle twitched. He pictured himself charging forward across the sand, his sword guiding him to calm the hurricane that began all those years ago, the torrent she had stoked with every lash and venomous whisper.

"Bend or be broken? That is your choice." Airth asked above the astonishment of the crowd.

Airth's words washed those images from Alexi's mind as Airth knelt before the Spessian Queen. The Commander of the End laid his sword in the sand and Alexi's brows furrowed beneath his helmet.

Surely this was no duel?

In mocking reverence, Airth drew his bronzed arms forward and lifted the river crown from her head in a weightless flourish.

His ebony cloak blocked Alexi's view as he rose from the sand. He held the crown high for all to see and only the crashing of the Carridean roared while the Spessian citizens gaped at the armies of the End and their queen brought low in the arena.

Alexi waited for him to crown himself King of Spessia, but as Airth lowered the crown, he studied the sapphires with disdain.

As if the blue gemstones were an insult to the golden locks that curled down his neck.

"An emperor does not wear the crown of a king."

In a forceful hurl, Airth pitched the diadem into the gaping surf.

"I ask again, bend or be broken? Your queen has betrayed you. The sails that carried my ships were woven by your hands. We wear ore mined from your riverbeds." Airth paused, and let his words fall upon the Spessian crowd.

The shifting anger of the theater was like a rising tempest.

"Will you bend your knee to the will of the Void or share the fate of your traitorous queen?"

As Allagria squirmed on her knees before the commander, Airth found his sword once more.

He stalked before the crowd with the confidence of a triumphant performer. He shouted with his arms outstretched, and pointed his sword to the sky.

"What do you demand of me? Do you wish to die as Spessians or live as Thyssians? Come down and fight for your queen!"

Alexi saw her now with eyes that hungered for any sign of loyalty in the audience.

The nobles who once relished in the glory of their kingdom wilted, and the men who had kissed the feet of her statue lowered their eyes.

The first cry was as faint as the flap of birds' wings.

"Thyssia!"

Then it swelled into a thunderous cry for blood. Each rising shout overwhelmed the call of the Carridean.

"Thyssia!"

She was defenseless in the presence of those who pretended not to see.

Black-robed alchemists slowly entered behind the procession, but these men and women were different. Their magic had robbed them of their hair and smudges of plum skin hung beneath their eyes. Their skin was so translucent that their skulls seemed only covered by marbled vessels of blue and purple.

The sound of chimes caught Alexi's attention–delicate golden chains connected to their wrists swayed in-step with their path towards their commander.

They had robbed the specter of her power. In the arena's sand, the She-Snake quivered on her knees.

Alexi's hand no longer hovered over his sword. He lifted the angled helmet, just enough so that his silver hair fell around his face.

He would not be the one to spill her blood. That would not be his way.

He would never let himself be like her again.

But he would let her see him in her utter humiliation, to behold his eyes as she knelt, helpless and afraid as he once did.

She would die and not a soul would fight for her.

He would stand in the helplessness of her eyes, knowing that all had abandoned their queen. He had no need for vengeance, because vengeance had already come for her.

He found her face again as Airth enraged the crowd.

Beneath the clamor for her head, this time, she saw him too. Her eyes widened, and her cries became louder beneath the sapphire gag.

The fire of countless nights, terrified and alone in the dark, burned in his chest. Alexi steeled every muscle in his face, staring with the eyes of death into his tormentor's face.

He would not take her life and ruin his future. He would only watch.

A glance was all he needed and as Airth drew back his sword, Alexi returned his helmet and hid his face.

In a searing glint of steel, as the sky looked down upon the theater, the terror in her unblinking eyes dissolved.

The Spessian queen's head fell onto the sand, but the roar of the crowd drowned out the thud.

In a monstrous yell, Airth bared his teeth.

"Thyssians! With your skill beside me, we shall claim every crown, every island for the people of our empire! The End does not yield!"

Chapter Forty-Three

Torin

Along the corridor, the evening sun poured through the Agametian glass, creating yellow ribbons of light.

The pitying warmth on his skin only deepened the doom in his heart. The clanking sway of the shackles at his wrists reminded him that there would be no fight or contest, only a sentence. With each step forward, the guards behind him moved in a pack of armored wolves.

Torin's footsteps echoed against the marble floor, drawing the attention of pious nobles, draped in swaths of autumn gold and mountain green, clustering around the entrance. Only shades of cowardice and envy surrounded him.

There was no sapphire or any shade of blue to remind him that all was not lost. Their gazes condemned Torin to death, and he pictured the sea to calm the panic in his mind.

Forced forward by the guards, his scuffling feet echoed in the hall, and the familiar tug at his ribs stifled his breath. As he sighed against the anger in his chest, the doors of the great hall parted, and the voices of the assembled evaporated in a sickening hush. His bones grew ridged as he moved through their stares.

The sea of gold and green nobles parted around him as the great wooden doors of the Hall of Justice closed with a sound that rattled stone. Xanthous beams of light bathed the hall through the round windows above, gazing down with watchful eyes.

All of it mirrored the gathering, with large daises rising above the crowd, and three humble stools claiming the center of the room. The only exception was the addition of two pedestals. The iron chain between his wrists dangled freely against his legs. His eyes focused on the seat reserved especially for the accused.

Beside the judge's seats, a small cushion waited for witnesses to kneel upon. It was a reminder to all who testified that liars would also kneel before the executioner.

The dust motes swirled in the amber light around the elevated thrones, and his grandmother's seat remained unoccupied. They had sent not a single soldier or royal representative from their house. Silhouetted by the sun, the throne of the Riverlands cast an imposing shadow, like the ruins of an ancient city.

As Torin lowered his gaze, his silver hair graced his open collared tunic, and they marched him forward as a guilty man.

The golden leaves and silver trunk of the Autumn throne served as a bitter reminder of their fallen relic. The young king appeared despondent, his eyes clouded with fog, and the only person beside the king was his commander.

Torin's persistent thoughts intensified as he passed the final throne.

Torin strengthened himself for the last time as he caught sight of the Mountain Queen.

His anger surged as his ragged breath threatened to break him.

She regarded him like an insect–no, less than an insect. To her, he was a sacrifice on the altar of vengeance. He did not waver under her gaze.

Instead, he stood with his head cocked in defiance, denying her any satisfaction of a reaction. Early in his life, he learned to conceal every flicker of fear and hope within the chambers of his heart. The guards pushed him toward his seat, but he did not avert his gaze.

As he stared back at the queen of the mountain, flanked by her emerald banners, he realized she was alone too, save for her bear. Bjorn did not stand beside his mother.

Theor stood with the sword of the Mountain drawn before their gray jagged throne. To bear the honor of commander was also the cruel privilege of an executioner.

Various stewards of the courts moved about the room, providing inks and quills to the scribes seated on the fringes. Their writing instruments moved furiously, scratching a long parchment. As the judges took their places, the attention of the entire room eased from his body like a boulder falling off his back.

He breathed calmly for just a moment before an iron hand forced his body downward into the seat.

Torin's skin crawled as the guards stepped away from the platform in a unified march.

Torin looked at the judge of his house and Sherat's eyes hung low in his sockets. The gods' sleep was already beckoning him and the elderly man slumped heavily against the back of his chair.

The judge of the Mountain Court rose from her seat, which paused the scribe's fervent scratching. Cassia announced to the entire room the expectations and laws of bystanders. Proclaiming that they would tolerate nothing but absolute silence.

Torin listened with clenched teeth as she listed the charges brought against him by the Mountain Queen.

"Kidnapping by force and intimidation, improper conduct with the member of a royal household, intent to disrupt political alliances, warmongering, conspirator of alchemists, crimes conflicting with the conventions of war..."

A burning laugh rumbled through his chest as she continued to announce the charges tacked to his name–the perfect blend of truth and lies. Even if he could refute one charge, there was enough evidence to damn him, regardless of the outcome.

He shut out her words as the charges became increasingly absurd and broad. She could find anyone in the room guilty.

Cassia took her seat, then the judge of the Autumn and Osiris took her place to address the assembly.

Yet, as he began his speech, Romulus motioned Osiris to ascend to the Autumn throne. A murmur of whispers swirled through the courts, and Cassia sharply reminded them of their oath of silence.

Torin attempted to study Romulus' lips, but the pounding of his pulse made it impossible to concentrate.

The king's countenance was pallid and marked with despair. Did he desire to duel and to claim Torin's life as the price of it all? Torin lowered his eyes.

The brown-haired judge of the Autumn Court descended the stairs and cleared his throat.

"At the behest of my King and Lord, His Majesty rescinds his right to injury or insult. We bring forward no charges to press on the heir of house Spessia."

A surge of both confusion and relief washed over him when Romulus glanced at him. Torin didn't see a king; he saw a wounded stag.

Pity welled up within him, and a seed of gratitude sprouted in his chest. They would not duel.

After a second chorus of whispers sparked in the pillar supported gallery, guards dragged two members from the room

As it was Sherat's turn to rise, the crowd silenced themselves, but the old man simply motioned for the trial to begin.

"Torin, son of Altimais, Grandson of Queen Allagria, Prince and Heir of house Spessia, Lord of the Carridean passage." Cassia began, "Do you wish to contest the charges brought against you?"

"All but one."

He envisioned Gailah's hand intertwined with his own as he guided her through the same room just a few days ago.

He relished the memory of dawn's gentle touch as it graced the curve of her cheeks and the blush beneath her skin. Every moment he had spent in her presence ached inside his chest.

Yet, a profound pang of regret seized him, a haunting realization of how deeply he wished he had taken her hand and danced with her when fate had given him the chance.

The court bellowed in response to the prince's words and Cassia shot them a glare that sent another handful of members escorted out.

"Please respond with decorum, Your Highness, yes or no will suffice. We consider elaboration to be the truth as you know it. I will ask again, "Yes or No?"

Impatience stained Cassia's words.

"Yes."

"Do you have any witnesses prepared to profess your innocence?"

From where he sat before the assembled court, he tried his best to hide the resignation in his voice.

"No. I have none."

There had been no time given or counsel provided. The hurried nature of it all made his insides knot. The Mountain Queen had not taken her eyes off of him, as if at any moment he would burst into flames at her command.

No, he would not erupt in a blazing torrent of injustice. Torin knew if he wanted to live, he needed his body to obey despite his heart clamoring for retribution.

"Very well, we shall proceed." She declared and glided slowly before the room.

Her questions began as a simple string of obvious inquiries. Questions only a fool could answer incorrectly. Like a serpent weaving through reeds, each question thereafter increased in deception and insinuation.

The wards in his mind wore down with each question. His jaw ached with every terse "Yes" and "No".

The questions taunted the loneliest parts of him.

"*Do you harbor any ill towards the new king of Autumn?*"

Torin blinked at the obscurity of the question. "No, I do not."

"Then you admit you abducted the Princess of the Mountain out of sheer desire and personal gain?"

He bit down on his tongue as his chest burned with the truth that, in every outcome, he was there. He would have taken her and fought for her. Whatever she decided, Torin was there because she needed him to be. He told himself that he did this for an alliance for his people, to change what the islands thought of house Spessia, but in the quietest corners of his heart, he knew he could not bear her hatred.

His ribs burned as he sighed, and his head ached from the bright yellow sunlight in the room.

He could no longer quell the anger in his voice.

"You are asking the wrong questions, honorable Cassia," He spoke through gritted teeth. "You are asking the wrong person the wrong questions. If you will not ask the only person who can assure you of my innocence...then do not waste your breath..."

Torin faced Katha's throne. The queen stopped stroking the head of her bear.

"You sentenced me to die the moment I begged for your help. From the moment I warned you of all of this, because I knew they would come for her, yet you have painted me as your enem—"

The whining hinges of the large doors echoed across the stone floors and their hateful eyes stopped looking at him. Every single person in the room turned their gaze. Katha's snow colored face blared against the green of her gown, as if a ghost stood behind his shoulder.

The hair along Torin's neck heightened with the murmurs in the room. His pulse resumed its frenzied beat as his sentence died in the air.

Blue.

Amid the crowd and their throngs of gold and green, Torin saw a shade of ethereal and indomitable, sapphire blue. Torin forgot what it meant to breathe.

Gailah stepped forward in a gown drawn from the river itself, as if it were sewn with every shade of water in the layers that flowed behind her. The princess' eyes were calm like an angry sea after a storm. Even the fabric attached to cuffs at her wrist rippled in her wake. She proceeded slowly towards the front of the room and it pained him to see how her movements siphoned her strength.

His heart beat like a banner in the breeze.

Gailah found him, and there was not a shred of fear in her cerulean eyes.

Torin's body commanded him to stand in her presence. At that moment, there were no judges or courts, no irons biting at his wrist. Despite the armored hands that tried to force him down, he fought to keep her gaze.

He could wade waist deep into the confidence in her eyes, terrifying and commanding all at once.

She ignored the flutter of the room and her mother's demanding voice. Gailah did not acknowledge the witnesses' pedestal. She skirted past it with her piercing eyes never leaving his.

She climbed the stairs below him and her gown rippled in a babbling river of fabric. Gailah took her place beside him and his heart beat so loudly she must have heard it calling to her.

Every part of him wanted to feel her in his arms.

Gailah's anger radiated from her skin and he longed to take her hand in his, but the irons clasping his hands together prevented him. He saw a band around her forefinger, the bruises that lingered across her body, and their twin wounds from the barbs that had struck them in the trees.

"You're breathing. You're here." Was all he could think to say, but Torin spoke in the voice of a drowning man.

"Of course I am," Her eyes flickered "because no one else is..." she whispered to him in that same armored defiance that heightened his pulse, but now, as she stood before the shock-filled room, there was a steadfast promise in her voice. "You asked me to expect only honorable things from you, and now I want you to expect that of me. I will not abandon you."

The ache in his chest was not from the pain in his ribs.

"Princess, you must kneel. You are not above the laws nor the truth of the gods," Cassia called out from her place among the judges.

Torin could only see blue as Gailah bridged the gap between his seat and the Mountain throne. What unsettled him was the way Queen Katha looked at her daughter as if it surprised her to see Gailah in attendance.

"I have no intention of kneeling before you or anyone else. I will not recount my story to you because you demand it from me. I will not strip my soul bare and recount the horrors that live in my mind." She turned her eyes towards her mother and her hands fluttered beside her gown. "No, Your Majesty, I will not be your witness. I will not condemn this man to die because he protected me when you would not. Your disdain wounds me deeper than any scar on my skin. You left me to the wolves.

You are my mother, you are my queen, and you abandoned me to your enemies...because you lied..."

Her voice quaked, and he saw Gailah breathe like she was summoning courage from the depths of her soul.

Katha rose with frightened eyes and colorless skin.

"Be silent." Katha commanded in a horrified whisper.

"You will hear me!" Gailah called out over her mother's voice and she shifted her shoulders towards Romulus.

"Romulus, I will not marry you." She tightened her fingers into fists. "I will not carry the deceit of my house. In good faith, I do not think you could ever wish to marry the daughter of your enemy."

"Gailah!" Katha shouted, and Gailah flinched. Anger burned through him as her distress and subtle movement spoke a thousand sorrows.

"My mother and queen let Alchemists experiment on your father's body and conjured his soul from the Void. She lets your mother rest alone with the gods while your father's body rots within our Chasm! Haydrian tortured the woman you loved because he wanted vengeance on the queen who betrayed him, executed him and exiled his equals. Do not marry me, do not marry a daughter of a servant of the Void."

Gailah's eyes fell on her mother. His heart cracked and his mind spiraled in free fall as her words shattered Romulus' face.

"Did the gods not command us to only serve them? I cannot stay silent. Mother, do not damn me to the fate you chose for yourself, but I will not let you kill him."

Silence, deafening silence rushed over the room. There was only a brief pause as Romulus stared at them, and in a blink, his eyes quickly flooded with rage. The king made a sound that could only come from a broken man.

Gailah gasped, but not at her mother's words.

Her fingers flew to the rune at her wrist, and the sound she made caused his knees to buckle. She clutched her arm and her voice cried out while she cradled her arm close to her.

Every thought fled Torin's mind as he kneeled beside Gailah. He searched her eyes but saw nothing but agony. He could not hold her, he could not protect her as the chains shook against his arms. Gailah's scream carved through him while chaos descended upon the Hall of Justice.

Lord Barrock restrained Romulus as his drawn sword slashed towards the Mountain Queen.

Curses fell in volleys from Romulus' lips as he called for Katha's head.

From her throned fortress, the queen stood and moved towards Gailah.

"Did he tell you what it cost me!?" Katha's words hung in the air like shards of glass. The queen withered against the stairs before the Mountain throne.

"Alchemy bears a terrible cost." Katha could not look at her daughter. Her eyes were wild, but she stared only at Torin. "Did Haydrian tell you what the voice in the shadows demanded for when I called out to Decius? When I begged the Void to surrender his spirit to his body? Did Haydrian tell you what I exchanged for the cost of Decius' soul?"

Torin's heart plunged.

Panic seized him as Gailah stumbled.

The clanking of chains at his wrists echoed loudly as he desperately reached for her.

The irons no longer mattered. He let them slice into his forearms just so he could keep her from falling to the floor. As her hands clasped onto his arms, she clutched him until her nails left marks in his skin. He did not care.

He would let her dig into his flesh if that was what she needed to stop the pain that tortured her. She could have what little was left of him if it meant her agony would end. She could have all that was left of him because from the moment she donned the colors of his people, his crown, she had already taken the rest. Gailah had captured every part of him, and he would fight for the rest of his days to prove that his heart was worthy of her.

A flash of dread consumed him as he realized Gailah's skin was prickled with sweat. The rune on her wrist blazed like a fiery beacon. Her silver hair rested against his as her fingers pressed into his shoulders.

Katha's words rattled through his ears.

"Forgive me, my daughter, for I did not know. He showed me a vision of a girl with silver hair standing beside a man in onyx armor, runes carved into his skin. Forgive me, I believed Torin to be one of them. Forgive me, please forgive me. I did not know. When I held my darling girl with silver hair, I wept. I knew they would claim you for themselves, for their order, for the price of my mistake, my terrible mistake. I let them cut off Haydrian's head because I could not bear the thought of losing you to them. I let them all die because I would not let them have you. I would let them all burn again because I would not surrender you to the Void. I am the one who broke the Mountain, and I failed to protect you before you drew your first breath. They are coming for you because you never belonged to me or to the Mountain. You belong to The End."

Shock surged up his spine, and terror gripped his entire being. Torin sought Gailah's gaze, but fear had taken hold of her body, wracked by the pain coursing from the rune blazing in torrents of heat. Heat that poured from her body and onto his skin.

Torin steadied her and the irons continued to bite into his skin. He held her and would not let the pain overtake her.

"Spessia has fallen!"

Torin knew the voice that cried out as the great wooden doors swung open.

His second in command, Lehgan, stood ragged and breathless in the evening sunlight. Soot covered his tawny skin, and smears of blood spattered his face.

"Torin!"

Their eyes met and as his dearest friend lurched forward, Lehgan collapsed against the marble floor.

Pronunciation Guide

People:

Katha: KAH-Tha-ah
Freyden: Frey-den
Aerin: Air-in
Bjorn: Buh-yorn
Gailah: Ga-ale-ah
Haydrain: Hay-dree-in
Trejen: Trey-jen
Senna: Sen-ah
Torin: Tor-en
Alexi: Al-ex-ee
Romulus: Rom-u-lus
Oxana: Ox-An-ah
Barrock: Bar-rOhck
Cias: Ky-us
Ellika: Ell-ick-ah
Regulus: Reg-u-lus
Altanah: All-tan-Ah
Tyraxus: Tie-rack-sus
Sefti: Seph-Tee

Tiranus: Tear-ran-us
Deren: Dare-in
Lyssia: Lie-See-Ah
Decius: Dee-See-us
Orla: Or-Lah
Their: Th-ay-or
Cassia: Cas-see-ah
Rorick: Roar-ick
Etilda: Ee-Til-dah
Airth: Air-ith
Lehgan: Lay-gan
Atraxis: Ah-track-is

Locations:
Islnadad: Isil-nah-dad
Ghobasi: Go-Bah-See
Nadr: Nah-der
Agametian: Agah-ME-Tian
Iosi: Eye-Oh-see
Spessia: Spess-see-ah
Misenia: My-Sen-ee-Ah
Thyssia: Thigh-See-Ah

Animals:
Kelligh: Kell-eye
Karak: Car-AHk

Misc:
Nactine: Nacht-een

THE SONG OF THE END

S.J. STILES

COMING 2025

SUBSCRIBE TO MY NEWSLETTER FOR MORE UPDATES ON RELEASES AND EARLY PREVIEWS

@THISTLEANDTHIMBLEPRESS

Acknowledgments

To Mel,

Thyssia would not exist if you hadn't read along every step of the way. Your feedback and counsel were so needed and invaluable. Thank you so much for taking the time to counsel my characters with some much needed therapy. Thank you for swooning, giggling, cringing, and screaming all the way through this book. As long as you keep writing, so will I.

To Aj,

Thank you for listening to my spiraling stories of islands that are only a figment of my imagination. Thank you for letting me share my creativity with you and for enabling my curiosities. The keyboard you gave me was the key to finding my story, and I will never forget that. I love you and I will never cease to be grateful for a husband that believes in me. You brought this dream to life.

To Mom,

You spent so many reading stories to us as kids, and now let me thank you for reading one more. I am so grateful for the wardrobes and hobbit holes that you led us to and for giving me the gift of books. Thank you for never holding me back and letting me read any book I could get my hands on.

I'm sorry I called Kelligh a kestrel, book two's ornithology will be better, I promise. ;)

I Love you.

To Sarah and Marlisha,

Thank you for putting up with my rambling questions and insecurities. You both were so incredibly helpful and I will always treasure your feedback.

About the Author

S.J. Stiles grew up in the fields of north eastern Ohio then settled her life in the hills of the Carolinas. She kept a journal of her thoughts and ideas wherever she went, sometimes on her phone or in a tiny book with a Parisian cafe on the cover. Every place she visited held fragments of a universe that demanded to be remembered. So she wrote them down in a journal full of archipelagos, continents, tragedy and hope.

Her debut novel, The Song of Thyssia is a summation of years of reading and dreaming but the first of many stories yet to come.

www.ingramcontent.com/pod-product-compliance
Lightning Source LLC
Chambersburg PA
CBHW020249030826
48979CB00030B/2666/J

* 9 7 9 8 9 8 9 6 4 9 4 2 6 *